ROBIN'S CAGE

BREANNE LEFTWICH

ISBN-13:
979-8-9867607-0-4 (Paperback)
979-8-9867607-1-1 (Ebook)

To my mom and dad who always provided me with everything I could ever need in life. Thank you for teaching me that I could be anyone or do anything with God's guidance and grace.

A special thank you to my childhood friend, Kensey, who has been the real MVP of support. I appreciate all the encouragement and love you've given me since I first told you I was publishing a book. Your help has meant the world to me, and now this book is at its best thanks to you!

Chapter One

The sun peeked over the flat plains of Garridan, encasing the city in its burnt orange glow as the cool breeze swept the changing leaves off the trees, signaling the end of October. I leaned against the brick chimney on our roof, taking in the sight as I did every morning. I remembered when I first arrived here six months ago and had been surprised by what I saw. It wasn't an advanced city with grand structures and unique features like I had envisioned but a normal one with traditional buildings, ordinary transportation, and a typical layout.

That wasn't where my misguided assumptions ended either. Garridan was no different than any other city. There were shops, restaurants, schools, and everything you'd find anywhere else. The adults went to work, and the children attended school. Despite having supernatural powers, people here lived in almost the exact same way others around the world did. It made the transition easier because it reminded me of home.

There *were* a couple differences though. The schools had specific classes for students to learn and use their powers in as well as an extra history class: the history of Garridan. Most people didn't have jobs that were directly related to their powers, but they learned to utilize them in their day-to-day activities anyway. It was intriguing to see how many ways a power could be used, and I was constantly in awe of the things the people here were capable of. It almost made up for leaving everything in Milton behind. *Almost.*

The sun began to glow upon the vast courthouse in the center of town. It was a beautiful building with a tall clock tower and the type of old characteristics I always fell in love with. I had spent a good portion of time there with my parents since that's where they, as well as all the Keepers of Balance, worked from. They were teaching me firsthand how they operated and what I would be doing when the time came for me to sit with them on the council. It was a lot to take in, but I was humbled by all the good that Garridan strived for.

"Knock knock," I heard someone say. I didn't turn around as Elijah came and sat beside me. "Hey, kiddo."

"Good morning," I greeted him as he handed me a cup of coffee. The warmth of it seeped into my hands as its sweet scent filled my nose.

We sat quietly next to one another as we viewed the artistic coloring of the sky as it was awakened. I leaned into him, sipping my coffee and breathing in the fresh breeze that always seemed to buzz around him. It was our daily routine that had formed unintentionally but I savored every second of it. I enjoyed the company of both my parents but there was something special about my time with Elijah. He filled the fatherless void I had always been subjected to and it was a wonderful feeling to be loved by him.

"Any big plans for the day?" Elijah asked after a while.

"Nothing out of the ordinary. Matthew and I were going to hit the gym then walk around downtown," I told him around a sip of my drink. "See if any shops call out to us today. Same as every Saturday."

Elijah looked down at the cup in his hand, his forehead scrunched, and seemed troubled as he struggled to reply.

"What's wrong?" I questioned.

"It's just . . ." he trailed off then looked at me, his eyes full of worry. "Your mother and I are concerned you aren't adjusting here very well."

"Why's that?" I asked softly, tearing my gaze away from his.

"You and Matthew have closed yourselves off to anyone else and you've gotten into a repetitive routine. You don't interact with any of the other students at school and you don't try anything new," he explained as I rubbed my lips together.

I couldn't argue with him. When we came here, Matthew and I had clung onto one another as we faced a new world and, in doing so, had created a wall around ourselves. It was easier to stick together than face the questions and judgements from other people our age.

"It's just simpler," I finally said.

"How so?" Elijah asked gently.

"The other kids don't understand us. They think Matth dangerous because he used to be a Cyfrin, and they thir misfit because I don't understand anything that happens here. We just don't fit in."

"I see," Elijah murmured, taking his reading glasses off.

"Not to mention, I'm going to be given a place of power in Garridan and a lot of them have strong opinions about that. They don't think it's fair that a newcomer should get to make decisions for them," I added.

"But you're not a newcomer, Robin. Garridan has always been your home as much as it has been any of theirs."

"But I didn't grow up here."

"There's plenty of children in that school who didn't fully grow up here. That doesn't matter."

"Yes, it does," I snapped, my frustration showing. "Maybe not to you but to them and to me it does. It doesn't matter how much history I study or how much time I spend with the Keepers of Balance. I can learn everything about Garridan but that doesn't make me any less of an outsider in their eyes."

"I suppose you have a point," he reluctantly gave in. "But I truly believe it doesn't have to stay that way. You and Matthew just have to try a little harder with them is all. Show them how amazing you are."

I nodded my head but kept quiet. I knew he was trying to be supportive, but his words didn't comfort me at all. I was a foreigner to this land and everyone in it. That wasn't going to change over a couple of exchanged pleasantries. I knew it would take time for me to fit in and be accepted but I wasn't sure I'd ever truly belong.

"Maybe you could join an extracurricular activity at school," Elijah suggested after my prolonged silence.

"Okay," I agreed, despite not wanting to, and he smiled widely. "I'll go talk to the counselor on Monday and see what's still open."

"Good!" he said, his tense shoulders relaxing again. "Your mother and I just want you to be happy here."

"I know," I told him, leaning into his open arm. He and iana had done everything in their power to make me feel at e here. The least I could do was put in the same effort.

e love you, kiddo," he responded, kissing the top of my

w," I repeated softly. "I love you both too."

After sitting down for breakfast and forcing a smile onto my face as the topic of extracurriculars came up again with Adriana, I made my way down the street to Matthew's house. His mom opened the door when I rang the doorbell, her blonde hair pulled back in a scrunchy. She smiled when she saw me, her light blue eyes crinkling around the edges.

"Good morning, Robin," she greeted me.

"Good morning, Susan," I replied, matching her smile. She was a tall woman with sharp cheekbones and small lips. Her face showed her age, but she embraced it.

"Would you like to come in?" she asked as Matthew peeked out from around her.

"We actually have plans, Mom," he told her as he pulled on his dark jacket.

I couldn't help but smile at him calling her 'mom'. It took him a couple of months to give in but now it flowed effortlessly from his mouth, and anyone could tell how much it meant to them both.

"Another time," I told her as she ruffled his floppy hair.

"Okay. Tell your mother I'm looking forward to our dinner party tomorrow," she replied.

"I will," I assured her. Matthew joined me outside and waved goodbye as we began walking away. "What's your hurry?"

"No hurry," he shrugged, and I raised an eyebrow.

"You used Claire's visual linking to spy on Felicity again, didn't you?"

"Maybe," he muttered. His older sister was a clairvoyant and had mastered multiple unique techniques; one of them being the ability to link her vision to someone else's so she could see through their eyes.

"I thought you weren't going to do that anymore. It only upsets you."

"I'm not upset," he denied, his face rigid.

"Clearly," I stated, and he huffed. "What happened this time?"

"She was on another date."

"Ah," I said, already knowing the spew that was about to leave his mouth.

"Not that I mind," he started, right on cue. "We agreed that we'd both move on and not hold onto hopeless ideals that we'd ever be together again."

"Of course not. Who wants that misery?" I asked sarcastically, thinking of Ben.

"But I just don't understand how she'd move on so quickly. And with so many people," he added in, glaring at the street as we walked. "It's not like I'm over here sleeping around. Our relationship meant something to me so it's going to take time to move on."

"Well, she *is* more approachable than you," I pointed out. "I don't think you could sleep around even if you wanted to."

"This isn't funny Robin," he snapped, his piercing eyes burning into me.

"I know it's not. I'm sorry. But this isn't the first time we've had this conversation. You know she loved you, but you're gone now and she's just trying to find a way to cope with it. You can't be upset with her for that."

"Says who?" he grumbled, crossing his arms.

"Me. So either stop being jealous or stop spying on her," I commanded, matching his stance as we had a stare down in the middle of the sidewalk.

He narrowed his eyes at me, and I lifted my chin in defiance, unwavering at the look that would have sent an unnerving chill through me not even a year ago. After a moment, he looked away and I smiled smugly.

"You're right," he finally sighed, running his hand through his hair. "It's just so hard. Do you not ever want to see how Ben is doing?"

"Of course I do, but what good would it do me? I'll just end up an irrational, obsessed, and jealous fool like you."

"Thanks," he said dryly.

"Anytime," I replied with a wink. "But for real, stop checking up on her. Claire can't tell you no, so stop asking."

"I'll try. Really, I will," he added when I gave him a pointed look.

"I guess that's all I can ask for. On a completely different subject, Elijah and Adriana are concerned about our adjustment here. Or lack thereof."

"So are my parents. Sounds like they've been conversing about it. I guess it's obvious we aren't fitting in too well."

"Do you think we ever will?"

"Honestly," he hesitated as he thought about it, "probably not without some divine intervention."

"That's what I was afraid of." I sighed and rubbed the back of my neck. "But I promised Elijah we'd start trying a little harder anyway. So do you want to sign up for an extracurricular activity with me?"

"No."

"Oh, come on!" I exclaimed in exasperation.

"No."

"Please!"

"Nope."

"Fine," I said curtly. "I'll just ask your mom."

"You wouldn't dare," he accused, narrowing his eyes at me.

"Try me," I shot back with a sly smile.

He looked me up and down, then shook his head with tight lips. "I really don't like you sometimes."

"But you love me," I reminded him as he began to walk away.

"Don't remind me," he huffed, and I smiled, grateful that I had him with me through this entire process.

Chapter Two

"I'm so glad you could all make it." Adriana beamed as we sat around our large dinner table. It was a casual affair, everyone speaking merrily with laughter filling the air. Matthew and I were as animated as anyone else. Our families were the one safe place for us to let our guards down.

"William, be nice to your brother," Malachi warned as the two battled for the last serving of ham.

"When am I ever not nice?" William shot back, and Claire snorted.

William was the eldest at twenty-three and had a dignified aura about him. He was serious in nature with the exception being when he was around his younger siblings. Claire was only a year younger than him, but her maturity level was far below that. Unlike her brothers, she was outspoken and spunky and didn't have any interest in growing up anytime soon. They both sported the Alastair's signature blue eyes and dirty blonde hair, but William's was neatly buzzed whereas Claire's sat short and wild. Matthew fit in perfectly with their family features, all three of them spitting images of their parents. The only difference between the five of them was Malachi's light brown hair tone.

"So, Robin," Malachi turned his attention towards me. "How's your training going?"

"Really well," I replied. "My trainer is pleased with my progress."

"Yes, she's all but mastered her hydrokinesis," Adriana added in proudly. "And her hand-to-hand combat is coming along greatly."

"It's still a work in progress," I clarified bashfully.

"It's definitely better than it was though," Matthew inserted. "She can actually block a hit now."

I punched him in the arm and smiled sweetly as he cursed at the force behind it. "But it appears you can't," I said.

He glowered at me as everyone around the table laughed. I couldn't say he was wrong though. My technique and performance weren't excellent but, compared to six months ago, it was a big step up. If need be, I could hold my own for at least a little while.

"How's school?" Susan asked.

"It's not too bad. I have all the classes I would've had in Milton with the exception of Garridan History," I replied as Matthew made a face.

Garridan History was typically taught freshman year. Since we weren't here then, we were required to take it now which meant a lot of humiliation for being seniors in a freshman level class.

"Robin is going to look into extracurricular activities tomorrow," Elijah spoke up.

"Oh, that's an excellent idea!" Susan exclaimed. She turned towards Matthew with a wide smile on her face. "You should join her."

I tried to contain a smirk as he fidgeted in his seat.

"I'm not really an extracurricular type of person," he said.

"It'll be so good for you though," Susan replied, her charm pulling him in. She had the ability of mind control and, despite not using it unless absolutely necessary, her charisma was unintentionally enhanced by it which often helped her get her way.

Matthew hesitated, then exhaled loudly. "Okay."

"Wonderful!" Susan clasped her hands together as the rest of her family shook their heads knowingly. They were no stranger to her shenanigans.

I grinned over at Matthew triumphantly and he gave me his signature glare.

"Where's Kesha tonight?" I asked William, missing his girlfriend's company.

"She had to work. Her boss is keeping her busy," he replied, staring his mom down.

"I told her she was more than welcome to take the night off and join us," Susan told him. "She's the one who chose to go in."

"Only because she knew it would make you happy," he pointed out.

"I can't deny that," she said with a smile. "She's a good girl. She knows how important it is for us to figure out our current project."

"What's your current project?" Claire asked.

"You know I'm not at liberty to talk about my work," Susan chastised.

"Go ahead and tell them," Elijah told her. "Malachi and William will know soon enough since they're in the guard. Matthew and Robin as well since they're working towards spots in the government."

"I'm not sure my boss would approve of that," she murmured playfully, a look of amusement on her face.

"*I'm* your boss," Elijah responded with raised eyebrows.

Susan grinned, then turned her attention away from him. "We've intercepted communication systems used by the Cyfrin. They've been speaking in code so we're currently trying to crack it," she explained excitedly.

"Once we do, we're hoping we'll hit the jackpot with information on some of the last kids that are still unfound or what the Cyfrin are planning next," Elijah added.

"It would be a huge advantage for us in defeating them once and for all," Adriana said.

"Do you think that's possible?" I asked. "I mean, they have a lot of followers. Not to mention, you guys thought they were gone before, and they weren't."

"Both of those things are true," Elijah nodded as he spoke, "but we've learned from our past mistakes with them. We have the upper hand in many departments and our guard is stronger than ever."

"Yes, we are," Malachi agreed. "The variety of skillsets we possess are mighty. Plus, with Matthew's insight on the Cyfrin, we know where their weaknesses lie. When the time comes to take them on, we'll be ready."

"Do you think that time will be soon?" Matthew questioned and the room grew silent as everyone considered it.

"It's hard to say," Adriana finally spoke up, folding her hands together and setting her chin against them. "But . . . Yes. I do believe they'll want to attack soon."

"Wait," I spoke up. "What do you mean? We aren't going to attack them?"

"No," Adriana replied. "We're safest behind the barrier. The few times we've made a strike against them, we've lost significant numbers. We learned very quickly that we have more of a chance of winning here than we do there."

"But if the Cyfrin know that, why do they keep attacking?" I questioned

"Because they don't want to be at a standstill," Matthew answered. "They want to take over the world, so they'll do whatever's necessary in their eyes to do that. Even if it means sacrificing some of their own."

I played with the food on my plate as I pondered what they were saying. "What if they don't come?"

"They will," Matthew told me with certainty.

"Okay, so what if they do but they can make their way into Garridan? Do you have plans for that?"

"The barrier is impenetrable," Susan assured me.

"What if they have something that can break through though?" I pressed.

"It's impossible," Adriana said.

"But-"

"We'll know more after we decode their conversations," Elijah spoke up, patting my arm reassuringly. "We can make sure they don't have any tricks up their sleeves or have a secret weapon we're unaware of. We always want to be absolutely ready with a foolproof battle plan so we don't repeat history."

"We want to have as little casualties as possible," Malachi added.

"This has gone on long enough though," Adriana murmured. "The Cyfrin's time is limited. They won't be a threat to us or the people of the world much longer."

"I'll toast to that!" Susan exclaimed, holding up her wine glass.

Everyone joined in clanking their glasses together, thrilled with the idea of defeating the enemy. Matthew and I gave each other the side eye, not as confident. I had no doubt Garridan would win in a physical battle, but I remembered how slick the three Keepers of Balance of the Cyfrin were. Some of their final words around me echoed in my head. They had a plan and were confident in it. Unlike Garridan, they weren't sitting around waiting for an attack; they were already plotting Garridan's demise. I only hoped they would slip up and let us know what that plan was once Susan's department figured out their code.

* * *

Matthew and I left the counselor's office with a list of extracurriculars we could still join, and we mulled over it halfheartedly as we walked towards Garridan History. There were numerous options to choose from but none of them screamed out at me as something I wanted to do. Most of the sports in school weren't accepting more players and I didn't have the availability to attend practices and games anyway. I was once again reminded of the many empty spots in my life that couldn't be fulfilled here.

"I miss basketball," I whined, thinking about my team and wondering how their season was starting out. My body ached for the competitive sports that it thrived from. Combat training kept me in shape, but it didn't give me the same high that a spectated game offered.

"Looks like water polo is still accepting people," Matthew joked, and I made a face.

"Pass. I like swimming and I like sports, but I don't like swimming sports. Do you think art counts as an extracurricular?"

"Technically it's a class. Besides, it doesn't matter what I think. It matters what your parents think, and they want you to join a club so you're interacting with people. You don't interact with people in art."

I sighed dramatically. "This sucks."

"Yep," he stated, unhappily eyeing the paper.

We sat down in our seats, putting the list away as Mr. Phipps entered the room and called the rowdy freshmen to order. When he finally got them under control, he instructed us to open our books to chapter sixteen.

"Today we are beginning our study of the guard," he began. "Over the next two weeks we'll be doing an in depth dig into every aspect of them but today we'll start with a broad overview. The guard is our only formal means of protection and has seen us through many battles during our existence. They're made up of three specialties: physical, mental, and weaponry. For each specialty there are two lieutenants and one captain that reside over it. Above them are four majors, three colonels, two lieutenant generals and then the general of the army. He is in charge overall and makes all the direct communication with the

Keepers of Balance. Can anyone tell me who the current army general is?"

A quiet girl with oversized glasses raised her hand. "Malachi Alastair."

All eyes swiveled towards Matthew, but he maintained his stone-cold expression, keeping up with his unapproachable demeanor. I saw the lightest change in his eyes, though, which showed me his interest was piqued at the possibility of learning more about his father.

"That's correct," Mr. Phipps told the girl. "The position of army general has been held by a member of the Alastair family for generations. The majority of their family lineage has possessed a defensive talent, making them suitable for such a thing. Even their name seems to predict that as their fate."

I raised my hand. "What do you mean by that?"

"The name Alastair is derived from Scottish origins meaning 'defender of the people'. It definitely plays into the idea that our names predict our gifts."

"Is that true?" someone else asked, sounding fascinated.

"There are many that believe it is. It's why some parents choose a name for their baby with the specific meaning of a power that they want them to possess," Mr. Phipps said, a smile playing at his lips. "But you'll never get a concrete answer on if it's real or just a myth."

Chatter broke out around the classroom as well as some laughter. It seemed as if everyone was intrigued by that possibility. Mr. Phipps tried to reign them in, but he was met by lots of pushback as students continued to talk over one another. He gave up and crossed his arms, leaning against the whiteboard as he observed their excitement. Matthew looked over at me with narrowed eyes, once again annoyed at being stuck in class with the freshmen because they often made it hard to learn since they didn't know how to listen. After a couple minutes, the chatter finally began to die down.

"I'll tell you what," Mr. Phipps spoke up as he tapped his finger on his chin. "Just for the fun of it, your homework tonight is to ask your parents their thoughts on the subject. See if they named you something with the meaning of a power they wanted you to have or if their parents did it with them. Then find out what the origin of your name is and why your parents chose it. We'll share in class tomorrow but for now, back to our books please."

It was an interesting theory, but I didn't see how it would make any logical sense. Then again, not much around here made any logical sense so maybe it could be real. Nevertheless, it was going to be a fun homework assignment and I was curious to see how my parents would answer. After class, Matthew seemed deep in thought.

"What's up?" I asked him.

"I'm just thinking about our lesson today," he replied.

"Thinking about your family history," I corrected, and he nodded, looking a bit sheepish.

"It's just cool to know my family has always been so vital to Garridan and that I come from a strong lineage," he told me, sounding proud. His face was lit up in a way I rarely saw, and it warmed my heart.

"It is!" I agreed sincerely. "You know, you've spent so much time getting to know your immediate family since being here but maybe it's time to get to know more about your whole lineage."

"I think you're right. I mean, my dad has power reflection abilities, William has force fields, and I'm a petrifier. If the three of us have such different gifts, imagine what the rest of our ancestors could do!"

"I can only imagine," I told him with a smile, and he grinned back at me. Having a family after being alone for so long had changed him in many ways and I was happy he finally knew what it was like to be a part of something bigger than himself.

Chapter Three

When Adriana, Elijah, and I sat down for dinner that night, I held my tongue for less than a minute before pouncing on them with my pre-thought-out interrogation.

"Have either of you ever heard the theory that your name decides your power?" I asked as we took turns scooping food onto our plates.

"Of course," Elijah chuckled. "Silly superstitions is all it is."

"You don't think there's any truth to it then?" I pried and he shook his head.

"No, I don't."

"Did your parents?" I inquired further and he scratched his stubbly chin thoughtfully.

"Not that I know of," he responded, sticking a spoonful of corn into his mouth and chewing slowly.

"How about you?" I turned towards Adriana who was buttering a piece of bread.

She took a bite before answering me. "My parents did believe in that possibility. It's why they named me Adriana."

"Really?" I asked, intrigued, and she nodded with a smile.

"Really."

"Do you know what the origin of your name is then?"

"I do. It's of Latin descent I believe, and it means 'of sea' or 'water'," she informed me. "They very much wanted me to inherit hydrokinesis from them seeing as how they both possessed it."

"And you did!" I exclaimed, causing her and Elijah to laugh.

"That I did," she said, pushing her long hair over her shoulders and pouring water into my glass with the tiniest flick of her wrist. "I preserved what they believed to be a pure bloodline due to my name and my name alone."

"Does that mean you believe in it too?"

"I lean a little towards that side," she admitted. "It's why we chose to name you Robin."

"It is?" Elijah questioned, watching her through squinted eyes. "I thought we chose it because it was your favorite name at the time."

"I may have had ulterior motives," she told him sheepishly and he raised his eyebrows in amusement

"Care to elaborate on that?" he pushed, and I grinned at his tone.

"Well, as you know, my parents were extremely strict with me and held me to very high expectations. I never had a moment of my life where I wasn't striving for perfection for them, and I didn't want that type of life for my child. I wanted my child to be free to be whoever they wanted to be," she explained.

"Free like a bird," I commented, and she nodded.

"Exactly. Besides that, robins symbolize hope and renewal in some cultures. When you were born, we were in the beginning stages of the war with the Cyfrin and I thought we could all use the reminder that there was still hope for our victory against them," she told us, her head dropping slightly. "But as it turns out, there was just hope and renewal for you and your life with other people."

My heart hurt for her as she remembered one of the biggest losses in her life. Elijah reached over and grabbed her hand, squeezing it gently. I followed suit, hoping we could be of some comfort.

"But I'm here now," I reminded her.

"Yes, you are," she agreed, taking a deep breath and composing herself. "But it's still hard to think about."

"Just think of it this way then: there's now hope and renewal for *us* as a family even after all the years we were apart," I told her and she nodded, tears pooling in her eyes. I stood up and walked over to her, wrapping her in a tight hug. Elijah joined in and clung onto us with his hands over our shoulders.

"I love you, sweet girl," Adriana whispered into my ear.

"I love you too," I told her.

"And I love you both," Elijah added, making us both giggle as we reciprocated his words. He often reminded me of an eager puppy. He was full of love and never wanted to be left out of what was going on. It was kind of humorous.

We sat back down and continued our dinner, discussing the name possibilities some more. After we finished eating, I headed upstairs to my room and curled up on my bed. Elijah and Adriana were two of the kindest, most brilliant people I had ever met, and I was lucky to have them as my parents. Despite that, I couldn't help but think about the other people in my life that I had lost to gain them.

I looked up at the pictures hanging over my bookcase. The one in the center was of my mom, Dawn, and I posed around last year's Christmas tree. A narrow shadow box sat under it, holding mine and Dawn's matching necklaces. I had finally taken them off the night before school started but couldn't bear to have them where I couldn't see them. Next to it was a photobooth reel of Felicity, Ben, and I at prom, making goofy faces and laughing. Despite how that night had ended, it was one of my favorite memories. The photos continued with some of just Ben and I, Felicity and I, Matthew and Felicity, Lizzie, and my basketball and swim teams. They stood as reminders of some of the best times of my life but also as reminders of what I had lost.

A lump formed in my throat as I grabbed my cellphone. I flipped to all the undelivered messages I had attempted to send to Ben or Felicity and ached to be able to speak to them. When I had first settled down in Garridan, I desperately tried to text, email, call, or instant message them continuously. However, the barrier that surrounded Garridan made it impossible for anything to go through which left me stuck with an empty hole inside that couldn't be filled. I knew it wasn't rational, but I typed out a message to Ben, letting him know how much I missed him and wished I was there, then hit send. Almost automatically a 'failed to send' response popped up and I tossed my phone to the side and grabbed a pillow, hugging it tight as I let the tears stream down my face.

That night, I tossed and turned as my dreams turned to nightmares and I watched as all my family and friends were kidnapped one by one. I desperately ran down an endless road of buildings, trying to locate them as their terrified screams echoed all around me. When the buildings finally ended and I was able to look around a corner, I saw all their lifeless bodies lined up on the ground in a straight line, their blood mixing together. I fell to my knees as three figures walked into the scene, and I quickly recognized them as the Cyfrin's Keepers of Balance. Toshiro and Mallory sneered at the bodies around them then looked at me as if proud of the suffering they caused. Alexander's face remained neutral but when he met my gaze, his eyes were full of sorrow.

"I'm sorry," he mouthed as I was yanked into a pit of darkness.

* * *

"Are you okay?" Matthew asked me the next day as we sat on a bench eating our lunch.

The fall breeze nipped at my nose, and I sniffled. "I'm fine."

He observed me for a moment then shook his head. "No, you aren't. You've been a walking zombie all day and your forehead is crinkled."

"What does my forehead have to do with it?" I questioned, smoothing out the lines on it subconsciously.

"You hold your stress in your face," he answered with a shrug. "Your forehead is only crinkled when you have something heavy weighing on your mind."

"You're very observant," I noted with a hint of annoyance.

"That I am. It's one of my finer traits that's helped keep me alive for so long. So what's wrong?"

"It's just . . ." I sighed and pressed my lips together as I contemplated my words. "What's the deal with you and Alexander?"

Matthew's whole body went rigid as he pulled away from me and went blank faced. I bit the inside of my cheek, hoping I hadn't struck a nerve.

"Where did that come from?" he asked, his voice strained.

"Honestly I've been wanting to know for a long time," I admitted, looking down at my hands. "Ever since I was with him at the Cyfrin compound and Mallory let it slip that you two had a history. I just didn't want to pry or bring back any unwanted memories."

"Then why ask now?" he demanded, his eyes staring right past my head.

"Because I had a horrible dream last night and he was in it."

"More like *because* he was in it," he stated, and I shook my head.

"No, actually. All three of the Keepers of Balance were there but he was . . . *Remorseful* of what happened in it. It's just like when I was with him in person."

"I'm not following," he said, now watching me with narrowed eyes.

"When I was at the Cyfrin compound, he was all over the place with his demeanor," I explained. "He seemed cold and distant at first glance but there was more than once when we'd be interacting, and he was decent to me. It was like he cared in his own weird way. I don't think he necessarily agreed with everything happening there. I feel like underneath his hard exterior, he's just a boy who needs guidance. Kind of like you."

"Don't compare me to him!" Matthew snapped. "I am nothing like him. You're just too compassionate, Robin. Or actually, better yet, you're just *gullible* because levelheaded people would know that one decent encounter with an evil psychopath doesn't make them redeemable. You can't save everyone, okay? Some people are just bad, and Alexander is one of them. Don't be stupid enough to let his charms work their wonders on you. He doesn't care, he was probably just trying to have his way with you."

I stared at him with wide eyes as my mouth fell open slightly. His words were like a slap in the face, and I took a deep breath as I tried to control the anger that was welling up inside of me.

"I may be too compassionate or maybe even a little *gullible* but at least I'm not a brooding prick that lies and lashes out at the people he claims are friends when things don't go his way," I told him hotly, my nostrils flaring as I huffed. "But maybe we aren't friends after all, though, because even after all this time you still can't be honest with me. After all we've been through together you still don't trust me."

His face contorted into shame, and he reached his arm out towards me. "Robin I-"

"Save it," I cut him off as I stood up, hurt and insulted. I waved my hand and drenched him with the water from a nearby fountain before turning on my heel and walking away with bruised feelings, angry thoughts, and a lot of questions.

Chapter Four

"Hi," I greeted Adriana as I walked into her office at the courthouse after school.

"Hey, honey. How was school?" she asked without looking up from the papers on her desk.

"It was okay. Matthew and I got into a fight," I told her, and she glanced up at me as I slid into the chair across from her.

"Oh no. I'm sorry to hear that," she said as she folded her arms over her desk. "What was it about?"

"Nothing important," I replied, picking at my green sweater.

"Well, I'm sure you two will make up soon. You can't seem to stay mad at one another for long," she reassured me with a comforting smile. I bit my lip as I hesitated with my next question. "What is it?"

"Is there any way I could go visit Milton?" I asked quickly before I lost my nerve.

Adriana's face turned serious, and I knew the answer that was coming.

"I wish there was, but you know how the council feels about that. Even if your father and I brought it up for a vote again, they'd deny it."

"It isn't fair," I muttered, swallowing around the lump in my throat.

"I know, honey. But the rules are there for our protection. Besides, your first goodbye was hard enough. I would hate for all of you to have to go through that again."

"It wouldn't have to be a hard goodbye if I could visit them consistently."

"I know but that's just not possible," she replied gently as she came around her desk and leaned against the front of it.

"Will it ever be?" I asked quietly, looking into her unearthly bright blue eyes that matched mine so perfectly.

"I don't know," she answered but I could tell that she wasn't being forthcoming. She knew it wouldn't ever be a possibility but was trying to spare me the disappointment. Garridan had to protect itself from the outside world, not because they could harm us but because being found out could destroy everything Garridan had always done to maintain the balance in the world. The secrecy wasn't truly for our protection like Adriana had said but for everybody else's.

"I just miss them," I finally murmured.

"It's okay to miss them. Just don't let it run your life. You'll only be as happy as you allow yourself to be."

"Excuse me, Mrs. Caldwell," a short, balding man said as he knocked on her door.

"Yes, Filipe?"

"Mrs. Alastair has requested your presence in her office. She made it clear it was very important," Filipe relayed as his glasses sagged on his nose.

"I'll be right there," she told him, and he scurried away as she turned her attention back to me. "Duty calls but we can talk more later, okay?"

"Okay," I said, allowing her to pat my cheek affectionately before heading off to find Matthew's mom.

I picked up my backpack and headed out of the building but when I made my way outside, I didn't feel like going home. Instead, I began moseying towards my favorite park that contained a small pond and walking trails. When I arrived, I sat down under the biggest oak tree that stood right next to the water on the opposite side of the trails and watched as people passed by. I absentmindedly played with the liquid in front of me, drawing it into different shapes before plopping them down on top of the scattered flowers that sat on the bank.

"Hey," I heard someone say.

I glanced over my shoulder and saw Matthew walking up. "Hey," I replied.

He stopped a couple feet away from me. "May I sit?"

"Are you going to insult me again?" I shot back and he ran his fingers through his hair.

"No, I'm not. I'm actually going to apologize."

"Then by all means, sit," I told him, motioning to the grass next to me.

He plopped down, watching the water ripple in the pond. "I don't know what to say."

"I believe the words you're looking for are 'I'm sorry'," I suggested sarcastically as I raised my eyebrows at him.

"I *am* sorry, Robin. I'm *so* sorry for lashing out at you and saying what I did. I got upset but it was no excuse to treat you like that," he apologized earnestly. "You aren't gullible or stupid. You're actually really good at reading people and I know you wouldn't fall for anyone's deceptions. You *are* too compassionate but that shouldn't necessarily be seen as a fault. I know it's just because you care and have a big heart."

"I do. Thank you for apologizing," I told him, watching as relief showed on his face.

"So you forgive me?" he questioned hopefully.

"Of course, I forgive you. I have a big heart remember?" I nudged his arm with my elbow. "I'm sorry I brought it up at all."

"No, you were right," he said with a shake of his head. "You're definitely nosy—don't get me wrong—but I know that you weren't prying just for the sake of curiosity. You deserve to know." He took a deep breath then sighed before speaking again. "When I was sent away from Garridan, I wasn't lucky enough to be adopted by a nice family like you were. I got shuffled around in foster care for years and it was really rough. I had no sense of stability or family . . . Until I met Alexander, that is."

"What do you mean?" I asked when he didn't elaborate.

"I was about five when we were placed in the same foster home," he said. "One day our foster dad decided I had stolen money from his cigarette box, and he had to punish me. Despite being only six at the time, Alexander stepped in and took my place. He endured every lash without a second thought. After that, he kind of took me under his wing and watched over me. He protected me from the dangers of our life. A year later, we were still joined at the hip. We only had one another but it was okay because we loved each other. We were brothers."

I watched as his distant eyes turned sad and I grabbed his hand in both of mine.

"Then his powers emerged and mine followed suit not long after. We were completely entranced by them, and we practiced in secret every day. We were convinced our brotherhood had formed them." He laughed dryly, shaking his head in disdain at the memory. "A couple months after we discovered our powers, we were yanked into a van on the way to school. Our heads were covered with bags and despite trying to fight, we both fell asleep."

“Darnell,” I murmured, remembering the man who had done the same thing to me the night I was taken.

Matthew nodded. “He has the power of somnokinesis which allows him to put other beings to sleep. It’s an excellent way to make sure someone who’s unwilling isn’t capable of resisting.”

“I remember,” I said as his face flashed in my mind. “What happened after you were brought to the Cyfrin compound?”

“We were deceived,” he stated softly. “We were kids with big dreams, and they played on that. They promised us family and safety with them, and we believed it.”

“You were young. You couldn’t have known any better.”

“It wasn’t all that bad at first. The Cyfrin leaders treated each child like their own. We were fed, clothed, and loved on. We went to school and training, and we shared a room in the castle.” His voice was distant, and his eyes were unfocused, as if seeing something far away. “We thought we were living the dream. But that all changed as we got older. We were slowly indoctrinated by their belief system and our training became a deadly game. Children died. Some of them by my hand.”

He swallowed loudly then took a shaky breath. “Everyone’s worth became based off their power levels. Alexander was on the top of that food chain since he possessed an elemental power, and it changed him. He turned cruel and brutal, hurting others for sport in the name of hierarchy. It made the leaders proud, and he yearned for their approval which made him even more dangerous. He did anything they asked of him. Despite all that, though, he never stopped looking out for me.

“My power is unique and strong which would’ve gotten me through but he’s the reason the Keepers of Balance thought so highly of me. He’s the reason I continued to live a life of luxury while so many others were beaten and starved as an educational purpose. He’s the reason I was forced to do things . . . Unthinkable things . . .” he trailed off, his jaw set, and his lips pushed together so tightly they turned white.

“Hey, it’s okay,” I told him, squeezing his hand gently.

He scoffed lightly. “Anyway, after he was given a seat with the Keepers of Balance is when we really had our fallout. I questioned their motives, and he didn’t like that. He told me to keep my mouth shut and stay in line otherwise he couldn’t guarantee my safety anymore. But I didn’t care. I spoke out against them and was punished time and time again. It got to the point that Toshiro wanted me killed but I guess Alexander couldn't really handle seeing me dead because he convinced him to give me a second chance. That's when I was told my redemption assignment."

"What was it?"

He looked over at me and smiled grimly. "You."

I raised my eyebrows, and he nodded his head in confirmation as I said, "That's when you came to Milton and turned my life upside down."

"That would be it."

"Did you know from the beginning you weren't going to succeed?" I questioned curiously.

"Not exactly," he said after a moment of hesitation. "I knew I didn't want to be a part of the Cyfrin any longer, but I wasn't sure I could actually leave, so you would've been the perfect way for me to get back in their good graces. However, once Felicity walked up to me . . . my fate was sealed."

I smiled at that. "She has that effect on people." We sat silently for a brief moment before I said, "I'm glad you chose to stay with us, Matthew."

"I am too. I guess I should be thanking Alexander. If it wasn't for him, I would've never met any of you or gotten away from Toshiro's rule."

"Do you really hate him?" I asked hesitantly and he began picking at the grass absentmindedly.

"No," he admitted with sadness in his voice. "I just hate what he's become."

"I don't think he's completely hopeless," I offered up. "He still has a conscious in there. I've witnessed it."

"That may be true, but it doesn't mean he's redeemable," he countered.

"You never know."

"It just makes me crazy that I still care about him. Even after all the things he's done or forced me into I just- he just- *ugh*."

"He's your family."

"Yeah. Unfortunately, he is," he agreed with a sigh.

"Thank you for telling me all this."

"Well, that's what friends are for. Right?" he replied, eyeing me, and I grinned at his subtle reminder of what I had said earlier.

"That's exactly what they're for," I agreed, leaning my head against his shoulder.

We sat like that until the sun began to set, both of us wrapped up in our own thoughts. I couldn't picture him and Alexander as little boys, innocent and untouched by the evil they grew up with. All I could think about was the growth that I had witnessed Matthew have in the short time I had known him. He had completely turned his life around, but it was obvious he was still haunted by his past ghosts.

Chapter Five

"Were our parents acting odd to you last night?" I asked Matthew the next week as we walked home from fencing class, our chosen extracurricular activity.

"You noticed that too," he commented, and I nodded. "Yeah, they're definitely hiding something."

"What do you think it is?" I questioned and he shrugged, pulling his hood up over his head.

"I honestly couldn't say," he answered as we walked up the sidewalk to my house. Before we reached the door, it flew open, and Elijah came running out with a bag.

"You can't come inside," he said, and I raised my eyebrows. "Claire has plans for you and Matthew so you both need to go to his house."

Matthew and I glanced at one another, then I said, "Uhm, okay. Can I at least get some clothes to change into?"

Elijah thrust the bag into my hands and smiled. "Already done." I cocked my head and scrunched my forehead as I looked him up and down, curiosity blooming at his odd behavior. He continued to smile innocently, then pushed us away with the force of air rippling from his hands. "Bye now."

"Bye," I offered up as we let the wind push us back onto the street. Without replying, he turned on his heel and went back inside as I stared at the closed door in bewilderment. "What the heck was that all about?"

"I have no idea," Matthew said, sounding just as confused as I felt.

"That was weird right?" I asked as we began walking.

"Definitely. Maybe Claire knows what's going on." We walked into his house and were greeted by quiet. "Hello?" he called out and a second later Claire popped up behind us.

"I've been expecting you," she announced ominously, her black dress highlighted with hot pink streaks. "Get changed. Mom laid out clothes for you. We're going to the movies."

"We're going to the *movies*?" Matthew asked suspiciously and she nodded with a sweet smile. "Why are we going to the movies?"

"Because you're my brother and I love you," she responded, and I rubbed my lips together to keep from smiling.

"That's bull," Matthew accused, crossing his arms.

Claire gasped and let a hand fly over her chest. "You doubt my love for you?" she questioned with a fake tone of hurt in her voice.

"No but I doubt your motives," he replied, rolling his eyes at her theatrics. "Why is everyone acting so weird?

"No reason." She shrugged. "Now hurry up before I sic a ghost on you."

She walked away without another word, and I leaned towards Matthew. "She can't really do that can she?"

"You bet I can!" she hollered over her shoulder, so we scurried up the stairs.

I went into the bathroom and pulled out the clothes in the bag, making a face when I saw what they were — a light blue, long sleeved dress accompanied by white leggings and wedged shoes. I changed into them and assessed myself in the mirror. It was a beautiful outfit that showed off my curves and brightened my already vivid eyes, but I couldn't figure out why Elijah sent this ensemble instead of a more practical option if we were just going to see a movie.

I splashed cool water on my face and pulled my hair out of its bun, patting down the crazier sections. When I opened the door, I found Matthew waiting in a dress shirt that nearly matched the color of my dress and grey slacks. I grinned as he shifted uncomfortably, pulling at the collar of the shirt.

"You look handsome," I complimented him as I stepped up and unbuttoned the top of his shirt. "There. That should help the choking feeling."

"Thanks," he muttered as he appraised me. "I have an awful feeling we're being set up on a date."

"You think so?" I asked in surprise.

"You don't?" he asked in response, and I shrugged.

"They know we're just friends. More than that, they know we're like family," I pointed out. "I don't think they'd try to set us up."

"Then what's with the matching outfits?"

"Family portrait?" I suggested, only half joking.

"I know you two are ready," Claire called up to us, and Matthew rolled his eyes.

"Don't you love having siblings?" I laughed, poking him in the side.

"It's a real treat," he replied sarcastically.

"I heard that," Claire said.

"You hear everything," he muttered, and I grinned. "Well, I guess we better go and find out what this is all about. Shall we?"

He held out his arm and I hooked my own around it. "We shall."

Claire took us to the movie theatre where we stood out like sore thumbs with our attire. Claire accepted the cat calls with winks while I looked down in embarrassment and Matthew glared dauntingly at those who tried anything funny. Luckily, most of our time was spent in the dark as the film played. After it ended, Claire rounded us up with a sly grin plastered on her face.

"Ready to go home?" she asked, and we stared at her, unsure if she was serious or not.

"We didn't really get this dressed up just to go to the movies, did we?" I asked in disbelief, and she shrugged without answering. Matthew and I exchanged a look as she began walking away.

"I'm going to kill whoever was responsible for this," he growled, and I almost agreed with him.

Claire drove to my house and instructed Matthew to walk me to the door. After we stepped out of the car, I scratched the back of my neck nervously.

"Maybe you were right after all," I commented.

"About what?" he asked.

"About this being a date."

"Well, they're going to be awfully disappointed then," he said, his lips pressed together as we stopped in front of my door.

"They'll get over it," I responded with a shrug, but my stomach churned with nerves at the newfound awkwardness of the situation. We stood there uncomfortably, neither of us knowing what to say.

"Well . . . Goodnight," he offered up.

We finally looked at one another, staring into each other's eyes as crickets sounded in the distance. A grin made its way onto my face and we both began laughing, the awkward moment passing away.

Claire rolled down the car window and yelled, "Take her inside!"

"Why?" Matthew shot back but she only glared at him. "Alrighty then."

The grin stayed on my face as I unlocked the door and opened it. We walked inside, greeted by darkness and silence.

"I wonder where my parents are," I said as I turned on the living room light.

"Surprise!"

My heart skipped a beat as people jumped out from behind walls and furniture, laughing as Matthew and I stood there frozen. I looked around and saw streamers and balloons hung around the room and a table full of presents in the corner.

Claire came up from behind and threw her arms around us in a hug. "Happy early birthday guys!"

"Happy early birthday!" everyone else echoed as our parents stepped up to us.

"What is going on?" I asked as I tried to breathe again.

"We wanted to throw you two a joint birthday party!" Susan explained with a smile. "You only turn eighteen once so how special is it that you get to share it with someone."

I looked over at Matthew. "Wait, when's your birthday?"

"In three days," he replied. "When is yours?"

"In five days," I responded with surprise. "How did I not know our birthdays were so close together?"

"Because we never discussed it," he said in a 'duh' tone and I made a less than attractive face at him.

"I know it's a little early, but we had a breakthrough with decoding the Cyfrin's messages so we're going to be all hands on deck at work for the next couple weeks," Adriana informed us. "But tonight is all about the two of you so go mingle. We invited the kids from your class."

"So it doubles as another attempt to get us 'adjusted'," Matthew commented, and they all looked sheepish at the accusation that was clearly true.

Matthew and I exchanged another look, neither of us thrilled with the idea of socializing, but I put a smile on my face anyway and did as I was told. I made the rounds around the room, thanking people for coming as upbeat music played in the background. I looked around as people laughed and conversed, seeming to be having a good time. Kesha pulled William into the middle of the living room and started dancing which quickly caught on with the other young people.

"Would you like to dance?" a boy with short black hair and milky brown eyes asked, holding out his hand to me.

"Oh um . . ." I bit my lip, wanting to say no but then I saw Adriana watching anxiously so I smiled at the boy and held out my hand. "Sure."

He twirled me onto the makeshift dance floor, and I couldn't help but laugh.

"I'm Martin," he said with a grin that illuminated his buck teeth. He stood just a couple inches taller than me with broad shoulders and a flat frame.

"Robin," I replied, returning his smile.

"I know," he assured me. "Actually, I think everyone knows who you are."

"Perfect," I groaned, and he chuckled.

"It's really not all bad, I promise."

"But that means that some of it is."

"Fair enough," he replied. "I was happy your parents invited me tonight. I've been wanting to talk to you for a while."

"Really? Why's that?"

"I find you interesting."

"You don't even know me."

"True. I guess it would be more appropriate to say I find your history interesting," he corrected. "I can't imagine how hard of an adjustment it was coming here after so long. I'm sure you could use a friend."

"I have a friend," I told him, nodding towards Matthew who had also been sucked onto the dance floor.

"It never hurts to have more than one," he said.

"Why didn't you ever talk to me before then?"

"I'm no good at talking to gorgeous girls," he replied, his eyes twinkling.

"Somehow, I don't think that's true."

"Alright, fine. Truth be told, I also find you intimidating. Your friend over there doesn't help make you any more approachable either."

I had to grin at that. "No, I guess he doesn't. But he's a good guy. He's all I have here aside from my parents."

"In that case I think you *both* need some more friends."

"I don't know if you've noticed but we're not exactly great at that."

"You seem to be doing fine with me," he told me with a shrug. "And I'd be more than happy to help you out."

"Really?"

"Really," he replied, his smile not faltering. "Consider me your first Garridan friend."

"I'd like that," I said, returning his smile.

"And if you're up for it, I could introduce you to some of my other friends," he offered. "Get you and home boy over there more social."

"I appreciate the offer. Thank you."

"Anytime!"

The night continued in a similar way with people coming up and offering good conversation or asking me to dance. It seemed there were multiple people who would've talked to us sooner had we made ourselves open to it. Maybe we had made our adjustment here harder than it needed to be after all.

Later on, Matthew and I got to blow out the candles on a huge, two-tiered cake then opened presents as everyone took a break from dancing and chowed down on the sweets provided. As the party was nearing its end, I realized I hadn't stopped smiling or laughing the entire time and I had actually enjoyed every moment of the evening. I walked to where my parents stood in the corner and encased them in a big hug.

"Thank you," I said with my head buried between them. "This has been the best night I've had in a long time."

"We're so happy you've had fun," Elijah told me, smoothing my hair down.

"I think you were right."

"About what?" Adriana asked.

"Our adjustment here . . . This was a good idea. I think it really helped."

They exchanged a smile and Elijah pulled me in for another hug. "We may not have a lot of parenting experience, but we're still usually right about everything."

I pursed my lips. "Maybe not *everything*."

"No, I'm pretty sure it's everything," he shot back with a grin, and I rolled my eyes.

"Okay," I muttered sarcastically.

Adriana let out a laugh and shook her head at our banter. "We love you, honey."

"I love you too," I replied. I turned around to gaze over the room but stayed wrapped in their arms. I watched as people slowly began to leave and saw Matthew leaned against a wall with his family surrounding him. I smiled as Claire smeared frosting on his face and they all laughed as he glowered at her. I wished I could freeze this moment and keep the memory alive forever because it was the first time in a long time I felt at home.

Chapter Six

The next day at school was different than it had been before. Instead of avoiding us, people greeted us in the morning or offered up small conversation. It was like a ripple effect throughout the whole school; since the seniors did it, so did the lower classmen. I had to admit it was a nice change. There were many who were still wary of us and continued treating us like the plague, but I brushed it off, grateful that we were starting to be accepted at all.

At lunch, Martin invited us to sit with him and his friends. Despite Matthew's hesitance, I accepted happily, and we joined them. They were a high-spirited bunch who constantly talked over one another, but I didn't mind because it meant I didn't have to add to the conversation. As they were laughing obnoxiously over a joke I didn't understand, a teacher walked up to the table, and they immediately grew quiet.

"Ms. Hayes," she addressed me, and I looked up at her in surprise.

"Yes," I acknowledged.

"Come with me please. You're needed in the office," she instructed before looking over at Matthew. "You as well Mr. Alastair."

Matthew and I exchanged a look then stood up, leaving our food trays where they sat. As we walked down the hall, my stomach churned at the familiarity of the situation. The last time I had been approached by a teacher and asked to follow them was when I found out my family had been killed by the Cyfrin. I tried to control my breathing, but it started coming out in little gasps as the trauma hit me all over again.

"Hey," Matthew said softly, putting his hand on my back. "It's okay. Everything is fine. Everybody's safe."

"How do you know?" I whispered.

He wrapped his arm around me and rubbed my arm as we continued to walk. "I just know."

When we arrived at the office, I saw Adriana waiting and I rushed over to her.

"Are you okay? Is Elijah okay?" I asked earnestly, looking her up and down as if I'd see open wounds on her person.

"Yes, yes! Everyone is fine," she assured me, and I sighed in relief as the weight on my heart lifted.

"But *something* is wrong," Matthew commented, eyeing her observantly, and she nodded her head once.

"We'll discuss it at the courthouse," she replied before heading for the door. Matthew and I followed instantly and hopped into the backseat of her car where it sat waiting out front. The ride filled me with more anxiety as deafening silence surrounded the space around us. Adriana appeared tense, her whole face scrunched up and her lip peeling from being bit so hard. She led us up to her office where Elijah, Susan, Malachi, William, Kesha, and two other Keepers of Balance waited.

"Hey kids. You remember Darby and Chang," Elijah pointed them out.

"Of course," I responded, offering them a timid smile.

"What's going on?" Matthew demanded, ignoring the pleasantries.

"Why don't you sit down," Malachi suggested, motioning towards two empty chairs.

I followed his instructions as my heart hammered in my chest and my palms sweated from the nerves I felt.

"I'll stand, thanks," Matthew replied, coming up behind me with his arms crossed.

"Suit yourself, son," Malachi acknowledged as Susan and Kesha stepped forward.

"As you know we had a break in deciphering the Cyfrin's codes," Kesha started, her glasses sliding down her nose. "Once we figured out one dialogue, it was a domino effect in learning the others."

"So you have their codes completely deciphered?" Matthew asked and she nodded, her hands fiddling with a strand of her dreadlocks.

"We've been listening in to their conversations and . . . it would appear it was all a trap," she continued.

I furrowed my brows and asked. "What do you mean?"

"She means that the Cyfrin purposely let us intercept their communications," Susan took over and Kesha backed away to stand next to William.

"Why would they do that?" Matthew asked, his eyes squinted.

"Because they wanted to get a message to us," she replied, and I glanced around the room. Everyone's solemn faces told me whatever the message was, it wasn't good.

"What was the message?" I prodded.

"It was an offer," Adriana answered quietly. "They're willing to give us the locations of the rest of the children they've found and the promise not to harm them or interfere in their lives in any way in exchange . . ."

"In exchange for Robin," Malachi finished.

My heart dropped into my stomach as it threatened to evict the food I ate at lunch, My mouth opened but no sound came out.

"You aren't going to agree to that, are you?" Matthew accused with a tone that sent chills up my spine as he put a hand on my shoulder protectively.

"Of course not!" Adriana exclaimed. "She's our daughter!"

"It does bring up a rather messy situation though," Darby spoke up, her greying hair falling into her dark brown eyes. "They also threatened to kill off those other children and more if we didn't accept their offer."

"But you can find a way to protect them," Matthew said to Malachi and William.

"Not if we don't know where they are," William pointed out.

The room erupted in possible solutions and ways to make the Cyfrin happy without trading me off to them, but I knew it would never work. Their rising voices became a tiny buzz in the back of my mind as my thoughts raced. Toshiro knew what he wanted, and he would have no problem doing whatever he deemed necessary to get his way. I knew he wouldn't stop with hurting the children of Garridan either. He would go after their families and friends as well. The only way to save all those people was to give him what he wanted: me.

I took a shaky breath and exhaled slowly, trying to get my bearings. I didn't want to go back. I didn't want to be with the people who killed my family and tortured my best friend. I didn't want to help them regain power by creating a pure bloodline and I definitely didn't want to give them the means to destroy the world. But if I only cared about what I wanted, innocent people would have their lives ruined and that wasn't right. Why should they have to suffer like I did?

"I'll go," I whispered. Everyone in the room continued speaking over one another so I raised my voice. "I said I'll go."

They all froze at my announcement, looking at me with different emotions plastered on their faces. Adriana and Elijah rushed towards me with panic-stricken ones.

"Honey, you do *not* have to go," Adriana told me, her voice fierce.

"More than that, you're *not* going to go," Elijah added, his bushy brows raised up above his wide eyes.

I licked my lips as I latched onto their hands. "I have to," I said, looking around the room. "It's my duty to Garridan."

"No, it's not," Matthew insisted, his voice urgent. "This is your *life* we're talking about."

"No, it isn't," I denied. "It's hundreds of other people's lives."

"Robin," Malachi spoke up hesitantly. "If you go, you may very well never make it back. You'll have no protection there or any guarantee of your safety if an attack is made . . . Which I guarantee will happen sooner rather than later."

"That's sort of perfect then," I said, bringing my attention back to my parents. "I'll go and you can get the locations of the other kids and set them up with protection. While I'm there we can figure out a way for me to get information back to you and you'll have the upper hand in the battle. Especially if you have a head's up on when they're going to attack. It'll give us a chance to end their terror once and for all so Garridan can live in peace again."

"It's not a bad idea," William commented, making himself vulnerable to threatening stares from half the room. "Well, it's not."

"Robin," Adriana choked out in a thick voice. "You realize how dangerous it will be."

"Yes."

"Are you sure this is what you want to do?" Elijah asked, his eyes full of sorrow.

I looked at my hands wrapped in my parents' and swallowed around the lump in my throat. Of course I didn't want to do it, but I was going to.

"Yes," I told him softly and Adriana closed her eyes as she leaned into him for support.

"Don't do it Robin," Matthew pleaded, crouching next to me.

"It'll be okay. Toshiro wants a pure bloodline. That guarantees my safety."

"No, it doesn't! It only guarantees he won't *kill* you. That doesn't mean he won't torture you to the brink of it if necessary."

"I only have to last until they decide to attack," I replied, refusing to look at him. I knew what I would see in his face, and it would only make the decision harder.

"We don't even know when that'll be! It isn't worth risking your life," he grimaced, his body radiating with displeasure.

"But it *is* worth everyone else's," I shot back. "I never understood choosing to save one over the many. I won't do that."

"You're a wise girl," Chang said quietly, his dark eyes soft as he looked at me. "Thank you for your sacrifice."

Matthew groaned at his choice of words and tears slid down Adriana's face. I knew I was hurting them, but it had to be done. However, I also knew it was a risk. I wasn't worried about being in the Cyfrin compound because Toshiro couldn't afford to kill me. I could last there as long as I needed to. I was worried about when the battle started, and I was on the wrong side of it. That was when I'd be fighting for my life.

"I have one request," I spoke up and all eyes turned back towards me.

"Anything," Chang offered with a wave of his arm.

"I want to go see Ben."

Chapter Seven

As the sun beat down over the flat plains of the south, we were already well on our way to Milton. Matthew was pacing around the floor of the plane, his nerves getting the best of him, and no one else seemed to be doing much better. Adriana and Elijah sat close to me, speaking in hushed tones as they both fidgeted mindlessly with one another's hands. Malachi and William were filling up on sweets as they discussed their surveillance plans once again, making sure there was no flaw in their protection of us while outside of Garridan territory.

We chose to go on Friday so Matthew and I would have the entire weekend with the people we missed most. No one was happy about my request, but I didn't care. This was my one act of selfishness, and I deserved it. I needed to go back and have one carefree weekend with happy memories before subjecting myself to the doom and gloom of the Cyfrin compound.

I played with my hair anxiously, my nerves no better than Matthew's. It seemed silly to be so flustered about seeing Ben, but I couldn't help it. All too soon, we were landing in a wide-open space and a soldier named Jenny masked the plane with her camouflage abilities.

"Be safe," Elijah told us as we got up to leave.

"And have fun," Adriana added with a soft smile.

I gave them both a hug then followed Matthew down the stairs with his brother and father in tow.

"Remember, you won't see us, but we'll be watching you at all times," Malachi said. "No one is getting through our lines so don't worry about that. Just enjoy yourselves."

"Thank you," I replied with a grateful smile. It was a little awkward knowing they'd be following us around, but it also relieved the stress of thinking someone from the Cyfrin could come in and ruin everything or hurt someone. After a half hour long car ride, we were finally in Milton, and I smiled at the familiarity of my surroundings.

"School has been out for a while," Matthew commented, and I nodded in agreement.

"Which means we have to track them down," I replied.

Matthew wiggled his phone at me. "I was just going to call her."

"You do that," I said with a roll of my eyes. "I'm going to swing by Ben's house and see where he is. I want to say hi to his family anyway."

"Meet you in a couple hours for dinner?" Matthew asked and I nodded, then took a deep breath.

"Good luck," I told him softly.

"You too," he replied. He got out of the car and sat down on a bench in front of the school, eyeing his phone. I shook my head and chuckled, hoping he'd really call her, then began driving towards Ben's house. When I arrived, I saw Mahka and Mr. Toves cutting firewood on the side of the house and Dakota sitting on a stool next to them reading. I opened the door and when I shut it behind me, all three of them looked up to see who had arrived.

"Robin!" Mahka hollered, running towards me with a wide grin on his face. He picked me up in a giant bear hug and spun me around, causing me to laugh.

"You've grown!" I exclaimed.

"You haven't," he replied with a wink, and I made a face at him.

"It's so good to see you," Mr. Toves told me as he stepped in for his turn at a hug.

"It's good to see you too," I said, my heart swelling with the truth of it as Dakota sauntered over. I wrapped one arm around him, and he smiled sheepishly up at me. "How is everyone?"

"We're all healthy and happy," Mr. Toves answered with a smile that crinkled his face. "How are you? How's your new home?"

"It's . . . different," I settled on, looking down at my shoes. "But I'm adjusting."

"I'm glad to hear it. Renee is at the store right now, but I know she'd love to visit with you. How long are you staying?" he asked.

"Just for the weekend."

"That's three nights you'll need a meal," he pointed out and I couldn't help but smile at his logic.

"Well, tonight I'm hoping to meet up with Felicity, but I would love to have dinner with you all tomorrow," I told him.

"I'll let Renee know," he said as a sparkle entered his eyes. "I know you'd rather see someone else right now though, am I right?" I nodded sheepishly and he continued. "He's down at the lake you two were so fond of."

"Thank you," I replied, giving him another quick hug before turning back to the car. "I'll see you guys tomorrow!"

I drove to the lake in half the time it should've taken me and was saying a silent prayer of thanks that I hadn't gotten pulled over. I parked the car behind the hill and jogged up it as the smell of musky water met my nose. When I reached the top, I looked around and saw Ben sitting by the lake, tossing rocks into it halfheartedly. I continued to watch him as I walked down the other side of the hill, my heart thumping wildly in my chest as I drew closer to him. I licked my lips and wiped my sweaty palms on my jeans before pulling up a small stream of water in front of him and twirling it gently.

His head shot up at the sight and he quickly stood as he turned around. When his amber eyes landed on me, he froze in disbelief. His jet-black hair was pulled back in a braid, showing off his features, and I smiled softly as my eyes brimmed with tears. I saw his lips speak my name. Then he was running for me. My heart swelled, yearning for him, and I met him halfway. We collided in a tight embrace, and I sunk into him, breathing in his scent as his arms pulled me closer. His lips were on mine then, moving fiercely as his hands traveled up my back and to my cheeks. I matched his earnestness as my body reacted to him, letting my fingers rest on his waist.

"Is this a dream?" he whispered, putting his forehead against mine. "If it is, I never want to wake up,"

"It's not a dream," I assured him, putting my hands on his wrists as he continued to hold my face in his palms.

"I can't believe you're here," he murmured, stroking my tear-streaked face with his thumbs.

"I can't either," I said softly, holding back a sob as my heart contracted in my chest. "I've missed you, Benjamin."

"And I've missed you, Robin. So much" he replied, pulling my lips back to his gently. "I have so many questions."

"I'll answer them all. But for now, just kiss me."

He gladly did as I said, running his fingers through my tangled hair. I let my hands run over his chest and he let out a sound of pleasure as I explored him. Somehow we ended up on the ground facing one another, trying to catch our breath as my head rested on my arm. His finger traced over my body, sending shivers down my spine.

"How much time do I get with you?" he asked.

"We're leaving Monday morning," I answered, and his lips pressed together.

"That soon, huh?" I nodded as his face clouded with sadness. After a quick moment, though, his signature grin creeped up. "Well, at least I get any time with you."

"There's the positive Ben I know and love," I said, and he chuckled.

"So how did you manage to get visitation rights?" he joked, and I hesitated as I decided what to say.

"It wasn't easy," I finally replied, knowing I couldn't tell him the truth. It was my burden to bear, and it would ruin our weekend if he knew. "But all that matters is I'm here. Oh, so is Matthew."

"That's great. Is he with Felicity?"

"If he didn't chicken out." I grinned, picturing him still sitting on the bench.

"How's everything going? How are you doing in Garridan?"

I looked away, rolling onto my back. "Honestly, it's been hard. Adriana and Elijah are great. They're so supportive and loving. Matthew's family too. But everyone else hasn't been so accepting."

"I'm sorry." He grabbed my hand, squeezing it gently.

"It got a little better this week. Our families threw us a joint birthday party and invited everyone in the senior class. It actually really helped the big divide that was between us and them."

"That's great then! Everything takes time."

"Yeah," I agreed. If I wasn't leaving Garridan, I might've actually been fully accepted by the end of the school year. "My training is going great too. It's been really fun seeing what all I can do with my powers. Even the physical training hasn't been terrible."

"I'm sure you've done great," he said, always the supporter. "Are you happy?"

I shrugged. "Some days, yes. Others . . . No."

"That's hard to hear . . . The only reason I can go on with my days is by knowing you're where you're meant to be. I want you to thrive there like you did here."

"It would be a lot easier if I didn't have to cut the people I love out of my life."

"I know but we can't change their rules. That make me even more thankful you're here right now," he said, giving me another kiss. "I honestly didn't think I'd see you for years, Robin, if ever."

His voice was thick, and I put my hand to his cheek, reciprocating his emotion. His face looked small and broken and I knew I was looking into his heart; what he had been going through the last six months. He was as lost without me as I was without him. Knowing that would only make the next goodbye worse than the first. Adriana had been right.

"Maybe I shouldn't have come back," I whispered, my chin quivering, and he looked frantic.

"No! No, don't say that!"

"I reopened healing wounds. It's going to be harder for them to heal this time, for both of us."

"I'd rather go through it all again if it means I get to see you, even if it's not for very long," he told me, and I closed my eyes as guilt filled me. "Hey."

When I opened my eyes again, he was staring at me intently, his face swimming with emotion. He pushed my hair behind my ear and cupped my face in his hand.

"You are worth all the hurt in the world," he murmured. "I'm a big boy. I can take it."

He leaned in and pressed his lips to mine softly. A tear made its way down my cheek, but I didn't care. I kissed him back, trying to transfer my love for him through physical touch instead of words. Ben was, and always would be, my happily ever after.

Chapter Eight

A couple hours later we were sitting with Matthew and Felicity in our usual spot at the diner. The laughter and conversation made it seem like no time had passed at all. We naturally fell into the sync we had before, and it felt good.

"How's basketball season going?" I asked as I chowed down on a plate of spaghetti.

"It would be a whole lot better if you were here," Felicity said with a roll of her eyes, her shoulder length hair curled and bouncing at the shake of her head. "When the five starters are playing it's not too bad but once we rotate people in it goes to hell in a handbasket. There's no way we're getting very far this year."

"That sucks."

"Yeah, it does," she agreed as Matthew gazed at her from his seat.

"How about the boy's team?" I turned towards Ben, and he grinned.

"Undefeated so far," he bragged, and Felicity threw a wadded-up napkin at him.

"That's great!" I exclaimed. "Think you'll take the championship this year?"

"Man, I hope so. It'd be a great senior year memory."

"How is your guys' school in sports?" Felicity questioned as Matthew and I exchanged a look.

"I'm not sure, actually," I confessed.

"We haven't exactly been paying attention to anything like that," Matthew added.

"Does that mean you're not playing any sports this year?" Ben asked me and I shook my head.

"We're in fencing if that counts," Matthew offered up.

"No. Not really," Felicity shot him down then turned a scrutinizing gaze towards me. "You love sports. Why didn't you sign up for any?"

I shrugged. "There were bigger things to focus on. Plus, team sports only work if your team meshes well. My presence wouldn't have allowed that."

"That's stupid," Felicity said bluntly, and I shrugged again.

"It is what it is, Felicity. I don't have the same life in Garridan that I did here. I have bigger roles to play there than a member of a high school sports team."

"Like what?" she challenged.

"Like a Keeper of Balance, a lawmaker, a peacekeeper," I replied. "I'm in training for physical combat, power control, and future government leader almost every day. My time is pretty much spoken for."

"Man, I'm sorry." She offered me a half smile. "I forgot how important you are there. It must suck though."

"It's not all daisies and rainbows," I agreed, looking at my hand in Ben's.

He gave it a comforting squeeze. "You're pretty much in the same boat, aren't you Matthew?"

"My priorities aren't nearly as important as Robin's but yes," Matthew replied. "Most of my free time is spent training for the guard and learning their routines and roles. It's demanding but luckily my father and brother are very helpful with it all."

"They're in the guard too?" Ben questioned and Matthew nodded.

"In it?" I scoffed. "His father *runs* it."

"Really?" Felicity jumped in, intrigued.

"Really," I answered. "He's the army general."

"That's awesome!" Ben exclaimed.

"Apparently Matthew's entire family lineage has always played a big part in the guard," I added, and Matthew grinned.

"That's cool," Felicity said. "How so?"

Matthew launched into the tale of his family history, proud and eager to share his knowledge with them. We all listened as he told us how it started with a very great grandfather a thousand years ago and the overview he gave of the people since then. By the time he ended with his father and brother, we were walking out of the diner and along main street.

"I think that's the most I've ever heard you talk," Ben joked, and we all laughed. "But seriously, you have a great family history. Always take pride in that."

"Oh, he does," I assured him. "It's actually really interesting watching the guard practice. Malachi and William are really strong."

"Do they practice often like a normal army?" Ben asked.

"I'm not sure about all the time, but ever since we've been there they have because they've been preparing," I replied.

"Preparing for what?" Felicity questioned and I bit my lip, knowing I had slipped up.

Matthew glanced at me then answered as discreetly as possible. "A battle with the Cyfrin."

"That doesn't sound good," Felicity said, her and Ben instantly concerned.

"It's been a long time coming," I told them. "It's inevitable if we're going to keep Garridan and the rest of the world safe."

"When you say 'we'," Ben hinted.

"The guard and the Keepers of Balance," Matthew clarified.

"Does that include you two?" Ben asked pointedly.

"Technically we're still just in training and not a part of either of those groups yet," I responded, lying by omission. "And we won't be for a couple years."

"That's a relief." Felicity sighed. "I can't imagine you two involved in a battle with those creeps."

Matthew and I shared a look, both hating that we had to lie to them but also knowing it was for the best. They would drive themselves mad with worry every day wondering if we were safe and that wasn't a life they could flourish on. If we wanted them to live their best lives, carefree and unburdened, they had to be kept in the dark.

"So what are the sleeping arrangements?" Felicity asked, changing the subject suddenly. "Is Robin or Matthew staying with me?"

Matthew choked on the water he was drinking, sputtering ineloquently as his face turned bright red. Ben and I laughed while Felicity arched her eyebrow in amusement.

"Guess that answers that question" she commented, observing him before turning her attention to me. "But that's okay. I'm dying for some time alone with you!"

"Sounds good to me," I agreed with a smile.

"We'll see you two tomorrow?" she asked Ben and Matthew.

"Bright and early," Ben replied, looking pained at the idea of leaving me.

"Bright and semi early," Felicity corrected, and he sighed.

"Fine," he relented as she glanced at Matthew.

"So you don't want to spend the night with me, huh?" she accused, and he tightened his jaw, preparing for the earful he was about to get.

I grinned at him as Ben wrapped his arms around my waist. When I looked up, he was staring at me with affection, and I reached up and let my lips linger on his. I let out a sigh of contentment as he connected our foreheads, our own special type of love language. I pulled away, knowing he never would, and smiled as I backed away. I pulled on Felicity's arm, taking her with me as I started down the street to her car, and she looped it with mine.

"You have no idea how happy I am to see you two," she told me.

"Believe me, I know," I responded.

"I've just been so lonely." Her bottom lip puckered, and I rolled my eyes.

"Yes, I'm so sure the queen of social has been lonely."

She made a face. "You know what I mean. Sure, I hang around a lot of people but it's not the same as being with my best friend or boyfriend."

I raised my eyebrows. "Is he still your boyfriend?"

"Of course," she told me, her forehead crinkling.

"That's not what I've heard."

"What do you mean?"

"Matthew told me you guys had agreed to 'move on and not hold onto hopeless ideals of being together again'," I quoted.

"I mean, we did," she admitted. "But he's here now which means it's not a hopeless ideal. It's possible for us to see each other."

I shook my head sadly. "No, Felicity. It really isn't. This was a one-time thing that only happened because something serious came up. After this trip, you won't see us again for a long time, if ever."

"That's what you said six months ago too," she reminded me.

"I know but it's the truth."

She shrugged so I decided not to press the matter. She would believe what she wanted to keep herself happy and I couldn't stop that.

"I've also heard you've been quite . . . How should I say this . . . *Promiscuous* since we've left," I said, eyeing her teasingly, and she gasped.

"Where did you hear that from?" Her eyes narrowed. "Ben."

I grinned and shook my head. "Nope."

"Well, you can't talk to anyone here so he's the only one who could've said something."

"It wasn't Ben."

"Then who? How?" she grumbled, folding her arms over her chest.

"That's a secret I'll take to my grave," I responded slyly. "So spill. Who, when, where, and most importantly *why*?"

She sighed then began her stories as we drove to her house. The rest of the night was filled with similar gossip, junk food, and very little sleep as we made the most of the time we had. I had missed her spirited and exuberant nature so much.

Chapter Nine

The morning air was frigid with a low blanket of fog covering the ground. The dying grass was damp but the blanket I sat upon protected my clothes from seeping in the moisture. The flowers between Mom and Dawn's headstones were fresh and too bright in the bleak surroundings but it brought me joy knowing people replaced them when they visited. I heard the crunch of feet on twigs behind me, coming closer with every step, then he was sitting behind me. His strong arms wrapped around me, and I leaned into his warm chest.

"Good morning, Benjamin," I greeted as he kissed the top of my beanie.

"Good morning, Robin," he replied, his voice low.

"How did you find me?" I asked, and he rested his chin on my shoulder.

"When Felicity told me she woke up and you were gone, it wasn't hard to guess where you came."

"You know me well."

He chuckled into my hair. "That I do. How long have you been here?"

"A couple hours. I just had so much to tell them."

"They would be proud of who you're becoming," he said, and I pressed my lips together.

"I'm not so sure," I replied meekly.

"Why's that?" he questioned, his eyebrows furrowing.

"My mom used to tell me that my greatest trait was also my biggest flaw. She'd tell me sometimes it was better to be selfish than selfless, otherwise I'd go through life giving up things for other people." Her voice echoed in my head as if she was saying it to me now. She was always so appreciative of me helping with Dawn, but she knew what I gave up to do that. I couldn't imagine what she'd say to what I was giving up now to help others.

"She had a point," Ben agreed. "It's a fine line. It's great to help others but sometimes you have to think about yourself and your future."

I looked down at my shoes. He didn't realize what an impact his words would have but they stung like a sharp knife. If he knew the situation at hand, he would beg me to be selfish, to forget about everyone else and choose to keep myself safe. A part of me wanted to be. To just stay here with him and be happy. But I knew I couldn't do that.

"Let's get out of here," I said, standing up suddenly.

He picked up the blanket and brushed it off before folding it over his arm. I grabbed his hand as he led me to his truck, looking back once to wave goodbye to my family. He opened the side door for me, and I hopped in, grateful to be out of the cold. He quickly circled around and started the engine, putting the heater on high, then pulled me over to the middle seat so he could wrap his arm around me. I looked up at him and he gently caressed my lips with his. When he pulled back, he grinned then leaned around me and pulled a small box enveloped with wrapping paper and a bow out of the glove compartment.

"Happy birthday, Robin," he announced, holding the box out to me.

My brows furrowed, confused for a moment, before I realized the date. Today was my eighteenth birthday.

"You didn't have to buy me anything," I told him, smiling sheepishly as I took the box.

"I didn't actually," he admitted. "It's a family heirloom."

"A family heirloom?" I looked at him, puzzled, and he nodded. "Then why are you giving it to me?"

"Because I love you and my parents know I'd choose to spend the rest of my life with you if I could," he replied which only confused me further.

"What?"

"Just open it," he insisted, seeming slightly nervous.

I did as he said and tore the paper off to see a black jewelry box. I glanced up at him and he nodded at me encouragingly, so I lifted the top to reveal a ring that made me draw in a breath. It was like nothing I had ever seen before with two soldered bands that had grooves niched into them to match the texture of tree bark. The bands arched in the middle, their twig like structure encasing an oval-shaped moonstone, and two bronze maple leaves accented it on either side. It was beautiful and unique.

"This was my great grandmother's wedding ring," Ben explained softly. "My great grandfather welded it for her himself. She passed it down to her son to give to his love as a promise ring who then passed it down to my dad for my mom and now, she's passing it down to me . . . For you."

My heart hammered in my chest as his words melted into me. The family history behind the ring was heartwarming and I wasn't surprised to see how well preserved it was. The Toves family was a sentimental bunch, and it was sweet to see how much they cared about traditions and one another. I blinked rapidly to keep the tears that were pooling in my eyes from falling as I took a shaky breath.

"It's beautiful but . . . I can't accept this, Ben," I whispered.

"Yes, you can," he disagreed earnestly.

"No, I can't. You know as well as I do that we can't be together, let alone get *married*," I told him, and he shook his head at me as a grin spread across his face.

"I'm not proposing to you, Robin. We're eighteen. That would be crazy."

"Then?"

"It's just a promise ring."

"A promise ring's intent is a promise to get married."

"Not this one," he denied.

"Really?" I asked almost sarcastically.

"Really. This one is just a promise of love. And no matter where you are or what you're doing, you can look at it and know that I love you and I always will you no matter where life takes us. Even if it's in opposite directions."

I swallowed around the lump in my throat and my chin quivered as emotions threatened to expose themselves.

"I love you, Robin," he reiterated, and I sniffled.

"I love you too."

"So you'll keep it?" he asked hopefully but I hesitated, not sure if it was the right thing to do. "Please. Keep it. You know my mom would be offended if you didn't."

"Okay," I finally accepted as a tear trickled down my cheek. "I'll keep it. Thank you."

He pulled the ring out of the box and placed it on the ring finger of my right hand. I held it up and admired it then turned towards Ben who was watching me closely.

"Do you like it?" he questioned, and I grinned at his nervous tone.

"I love it. Really," I assured him, giving him a quick kiss on the cheek. "I'll treasure it forever. I'm surprised your mom gave it to you though."

"She actually gave it to me right after you left," he admitted as he began driving. "I was a mess, and she knew how hard the separation was, so she told me to give it to you the next time you came to visit. She did clarify first that it wasn't for engagement purposes."

I laughed at that, just picturing her lecturing him about marriage at our age.

"I'm just grateful I got to give it to you at all," he said.

"I am too," I replied, genuinely moved by the inanimate object that now served as representation of his love for me, "but if we're giving promises, I feel like you should have something too."

He grinned over at me then reached into his coat pocket before holding his palm out. Sitting upon it was a keychain that had a faded green friendship bracelet looped into it. There were two silver animals in the middle of the fraying string, a bear and a giraffe, and I recognized it instantly.

"Is that-" I started.

"The friendship bracelet you made me when we were eight," he confirmed as I took it from him.

"I can't believe you still have this," I said, smiling at the memories it brought back.

"I found it the beginning of last year in our hangout spot and hung onto it. I was hoping it'd bring me good luck in getting you to be my friend again," he explained.

"It looks like it worked," I noted, and he chuckled.

"It went beyond what I expected of it," he joked. "Now it's always in my pocket."

"Really?"

"Really," he replied, taking it back from me and rubbing his thumb along the animals. "It was a reminder to me that you were in my life again and now it serves a different purpose twice as important."

"You know, you're quite the romantic," I commented, and he winked at me.

"Just don't tell anyone else," he requested playfully. "It would ruin my reputation."

I snorted. "Anyone who's met you knows you're a romantic."

He shrugged. "Worth a shot."

"Hey, do you mind if we stop by Lizzie's really quick?"

"Of course," he agreed, instantly changing course.

When we arrived, I was met by her wild light blue hair, tears, and a long hug. She invited us in for breakfast where we repeated the conversation I'd had with everyone of how I was doing and adjusting. She eagerly showered me with clothes she had bought for me for my birthday and professed how grateful she was that I had made the trip. An hour later, she saw us off with full stomachs and the promise from me that I'd try to come back again sooner rather than later. I sat back in contentment as Ben drove us towards Felicity's house. I was looking forward to lounging around with them and enjoying the next day and a half while I could.

Chapter Ten

"That is absolutely stunning," Felicity gushed, holding onto my hand tightly when I showed her the ring. I gave her a rundown on the conversation that came with it, and she held her hand up to her chest, eating it up. "That is the most beautiful story I've ever heard!"

"I know," I agreed, sighing at the romantic notion. "I just wish things had turned out differently. It's like the two biggest parts of my life are battling for first place but no matter what, I lose a part of me — Ben or my heritage."

"I wish I could make it better. I can't imagine how difficult all this has been for you."

I smiled at her sadly. "Thanks. But anyway, how was your morning with Matthew?"

"Not as perfect as yours and Ben's but it was still really great. It felt like old times with him hanging out with me and my parents on the weekends."

"That's great. This weekend was good for everyone."

"Yeah," she said, looking away.

I eyed her, trying to figure out what she was thinking. "What's wrong?"

"It's just . . . After this weekend Matthew and I are officially done."

"I thought you two were already done," I pointed out.

"I think we agreed to be done but didn't really mean it, you know? I think we both held onto the hope that we could be together again."

"What changed between yesterday and today?" I questioned, referring to the hope she seemed to still be holding onto when we were talking last night.

"I really can't explain it," she said, twirling her finger around a strand of hair. "Matthew and I had a serious conversation this morning about everything. He told me about Claire spying on me. Thanks for not spilling the beans about that by the way." She looked at me with a brow arched accusingly and I smiled sheepishly as she continued. "Neither of us have been very good these past six months. He's invaded my privacy because he wanted to be here with me, and I slept around as payback for him not being here. It isn't really a great setup.

"Besides, we're on completely different paths now and want different things. I want to go to college and have fun with no strings attached. Matthew wants to join the Garridan guard and put down roots there. We're never going to have a future together. So, after this weekend, no more. No more heartbreak, no more tears, no more hope. We're both moving on."

"Oh, Felicity," I murmured, wrapping her in my arms as she began to cry. I patted her hair and shushed her as she sobbed. "For what it's worth, I think you're both very brave for making that decision."

She sniffled and looked up at me. "Yeah?"

"Yeah," I replied with a gentle smile.

"Thank you," she said before sitting up and wiping her face with her sleeve. She plastered a smile on her face before going to sit at her vanity to retouch her makeup. I watched her with sadness, knowing it was the best thing for them both but hating how much it hurt them. She did what I should've done with Ben, but I wasn't as strong as she was. I wasn't ready to let go.

"Have you decided on a college yet?" I asked, not wanting to think about Ben anymore.

She looked at me gratefully then listed off her options thus far. When all traces of tears were off her face, we went downstairs and joined the boys and her parents in the living room.

"What would you kids like for dinner?" Annie asked as I sat next to Ben in the loveseat.

"I actually promised Ben's parents I'd have dinner with them," I told her.

"I know," she said with a smile. "They called earlier, and we invited them here so we could all spend some time with you. I also invited Lizzie."

"That sounds amazing," I replied sincerely. "Thank you."

"Of course. So any requests?" she questioned, looking around the room.

"How about steak and ribs," Felicity suggested, and everyone nodded in approval.

"Perfect," Annie declared. "I'll send Betty out to the store, and we can eat at five. Ben's family and Lizzie will be here in the next hour or two."

"Great. Thanks, Mom," Felicity said. "You guys want to play some board games?"

"I'm in," Ben declared, and I nodded in agreement.

"Only if we get a rematch in Uno," Matthew spoke up and Felicity grinned.

"Uno it is," she announced.

We spread out along the floor around their wooden coffee table while Annie went and pulled the games out of a closet. Ben leaned in towards me, eyeing Matthew and Felicity who were sitting a good distance apart but smiling happily.

"Why do I feel like there's a story there?" he asked me quietly.

"Because there is," I replied softly. "I'll tell you later."

He nodded in agreement before pulling my hand into his lap as Felicity shuffled the cards. The next hour flew by with lots of laughter and yelling as insults were thrown around the table. When Ben's family arrived, Mahka and Dakota joined in on the games. Dakota whooped us all in Trivia Pursuit as the grownups stood around watching and sipping on drinks.

"How about the adults play against Dakota," Ben suggested as they laughed at us. They all glanced around then accepted the challenge, determination in their eyes. In the end, Dakota beat Lizzie by just one point and grinned wildly at his accomplishment as they all grumbled.

"Dinner is ready," Betty announced from the kitchen.

Everyone began filing into the dining room, but I pulled Mrs. Toves to the side.

"I just wanted to tell you thank you," I said, holding the ring up between us. "But are you sure you want me to have this?"

She smiled at me and patted my cheek lovingly. "There isn't anyone I'd rather it be passed down to. You and Ben have something special."

I looked at the ring in between us, still torn. "I know we do but . . . There's no guarantee that we'll be together forever. I'd hate for your family heirloom to be taken outside of the family."

"That ring is a symbol of love and Benjamin loves you," she stated. "That's all that truly matters. It may have been in our family for three generations but that doesn't mean it has to stay there. Even if you and Ben end up on different paths in life, I know that ring will be cherished and loved by you then by whoever you choose to pass it down to."

I wrapped her in a long hug then whispered, "Thank you."

"You're welcome. Now, let's go eat," she said, smiling as I put the ring back on my finger.

I walked around the dining room table to sit next to Ben who gave me a questioning look, but I just smiled at him without offering up an explanation. The food was passed around and I loaded my plate with the homemade goodness that left my mouth watering.

"So, Robin. Matthew," David addressed us. "How are you two doing at your new school?"

"Really well," Matthew automatically answered, and I nodded my head in agreement. They waited for us to offer up more but when we didn't, Mrs. Toves spoke up.

"How are your grades?" she asked.

"They're good. All A's for me," I told her.

"Mostly B's on my end," Matthew admitted.

"How about activities? Are you two doing anything of interest there?" Annie questioned.

"Oh lots," I spat out and Matthew raised his eyebrows at me.

"Like what?" Annie prodded and I internally kicked myself. We couldn't very well tell them about our training activities. I shot Matthew a pleading look and he quickly came to my rescue.

"Well, we both joined a gym there. We're spending a lot of time working out and doing kickboxing," he told them, spinning our real doings into something they could hear.

"We also joined a fencing class," I added.

"That sounds like a lot of hard work," Mr. Toves spoke up. "What do you do to relax?"

"We've immersed ourselves in a history class," Matthew answered. "It's been fun learning different things."

"And we joined a roleplaying group," I said. "Our current theme is supernatural powers."

Felicity choked on her water and Ben cleared his throat at my statement. I couldn't help but grin at their reactions of me coming so close to the truth without anyone really knowing what I was talking about.

"Well, that all sounds great," Lizzie offered up as Felicity and Ben were given looks of disapproval. "I'm glad you two seem to be doing so well."

"We are," Matthew confirmed.

"And your families?" Mrs. Toves asked.

"My parents are wonderful," I told her with a smile. "They've been extremely supportive throughout this entire thing. Matthew's too."

"I still find it so amazing that your families lived in the same city," Annie commented in awe. "What are the odds of you both finding out you're adopted and your birth parents being from the same place?"

"It's definitely a unique situation," I said.

"We're just thankful we didn't have to go through everything alone," Matthew added in, trying to end the topic before anyone started to question our story.

Luckily, the doorbell rang, and Annie excused herself to go answer it. I faintly heard her talking to someone, then the sound of her heels came towards us followed by another set of shoes. I looked at the door to see her walk in with Malachi at her heels and my breath caught in my throat.

"Dad," Matthew said, standing up and instantly surveying his surroundings for possible threats.

He smiled meekly at the adults in the room, clearly uncomfortable with being in the room. "I apologize for intruding. I'm Malachi, Matthew's father. Also, the chaperone on this trip."

"It's very nice to meet you," David told him, standing up to shake his hand. "Would you care to join us?"

"Thank you but no. I'm afraid there's an emergency back home," he replied, looking from Matthew to me. "We need to leave right away."

My mind raced at his words, trying to figure out what could've possibly happened for him to show himself and end our trip a day early. Ben tightened his grip on my hand then looked at me with panic-stricken eyes.

"I'm so sorry to hear that," David expressed, and Malachi nodded his head with a forced smile in acknowledgement.

"We have to go right now?" I asked softly and he nodded his head again.

Annie eyed us all carefully then turned to Malachi. "How about we get you all some plates for the road while the kids say goodbye."

He hesitated so I shot him a pleading look. He watched me for a moment, his bushy eyebrows drawn in tight. "Okay," he finally agreed. "But ten minutes is all we have to spare."

The room was silent as he and Annie left the room. All eyes were on Matthew and me as we stood up. I walked around the table quickly giving everyone hugs and telling them goodbye. I watched as Matthew offered Felicity his hand for a handshake, but she grinned and pulled him into an embrace instead. When she let him go, she turned to me, and I hugged her tightly.

"I'll miss you," she whispered in my ear, and I nodded, too choked up to respond. As she and Matthew headed outside, Ben took my hand and guided me out of the room so we would have a moment alone.

"I don't want a long goodbye," I told him, my heart already aching with the thought of leaving him.

"Then a short one it is," he replied, cupping my face in his palms, and pulling my lips to his.

I focused on him and only him as he held me — his scent, his taste, his body against mine. I memorized everything I could to keep it fresh in my mind as long as possible. When I backed away from him, his face was contorted with torment. I held up my hand, the ring facing him, and smiled a smile full of heartbreak. He put his hand in his pocket, coming out with the tattered friendship bracelet, and smiled back. This time, no words were said. No words were needed. I turned around and walked out the Larson's front door without another look back.

Chapter Eleven

"What's going on?" Matthew demanded as soon as we were in the car with Malachi and William.

Malachi clenched the steering wheel, his mouth pressed together tightly.

"The Cyfrin reached out to us again and upped the timeframe," William answered, his voice as hard as steel. "They want Robin there by noon tomorrow otherwise no deal and they start picking the kids off one by one."

"But they agreed to a week," I said, suddenly nauseous.

"Well, they changed their minds," William seethed.

I looked over at Matthew and his face was as distraught as mine.

"So we're taking her there now?" Matthew asked.

"No. First back to Garridan to meet with the council," Malachi replied. "We need to make sure everything is hashed out before we send her there. We'll be leaving before first light tomorrow morning."

My dry throat yearned for relief as I tried to say something but failed. I took a deep breath to try to calm the stress that filled me. I knew this was coming. I had already prepared myself for it. Just because the timeframe had changed didn't mean the situation was any worse, so I inhaled once more and let determination take over.

"Let's get it done then," I said firmly with authority.

Malachi met my eyes in the rearview mirror, and I could feel William and Matthew staring at me too. They all seemed surprised by my demeanor change but didn't question it as we drove to where my parents waited.

"Everything is going to be okay," Elijah promised as we all buckled in.

"I know it will," I told him. "This is what I signed up for. I'm ready."

He pushed my hair behind my shoulder, his eyes brimming with tears. "You're a very courageous young lady. I'm proud of you."

"Thank you," I replied, his words tugging at my heartstrings.

"Are you sure you want to do this?" Matthew asked, and I nodded once.

"It's already done, Matthew," I responded. "I need you to support it, not try to discourage me. You of all people should understand why I'm doing it. You've done it before too."

His face hardened at my comment, but I didn't falter as I stared at him. I could feel all sets of eyes on me as I challenged him, his face masked with unhappiness.

"Fine," he finally said, his voice gentler than I had expected. "But I'm not looking away first."

"Really bro?" William spoke up as one side of my lips turned up in a smirk.

"Look away or get wet," I threatened, and he snorted.

"Look away or get petrified," he shot back with raised brows.

I pursed my lips for a moment but knew I lost. I narrowed my eyes then looked towards Elijah and Malachi who were watching with amusement. I could feel Matthew's boastfulness radiating from him, so I shot him the bird and half the plane started laughing.

* * *

It was late when we arrived back to Garridan, and the streets were quiet as everyone rested in their homes. We went straight to the courthouse and stood before the Keepers of Balance in their main chambers where four desks, one per element, were set up along the front of the room in a half circle configuration. Elijah and Adriana took seats at their appropriate sections as the rest of us stood in front of the desks. I once again noticed how each group of four wore similar hues to their given element.

"I assume you're up to date on the situation," Darby spoke up and I nodded. "Good. We have some last-minute details to go over then you'll be sent to the Cyfrin if you're still willing."

All sixteen members of the council watched me expectantly for my answer and I nodded once again.

"We need to hear you say it," a balding man named Peter informed me.

"Yes. I'm willing," I said out loud.

They all appraised me with different expressions; some grateful, some uncaring, and some nervous.

"You understand the plan?" Peter asked.

"Yes. Stay on the Cyfrin's good side and off their radar. Get them to trust me and send information back that could be useful to defeat them," I summarized. "Was it decided how that would be done?"

Darby motioned towards the doors and a moment later Claire strutted in with a cocky grin on her face.

"Claire?" Matthew questioned and she threw him a sidelined wink.

"Ms. Alastair has been practicing with Mrs. Welch the last couple months," Darby began.

"She's an older lady. The only other clairvoyant besides myself," Claire explained to me with a wiggle of her brows.

"Yes. She's been helping Ms. Alastair perfect her skills and, lucky for us, she's just honed in on a new one," Darby continued.

We stared at Claire in wonder, waiting for her to enlighten us with the details.

"Well, what is it, Claire?" Malachi asked when she didn't offer up an explanation as she savored the attention.

"Your amazingly talented daughter can now astral project," she told him triumphantly. "So far I've only been able to hold out for ten minutes at most but that'll be more than enough time for some correspondence with Robin."

"Will I be able to see you?" I questioned.

"Oh, for sure. I've been working on only allowing one individual to see me while staying hidden to others but I'm not quite at that level yet," she admitted, sounding displeased. "So we'll have to keep our meetings limited to night when you're alone."

"Okay," I nodded, a sense of relief running through me knowing that I'd be seeing a friendly face. "How often should I expect you?"

"Twice a week," Peter answered for her. "Every Monday and Friday she will come to you and hopefully you'll offer her something of substance."

"She'll do what she can," Adriana told him harshly, his belittling tone putting her on the defensive. "None of us expects Toshiro to offer up anything useful right away. If at all."

"She can always snoop around then," Peter replied.

"No, she can't," an air element named Jose disagreed. "She needs to be careful and earn their trust. If they catch her nosing around, it'll only put them on the defensive which will ruin our entire plan."

Peter continued to grumble nonsense at them, clearly unhappy with the plan, as Claire came up next to me.

"I'll come visit you every day the first week," she told me quietly. "I know you'll need a friend."

"Thank you," I responded, smiling at her gratefully.

As the adults continued their disagreement, she leaned in closer to Matthew and me. "After a bit more practice you know what else I should be able to do?"

"What?" Matthew asked.

"Take someone else into the astral realm with me," she replied.

"You could bring Matthew to visit!" I exclaimed in a hushed tone, and she nodded which caused Matthew to smile widely. "When do you think you'll be able to?"

"Why? Am I not enough?" she shot back with pursed lips. She must've seen the panic on my face because she suddenly laughed. "I'm joking."

Matthew rolled his eyes, and I bit my lip as a sudden thought popped into my head. "Could you let me come back and visit my parents?"

Her face twisted into disappointment. "No, I don't think so. I think I have to be with the person physically to detach them from their consciousness."

"Oh, okay," I replied, matching her disappointment. My eyes shot up to the Keepers of Balance as my name was called. "What?"

"Do you have any questions?" Elijah asked, his voice gentle.

I thought about it for a moment then spoke up. "What happens when a battle starts?"

"None of us can honestly tell you for sure," Chang answered. "It depends on what Toshiro does with you and how long you've been there. I don't think he'd trust you enough to fight alongside of them so he may lock you up somewhere. If that's the case, your best option is to try your hardest to escape and make a run for it while you can."

I glanced at Adriana as she rubbed her lips together, clearly nervous, then towards Elijah whose face was full of concern. I knew when the time came, they wouldn't leave me. They'd fight to find me. The session came to an end after that, and they both walked straight to me.

"Let's get you home," Adriana said as she wrapped her arm around me. "You need to try to get a couple hours of sleep."

"We'll meet you at the landing strip at five," Malachi informed them, and they nodded.

"You're coming right?" I asked Matthew.

"Of course. I'd never let you do this alone," he responded, and I smiled at him gratefully as Adriana ushered me away.

We walked home in silence, both of them holding one of my hands. It seemed almost comical that at eighteen I'd be walking in between them with our hands intertwined but I didn't care. All I cared about was how much they loved me.

"Do you want anything to eat?" Elijah offered as we walked in the front door. "I can whip up some of your favorites."

"No, thanks. I think I'll just head upstairs and try to rest my eyes a little bit," I told him. "Maybe you can have some ready before we meet the Alastairs though."

"That I can," he replied, kissing the top of my head. "Goodnight, kiddo."

Adriana followed me to my bedroom and sat on my bed as I took my shoes off. "How are you doing, honey?"

"I'm okay."

"The truth," she said, eyeing me, so I sat down next to her and sighed.

"Don't get me wrong, I'm scared and not happy about what's happening, but I really am okay. This is something that needs to be done so I'm just going to stay focused and get it done," I told her, twisting the ring on my finger.

"I noticed that on the plane," she said, motioning towards the ring and I smiled down at it.

"It was a birthday gift from Ben."

"It looks old," she observed bringing my hand closer to her face so she could see it better.

"It was his great grandmother's. It's a promise ring."

"It's beautiful," she responded, but her eyes were troubled.

"Don't worry. We aren't planning to do anything dumb," I assured her, and she smiled softly.

"That isn't what I'm worried about. I'm worried that you're setting yourselves up for heartbreak."

"We've already experienced our heartbreak," I replied, leaning into her. "Twice. This is just a reminder of his love for me not an expectation that we're going to have a life together."

"I wish our laws could change," she murmured quietly.

"Have they always been this strict?" I questioned and she shook her head.

"A long time ago we lived amongst the normal world. We were coworkers, neighbors, and friends and we lived in peace."

"Really?" I asked, intrigued by this new information. "What changed?"

"Fear," she stated bluntly. "A Welsh man heard stories of our ways and created a movement against us. He made horrible accusations and unfortunately many people got scared of what we could do. Even our closest allies grew weary of us. They started calling us Cyfrin."

Surprise filled me. "Cyfrin?"

"Yes. It's a Welsh term for sorcerer," she explained. "Eventually, the fear grew too strong and the harmony we had with people vanished. Our people unanimously decided to go into hiding in order to save both ourselves and the people who were willing to fight and die to get rid of us."

"Wow."

"Ever since then, we've been here hiding and helping. Tales of our kind have become fictional stories of entertainment rather than the warning folklore they started as," she continued. "It would be nice to allow our people to mingle and see the world but the fear that lives inside many is just too big. We would only be repeating history."

"I understand. It sucks but you're right. You have to protect your own. Is that how the Cyfrin got their name?"

She nodded. "They adopted that old term since it brought such fear into people once upon a time."

"Of course that's why," I murmured, unsurprised, and she put her arm around me.

"We can talk more later. Try to get some sleep, honey," she instructed. I placed my head on my pillow and pulled the covers over my shoulders as she brushed my hair away from my face. "I can't imagine how hard leaving everything behind has been for you but I'm glad you've been here with us."

"I am, too," I responded.

She gave me a kiss on the cheek then left the room. I closed my eyes and shifted around to try to get comfortable. I knew the next couple hours would go by too fast and I'd soon be awakening to my next new reality.

Chapter Twelve

The plane was ready for us when we arrived, and we boarded immediately. The trip was filled with silence the majority of the time as Matthew and I played a card game halfheartedly. As we began to descend on our destination, I spoke up.

"I know you're delivering me to Toshiro directly but let's say our goodbyes now," I requested. "I can't afford for them to think of me as weak, so I need this exchange to be professional."

"A very smart tactic," William approved.

"I agree," Adriana added as Elijah and Matthew nodded in agreement as well. "Besides, we'll be seeing you again soon enough."

"Yes, you will," I said with a confident smile that hid my worries. None of us knew how long it would be until we saw one another again.

"Be safe," Elijah murmured in my ear as he gave me a tight hug.

"I will. I promise," I told him. "And thanks again for the parting breakfast."

He grinned at my referral to the abundance of food he had made throughout the night. It was a whole feast just waiting for me when I woke up, but I couldn't manage to eat much of it. Adriana wrapped me in her arms next but didn't say anything, her unspoken words already in my heart.

"Remember all the tips I gave you," Matthew said as we exited the plane and began our walk.

"Trust me, I've been replaying them in my head already," I assured him.

His breakdown on the three Keepers of Balance's strengths and weakness would come in handy the next couple months and allow me to play on them as I needed to. It was a big advantage having Matthew's knowledge.

"And, please, for the love of everything good in this world, don't let your compassion blind you when it comes to Alexander," he pleaded quietly so no one else would hear.

I glared at him, but he didn't falter in his seriousness, so I rolled my eyes and told him what he wanted to hear. "I won't," I said tersely, and he nodded in approval. "Hey, keep an eye on my parents, would you?"

"I will," he promised as we came into the town of the Cyfrin compound.

People eyed us with hateful looks as we walked by. Malachi and William were in the lead, watching for any potential signs of hostility, followed my parents, then Matthew and I, and two more guards bringing up the rear. We all held our heads up high and kept our eyes forward, refusing to engage with the threats thrown our way. Soon we were approaching the castle gates and they automatically opened to allow us through.

Standing at the top of the steps that led into the castle were the trio I had come to loathe: Toshiro, Mallory, and Alexander. Unlike the unity in appearance of Garridan's Keepers of Balance, they each embraced their own unique style. Toshiro looked the same as he did when we had first met with his shaggy hair seemingly untouched and a sleek, blue business suit. The triumphant look on his face as he eyed us was complete with a smirk and upturned nose as he jeered.

Mallory's fiery auburn hair was still a mess around her head, but her facial features had noticeably matured in the last six months. Her fair skin contained more freckles, and her signature sneer was on her face. She sported clunky combat boots and army green pants with a black crop top. It was a more grown-up style than she had been showing off during our last interaction.

Then there was Alexander. Gone was his mini afro and in its place was a crisp and clean buzzcut with a light fade. His facial hair was also gone as if recently shaved, showing off his deep jaw line. His caramel skin radiated against the peach crew shirt he wore, and his dark jeans had holes in the knees. Our eyes met and for a brief moment his bored expression was replaced by one of enchantment as he watched me ascend closer. Toshiro cackled loudly, and my gaze jumped towards him

"Welcome back, my dear," he greeted me with a wide smile.

"Toshiro," I acknowledged, keeping my voice professional.

"I'm so very glad your leaders accepted our proposal," he continued.

"The Keepers of Balance had nothing to do with it," Elijah spoke up, his voice stern. "The decision was Robin's and Robin's alone."

"Oh, my," Toshiro gasped theatrically, eyeing me up and down as he stroked his chin. "I always suspected you were the martyr type."

"I'm not a martyr," I denied briskly.

"Just what a martyr would say," he noted gleefully, and I fought the urge to make a face as he brought his attention to Matthew. "And you just can't seem to stay away, can you Matthew?"

I saw Malachi tense up and William very lightly nudged him with his elbow to remind him to stay calm. I couldn't imagine the amount of restraint it took Malachi to not attack the man who kidnapped and tortured his son for years while they searched blindly for him. I glanced at Matthew, and he gave me a barely visible nod as a gesture of encouragement to continue so I looked forward with my head held high and stared directly at Toshiro.

"I believe you have something for my people," I hinted which caused him to grin wider.

He snapped his fingers, and someone walked up to him with a flash drive. "And here it would be."

William walked up the rest of the steps and took it from him. "How do we know the names and locations of the lost children are on here?"

Toshiro huffed and put his hands on his hips. "It's those type of questions that make me think you don't trust me."

"We *don't* trust you," William spat out and Toshiro shrugged nonchalantly.

"Well, if it's not on there I guess you can always come back and try to storm my compound," he said.

"Toshiro," Adriana spoke up, her voice as hard as steel.

"Oh, bother," he groaned with a roll of his eyes. "Someone bring me a computer."

Less than a minute later, a woman ran up with a laptop and held it out to William. He took it from her and inserted the flash drive. After a moment of tense silence, he pulled it back out.

"It's all there," he confirmed, and Toshiro sighed.

"Just as I said," he pouted. "You got what you came for now it's your turn. Hand over the girl."

I stood up taller and set my jaw as I took a deep breath. I gave Matthew's hand a quick squeeze then walked past my parents and Malachi without giving them a second glance. I kept my gaze steady on Toshiro, my eyes offering him nothing into what I was feeling, and he motioned me towards Alexander. I silently walked to Alexander's left side and could feel him watching me as I turned around to face the people I had just left. I refused to look at them, and Toshiro chuckled.

"You are a brave one, aren't you?" he commented, and I slid my eyes to him for a split second to see him watching me with glee. "Oh, just thought you'd like to know there's no point in trying to contact her through dream projection. Darnell will be putting her to sleep every night."

Panic filled me and it took everything I had to keep a straight face. If Darnell used his powers on me, I wouldn't be awake at night for Claire to come to me which meant our whole plan had just crumbled. I shot a look at Adriana, and she shook her head at me. I wasn't sure what it was supposed to indicate so my panic continued to grow.

"It would appear we are done here," Toshiro announced He waved his arms and his guards started advancing towards the group on the stairs, forcing them back. We stood there and watched as they were pushed out of the castle gates and followed as they retreated the way they had come. Within minutes, they were out of sight completely and Toshiro clapped his hands.

"That was fun now, wasn't it?" he asked, and Mallory snorted as they all turned towards me. "Alexander will show you to your room then we'll have lunch and catch up."

"I think I remember the way," I popped off.

"I don't think so," he denied, grinning slyly.

"You have a real room," Alexander informed me quietly.

"Oh," I murmured, not expecting that.

"It's also stocked with everything you'll need," Mallory said. "Clothes, toiletries, all that garbage you couldn't bring with you."

"Thank you?" I said hesitantly but it came out more like a question.

"We take care of our own," Toshiro responded, and I didn't miss the underlying meaning behind his words. "Now hurry up. Anyone late to lunch will be severely punished."

My eyes jumped back and forth worriedly before Mallory laughed.

"He isn't serious," Alexander told me.

"This time," Mallory added with a wicked grin before she and Toshiro headed into the castle.

I looked up at its massive exterior, once again awed by its old charm.

"Care to see your room?" Alexander asked and I saw him observing me when I glanced his way.

"Sure," I replied, and followed him as he began to walk.

He led me up one of the staircases in the foyer, his hands clasped behind his back.

"Is it true?" he suddenly asked.

"Is what true?" I questioned.

"That *you* made the decision to come back here," he clarified, eyeing me intently.

"Yes, it's true," I confirmed, and his brow furrowed.

"Why?"

"Because it's what needed to be done and I knew the leaders in Garridan wouldn't go for it. At least this way no one has to feel guilty for the decision."

"But you're giving up your entire life."

I shrugged. "It's not the first time. Besides, my life is little compared to that of a couple hundred."

Alexander continued to appraise me, but I couldn't tell what he was thinking as we stopped in front of a set of double doors with an intricate design on them. He opened them and stood aside for me to enter and when I did, my mouth dropped open in awe. The room wasn't massive, but it was bigger than I'd ever had before. There was a four-poster king sized bed with a translucent curtain tied up at each post to my left and a bay window with a multitude of pillows straight ahead. A vast fireplace sat in the center of the wall opposite the bed with an old couch in front of it, a bookshelf lined with older reading material to the right, and a flatscreen tv above it.

"This is lovely," I said as I walked around the room. A wardrobe stood in the corner, and I opened it to see it stocked with a variety of clothing.

"We attempted to pick out your usual fashion taste," Alexander informed me, still standing in the door frame.

"Thank you," I responded, though it felt weird to express any sort of gratitude to any of them.

"The on suite is right off the door there," he continued, motioning towards it. I walked over and peered in where my eyes were met with a simple clawfoot tub with a shower head positioned above it, a toilet, and a large vanity with an oval mirror. "All the toiletries should be the same as what you use."

I glanced over my shoulder at him suspiciously. "How did you know what toiletries I use?"

"Do you really want to know?" he questioned, and I hesitated before shaking my head. Maybe some things were best left to the imagination.

"Can I have a minute alone?" I requested.

"Certainly. I'll be back by in fifteen minutes to accompany you to the dining room," he replied.

He closed the door behind him, and I climbed onto the silk sheets that covered the bed. I grabbed a pillow and hugged it between my arms as I let the tears I had been holding in for days freely slide down my cheeks.

Chapter Thirteen

I allowed myself to cry for only ten minutes before picking myself up and going into the bathroom. I splashed some cool water on my face then patted it dry with one of the soft towels that were folded neatly on a shelf. At least my accommodations were better than last time. I viewed myself in the mirror, noticing the heavy bags under my eyes and the stress lines on my forehead. I ran my fingers through my tousled hair, pushing the harsh waves behind my ears. A knock on the door met my ears and I tried to think positive thoughts to help get me through the day.

"Robin," Alexander called out as he opened my door and walked in.

I walked out of the bathroom with my eyes in slants.

"Okay, I understand I'm basically a prisoner here but let's get one thing straight," I told him as I advanced with my arms crossed. "You do *not* open my bedroom door without my consent. Okay? What if I was in the middle of changing or showering or-"

"Or doing something you need to hide from us," he cut me off, staring at me pointedly.

"If there's never going to be any trust, what am I even doing here?" I shot back.

"Trust must be earned."

"Do you enter Mallory's room without permission?"

"Please. She would torch my head off," he muttered.

"I won't torch your head off, but I *will* drown you unless that same respect is given to me," I threatened, staring him down.

The side of his mouth twitched slightly as if he was holding back a smile. "I'll talk to Toshiro about it," he offered, and I scoffed.

"Do you do anything without Toshiro instructing you to?" I accused, playing at his ego like Matthew recommended. "Or are you just his little yes-man?"

He narrowed his eyes. "I know what you're doing."

"But it's the truth," I pressed.

"Fine," he said after a moment of silence. "No one enters your room without permission."

A half smile crept onto my face in triumph. "Thank you."

"You're manipulative."

"No worse than any of you." I shrugged, and he smiled softly at me.

"You're going to do just fine here," he prophesized before turning on his heel and walking out of my room.

I jogged to catch up to him, but he remained silent as we headed to the dining room. Toshiro and Mallory were already seated, their plates empty as they waited for us.

"Hello, dear," Toshiro greeted me. "I trust your new room is up to par."

"They are," I confirmed.

"Excellent. If you have any needs don't hesitate to tell Roxy," he said.

"I'm sorry, who?"

"Your servant," Mallory answered in a 'duh' tone.

"I'll introduce you after lunch," Alexander offered but I was too unhappy with Mallory's term to reply.

"So how have you been?" Toshiro asked and I eyed him suspiciously, the small talk putting me on edge. "Don't look at me like that. You're here to stay which makes you family. You might as well jump right in." I continued to scrutinize him, so he sighed heavily. "Fine. Mallory, would you like to tell Robin your plans for the evening?"

"You and I are having a slumber party," she informed me, looking less than pleased about it, and I raised my brows at her. "So you aren't alone on your first night in your room."

"Speaking of which, Robin has requested that no one enters her room without her permission," Alexander announced. "I told her we would abide by that rule."

"Did you now?" Toshiro asked, his eyes narrowing ever so slightly. "And why would we do that?"

"Well, she did threaten to drown me," he replied, and Toshiro let out a chuckle.

"In that case, privacy it is." He gazed at me intently. "However, if you try any funny business or attempt to misguide us, you'll endure worse than a lack of privacy."

I met his gaze while keeping my expression blank and repeated the words I once spoke to him so long ago. "You'll receive no trouble from me."

"Excellent," he emphasized slowly before his oddly bubbly demeanor came back. "You know, Alexander was very pleased to hear you were coming back."

"Are you sure it wasn't you?" I responded sarcastically.

"Oh, I'm very pleased you're here but for business purposes only," he replied, and I held back a look of disgust knowing he was referring to his sick plans of reproduction. "However, Alexander seemed to very much enjoy your company."

"I was only here for a couple days before," I reminded him. "And we were hardly around one another."

"Au contraire. It was very much enough time for him to be smitten by you," he said, and I rolled my eyes.

"Listen, I know you have this big plan for me to have a kid with him in the future, but could you spare me the ridiculous attempt of convincing me that there's any type of feelings between us," I spewed in annoyance. "Because trust me, there isn't."

Toshiro cocked an eyebrow then pursed his lips as he attempted to hide a smile while Mallory cackled. I glanced over at Alexander, and he sat stone faced as he shifted uncomfortably in his seat.

"You idiot." Mallory snorted, and I tried to wrap my mind around what was happening as Alexander excused himself from the table.

"What did I do?" I demanded as Toshiro and Mallory watched me with amusement.

"You bruised his ego," Mallory informed me with a grin.

"How?" I asked, still confused.

"He really is smitten by you," she answered, and I pulled my eyebrows together as his behavior suddenly made sense.

"Oh," I muttered, feeling equally as uncomfortable as Alexander had appeared.

"He's wants to woo you," she continued, batting her eyelashes quickly.

"Unlike myself, he appears to want to procreate out of love," Toshiro said, his voice hinting at annoyance. "He doesn't want to force you into anything."

"Well, at least there's one gentleman here then," I commented. "But I don't plan on being wooed by anybody."

"Play your cards smartly, Robin," Toshiro warned.

"What's that supposed to mean?"

"You two are going to produce a bloodline whether you like it or not. Wouldn't it be better if you did it with someone you cared about?"

"You're telling me to fall in love with him so the baby making process would go smoother?" I asked in disgust.

"I'm just saying you should open yourself up to the possibility that you could be happy here if you tried," he amended. The tone in his voice sounded genuine and I paused as I considered if he could be or not. I leaned towards not with what I knew of him but kept my mouth shut as he turned his attention towards Mallory who was playing with the fire on the candles.

After lunch, I made my way back to my room. I looked through the clothes I had been given then flipped through some of the pages in the dusty books. They were all classics that I had no interest in, so I ventured out to go to the library. After going down the stairs, I turned into the hallway opposite of the dining room. I tried to recall where the room was but ended up getting turned around in all the different corridors. I rounded another corner and let out a frustrated groan when all I found was a room full of artifacts.

"Can I help you with something?" a smooth voice asked, and I looked behind me to see Alexander standing at the end of the hallway. He began walking towards me as I clasped my hands together

"I was just looking for the library," I told him, and he appraised me with an amused expression.

"You're a far way off," he informed me, and I groaned again.

"Of course, I am. These hallways need road signs or something."

He chuckled at my comment. "I'll be sure to bring it up at our next meeting. Until then, would you like me to take you to the library?"

"That'd be great. Thanks."

We began walking back the way I had come with silence surrounding us. I fiddled with my fingers anxiously as the quiet became too awkward for me to bear.

"I'm sorry," I blurted out and he glanced over at me.

"For what?"

"Bruising your ego," I replied, and he raised his brows at my wording. "I mean for hurting your feelings."

His eyes appraised me in amusement once again, a look I was getting used to from him at this point. "You didn't hurt my feelings. Or bruise my ego."

"Then why did you leave?"

"It seemed a little invasive of a topic for casual talk."

"Oh," I said softly, looking at the portraits on the walls we passed.

"It isn't something I want discussed so freely," he added. "Toshiro may have created that plan, but it doesn't give him the right to infringe on our privacy."

"Do you agree with his plan?" I asked, suddenly curious about his thoughts on the subject. When Toshiro announced it to me the first time I was here, I had just assumed he was on board with it but now I wasn't so sure.

He hesitated, his eyes tightening as he considered his next words. "I agree that we need pure bloodlines in order to achieve our maximum strength in lineages," he said slowly. "However, I don't agree with the way he wants to go about it. I understand we're limited on our choices, and you were a rare find so he wants to make sure we seize the opportunity but . . ."

"But?" I pried as I stared at him.

"But I don't think that's something someone should be forced into," he finished. His words surprised me, but they reinforced my idea that he still had some redeemable qualities and wasn't all bad like Matthew claimed. He still had some good in him which meant he could still be saved. If Matthew could hear my thoughts right now, he'd petrify me.

"So are you planning on disobeying him then?" I questioned quietly.

"No. I'm being naïve and hoping for a different outcome."

"Which would be?" He set his jaw, his lips pressed tightly together as he stared ahead. I cocked my head to the side as the realization dawned that he was embarrassed. "You can tell me."

He gave me the side eye and I smiled encouragingly. After another minute of assurances from me, he finally sighed and caved in to my coaxing.

"I'm hoping you'll *choose* that path," he admitted, his voice low and his eyes looking just past the top of my head.

"Why would I do that?"

We came up to a set of doors and he opened them to reveal the library, then turned back towards me. He grabbed my hand and held it up to his face, gazing at the promise ring from Ben.

"Your heart belongs to another," he noted quietly. "But maybe one day it can belong to me." He stared into my eyes as he held my hand and my breath caught in my throat at the intensity of his gaze. His deep brown eyes were wistful and full of longing, as if he yearned for a love he never received. He very slowly tucked my hair behind my ear, causing goosebumps to run along my arms, then dropped both his hands next to his sides. "I won't force myself on you. I never will. But maybe you can learn to love me. And I could learn to love you."

He walked away briskly, and I stared after him with wide eyes as my mouth dropped open. This wasn't what I had expected when I volunteered to come here, and I wasn't sure if that made it easier or worse.

Chapter Fourteen

Later that evening, I skipped out on dinner, choosing to lay in bed instead as I pondered the day's events. A knock at my door startled me but I rose to my feet and went to see who it was. When I opened the door, Mallory stood there in deep red pajamas with her arms crossed.

"Are you going to invite me in?" she demanded.

"Uh . . . Yeah. Come in," I offered, stepping aside.

"Let's get this fun filled evening over with," she grumbled as she made herself at home on my bed.

I closed the door then slowly walked back to the edge of the bed, sitting down awkwardly. "You don't have to do this."

"Unfortunately, I do," she replied, turning on the TV and flipping through the channels.

"Okay then." I rolled onto the available pillows and gazed at the show she had chosen. "This is a good show."

"Yeah, it's one of my favorites," she said absentmindedly.

"Mine too!" I exclaimed with a smile.

She looked over at me in disgust. "Don't sound so excited. That doesn't bond us."

"Are you always like this?"

"Like what?" she shot back with narrowed eyes.

"Rude, unpleasant, snippy, hateful" I answered, and her lips twisted into a grin.

"Pretty much."

"Did your parents raise you that way or was it Toshiro?"

"Neither. My parents died when I was like five or something. They don't get any credit for raising me." Her hostile tone was like a slap in the face, and I stared at her in shock as she continued. "And technically Toshiro didn't raise me. Nannies did. They were horrible."

"Did they mistreat you?" I asked in concern, and she laughed.

"Oh, please. They were nothing but polite and respectful.".

"Then how were they horrible?"

"Because they were polite and respectful," she said simply. I watched her for a long time as she adamantly ignored me. I didn't understand how someone so young could be so vile. "Why don't you take a picture? It lasts longer."

I quickly averted my gaze, her point getting across. We sat sprawled out along the bed in silence, the only noise coming from the television. When the clock struck ten, another knock sounded at the door.

"Come in!" Mallory yelled.

The door opened and Darnell walked in with the same pleasant smile he always seemed to have.

"Hello ladies. Robin, it's good to see you again," he greeted me. I offered him a small smile then realized why he was here. "I'm afraid it's bedtime."

"For you, not for me," Mallory informed me with a sneer. "I'm going back to my room."

"I thought we were having a slumber party," I said, though I was perfectly fine with her leaving.

"Slumber parties end when someone falls asleep." She jumped off the bed and sauntered out of the room without another word.

"Sorry about this," Darnell apologized to me.

"It's not your fault."

"Why don't you make yourself comfortable. You probably won't move all night."

"I remember," I murmured as I got under the covers. "I'm ready."

"Goodnight, Robin," he whispered as his finger trailed over my head.

"Goodnight, Darnell," I replied as my head became foggy. My eyes quickly grew heavy, and I fought to keep them open as I watched Darnell exit the room. I blinked once. Twice. Then darkness overcame me.

* * *

When I woke up the next morning, the familiar taste of metal lingered on my tongue and my head was hazy from the magic Darnell used. I groaned as I sat up and looked at the clock to see it was only six in the morning. I rolled out of bed and jumped in the shower to clear my head. I was disturbed to see all the exact soaps and hair products I used lined on the shelf. When I was finished, I wrapped my hair in a towel and went to pick out some clothes. As creepy as all this was, I couldn't complain about the wardrobe selections as I pulled out a pair of skinny jeans and a light blue blouse that closely resembled one hanging in my own closet.

My eyes lit up at the selection of shoes lining the bottom of the wardrobe and I picked up a pair of dark boots and slid them on. I freed my hair from the towel and quickly ran a brush through it to get the tangles out then scrunched it up to help get more curls instead of frizz as it dried. When I was done, I walked towards the door where I saw a paper sticking in from the bottom. I bent down to pick it up and unfolded it to see a lightly detailed, hand drawn map of the castle. A single sentence sat in the bottom right corner:

So we don't have to put road signs in our home
– Alexander

A smile tugged at the corners of my mouth as I folded it up again and sat it on the bookcase. It was an unexpected gesture, but I appreciated it, knowing it would come in handy in the coming days as I learned my way around the castle.

"Robin."

A scream escaped my mouth as I whirled around. Standing in front of me was a translucent version of Claire who had a big grin on her face. I brought my hand up to my chest as I urged my heart to slow back down.

"You scared me!" I exclaimed in a whisper, and she chuckled.

"Clearly."

"What are you doing here?"

"I came to check on you. Since we can't meet at night like we planned, I figured the best time to try to get you alone was in the morning." She glanced around the room before her eyes landed back on me. "Seems I was right, as usual."

"Robin, are you okay?" Alexander called out from the other side of the door, concern in his voice. My eyes widened in panic, and I ushered Claire into the bathroom. "Robin?"

I ran to the door and pulled it open, turning my face as innocent as I could manage. Alexander poked his head in, his eyes scanning every inch of the room.

"I heard you scream," he said, stepping around me.

I let out a breathy laugh. "Yeah, I uh- I thought I saw a mouse."

Alexander cocked an eyebrow at me. "A mouse?"

I nodded vigorously as he continued to scan my face. "It was just a cord though."

"I don't believe you," he informed me as I started to squirm under the intensity of his gaze.

"That sounds like a personal problem."

He folded his arms over his chest. "Do we need to revoke your privacy privileges on day one?"

"No!" I threw my hands on my hips and glared at him with my chin set high. When I spoke again, I raised my voice in hopes Claire would hear. "If you don't believe me, just look around the room. There's nothing here to hide."

"I think I will." He turned around and slowly sauntered around the room, looking between every nook and cranny where something could be hiding. He rustled through my wardrobe, feeling inside every shoe and pocket, before looking under the bed.

My hands began to sweat as he stood up and headed for the bathroom. He pushed open the door and I scurried up behind him, letting out an inaudible breath of relief when I saw the empty room. He glanced at me with tight eyes then continued with his search. After digging through the bathroom, he stood there, his face still full of doubt.

"You forgot to check the toilet," I popped off with, matching his stance.

"You really enjoy challenging people, don't you?"

"Only when necessary. Now are you taking me to breakfast or not because I'm starving." I turned on my heel and marched away from him, finally able to breathe easier. Meeting with Claire would be more difficult than we had anticipated. I only hoped she'd keep trying. When I rounded the corner of my door into the hallway, I bumped into someone, causing them to drop a stack of silver trays that loudly clapped on the hard floor.

"I'm so sorry!" a woman exclaimed, automatically kneeling to pick up the mess. She was about my size and appeared to be in her mid-twenties with oily hair pulled back taut and a bare face that was shrunken back in fear. Her light green eyes skittered around as she kept her gaze down.

I knelt next to her and placed my hand on her shoulder. "Hey, it's okay. It was an accident. Besides, it was my fault."

She watched me from the corner of her eye, as if unsure of my sincerity. I opened my mouth to reassure her again, but Alexander's harsh voice sounded instead.

"Clumsy idiot. Do you know who you just ran into? You're lucky I don't send you to the dungeon," he hissed at her as my mouth fell open in shock.

"Hey, it wasn't her fault," I told him as her body quivered.

Alexander shot me a glare with eyes so full of hate I fought the urge to cower myself. He grabbed me by the arm and yanked me off the ground.

"There is a time and place for your mouth, and this isn't it," he snapped, his face close to mine. "Don't ever undermine me around a servant. And don't *ever* get friendly with them. Do you understand?"

I swallowed loudly, nodding my head slightly as I fought off the battling urges to cry or punch him. Neither would benefit the situation. He turned back to the servant as he let go of my arm.

"Robin, this is Roxy, your servant," he told me as he continued to look down on her.

"It's nice to meet you," I offered up, causing myself to once again be subjected to a heated stare from Alexander.

"She's your *servant*. It's not nice to meet her."

I fumbled for words, not sure if I should say anything at all. "Why not?"

"Because she is below you. It's nice for her to meet you, not the other way around. Got it?"

"No. I don't actually," I replied, causing him to take a deep breath.

"Walk with me," he instructed, turning me around so we were heading down the hall away from Roxy.

I glanced back and met her eyes, offering a timid smile before looking back towards Alexander.

"You're new here and as such, you don't know or agree with our ways. So I'll give you a little wiggle room until you adjust," he told me with a voice much lighter than he had been using. "We rank people based off their power level. High power results in high standings. Low power results in low standings. The lower the power, the less you are."

"That's a terrible way to view people!" I chastised, despite already knowing that from what Matthew had told me, but he merely shrugged.

"To you, maybe. But it's the way we live here, and you'll be smart to learn that sooner rather than later. Servants are the bottom of the barrel; they're scum and will be treated as such." He stopped walking and looked me dead in the eye. "When people get out of line here, terrible and painful things befall them. I don't want to see that happen to you. So, please, don't fraternize with Roxy or any of the other servants. Okay?"

I tore my gaze away from his before nodding in agreement. It wasn't what I wanted to do but I knew I had to do what needed to be done in order to stay on his and Toshiro's good sides. I had to get them to trust me. The existence of Garridan depended on it.

Chapter Fifteen

When we walked into the dining room, I was surprised to see the table full of people. Alexander pulled my chair out for me, and I sat down as my gaze jumped from one person to the next. I only recognized two of the ten newcomers: Darnell and Serafina. I noticed that five of the individuals appeared to be around my age and they sat with their eyes cast downward, their dirtied bodies stiff.

Serafina's small lips pulled back around her teeth in a vicious smirk at seeing me. Her pale complexion still sat offputtingly against her black hair and sharp facial features. I averted my eyes from hers quickly, her face already seared into my nightmares.

"Good morning lovebirds," Toshiro sang out and I fought the urge to shoot him a glare.

"Toshiro," Alexander acknowledged.

"We have some introductions to attend to!" Toshiro announced. "Robin, you already know Darnell and Serafina. This is Arthur, Monique, and Isaac."

Arthur was a short man with wild, brown hair and a long, scraggly beard. A pair of round glasses sat upon his button nose, magnifying his dark blue eyes as he nodded at me.

"You're the man who tracks power surges," I noted.

"That's correct," he confirmed in a gruff voice.

"Monique is the head of our guard. She possesses the skill of weapon physiology," Toshiro informed me.

"What's that?" I asked as I took in her appearance.

For the head of the guard, she looked nothing like I expected her to. She was skinny and gorgeous, her black hair naturally curled and running down her back in a thick curtain. Her brown eyes were framed with long lashes and her lips puckered in a natural smile as she stared at me.

"She can turn into any weapon she desires," Toshiro explained, and my eyes widened. That was an unsettling thought. "And Isaac has power cancellation abilities. He can stop anyone's powers while they're trying to use them."

"Wow," I heard myself say, and Isaac chuckled.

"Nice to meet you," he told me, his blue eyes dancing. He looked tall and muscular with a buzzed haircut and clean-shaven face. I noted the scars that ran down his neck and arm, wondering where he got them, before realizing his other arm was missing. I looked away but not before he noticed. "Lost it in a battle," he said with a grin.

"Nearly lost his life too," Monique spoke up, shaking her head in disapproval.

"What doesn't kill you makes you stronger," he shot back, wiggling his brows at her.

"Alright, that's enough," Toshiro instructed, raising his arm to silence them. "Let's eat, shall we?"

"Who are they?" I asked, and all heads turned towards the scraggly bunch at the opposite end of the table.

"I'll introduce you to them later in class," Alexander answered.

"Class?"

"Yes. Training, history, all of the good stuff that comes with newcomers," he replied.

"Newcomers," I repeated. I looked at them once again before a lightbulb clicked in my brain and I gasped. "They're Garridan children?"

"Yes."

I whirled around, slamming my hands on the tabletop as I stood up and glared at Toshiro. "We had a deal!"

"Oh, calm yourself," he said, shaking his head belittlingly. "These five were taken prior to the agreement taking place."

"Send them back home!" I demanded, knowing how scared and confused they must be feeling. Anger rose like bile in my stomach at the thought of what they'd already gone through.

"Don't be ridiculous," Toshiro scolded. "We put a lot of work into finding them."

"They don't belong here! You can't just kidnap them and keep them locked away!"

Alexander placed his hand on my arm, a warning signal to stop while I was ahead as the Cyfrin members watched me with amusement.

"Their accommodations are about to drastically change," Toshiro assured me. "We only kept them in the cells the last couple weeks to pacify them. We didn't want them trying to escape before they realized we could kill them as easily as we breath."

"Now that they know that, they won't run," Mallory clarified.

"So you've instilled them with fear," I spat out.

"The one way to ensure their safety," Toshiro said. "Now, please, sit. Let's eat. Then you and Alexander can take them to their new rooms before the start of their training."

I slowly sank back into my chair, my eyes drifting towards the young adults. I caught Alexander shaking his head at me from the corner of my eye, so I brought my gaze back to my plate. I'd get to talk to them soon enough.

* * *

"Don't speak," Alexander murmured in my ear as we stood from the table.

I internally sighed, getting annoyed with how often I was being told to hold my tongue. But I'd argue with him about it later. Right now, a more pressing issue was at hand.

"Please, follow me," Alexander told the group of five.

There were two girls and three boys, all as different as could be. They rose from their seats, their heads still cast downward, and I suppressed the urge to comfort them. I walked next to Alexander with them trailing behind us as he led us up the stairs to the opposite corridor of where our rooms were. He stopped between two doors where guards were already positioned.

"This room is for the girls," he announced, motioning towards the door on his left before raising his hand to the other side. "And this one is for the boys. You have one hour to shower and change before you'll be brought to us. Make sure you're ready."

He motioned me forward and we walked around them as the guards opened their doors. When we were well past their earshot, I whirled on him and poked my finger into his chest.

"What's the big idea with always telling me to shut up?" I accused, causing him to cock an eyebrow in amusement.

"I don't believe I've once told you to shut up."

I rolled my eyes. "You know what I mean."

"It's for your own good," he said as he pushed past me.

"Well, there's a nineteenth century stigma for you," I scoffed but he only shrugged.

"You may not like it, but it's the truth. I'm only trying to protect you."

"I don't need your protection!" I yelled in exasperation.

He sighed heavily before meeting my eyes, his eyes surprisingly gentle. "Yes. You do."

I pressed my lips together, his expression weakening my annoyance. "From what?"

"From Toshiro and everyone else here who would have you permanently silenced for slipping up. The people here aren't what you're used to, Robin. If you don't agree with them, you're the enemy, and they won't be forgiving of it. You can act out around me but no one else. In front of the rest of them, you need to be molded. You need to be one of us. It's your only chance at survival."

His tone was soft but there was an underlying bite to it that made me question how personal his statements were to his own experiences. Maybe these were words of advice from personal knowledge and it's how he survived so long ago. If that were true, his own acting ended up becoming his reality.

"I won't apologize for being hard on you," he continued. "It's the only way to keep you safe."

Despite the dominative aspect of his behavior, I couldn't help but be appreciative of his reasonings. It was a nice feeling to think that someone was watching out for me here, even if I considered him one of the bad guys.

"Well . . . Thank you," I said softly.

"Thank you?" he repeated, taken aback.

"Yes, thank you."

"You're welcome." He looked puzzled as we continued on our way, so I changed the subject.

"Oh, and thank you for the map," I told him with a grin which he returned with a gleam in his eye.

"I already marked all the appropriate places I assumed you'd be needing directions to."

"I'm sure it's going to come in very handy."

"Good."

"So what exactly are we going to be doing with those other kids?" I asked.

"First, we'll start with the basic introductions: names and powers. From there we'll give them the history of the Cyfrin and what our base of operations is as well as how things are ran and managed. After that, we'll begin power and strength training."

"Is this what you went through when you and Matthew were brought here?"

He nodded. "Basically. Although, since we were so young, we also had normal school classes. Math, science, literature, the works." He gave me a sideways glance, his brows furrowed. "Matthew told you about that?"

"Yeah. He did."

"I'm sure he filled your head with how horrific of a person I am," he said dryly.

"No," I replied, unconvincingly.

"I know you're lying."

"Okay, he definitely threw out some insults," I amended. "But it wasn't all bad. Really."

He looked down at his hands and licked his lips before asking, "How is he?"

The side of my mouth lifted in a small smile. "He's good. Happy. He fits right in with his family."

"Really?"

"Really."

He nodded his head a couple times before clearing his throat, the sentiment in his eyes falling away as he pushed open a door. I stepped into a large room lined with tall windows that almost met the cathedral ceilings. A long bench sat against the wall closest to us and different types of workout equipment stood stagnant near the back of the room. The cold, concrete floor was covered with multiple worn-out carpets, and it smelled heavily of mildew.

"Welcome to the training room."

Chapter Sixteen

My nose scrunched in disgust at the odor that filled it. "This room is in a serious need of a renovation."

Alexander shrugged. "It performs its purpose regardless. Besides, we won't be here much longer anyway."

"What do you mean?"

"Once Garridan is demolished, Toshiro wants a more public castle. He has his eyes on the one in England currently. That way we're front and center to the world while we take it down."

I pushed down the anger that rose in me at the thought of the Cyfrin getting that far with their plans. I couldn't allow them to succeed. I wouldn't.

"Why do you think you're better than them?" I questioned.

"Because I am. We all are. We're the reason they live such comfortable lives and what do we get in return for it? Nothing. In fact, we have to hide from them. It isn't right," he replied, shaking his head. "Let me guess. You don't agree."

I cast my eyes downward as the lie slipped through my lips with ease. "It really isn't my place to disagree anymore, is it?"

"No, it isn't. And you'd do well to keep up that charade," he said, cocking his head to the side as he saw through my act. We stayed silent for the remainder of the time we waited for our unwilling guests to arrive. When they walked in, clean and in new clothes, Alexander directed them to sit along the bench as we stood in front of them.

"Welcome to the Cyfrin," Alexander began.

"Welcome? We've been here for weeks," a girl with strawberry blonde hair and a deep scowl muttered.

Alexander's icy stare shifted over to her. "What's your name?"

"Emery," she responded, her light blue eyes narrowing at Alexander's hostile tone. Suddenly, she bent over and clutched her chest, her breath coming out in short gasps before she began gagging.

I took a step towards her, but Alexander held his arm out to stop me. I watched helplessly as Emery dry heaved, my own stomach churning at the sight.

"We have to help her. She's choking!" I exclaimed.

"That she is," Alexander mused as Emery coughed out multiple specks of green that floated to the floor.

I stared at them in confusion. They were leaves. I glanced over to Alexander, realization dawning. He was doing this.

"Since someone decided to get lippy early on, you'll all be learning a valuable lesson," Alexander spoke harshly. "Step out of line and you'll be punished. Right now, Emery has the roots of a plant tightening around her heart and lungs. She could easily be dead in the next minute if I continue . . . But I won't. Not this time."

As soon as the words were spoken, Emery inhaled deeply, her deprived lungs aching for oxygen. She was still holding her chest, but her face was already beginning to turn a lighter shade of red.

"Emery just used up your one freebie," Alexander said, his cold gaze jumping from one person to the next. "Don't step out of line again."

I watched him in horror, petrified by the horrendous stunt he just pulled. His face showed no remorse as he began pacing in front of the group, his hands clasped behind his back.

"Let's jump right in. My name is Alexander, and I am one of four Keepers of Balance here. The Keepers of Balance are in charge. We are the law, the jury, and the judge. We possess the most important powers of anyone: one of the four elements. As you may have guessed, I have the element of the earth. Robin here possesses the one of water."

A chubby boy with greasy, brown hair and acne slowly raised his hand, fear written all over his face, and Alexander arched an eyebrow at him.

"Yes?" he questioned.

"Are we allowed to ask questions?" the boy asked, his voice barely over a whisper.

"Depends on the question," Alexander replied, folding his arms over his chest.

The boy opened and closed his mouth several times, unsure if Alexander's answer was giving him permission to speak or not.

"Ask," Alexander commanded.

"Why was she being introduced to people this morning if she's a leader here?"

"Because she's been here for less time than you have," he answered, causing furrowed brows all around. "We'll get back to that later. For now, it's time to learn your history. The Cyfrin broke off from a society called Garridan twenty years ago. The Cyfrin, as well as Garridan, are made up of a civilization of people with supernatural powers. We broke away from them because our views differed from theirs. They wanted to be complacent while we wanted recognition for the works we do for the world. As you can imagine, this caused tensions which ended up leading to war.

"Due to this, the leaders in Garridan threw out their children, casting them off to live in the normal world without their powers. The Cyfrin have worked diligently to rescue all those children over the years and bring them back to the life they should live in. One where they possess their powers and roam as a hierarchy in this world. Unfortunately, it wasn't an easy task and many of you fell through the cracks. However, once your powers were activated, you sent us a beacon to find you which brings us to why you're here.

"Over the last year or so, you've all discovered you have a supernatural power of some sort. You aren't crazy. It's real and it's meaningful. It's the very best part of you and we will train you to use it to the best of your abilities. We'll train you to become one of us. Someone worthy. Now, state your name and your power for Robin's benefit. I already know everything there is to know about each and every one of you." Alexander pointed to the right end of the bench. "Begin."

The person I could only describe as a man stood up, hovering over me by at least a foot. He was brawny with wide shoulders and buff arms. He had dark brown skin with cool, jewel undertones and deep brown eyes that sat under a full set of lashes. His wide nose sat nicely accented by his full lips while his coily hair fell over his forehead. He looked from Alexander to me, then opened his mouth to speak.

"My name is Andre Crossley and I have dream premonitions," he said in a deep voice.

"How old are you?" I asked, curiously.

"Twenty-one," he replied.

"Next," Alexander cut in. Andre sat down and the shy boy stood up.

He fiddled with his fingers, his dark green eyes never sitting still as he bit his skinny lip. "My name is Toby, and I can control metals."

"Also known as ferrokinesis," Alexander inserted. "Next."

"Wait," I told him. "I want to know how old they all are."

"Why?" Alexander questioned.

"Because," was all I offered in response.

"Very well. Your age, Toby?"

"Sixteen," he answered before sitting down quickly. It explained his awkward deposition. He was still going through puberty. That meant he was one of the youngest babies that had been sent away. He had to have been just a couple months old.

The next boy was average height and weight with succulent, light brown skin; curly, brown hair that sat high on his head with side fades; and light brown eyes that were covered by thick eyebrows. A light mustache sat at the end of his upturned nose with a five o'clock shadow around his sharp jawline.

"I'm Mateo and I'm a shapeshifter," he said with a thick accent. He looked over at me and I nodded my head in encouragement. "I'm eighteen."

"Next," Alexander demanded, and the girl he had previously tortured stood up.

"I'm Emery, I can control electricity, and I'm twenty," she said, her voice hoarse from the leaves that had climbed their way up her throat. She was short and curvy with a round face and a button nose. Her thin lips sat shapeless on her pasty skin, seeming to be set in a permanent scowl. I was already concerned she was going to get herself killed.

The last girl stood up hesitantly, her chin length hair demanding attention with its faded turquoise shade that brought out her wide, blue eyes. Her ghost white skin was nearly translucent on her skinny frame with the exception of her oval face that possessed a red hue. A piercing sat in the side of her pointy nose, and I could see multiple tattoos that I would've expected to be on the girl with the attitude.

"My name is Kodi, and I can talk to animals," she mumbled. "And I'm nineteen."

"This is a very diverse group, so we'll have individual training sessions alongside the group ones," Alexander said as Kodi took her seat. "We want you all to feel at home here but remember trust is earned. You'll only be given so much freedom until the time comes when we can consider you family."

If I didn't know any better, I'd believe he was sincere. His point of view of the Cyfrin's history was manipulative and I knew these children of Garridan deserved to know the truth. They were wanted and loved by their birth families, not cast out like some rejects. I wanted to get to know them so I could help keep them safe. I just wasn't sure how to do that in a way that wouldn't get us all in trouble. As Alexander continued to speak on the expectations of the Cyfrin, I pondered how I could get some time alone with the newcomers. An idea flashed in my mind, and I smiled hopefully.

"Hey," I nudged Alexander, a motion he clearly wasn't accustomed to as he stared at me with a taken back expression. "Can I talk to you for a minute?"

I walked away from the group, and he followed as he said, "I hope this couldn't have waited until another time."

"No, it couldn't. I don't think we should start their training today," I told him.

He raised his eyebrows at me expectantly. "And why not?"

"I don't know how things around here worked when you kidna- I mean *rescued* younger kids but they're all adults or close to it. They aren't going to be as easily manipulated as children are, and you can't just threaten them and expect it to be effective. If you want them to truly be on your side, and become open minded to your cause, you have to try a different approach."

"I suspect you have something in mind," he said, and I nodded.

"I want to have a group therapy session."

"I beg your pardon?"

"I want to sit with all of them and just let them tell their stories. How they were raised, where they're from, what they went through when they were brought here, that sort of thing."

"That seems juvenile."

"Please? It could help."

"I don't see how."

"It'll be a way to get them to open up and trust one another so they don't feel so alone. Once they realize they have people who understand what they're going through, it might be easier.

Especially if I tell them my story, too, so that they can relate to someone who's already been through what's happening to them."

"I don't think your story is the most comforting to hear if we want them on our side," Alexander commented, his lips pushing together.

"I won't tell them the bad things," I assured him. He watched me for a moment, observing my anxious face. "Please? You can listen the whole time and if you hear something you don't like you can shut it down. But there's no harm in trying it my way, is there?"

After another minute of deliberation, he sighed. "Fine. Let's try it your way."

Chapter Seventeen

Alexander sat on the bench with his arms crossed in front of him as I sat the group in a circle on the ground. None of them looked pleased by what was about to take place, but I didn't care. I knew it would be good for them in the long run.

"Okay, who wants to start?" I asked with a smile. When no one volunteered, I decided to pick. "Andre, how about you?"

"Is this really necessary?" he asked, his face full of disdain.

"I think it is. Your whole world has been turned upside down. You can't tell me it wouldn't be nice to know you aren't going through it alone," I said, looking from one face to the next. "We all need a friend in this life."

Toby's hand slowly raised, surprising me. He would've been the last person I'd expect to speak willingly.

"Go ahead, Toby," I encouraged.

His eyes skirted around the room, still unable to make eye contact with anyone. "I've never had any friends."

His sad tone made my heart swell. I reached out and grabbed his hand. "I'll be your friend."

He finally looked over at me and a timid smile crossed his face. "Really?"

"Really." His smile widened and I returned it. I could tell he was the type of kid that just needed acceptance. "Why don't you tell us about yourself. Your family, school, where you're from. That kind of stuff."

"I don't have a family. I've been in foster care my whole life," he said quietly.

"I don't have a family either," Emery spoke up, offering him a comforting look, which was another unexpected surprise. "I aged out of the foster care system over a year ago and have been alone ever since."

"I think that's what's going to happen to me too," Toby replied, looking near tears.

"Don't give up hope," Andre inserted. "I was your age when a family adopted me. I still live with them while I'm going to college. Or I *did* before I was abducted by these psychos."

I glanced at Alexander who was glaring at Andre, and I bit my lip. I caught his eye and shook my head slightly, my eyes begging him to let them speak their minds for the moment. His eyes hardened but he sat back against the wall, looking towards the back of the room, so I quickly diverted the conversation back to safe topics.

"See, Toby. You aren't alone even with that," I told him. "What else can you tell us?"

"I'm from Indiana and I don't do great in school. I get bullied a lot because I like manga and video games," he answered.

"Hey, I do too!" Kodi exclaimed, and I relaxed a little bit. They were already finding common ground. Maybe this would work out better than I had hoped.

"You didn't say anything earlier about foster care," I commented to her. "Do you have a family?"

"Yeah. I got adopted when I was little," she responded. "My parents are great."

"Any siblings?" I asked.

"Nope, just me."

"Where do you guys live?"

"Montana. But I was supposed to be moving to Tokyo in a couple months for a study abroad program."

"Oh, wow. That's exciting! I've always wanted to visit other countries," I told her, and she nodded, looking away. Another dream taken away by the Cyfrin's actions.

"I'm from Costa Rica," Mateo told me. "It's beautiful there. You'd like it."

"I'm sure I would," I agreed, then my brow furrowed, and I looked to Alexander. "Weren't all the Garridan children placed in foster cares in the United States?"

He nodded but stayed silent.

"I was adopted before I can remember and not long after my family moved back to Costa Rica," Mateo explained, seeing my confused expression. "It's where they were originally from."

"Oh, okay," I said with a nod. "That makes sense. What's your family like?"

"Big," he replied with a chuckle. "There's nine kids, all of us adopted."

"Think they'd want a tenth?" Toby half joked, and Mateo grinned at him.

"I'm sure they would," he told him as Alexander stood up with a huff.

"I'll be right back," he announced, not giving us a second look, so I ignored his outburst as he walked to the doors.

"Do either of you want to tell us about yourselves?" I asked Emery and Andre.

"Nope," Emery replied, hunched over, and messing with her shoe. She was going to be a work in progress.

"I'm from LA," Andre offered up. "I'm majoring in engineering, and I like sports."

"Which ones?" I asked.

"Any but I'm partial to basketball," he responded.

"I am too," I told him. "I was on my school's varsity team up until my senior year."

"Why did you quit?" he asked.

"I didn't exactly," I said, looking down. Since Alexander wasn't in the room, I found it safe to continue with the truth. "I had to leave for Garridan the end of my junior year and couldn't go back home."

"The place we were all born?" Mateo asked and I nodded. "I thought that guy said we weren't wanted there."

"That isn't entirely true," I admitted.

"I don't understand," Toby said.

I glanced at the door, anxiety settling in my chest as I debated what to do. They needed to know the truth, but did I have enough time to tell them? Could I trust them to keep quiet about what they learned?

"What aren't you telling us?" Emery asked accusingly.

I licked my lips then decided to go for it. "A lot. But it's really sensitive information. I want to tell you and you need to know but . . ."

"But?" Andre pressed.

"But if you slip up and say something, I'll probably wind up tortured to the brink of death and who knows what will happen to you," I told them. "The people here are dangerous. You already know that, but you don't know to what extent. You're being fed lies so you'll be complacent."

"Then tell us the truth," Mateo insisted, his eyes wide.

I swallowed loudly, unconfident in my decision. "If I do, you all have to promise not to say a single word about it. You need to do as your told and stay in line. You have to act like you're adapting here."

"We promise," Kodi said for them all, and after another quick deliberation, I started.

"Not everything Alexander said was a lie," I told them, speaking quickly and quietly. "The Cyfrin did break off from Garridan because of different ideals but it wasn't as innocent as recognition for the works they did. The Cyfrin want to rule the world. They think they're royalty compared to normal people and that normal people's rightful place is as their servants. The only reason they've failed at taking over the world is because of Garridan's interventions. They've been trying to take down the Cyfrin for decades now."

"And what about us?" Andre asked, his voice hard.

"The Cyfrin started targeting the children in Garridan when the war first started. The council decided the only safe place for them was in the normal world, so they stripped them of their powers and placed them in homes across the states. They didn't cast us aside; they wanted us. They all wanted us. But we weren't safe. They sent us away to protect us."

The expressions across the room reminded me much of my own when I first learned everything from Matthew. I wished I could ease their feelings, but I couldn't. I had to finish.

"Unfortunately, things didn't work as well as Garridan had hoped. The Cyfrin had a man who could locate power surges which led them straight to these defenseless kids and they kidnapped them. They brought them here and raised them as their own. Garridan began trying to bring their children home a couple years later but so many had been adopted or shuffled around foster care that they couldn't find them all. I was one of those kids and so are all of you."

I saw tears in Toby's eyes and the other's looked shaken. Telling them was the right thing to do.

"So how did you end up here then?" Kodi asked.

"It's a long story for another time. What matters right now is that you know the truth and you can help me," I responded.

"Help you how?" Emery questioned.

"Garridan suspects that the Cyfrin are going to attack them sometime soon. The guard there is already preparing and want it to be the last battle. They're ready to finally take down the Cyfrin once and for all. So I need all of you to follow Alexander's training and learn everything you can about your powers and physical combat so you can fight when that day comes," I told them.

"You want us to fight in a war?" Toby asked in a small voice.

"No. I want you to fight to get out of here to safety. If we can just make it to Garridan's side, we'll be okay," I explained. "I know this is a lot to process but you need to make your decision now. Are you with me or not?"

They all nodded their heads, none of them with that much conviction, but it was better than nothing. I realized that my own safety was no longer a priority when the day of the battle arrived. Their safety was.

"I know you don't know me, and you have no reason to trust me, but I promise you I'll do everything in my power to get you all out of here safely. I won't leave any of you behind," I said, holding eye contact with them one by one. "We just have to make it through the next couple months or however long it is until the Cyfrin attack."

"Together?" Toby asked, his squinty eyes full of affection. It appeared I had at least one of them on my side.

I smiled at him reassuringly. "Together."

Chapter Eighteen

"How did the first day of training go?" Toshiro asked as the same group from breakfast sat around the table for dinner.

"Surprisingly well overall," Alexander replied.

"Really? No need for intervention?" Toshiro pressed.

"Only once," Alexander answered, and Toshiro began to clap gleefully.

"Which one got the death grip thrust upon them?" he continued, thoroughly happy by the idea.

"Emery."

Toshiro's gaze jumped from one newbie to the next, his eyes sparkling as he tried to guess which one of them it was. He pointed at Emery, and she glared at him.

"What?" she spat out, making him grin maliciously.

"Are you Emery?"

"Who's asking?"

I shot her a look, wishing she'd keep her mouth shut before they shut it for her. Toshiro eyed her with an indecipherable expression.

"I like her," he finally announced, to which she rolled her eyes.

"Wonderful. My life is complete now," she said sarcastically.

Everyone's gaze shot back and forth between her and Toshiro, wondering how long he'd let her go on before silencing her. To my surprise, he didn't reprimand her.

"You can control electricity, correct?" he asked.

"Apparently."

"I think you could have a high place in our guard with a power like that."

"Joy."

"Alexander, make sure you whip this one into shape. She could be of great use to us," Toshiro said, his gaze shifting away from Emery. "Robin, what do you think of our new guests?"

"They seem to have great potential," I responded to which I received approving glances.

"I don't see the chubby one lasting," Serafina snorted, and Mallory laughed. They were two peas in a pod with their vile behavior.

"His name is Toby, and his power is more valuable than yours," I heard myself saying, instinct taking over to stand up for him. It may have been the wrong move, though, as everyone eyed me with judgement.

"You better watch how you speak to me," Serafina hissed as she glared.

"Actually, you better watch how you speak to her," Alexander said, his hard gaze intent on her. "She's a Keeper of Balance. It doesn't matter how long she's been here. She outranks you, Serafina."

Serafina looked down, her mouth set in a tight line. I could see her seething, but she didn't argue.

"You'd be wise not to threaten her again either or I'll let Dante take care of you," Alexander added.

"He's our torture specialist," Mallory informed me, seeing my confused look.

"You have a torture specialist?" I asked quietly as Toshiro started speaking again.

"Duh," she said, rolling her eyes as I sat there disturbed by that fact.

As I ate my food, it became increasingly hard to pull my wrist up to my mouth. My forehead scrunched as an invisible barrier seemed to be pulling at my arm, keeping the fork from reaching its intended destination. I yanked a little harder, but the barrier was suddenly gone, and I began to choke as the food was shoved into my mouth. I coughed violently and took a swig of water, trying to help ease the pain in my throat as I glared at Serafina. She smirked at me as Alexander began to realize what was going on. His eyes blazed and he opened his mouth to, no doubt, banish her to Dante's dwelling but I put my hand up to stop him.

"Please, allow me," I told him, much to the confusion of everyone else. I gathered the moisture in the air, letting the icy feeling I loved creep through my body, before shoving it at her with so much force that her chair was shoved into the wall.

She fell over, soaking wet, and let out a scream that reminded me of a banshee. "You'll pay for that!"

I matched her previous smirk as Isaac, Monique, and Darnell started laughing. Alexander gave me an approving look, trying to stifle a grin of his own while Serafina stood up in a stance that was prepared for a fight. Toshiro raised his arm up towards her, and she looked down.

"We don't tolerate lawlessness," he told her. "You should know better."

"She did it, not me!" she hissed back.

"You challenged her. Don't be so daft as to think I didn't see what you were doing to her. Robin was simply giving you a taste of her power since you seem to be under the impression that she isn't your leader," he said, his voice hard. "I think some time with Dante would do you some good."

Her eyes widened, the quickest flash of fear showing before her face became expressionless.

"I think she learned her lesson," I spoke up, not wanting anyone to be subjected to their type of punishment. Not even someone as nasty as her.

She scowled at me. "Don't try to do me any favors."

"Monique, escort Serafina to the dungeon," Toshiro instructed.

Everyone kept their eyes down as the two left the room, the mood suddenly uncomfortable. Toshiro looked to where the trainees sat and cleared his throat.

"This is a good lesson for you all. It doesn't matter who you are or how high you rank. If you disobey the laws or cause trouble, punishment will be given. Remember that as you continue with your training and we start to loosen the reigns on you," he said. "Understood?"

Silent nods answered him, none of the five brave enough to speak. I hated to think it but maybe this would get through to them just how serious of a situation they were in. Maybe this would push them to my side. After dinner, Alexander and I escorted them back to their rooms. To his annoyance, I wished them all good night before they shut their doors.

"Would you like to go on a walk through the gardens with me?" Alexander asked as we ventured back down the hall.

"Oh, uhm, that-that would be nice," I said, tripping over my words. "But I was actually hoping for some time alone before Darnell has to put me to sleep. It's been a long day."

"Oh," he murmured, sounding disappointed.

An unexpected feeling flooded through me, and I had the sudden yearn to reassure him. "We could go tomorrow instead though."

One side of his lips lifted in a half smile. "Tomorrow it is."

We stopped in front of my door and my hand hovered over the doorknob as he lingered next to me. I watched as he opened his mouth to say something then decided better and pressed his lips back together.

"Is something wrong?" I pressed.

"Not exactly," he responded.

"Then?"

He hesitated before saying, "You need to be careful around Serafina. She's a loose cannon and she seems to have it out for you for some reason."

"Won't her little session tonight take care of that?" I asked dryly as my stomach churned.

"No. Probably not. She's sent to Dante every couple of months for stepping out of line. If she wasn't so useful to Toshiro, he would've killed her by now."

"Oh."

"Just . . . Don't ever be alone with her, okay?" he requested, concern apparent in his voice. "I know you can take care of yourself, but I also suspect you won't do what's necessary to keep yourself safe if someone is attacking you."

"By necessary you mean?"

"Terminating the threat." I bit the inside of my lip and looked away. "I know you think I'm a monster for thinking that way," Alexander said quietly.

"No," I denied softly. "Just misguided." I offered him a small smile then opened my door. "Goodnight, Alexander."

"Goodnight," he responded, watching as I stepped into my room and closed the door.

I put my forehead against the door as thoughts whirled in my head. He had his sweet moments just as much as he had his bad. Surely that meant there was hope for him. I sighed then turned around with my eyes closed as I leaned against the door.

"Who was *that*?"

My eyes flew open, and I saw Claire lying on my bed, the pillows visible through her.

"Are you crazy?" I hissed quietly. "He could've seen you!"

"Oh, please," she said with a roll of her eyes. "Do you really think I'm that careless?"

"Uh, yeah. I do, actually."

"That hurts, Robin. That truly hurts," she told me, her hand on her chest with pouted lips. I think she had Felicity beat in the drama department by a long shot.

"How long have you been here?"

"I've been coming every thirty minutes to make sure I didn't miss you again. We definitely need a set time to meet because this is exhausting."

"Come in the mornings. It would've been fine this morning if I hadn't screamed," I admitted.

"Causing Mr. Yummy to come running to your rescue," she said with a wiggle of her eyebrows. "So again, I ask, who is he?"

"That's Alexander."

"*That's* Alexander?" she repeated with gleaming eyes.

"Yes."

"Yeesh. Who *wouldn't* want to have a baby with him?" she said with a devilish smile.

"Me," I replied, my voice like steel as I crossed my arms. "This isn't a joke, Claire. This is my life. Not to mention he hurt your brother. Can't you ever be serious?"

She looked away, my words hitting her hard enough to provoke an apology. "Sorry. I didn't mean to hurt your feelings."

"You didn't hurt my feelings. It's just not a game. Yes, he's cute, but is that really all that matters to you?"

"Maybe."

"Claire," I said with a roll of my eyes, and she grinned at me sheepishly.

"How are you doing?" she asked.

"I'm okay. Almost everyone has been polite and welcoming. Alexander is trying to give me tips on how not to end up in the torture chamber, but it's hard to keep my mouth shut when there's so many bad things going on."

"I bet," she sympathized. "But even if it goes against your instincts, you have to stay on their good sides."

"I know." I sighed heavily. "I'm trying."

"I'm sure you are."

"I miss everyone there already."

"We all miss you too. Everyone's been going stir crazy waiting for me to get to talk with you."

I smiled, warmed by knowing that they cared and worried. "Well, you can tell them I'm okay."

"Trust me, I will. Oh, and just because Peter will hound me, have any useful information yet?" she asked with a roll of her eyes.

"Maybe not useful but I do have some information they'll want to know."

"Really? What is it?" she pressed eagerly.

"The Cyfrin have five Garridan children here that they abducted over the last couple weeks. It was done before the deal was made though."

Claire scoffed. "Of course. They would get around something like that. Do you know their names so we can tell their families?"

"Only their first names aside from one."

"Well, that might still help. What are they and how old?"

I relayed the information, and she repeated it back to me to make sure it was correct. Her figure started to fade even more than she already was, and she yawned.

"Are you okay?" I asked.

"Yeah. I just need to go back to my body. It's gone through a lot today."

"I'm proud of you," I told her, and she smiled at me.

"No, I'm proud of *you*," she responded. "Hang in there. I'll be back the day after tomorrow."

"Why not tomorrow?" I asked in disappointment.

"My body needs time to recuperate. This isn't easy," she replied. "But it'll get better as time goes on."

"Okay. I'll see you soon then."

"Bye, Robin," her voice said as her body disappeared completely.

I sprawled out on the bed, already missing her. I couldn't wait to be back in Garridan with everyone. A person could only handle giving up people so many times and I was close to my breaking point. I turned the TV on and stayed laying there until Darnell knocked on my door, ready to end my day.

Chapter Nineteen

"Harder! Faster!" Alexander yelled at Kodi, whose face was beet red and dripping with sweat.

She continued to hit the punching bag in front of her, but her motions were getting weaker and slower. Alexander had summoned her two hours before the others and had been working her like a pig ever since she walked through the doors.

"She needs a break," I told him.

"She doesn't have time for a break," he responded. "Her power is useless unless we're visiting a zoo. She needs to offer physical competence otherwise she will fail and become nothing more than a servant."

The way he said it made me think he didn't want that to happen. It was as if he was pushing so hard in order to make sure she didn't end up some place she'd be treated poorly.

"Why do you care?" I asked, and he gave me a look.

"I don't."

"Yeah, you do," I replied softly as I stared at him.

He clenched his jaw then looked at Kodi. "Go. Five-minute break. Not a second more." After she stumbled to the bench, he turned towards me with narrowed eyes. "What do you want from me?"

"The truth. You can't tell me you don't care. Why else would you be pushing so hard?"

"Because it's my job to make sure they're useful."

"That's true. But I don't think that's the only reason. You want them to succeed."

"Of course, I do!" he quietly yelled. "Do you think I like it when one of our own is beneath us? When they're no better than a regular person? Every servant in this castle is a disgrace to our kind. They failed us. I don't want that for any one of us, but it happens. I can make sure it happens less frequently, though, by training newbies."

I eyed him, mixed emotions running through me. His explanation was so misguided but the intentions behind it were kind. He was constantly walking the line of doing bad things for what he perceived to be a good reason.

"What?" he asked, crossing his arms.

"You're just very complicated," I responded. "It's hard to figure you out."

"Maybe you shouldn't be trying to figure me out then."

"Maybe not," I agreed. "But I think you want me to."

He turned away from me. "Thirty more minutes with Kodi. Then we'll bring the rest in."

* * *

After lunch, we were all gathered in the training room again with Alexander in the center.

"Today's schedule will be your permanent one for the time being," he said. "Breakfast, then physical training. Lunch, then power training. After dinner, you'll have the evenings to do whatever you wish with an armed escort. Get used to it. Now, who would like to demonstrate their powers first?"

Just like yesterday, no one volunteered so Alexander pointed at Andre.

"My powers don't work on demand," Andre informed him.

"Then do enlighten us on how they work," Alexander responded.

"It only happens when I'm sleeping. Something specific will happen in my dreams and within the next couple of days, it'll repeat but in real life."

"Precognitive dreaming," Alexander mused. "Interesting."

"Is that even something that can be further developed?" I questioned.

Alexander nodded. "Very much so. With the right teaching, he can call on it to happen while he's awake, find specific subject he wants to see the future of, and see far past a couple of days."

"Really?" Andre asked, his interest piqued, and Alexander nodded again.

"It's usually best for this kind of power to be trained by someone with a similar power. However, we haven't had a future seeker in a long time, so we'll have to figure something out to help you. For now, can you tell us a premonition you've had that will happen so we can watch for it?"

"Last night I had one about that red headed, angry chick," Andre replied.

"Mallory?" I asked.

"Yeah, her. She's going to burn a book in the library," he continued.

"Why would she do that?" I questioned, and Alexander rolled his eyes.

"Because she's crazy. But that's what we'll watch for and see how long it takes to happen," Alexander told us. He looked to Kodi who was next on the bench. "Seeing as your power can't be grown or shown with no animals around, we'll skip you. Mateo. You're up."

Mateo stood and stretched his arms out in front of him, shaking his hands out when he was done. He grinned and I could tell he was enjoying the attention.

"What would you like to see?" he asked, causing Alexander to cock on eyebrow.

"What can you shapeshift into?" Alexander questioned.

"Animals," he answered.

"What animals?"

"So far any that I try."

"Start simple. Dog," Alexander requested.

Mateo's body vibrated rapidly for the briefest second, becoming just a blur in front of my eyes. Then he shrank down onto all fours, his limbs growing smaller and his skin sprouting hair. Before I knew it, the boy was gone and in his place was a fluffy golden retriever with its tongue sticking out.

"Wow," I breathed, my eyes wide with awe.

"Does it hurt?" Toby asked, his eyes wider than mine.

Mateo barked in response, and we all stared at him, waiting for the words that never came.

"He said it does but in a feel-good kind of way," Kodi informed us.

Alexander glanced between her and Mateo before asking him, "You can't talk?"

Bark. Bark.

"He can but it translates to whatever animal form he's in," Kodi answered.

Emery snorted. "That's awfully inconvenient."

Mateo growled, baring his teeth at her.

"I'm not repeating that," Kodi muttered.

"What'd he say?" Emery asked with narrowed eyes.

"Nothing," Kodi insisted as Alexander observed her.

"Maybe you'll turn out to be useful after all," he commented, his finger tapping his chin. "Neither of you are very useful on your own but together you could be a good team."

Mateo rose on his hind legs, growing five times my size as the cute puppy turned into an angry brown bear with an unhinged jaw. He let out an earsplitting roar, his hot breath wafting over me as spit dripped from his teeth.

"I don't think he liked you calling him useless," Andre said, his deep voice higher than usual.

"Yeah, basically," Kodi confirmed, her face covered in fear.

Alexander seemed to be the only one of us unfazed and his lips turned up in a smile. "With the right training, and Kodi's translations, you might just wind up an asset after all."

Mateo let out a long breath from his snout as if agreeing then turned towards Kodi and gave her a wink. I let out a shiver, the sight of a bear doing such a human action leaving me uneasy.

"Bird," Alexander said, and Mateo's shape instantly shrank into a ruffly feathered toucan.

We all took turns requesting an animal before Alexander told him to shift back. When he did, his face was withdrawn with bags under his eyes, and he slumped forward lightly.

"The fatigue you feel will get better with more training," Alexander told him, and he nodded slightly as he leaned against the wall. "That goes for all of you. Toby, you're up."

Toby got off the bench and wiped his clammy hands against his jeans. "I don't know what to do," he admitted, looking down.

"Well, what were you doing back home?" I asked. "Why don't you show us that?"

"Okay," he whispered. He looked around then walked to one of the exercise machines. He put his hand palm against it and suddenly disappeared.

"Whoa," Mateo said from behind me.

"How'd you do that?" Emery asked. "I thought you could control metal."

"I can," Toby replied. "But I can do this too. It's what I did the most at home so the older boys couldn't hit me."

"We call it ferrokinetic invisibility," Alexander informed us. "He can turn invisible by touching the metal but only while touching it. The second he lets go, he's visible again, so it isn't a particularly useful skill."

"It was to me," Toby murmured as his body appeared in the same spot it had gone.

"Show me a skill that will be useful to *me*," Alexander commanded, and I narrowed my eyes at his snarky behavior.

Toby lifted his arm, bringing the weight machine with it, then condensed it into a ball with his hands. He turned around in a circle once before throwing his arm forward and hurling the squished metal directly at Alexander. I gasped but, without even blinking, Alexander raised his arms, pulling a wide tree trunk from the concrete floor. The ball hit it with a loud crack, causing the tree to sway and branches to scatter on the ground. Alexander glanced around the trunk at Toby who refused to meet his eyes.

"Not bad," he said before waving his hand over the tree and shrinking it back into the ground. "Seems like there's some anger in there after all. I'm interested to see how you progress."

Toby inched past him without a word and sat back on the bench. I walked over to him and put my hand on his back as Alexander called Emery up. She stared at him blank faced before raising both arms over her head. The lights in the room all flickered before going out completely. When I looked back at Emery, her hands were consumed by balls of intricate, glowing lines I could best describe as lightning bolts.

She stared at it, mesmerized, her eyes glowing in the light. She let it travel up both arms, seeming to savor the feeling it left behind. It expanded off her and I could feel my hair standing up on end as she continued to let it grow. Just when I didn't think I could take the static feeling any longer, she let out a loud yell. She cast her hands forward and the fizzling energy ran off her fingers into the wall. The windows shattered against the force and, after a moment of quivering, part of the wall collapsed. She glared at Alexander from the side of her eye as he stood looking as stunned as any of us.

"You're quite powerful," he told her.

She sent a small zap onto one of the leftover branches and it sparked. "I know," she said.

"Am I the only one who's scared of her?" Mateo whispered, and most of us shook our heads.

Emery was a force to be reckoned with.

Chapter Twenty

I looked down at the map in my hands, confirming the corridor I was supposed to turn down to meet Alexander. The halls were mostly empty with the occasional person walking past me in the opposite direction, but none returned the greetings I offered. The people here weren't very friendly. As I was about to turn another corner, voices made their way to my ears, and I paused, recognizing them.

"You were right about Emery," Alexander was saying. I inched forward, making sure to keep out of sight as they continued. "She could be more valuable to us than our whole guard combined."

"When will she be ready?" Toshiro asked.

"She's already extremely powerful but after a couple weeks of training, she could do it," Alexander replied. "I'm sure of it."

Do what? What were they planning to do with her powers?

"Excellent," Toshiro said, the sneer on his face evident in his tone. "And what do you make of Robin thus far?"

"It's obviously an adjustment for her here but she hasn't given me any pushback since I laid out the ground rules." *He was lying.* "She's been extremely helpful in the training process, and I think she was sincere when she said we'd get no problems from her."

"Do you think she'll do what needs to be done when the time comes?"

"No. She won't. Not yet anyway. She's only been here a couple of days. We need more time with her before I can give you the answer you want."

"And if you can't?"

Alexander hesitated before answering. "I don't know."

"Yes, you do. If she isn't willing when the time comes, she'll be locked away. We might do it anyway. We can't risk her losing us the war."

"She'll never forgive me for something like that," Alexander murmured, his voice sounding torn, and I desperately wished I knew what they were talking about.

"That isn't my problem," Toshiro replied in a cold tone. "I told you to do whatever was necessary to get her on our side, not just compliant, and so far, all I see is your failed attempts at flirtation."

"I'm not flirting with her," Alexander denied.

"You got that right. You're about as romantic as a toad."

I peeked around the corner to see Alexander glaring menacingly at Toshiro with his hands balled into fists, but Toshiro was unfazed.

"Is that your grand plan then?" Toshiro asked. "To make her fall in love with you so she'll be on our side?"

"Of course not!"

"Then what, pray tell, are you doing?" Alexander looked away with a tight jaw, and Toshiro cocked his head, his eyes thoughtful as he studied him. "My dear boy," Toshiro tsked, shaking his head. "You're *actually* falling for her, aren't you?"

Alexander didn't reply, keeping his eyes on the floor as Toshiro sighed. He put his hand on Alexander's shoulder and squeezed it. "Your number one priority is our mission. We've worked too long and too hard for you to lose focus now."

"I'm well aware."

"However, with that being said," Toshiro paused and sighed again, "I know certain things can happen when you spend so much time with someone and you'll be spending the vast majority of yours with her so . . . Good luck. I hope you succeed in your personal endeavors. As long as it doesn't interfere with our plans."

Toshiro turned towards where I stood hiding and began walking my way. I looked around frantically then jumped behind the floor length curtains that hung against the window nearest me. I held my breath and closed my eyes as his footsteps neared. My heart beat rapidly as he passed me by, not slowing at all. When he was far enough away, I let out a loud sigh. That was a close one.

As I stepped out from behind the curtain, my brain jumped around all the things it had just witnessed. Toshiro was uncharacteristically kind at the end of his interaction with Alexander, and it was a hard thing to swallow. If I hadn't heard it myself, I wouldn't believe he was capable of such support. Then again, he *had* raised Alexander from a young age so maybe he did possess a paternal feeling towards him. He sounded sincere but that only left me mulling about the topic even more.

Alexander had feelings for me. Real and true feelings, not just artificial ones pushed on him by Toshiro. Butterflies fluttered in my stomach, and I found myself smiling at the idea. I looked down at my hands and the ring on my finger caught my eye. Guilt instantly overwhelmed me as I thought of Ben. How could I even think about another guy when I loved him? I shook my head as I silently chastised myself. That was the last thing that should be on my mind anyway. I was here for a reason. Not to mention Alexander was the enemy. The first part of their conversation is what I should be focused on.

As I began walking again, I thought about how I could get more information on what they wanted Emery for. It had to be something big and deplorable. With her abilities, it could be a range of things and frivolous information like that wouldn't help Garridan. I had to figure out what their plan was exactly. When I rounded the last corner and saw the side exit Alexander had instructed me to, I folded up my map and placed it in my coat pocket. I pushed open the door and was hit by a strong wind as I stepped outside. A small shiver left my body at the temperature of it.

"It's starting to get colder and colder," Alexander commented.

I looked to where his voice came from and saw him leaning against the wall next to the door.

"It sure is," I agreed as he pushed himself to a standing position.

"I thought you'd like to see the garden at night," he said, beckoning me towards him.

I followed him to the edge of the vast balcony and a smile crept onto my face. Below us, the garden was lit up by ground lights. The intricate walkways were lined with them every couple of feet, making sure nothing was left unseen. Towards the back there was a wood pergola with seating underneath and on the other end was a swing lined with ivy. The center of the garden held the fountain I remembered going to the last time I was here. Despite winter nearing, all the shrubs and flowers were in perfect condition creating a beautiful display of color.

"It's breathtaking," I finally said, the sight amazing me.

"Thank you," Alexander replied, and I looked up at him in confusion.

"What?"

"The garden is mine," he explained. "I designed every inch of it and make sure it stays maintained."

"Oh. That explains why all the greenery isn't dead."

Alexander chuckled. "That would be exactly why."

"So you like to garden," I remarked, a grin playing at my lips.

"Is there something wrong with that?" he asked, sounding amused.

"No, no. Of course not. I just wouldn't have pictured it as a hobby for you."

He raised his eyebrows. "You do realize my power basically makes me one with the earth, right? That includes flowers and bushes."

I looked away as heat rose in my cheeks. I guess that should've been kind of obvious. Alexander smirked at my expression then asked, "What would you picture as my hobby then?"

"Honestly, I don't know," I admitted. "I can't really picture you doing anything normal."

"Why not?"

"Because you're *not* normal. You live in a castle and have magic powers and evil plans. No one pictures the villain doing day to day activities."

"Villain," he repeated quietly, and I pressed my lips together. Luckily, he didn't press the subject. Instead, he asked, "How are you holding up?"

I shrugged. "Do you care?"

"I wouldn't be asking if I didn't."

"Are you going to reprimand me if I give the wrong answer?"

"No. I'm just trying to be a friend."

I looked over at him. "Are we friends?"

"Maybe not yet but . . . Hopefully we can get there. Everyone needs a friend in this life, remember?" he said, quoting my words from the other day. "So how are you doing?"

After a quiet moment, I responded truthfully. "It's hard."

"It'll get better," he assured me.

"Will it? We both know I'll never agree with what the Cyfrin want to accomplish. I'll always be an outsider pretending to be something I'm not just so I don't die. What kind of a life is that?" Alexander stayed silent so I pressed on, letting my thoughts spill. "But then again, it's really no different than when I was in Garridan aside from the dying part. Even there, I wasn't happy. I was an outsider just pretending to understand what was going on.

"Ever since my powers came, my life has been a series of heartbreak. No matter where I am or what I'm doing, I'll always be missing a part of me. If I'm in Garridan I'm missing my best friend, my boyfriend, my school, my normalcy . . . But if I'm in Milton I'm missing my parents, and Matthew, and this beautiful thing that makes me special and whole." I raised the water from the fountain as I said it, letting it dance in the moonlight. I watched it, loving the way it flowed with just a single thought. I smiled sadly at it then settled it back in its home before taking a deep breath. "Maybe I'm just not destined to be happy. Maybe I'll never stop having things taken away from me."

Alexander put his hand on my shoulder, and I stared at it before looking up at him. His brows were pulled together in concern and his eyes assessed me carefully, making sure I was okay.

"What more are you going to take away from me?" I whispered, and he dropped his arm.

"What do you mean?"

"My parents? Matthew?"

"I would never-,"

"I heard you and Toshiro talking earlier. What does he want Emery for? What are you planning to have her do? Whatever it is, it's going to hurt Garridan, right? Which means it'll hurt everyone *in* Garridan." His eyes hardened but I saw the smallest flicker of guilt in them. I rubbed my lips together and swallowed around the lump in my throat. "You would never, huh?"

I shook my head then turned around to go back inside as tears threatened to expose me.

"Robin," he called out, but I didn't give him a second look as I closed the door behind me. This wasn't how I had planned to have this conversation and I kicked myself for letting my emotions get the best of me. I was failing Garridan. If something happened and people got hurt, it would be all my fault.

Chapter Twenty-One

Alexander and I were walking side by side with our trainees behind us. We hadn't spoken all day and the atmosphere was tense. As we were going by the library, my nose was accosted by the smell of smoke. I stopped and looked around, trying to locate the source.

"It's Mallory," Andre said, his voice ominous.

Alexander scrunched his brows, then walked to the library doors, opening them up wide before stepping in. The rest of us followed slowly, watching as he walked to where Mallory sat in the middle of a circle of burning books. Mallory's eyes reflected the light coming from the fire as she stared at it wordlessly. She seemed to be in her own world, enchanted by her inferno.

"Hey, Mal," Alexander greeted her cautiously. "What are you doing?"

"Watching the world burn," she replied quietly.

"I don't know about the world, but you definitely got some books burning," Alexander told her.

She smirked but it didn't reach her eyes like normal. "The whole world is found in books, big brother. It's symbolic."

"You're psychotic," he said with a shake of his head,

"Aren't we all?"

"I suppose that depends on the point of view of whoever you're asking. I'm sure they all think we are," Alexander nodded his head at us, and Mallory's eyes hardened when she saw we were there.

"Why do we care what they think?" she spat out.

"We don't," Alexander replied, his eyes skimming over us. When they landed on me, his demeanor wavered but he quickly looked away to hide it. "Don't burn down the castle."

"Oh, please." Mallory rolled her eyes then twisted her wrist, extinguishing the flames. "Can I watch training today?"

"Only if you're going to be helpful."

"I'll make them cower with my fire balls."

"Excellent. You can join us." They strode out of the room, knocking us out of the way as they passed.

"They're joking right?" Toby asked nervously as they all looked to me for an answer.

"I honestly don't know," I admitted.

"This place is a nut house," Emery muttered, and I couldn't disagree as we followed to the training room.

The trainees lined up in their usual spot along the bench and Mallory slowly walked in front of them with her hands behind her back in a fashion much similar to Alexander.

"Who here thinks their power could be a match for mine?" she asked. When no one answered, she sneered. "Correct. None of you could beat me in a fight. However, some of you could definitely hold your own for at least a little while. One of you could even outwit me." She stopped in front of Andre. "If you grow your power to where you can predict my moves before I do them, you could survive an attack from me. But right now, you're useless. Kodi and Mateo, useless. Toby and Emery, let's see what you got."

"I don't want to fight anybody," Toby said, his voice shaking.

"Too bad. That's what you're here for so get used to it," Mallory told him. "Get up."

Toby slowly rose to his feet next to Emery but kept his head down.

"You have to look at your attacker if you plan on living," Mallory said but Toby didn't divert his gaze from the floor. Mallory tightened her eyes, her face unhappy. "Fine. Then fry."

She pulled out a lighter from her pocket and flicked it on, pulling the flame from the spout and growing it in her hands before placing the lighter back where it came from. I stared at her, realization dawning on me that she had to physically have fire in front of her to control it. She was limited. She thrust her hands out, and the fire leapt out of them towards Toby's unsuspecting body.

"No!" I yelled, reacting instinctively, and pulling a shield of water in front of him. The fire sizzled out as I pushed the water onto Mallory, making sure every inch of her was wetted down.

Everyone stared at us with wide eyes as Mallory turned on me, seething in every way.

"What the hell is the matter with you?" she yelled at me, her usually curly hair flat and sticking to her head.

"You can't attack an unarmed person!" I yelled back.

"He isn't unarmed. He could've easily blocked that!"

"But he wasn't going to! Not everything can be taught with force and violence."

"That's how we do things around here."

"Well, maybe it's time for that to change. I'm not going to let you hurt him. Or any of them for that matter."

Mallory glared at me, her look capable of death. "I'm above them. I can do whatever I want."

"All you people care about is hierarchy!" I cried out in exasperation. "If that's the most important thing to you, then fine. Guess what? I'm above you. So get out."

Mallory scoffed and folded her arms. "You are *not* above me. We're equal."

"If we're basing it off of power level, which is how things are done here, then no. We aren't equal. I can conjure water anywhere at any time to control which means I'm unlimited in what I can do. You're not. You can't conjure fire. You have to have a source. Right? Which means if something was to happen to that source, you're useless." Mallory visibly swallowed and pursed her lips, so I continued. "Take right now for example. Your lighter is drenched with water. It can't work. So what good are you? What are you going to do to fight me off? To fight any of us off?" I stared hard at her as she looked away and I let out a single humorless chuckle. "That's what I thought. Now get out."

She glanced over to Alexander, but he was too busy staring at me.

"This isn't over," she told me before stomping out of the room.

I turned towards the trainees and looked them over. "Listen, I know what you're going through, and I know it's unbearable. Not even a year ago, I was in your shoes. I had just found out I had a supernatural power, and I was being told I had to learn how to use it to fight for my own safety. I know it isn't easy and I know you might not want to do it. But that's too bad. Right now, your *life* is on the line." I remembered the words Matthew spoke to me when I hadn't wanted to learn and repeated it to them. "You each need to explore the depths of your powers and use it to your advantage. If you want to survive, if you want a chance, you *have* to fight back. Help me help you. Please."

* * *

"That was quite the tactic," Alexander said after our training session ended productively.

"It wasn't a tactic," I denied. "They needed to hear it."

"Well, no matter, it worked. They all seem much more open to what we're teaching them."

"Good. They need to be. It's the only way they won't get killed here."

"You're quite the leader," Alexander commented, glancing at me from the side of his eye.

"I'm not a leader. I just can't watch them get hurt," I replied, and the corner of his lip turned upward.

"You may not see it, but it's true. You're a natural born leader and your compassion is your greatest asset."

I snorted. "Really? Because I've been told by more than one person it's my biggest flaw."

"You're not associating with the right people then," he said, and my brows furrowed. "You did good today. Just accept the win."

"Fine. Thanks," I finally relented as we stopped in front of my bedroom door. "I'll see you tomorrow."

"Wait," he said, holding out his hand. "We need to talk about what you overheard the other day."

"You're going to tell me what your plan is for Emery?"

"No. I meant the other subject matter."

"I'm not interested in that."

"Aren't you?"

"No."

"You're lying."

I hesitated. "Maybe. But it doesn't matter. I don't care if you have feelings for me."

"Because the feelings aren't reciprocated?" he asked. I looked away without answering so he pressed on. "Will they ever be?"

"No," I replied softly. "Not in a world where Ben exists."

"I don't believe that. You can't deny the possibility of it happening when I've already stirred up something in you."

"You haven't," I denied, shifting uncomfortably.

"You're lying," he repeated, his voice earnest and his eyes intent on mine. "I see the way you act around me sometimes. You may love Ben but . . . I think you might like me too."

As he continued to watch me, I noticed how full his lashes were, framing the brown iris in a beautiful fashion. I swallowed, diverting my gaze again. "Even if I did, which I'm not saying I do, it doesn't matter."

"How can you say that?"

"Because Toshiro was right about something."

"What?"

"Our number one priority is our mission," I repeated Toshiro's words. Little did Alexander know that our missions were two entirely different things.

"Our mission will be over one day," Alexander pointed out.

"It won't matter then either."

"Why not?"

"Because you were right about something too."

"What?"

I looked up at him and took a shaky breath. "I will never forgive you if you succeed at destroying Garridan."

This time, he looked away, but not before I saw the hurt in his eyes. He was convicted by my words. I walked into my room and shut the door as I replayed his reaction in my mind. Maybe having him fall for me would work in my advantage. It could allow me to get closer to him which would mean I could possibly convince him he was doing the wrong thing. Or maybe it would allow me to make him feel enough guilt to second guess whatever they were going to do. I just hoped I didn't become a victim of my own plan.

Chapter Twenty-Two

As the next couple weeks passed by, Alexander shut me out. My words had impacted him more than I had thought they would. He still escorted me to all our necessary engagements, but the walks were filled with silence, nothing more than the sound of our shoes on the concrete filling the halls we passed through. There were times I could feel his eyes on me, though, sneaking glances when he thought I couldn't see.

I took a more active role in training, knowing they needed my guidance more than Alexander's and it showed. Each trainee was more focused and driven as they willingly worked on expanding and being in touch with their powers. My speech seemed to have gotten through to them and, despite it being a slow and tedious process, they were all showing improvement. I couldn't say the same for their morale. Aside from Mateo, who was friendly with everyone, none of them interacted unless we forced them together, and I knew that would be a problem later on. They all needed to trust one another when the time came so something had to be done.

"I'm going to have Kodi and Emery sleep in my room tonight," I told Alexander.

He eyed me dubiously. "Why?"

"Sleepover."

"Why?"

"I'm a girl. They're girls. It's what we do," I said with a shrug. "And none of us have had any fun in a good minute. They've been working hard; they deserve some relaxation."

"And what about the boys?"

"I'll have a sleepover with them tomorrow night," I joked.

He narrowed his eyes, not appreciating my humor. "No."

"Then you can have a sleepover with them," I suggested with a smirk.

"No."

"Fine. I'll figure something else out for them. But I need Darnell to not put me to sleep tonight," I requested which was met with another look. "Oh, come on. It's one night. It's not like

I'm going to be sneaking out the window or performing mass genocide. It's a sleepover."

"Fine. But don't come crying to me when you're dead on your feet tomorrow."

"What do you mean?"

"Long term use of somnokinesis tends to have an ill effect on a person's ability to sleep on their own," he explained. "The inner demons your dreams can't work through all build up and try to come out at once. It's usually pretty brutal."

I crossed my arms over my chest. "And yet you all chose to do this to me anyway."

"The pros for us outweighed the cons for you."

"Of course they did." We stared each other down for a moment but I finally looked away, not in the mood for any more fighting. "I'm going to get the girls. You know where we'll be if your distrust becomes too much, and you need to check up on us."

I turned around and walked away as I desperately ached for the company of Felicity. She's the only person I could talk to about Alexander with no judgement and honest opinions. I needed her guidance before it all became too overwhelming but, unfortunately, that wasn't going to happen. I nodded at the guards outside of the trainees' bedrooms then knocked on the girls' door. When it opened, Emery looked out with an unfriendly expression but when she saw me it softened slightly.

"Oh, it's just you," she said, running her hand through her messy hair.

"Just me," I confirmed with a smile. "I came to see if you and Kodi wanted to have a sleepover in my room tonight."

Kodi came up behind Emery, her face showing interest, but Emery just scoffed and asked, "Really? A sleepover?"

"It'll be fun," I insisted. "I know it seems strange considering the circumstances, but I figured we all deserved a little break."

"Yes, braiding each other's hair and gossiping will make life so much better!" Emery exclaimed in a giddy voice, her sarcasm overwhelming.

I rubbed my lips together then shrugged defeatedly. "You don't have to. I just thought it would be a nice change."

I took a step back, prepared to walk away, but Kodi jumped around Emery with her hand up. "Wait! I want to go."

"Really?" I asked.

"Really."

A smile crossed my face. "Okay! Why don't you get in your pajamas then we'll go."

"These are my pajamas," she said, looking down at her usual grey sweats and black t-shirt.

"Oh. Well, then, I guess we'll go now," I said, holding back a grin at her lackluster fashion choices.

She slipped on some sandals and walked out the door. "Bye, Emery."

"Wait," Emery spoke up. I looked over at her and she rolled her eyes. "I guess I'll come too."

"Don't do me any favors."

"I *want* to come," she said.

"Yeah, that sounded convincing," Kodi snorted, and I couldn't help but laugh.

"Get your shoes and let's go," I told Emery. Five minutes later we were in my room, sprawled out on the bed. "What do you guys want to do?"

"We could braid each other's hair and gossip," Kodi suggested, her own sarcasm coming through.

Emery glared at her, and I bit my lip to stifle a grin.

"Do you guys like games?" I asked. "I had Roxy bring some up earlier."

"Is there Uno?" Kodi asked. "I love Uno."

"I think so!" I replied, getting off the bed and going to the stack of games that sat on the couch. I grabbed the cards then shuffled them when I got back on the bed.

Emery sat stiffly, staring at them as I passed them out.

"Is something wrong?" I asked her.

"No," she responded. "It just feels childish."

"That's not a bad thing. We all need a break from being an adult sometimes."

"You don't get the luxury of a break when you live on the streets."

Kodi and I exchanged a glance, unsure whether to pry or not. "I can't imagine how difficult that must be," I finally settled on saying.

Emery shrugged, her face indifferent. "Life is difficult for everyone in some way or another."

"I suppose that's true."

We played quietly for a while, trying to warm up to one another. It was different from the last time I had played this with Ben, Felicity, and Matthew. But that seemed like a lifetime ago anyway. After a couple hands, I noticed Kodi kept throwing me glances.

"What's up?" I asked her.

"What?" she responded.

"You keep looking at me. What's up?"

"Oh, sorry, it's nothing."

"Are you sure?"

"Well, it's just . . . You never told us how you ended up here," she admitted. "We all know you're different from the rest of the Cyfrin but it's still hard to trust you when none of us can figure out what your story is."

That explained a lot.

"My story is very similar to yours in ways," I told her.

"And in other ways?" Emery asked.

"It's a lot different," I answered. They both looked at me expectantly, the game forgotten, so I shifted into a seated position. "Do you want the short version or the long version?"

"Long," they said simultaneously so I launched into my tale starting with meeting Matthew and ending with the Cyfrin's offer to Garridan. Emery's face continued to get more disgusted as the story progressed while Kodi's became more sympathetic. When I finished, they both just stared at me while they processed everything.

"You've had one hell of a year," Emery said.

"Yes, I have," I agreed with a sad smile.

"I'm sorry about your mom and sister," Kodi told me, and I looked down at my hands, holding back the grief that always threatened to overwhelm me when speaking about them.

I swallowed, trying to keep the tears from springing into my eyes. "Me too."

"I don't know how you can stand to be around them," she continued.

"It isn't easy," I admitted.

"But you do it," she pointed out and I nodded.

"I have to. For you guys and for Garridan and for the rest of the world. If we don't stop the Cyfrin, the whole world is going to pay the price."

"Does that mean you have a plan to stop them?" Emery asked, and I hesitated.

"Yes and no. Garridan is fully prepared for another battle, but my intel will hopefully give them the edge they need to end it once and for all," I answered. I sighed heavily and rested my chin against my hands. "The only problem is I haven't had any luck getting any information."

"I might be able to help with that," a muffled voice said from under the bed.

All three of us gasped and quickly stood up, eyeing the floor.

"Who's under there?" I demanded, my hands up and ready for anything. I watched as feet popped out from under the bed skirt, the person shimmying out and standing up.

"Mateo?" I exclaimed before sighing in relief as he ran his fingers through his hair sheepishly.

"Hi," he offered up.

"How long have you been under the bed?" Emery asked, her hands on her hips.

"How long have you been on top of the bed?" he asked.

"You heard everything?" I questioned, heat rising to my cheeks at the details I had given to the girls about Ben and me.

"Yeah."

"Shame on you for eavesdropping, Mateo," Kodi chastised, and he smiled unapologetically. On the plus side, it was one less person I had to gain the trust of.

"How did you get in here anyway?" I pried.

"I came through the vents. You can get almost anywhere in this castle through the reworked duct system."

"Correction: *you* can get almost anywhere through the reworked duct system," Kodi pointed out.

"The perks to being the size of a mouse," he replied with a laugh. "But that brings me back to what I said before. I can help."

"Help with what?" Emery questioned.

"Getting information for Robin," he answered, looking to me.

When it clicked in my mind what he meant, I smiled. "You can eavesdrop on Toshiro!"

"Exactly!"

"And people thought your power would be useless," Kodi teased.

"This is a game changer," I told them, a weight lifted from my shoulders as I finally saw some light at the end of the tunnel. "We get some useful information, Garridan wins."

"Which means the world is safe," Emery concluded.

"And we get to go home," Kodi added.

We all exchanged excited glances, hope igniting in all of us. Mateo had just given us the possibility of foolproof success and I couldn't wait to tell Claire. Her visits were always depressing when we got on the subject of why I was here. Peter was extremely unhappy that we hadn't had any sort of major breakthrough yet but, luckily, none of the other Keepers of Balance seemed too upset about it. They knew it would take time.

After visiting with us for a while longer, Mateo snuck back to his room with the promise of relaying everything to Toby and Andre. There was no doubt in my mind that they'd be on our side which meant we were officially a team conspiring against the Cyfrin. Training would be more intense than ever before but hopefully our personal relationships would grow from here.

Emery and Kodi fell asleep after midnight, leaving me tossing and turning in the bed with just my thoughts for company. My mind was a whirlwind of 'what ifs' as people's faces came and went from my mind. My mom and Dawn, Ben and Felicity, Adriana and Elijah, Matthew, and so many others. It was as if all the people I had ever loved were haunting me, their voices calling out to me all the different ways I would fail them if I hadn't already.

You won't save Garridan, Adriana told me.

You'll be the reason I'm a servant, Felicity said.

You'll break my heart, Ben accused.

You got me killed, Dawn's sweet voice whispered.

I shot up, breathing heavy as sweat poured down my back. I put my hand over my mouth as a silent sob tore through me, then I swung my feet out of bed. I pulled on my slippers and quietly sauntered out the door so I wouldn't wake Emery or Kodi. Tears slid down my face and my lip quivered as my mom's voice told me what a disappointment I was. I began walking to try to silence the voices as they grew louder and more intense.

Despite it being the middle of the night, lights filled the castle, illuminating it so nothing could go unseen. It was eerily quiet, though, causing my soft footsteps to sound loud. Before I knew it, I was at the side door that led to the balcony. I pushed it open,

letting the cold of the night embrace me as it nipped at my bare arms. I walked to the edge, standing rigid as I stared at the beauty of the garden below. I took a deep breath, the motion hurting my throat, as I allowed the frigid air to numb my feelings along with my fingers. My shoulders tensed up even more and the tears that dried against my face wouldn't stop falling.

"You'll catch a cold out here dressed like that."

I whipped my head around and saw Alexander walking towards me bundled in a coat with another one in his hand. I looked back to the garden as he came up behind me. He draped the jacket over my shoulders then stood next to me.

"What are you doing here?" I asked quietly.

"Waiting for you."

"How'd you know I'd come here?"

"Just a guess. Most people try to find peace from the nightmares, and you seemed to like it here," he told me. "I told you the long-term effects of somnokinesis were rough."

"I thought you said not to come crying to you about it."

"I did . . . But I came to you. I knew you'd be suffering. I couldn't let you do it alone."

"Will it stop?" I whispered, closing my eyes as my head threatened to explode.

"Not tonight," he replied, his voice sympathetic. "But tomorrow Darnell will put you to sleep again, and you won't have to deal with it anymore."

"Can he do it now?"

"What?"

I turned towards him as another sob tore through my chest. "Make him put me to sleep now. Please. I can't handle this. I can't."

"Okay," he agreed softly, putting his hand on my arm. "Okay."

He led me inside as my heart cracked a little more with each voice that threw a new accusation at me. It was as if they wanted to break the little bit of happiness that I clung onto. They were trying to ruin the good memories I had left. But they wouldn't win. Not tonight. Tonight, I was going to sleep.

Chapter Twenty-Three

"Up until this point, we've been practicing your training alone or on dummies," Alexander said. "But today, that changes. Today you'll start going head-to-head with one another."

"What if we hurt the other person?" Andre asked.

"Then that means they need to get stronger." Concerned looks were exchanged amongst the trainees, none of them thrilled with the idea of fighting each other. Alexander sighed heavily, his face bordering on annoyance. "Listen and listen closely. You have to learn that what we're doing in here is in preparation of what you'll be expected to do out there. You can't hold back otherwise you'll fail. And failure will not be tolerated. Andre, Emery. You're up."

Andre's face turned to bewilderment. "I'm not fighting her. She's half my size!"

"And you think that means you'll have an advantage?" Emery asked with a scoff, cocking her brow at him. "Step up, big boy. Let me show you how it's done."

She walked into the middle of the room as Andre stared after her with disbelief. He glanced over at me, and I shrugged, knowing he wasn't getting out of it. Emery had her eyes on him, intent and a little playful, as he sauntered across from her.

"What are the rules?" Emery asked.

"Don't die," Alexander replied, leaning against the wall with his arms folded.

"Excellent," she said as a smirk crept onto her face.

Andre's eyes followed her every move as she lingered in front of him, his lips set in a tight line. Emery circled him once, twice, three times then suddenly lunged out, kicking him hard behind the knee. Andre was caught off balance, the move making him kneel on the ground as Emery took a cheap shot, bringing her elbow down on the back of his neck. Andre let out a grunt as he fell further towards the ground before Emery repeated the move and he was sprawled out on the mat.

Emery's eyes glistened as he looked up at her, giving her a small nod of approval for being able to take him down. He stood

back up and I saw his fingers twitching at his side, anticipating her
attack this time. When she sprang forward with her leg up to kick him in the stomach, his hands latched onto her calf, and he yanked it forward causing her back to smack into the ground. The wind was knocked out of her, and she lay there stunned for a moment before she pushed herself back up. She stood across from him again before attempting an uppercut to his jaw. He easily caught her wrist and yanked her around, pinning both arms behind her back just hard enough to leave her immobile.

"I win," he murmured close to her face as she struggled to get out of his relentless grip. He looked over at Alexander. "Are we done here?"

"You could pummel her," Alexander said, and I could barely detect the sound of sarcasm.

"No," Andre replied, letting go of Emery's arms.

She looked displeased with losing but her eyes were still lit up in a way I hadn't seen before. "If this were power training, I would've fried you," she told Andre.

He let out a chuckle and said, "I don't doubt that," before they took their spots back in line.

"Clearly that was an unfair pairing, but it was done with the idea that you won't be sparring against people equal to you in a real fight," Alexander said from where he stood. "Emery never had a chance against Andre, but she did start out with the advantage. When you're on a battlefield, all bets are off. You'll have to fight dirty in order to survive. Remember that."

"If we were in a real fight, why wouldn't we just use our powers?" Mateo asked.

"Preferably you would. However, some powers are no good in a fight," he replied, looking to Kodi. "And there are some people who you'll be unable to use your powers against. For example, Isaac who can cancel your power temporarily or the general of the Garridan guard who has the ability of power reflection. In those circumstances, all you'll have at your disposal is your own strength and skill. That's why it's important that you take your physical training just as seriously as your power training."

After his explanation, he called on Mateo and Kodi to go next. They both grinned, clearly excited to show the other one up. Mateo quickly pounced on Kodi, knocking her to the ground, but she wrapped her legs around his waist and swung him around to where she sat on top of him. They repeated this several times, rolling around on the ground and bumping into things before it somehow turned into a slap fight. Neither one wanted the other to get the last hit, so they became more aggressive, their bare skin paying the consequences as Alexander watched with disapproval.

He rolled his eyes and waved his fingers in opposite directions, causing two vines to wrap around their torsos and yank them apart. "You're all ridiculous. You really think a slap fight is going to save you?"

"Come on, Alexander," I spoke up. "They aren't stupid, and they aren't weak. They just don't want to fight each other. We should go back to the dummies. That's more effective than this."

"I have a better idea," he replied. "I'll just bring in outside opponents."

"But they'll get hurt!" I exclaimed.

"That's the point, Robin," he said harshly. "How do you expect them to survive out there if we don't prepare them in here?"

I bit my lip, knowing he was right. I had to know that they could take care of themselves whenever the battle began. "Fine. But I get to choose the opponents."

Alexander raised his brows at me, amused as usual. "I don't think so. You'll choose people who won't give enough of a fight."

"And you'll choose people who will kill them," I shot back, crossing my arms.

He eyed me for a second then matched my stance. "I'll fight you for it."

"What?"

"You and me, right now. You win, you choose. I win, I choose," he explained. He waited with a smirk on his face, which made me *want* to pummel him.

"Deal," I said, and his smirk disappeared.

"What?"

"Deal," I repeated, pleased by the shock on his face. He had been expecting me to back down.

He took a deep breath, his eyes tightening as he weighed his dilemma. He didn't want to fight me, but he couldn't go back on his word now. It would make him look weak.

"Fine," he stated, motioning towards the mat in the middle of the room.

We both sauntered over, neither of us pleased with what was about to happen, but this was my chance to show him I was worth more than the pawn the Cyfrin wanted to use me as. I wouldn't sit in the background while he hurt the people I loved, and that included the five trainees I had grown to care about. He watched me with fervent eyes, offering me one more chance to back out, but I held my ground. He let out an unhappy breath, then stepped forward to make the first move as I focused on his position. He shifted his leg forward slightly, his torso retracting in the opposite direction, and I immediately ducked as he threw his weight into a punch aimed at my face.

I drove my elbow into his stomach as I came back up and a grunt escaped his mouth. He swung his leg around, landing a blow straight to my ribs, and I cried out as the pain radiated through me. We sparred for a solid minute, neither of us getting a good hit in until I dropped my arm too soon and his fist connected with my eye. I took a step back, my hand automatically reaching up as my face throbbed and my vision blurred. Alexander took the opportunity to sweep my feet out from under me and I fell onto my back, the breath forced out of my lungs.

Get up is the only thought that flew through my mind as he came for me again. I wouldn't lose. I pushed myself off the ground, barely dodging a blow to my stomach from his foot. I blocked his next punch with my forearm, ignoring the sting that came with it, as I used my opposite arm to land a punch to his face. He stumbled back, surprised, and I used his lack of balance to drive a kick into his chest, knocking him to the ground. I pulled my foot back and used all the force I could muster into kicking the side of his head.

Blood dripped from his face as I went to repeat the motion, but he caught my ankle in his hands and pushed me back, giving him time to get off the ground. His elbow connected with my face, and my eyes watered from the impact as my nose started to bleed. He rushed towards me, and we fell to the ground, struggling to overpower the other as Mateo and Kodi had earlier. He finally pinned me on the ground, holding my hands above my head.

"Pinned ya," he whispered, and I was brought back to the first time I was in the Cyfrin compound, and he had said those words to me.

Little did he know that I was stronger now than I was then, and I said a silent thanks to Matthew for all the hours of training he forced me into. I forced my head up, slamming my skull into his nose, then maneuvered out of his grasp the way I had practiced so many times before. I brought both feet under his torso and pushed him off me before kneeling on his chest with one knee pressed against his throat. He tried to throw me off balance but my weight on his chest crippled him as he struggled to breathe.

"Do I win?" I asked, breathing heavily, as his face started to turn red.

He nodded once and I slid onto the ground next to him as he began to cough. I wiped at the blood from my nose then leaned back against my hands. I closed my eyes as my head pounded and my body ached. When I opened them again, Alexander was watching me with a half-smile playing at his split lips.

"What?" I questioned, not expecting that reaction from him.

"You're very impressive," he answered.

"I had a good teacher."

He nodded, seeming to know who I meant. "I believe you did."

I furrowed my brow, confused by his demeanor. "Why aren't you angry?"

"You put up a good fight," he replied with a shrug as I continued to stare at him.

"Did you let me win?" I asked, appalled.

"Does it matter?"

My mouth opened and closed a couple times, but I was too dumbfounded to speak.

"You have excellent technique and you got in some good hits," Alexander continued, motioning towards his bruising temple. He leaned in closer to me, his voice soft so no one else could overhear. "But I've been doing this a lot longer than you. You could never really beat me in a physical battle."

"But . . . *why*?"

The back of his fingers brushed against my swollen eye lightly. "You have a lot of motivation that drives you. I know you would've kept going until you physically couldn't move anymore, and I couldn't do that. I couldn't hurt you anymore than I already did."

I looked down at my feet, upset that I didn't really beat him. "Do I still get to choose their opponents?"

Alexander chuckled then nodded. "Yes. Just make sure they'll present a challenge. Don't be the reason they're unprepared for a fight."

"You mean *the* fight," I corrected, knowing he meant the battle against Garridan that was brewing, and he nodded before standing up. He offered me his hand and I took it, wincing at the pain that came with the movement of getting up.

"Thanks to Robin I won't sic Serafina or Mallory on you tomorrow. But you *will* be presented with people of equal or slightly greater skill. Be prepared to hurt," he told the trainees. "The rest of the day is yours. Enjoy it while it lasts."

"Why?" Emery asked suspiciously.

"Because I have meetings I have to attend," he replied.

I glanced over at Mateo, and he nodded his head, already on the same page as me. Information was right around the corner.

Chapter Twenty-Four

"That was one heck of a fight," Mateo commented as Andre tended to my wounds. "How did you learn to fight like that?"

"Same way you guys are," I replied, wincing as the warm cloth stung the cut by my eye. "Remember my friend Matthew who I was talking about the other night?"

"The one that was from here, right?" Toby interjected, confirming that Mateo had relayed my story.

"That's the one. He trained me initially and then when we were in Garridan we practiced almost every day with trainers from the guard," I explained.

"That means we'll be that good someday too," Mateo said, punching the air, and I couldn't help but grin at his high energy as he pulled Toby into a headlock and started a brawl.

"You're lucky you don't have any broken ribs," Andre murmured as he gently ran his hand over my ribcage, causing me to hiss in a breath.

"Lucky Alexander took it easy on me," I replied with a grunt, still unhappy with that fact.

"This is taking it easy?" Andre asked, gesturing towards my bruised face.

"He could've done much worse."

"That doesn't win him any points in my book."

"He's not all bad," I told him quietly.

"I'm sure he's not, but by my definition not all bad is still bad."

"He's just been misguided."

"I'm not saying it's his fault that he is the way he is," Andre amended. "But that doesn't change the fact that he *is* the way he is."

"What if he could change?"

Andre put down the cloth and sat in front of me, his eyes soft. "Do you think he could?"

"I don't know," I admitted.

"But you wish he would."

"Of course I do."

"For you?"

"What do you mean?"

"I see the way he looks at you. He cares about you. The question is, do you care about him too?"

His question threw me off and I stuttered around an answer. "I mean, I-I do but not in the way you're implying."

"Are you sure?" he pressed, his face nonjudgmental.

I looked away, unable to answer his question. "You should be majoring to be a psychologist or a doctor," I told him.

He smiled at me gently, letting the other topic wash away. "It's never too late to switch."

The doors to the library opened and Emery and Kodi walked in.

"They're heading for the throne room now," Emery informed us.

"Guess it's my time to shine," Mateo said, winking at us.

"Be smart," Kodi told him with a knowing look.

He scrunched down, shrinking smaller and smaller until he was the size of my palm. He squeaked up at Kodi then ran off, his little paws tapping the ground silently.

"What did he say?" Toby asked.

"He said he's smarter than all of us combined," Kodi relayed with a roll of her eyes.

"If he's so smart, why didn't he just turn into a bat so he could hear their conversation from here?" Andre questioned, and we all grinned at his logic.

We settled in on the floor around a small pile of books, flipping through them aimlessly. After a while, the silence became too much.

"How long do we have to wait?" Toby whined.

"Their meetings could last all day," I replied, and he sighed. "You don't have to wait here if you don't want to."

"I'd rather be bored here with all of you than on my own," he said, pulling at the frayed carpet. "Why aren't you in there with them though?"

"They don't trust me. They won't let me into any meetings or give me any kind of sensitive information. They won't even let me perform the duties of a Keeper of Balance. Even though the Cyfrin compound needs it."

"What do you mean?" Kodi asked.

"Have you noticed how the land here is dry? Or how it never rains? Or how the stream on the north side sits stagnant?" I asked, pointing out just some of the things that were being effected by the lack of a water element in their midst.

"I never really paid attention," Kodi admitted.

"I never would've before either but now I'm programmed to see it. The Keepers of Balance take care of the earth by helping the natural order of things," I explained as they listened intently. "As a water element, there's things I can do alone such as purify water sources or make rivers flow. But there's a lot of things that require two or more elements working together to be performed."

"Like what?" Emery asked.

"Well, one example would be the rain. I can bring moisture to the air, but an air element has to form the clouds for the water droplets to keep growing in until they're ready to fall."

"That's so cool!" Toby exclaimed and I smiled, pride filling me once again at the importance of my abilities and the good it was used for.

"If you control it then why are there droughts in some places?" Andre asked.

"There's only sixteen Keepers of Balance in Garridan. Four of each element. It's not easy to maintain every area while also dealing with things like the Cyfrin," I pointed out. "They try to do all they can, but some places do get lost in the shuffle."

"So I'm assuming they don't take care of the land the Cyfrin sits on," Andre observed.

"No, they don't. And since the Cyfrin are lacking a water element, they're paying the price."

"I'm surprised they don't let you do that stuff and just leave you out of the meetings and what not," Emery commented.

"Unfortunately for them, it's not that simple. I still don't fully understand it myself, but the Keepers of Balance have to be in unity with one another to be productive. If Toshiro and I tried to bring rain but he only thought of how he couldn't trust me, he could overcompensate and cause a tornado." My eyes jumped from one face to another, taking in their bewildered expressions.

"So not only are you to thank for the good elements, you're also to blame for the bad," Emery said slowly before scoffing.

"No one can be in unity all the time," I responded with a shrug. I listened as they broke out in chatter, pointing out different things and asking more questions. I answered them the best I could, but I was just as mystified as they were on some things and had to remind them I was still fairly new to it all as well.

After a moment of silence lingered, Toby looked up at me again. "What happens after the battle between Garridan and the Cyfrin?"

"As long as we win, which we will, we'll all get to go home," I answered.

He looked down. "I don't want to go back to the group home."

"Well, good. Because I meant home as in Garridan," I said with a soft smile.

"Really?"

"Really," I assured him, and a smile lit up his face.

"What if we want to go back to our real homes?" Kodi asked quietly, her face withdrawn.

"I'm not sure," I replied slowly. "The people of Garridan are really caring and selfless. As all the kids they sent away got older, they decided to leave them be once they found them and knew they were safe. They didn't want to steal them away from the only life they knew. But since you all have your powers . . . I'm not sure what they'll want to do."

"Shouldn't it be our choice though?" Kodi pushed.

"It definitely should. I'm just not sure it's that easy." She looked away so I rushed to continue. "But they're really fair people. If you don't want to stay in Garridan, I don't think they'll make you. They'll probably just take your power away first."

"They can do that?"

"They did it before so I don't see why they couldn't again."

"That doesn't seem very fair."

"What doesn't?" I asked.

"Choosing between keeping our power or our families," Kodi clarified, and I nodded absentmindedly.

"I know what you mean," I murmured, my own inner battle always at the back of my mind.

"Guess you two lucked out in that department," Kodi said to Emery and Toby.

"Excuse you?" Emery asked, narrowing her eyes.

"I just meant you don't have to worry about that which is nice," Kodi explained hastily, realizing she said something wrong.

Emery's eyes blazed, her scowl menacing. "Oh yeah, how *nice* that we grew up jumping from one foster home to another. How *nice* that we endured abuse and torment for no reason. How *nice* that we were forced into the wrong crowd because no one had high expectations of the problematic foster kid. How *nice* for us that we were kicked to the street the day of our eighteenth birthday with nothing but the clothes on our backs. Yes, really, *we're* the lucky ones." Her face was red with anger, and she stood up then stomped out the door.

"Emery, wait!" Andre called out, getting up and following her.

"I-I didn't mean to upset her," Kodi told us, her eyes filling with tears. "I didn't mean it the way it came out. I just meant . . ."

"I know what you meant," I told her, sliding over, and putting my arm around her shoulders. "You were blessed with a happy life after Garridan just like I was. But that doesn't make our struggles any less relevant."

"She's right," Toby agreed, sitting on her other side.

"You're not mad at me?" she asked, and he shook his head.

"Of course not," he replied, taking her hand in his own. "I can't imagine how you feel being taken from your family. And knowing you either can't see them again or can't keep your power. It's like it's a part of you already. I don't think I'd ever feel whole without mine again."

"That's exactly it," I told him quietly. Just then, something scaley rubbed against my leg and I let out a yelp, kicking at it as we all jumped up. The snake flew through the air, stretching out and landing on four limbs.

"Hey! That hurt," Mateo complained, rubbing his neck.

"Maybe you should be careful what creature you creep up as then," I shot back.

He sauntered over, his mouth turned down in a scowl that looked unnatural on his face. When he saw the tears on Kodi's cheeks, his expression instantly changed to concern. "What happened? Are you okay?"

"I'm fine," she assured him, swiping at her face. "I just said something stupid and made Emery mad at me."

"Oh, well, it doesn't usually take much," he said, plopping down. "What did you say?"

"I'll tell you later," she responded. "Did you overhear anything useful?"

"Not particularly. These weren't battle plan meetings," he told us.

"Then what kind of meetings were they?" I questioned.

"Party planning meetings," he replied with a grin.

"I'm sorry, what?"

"They're planning a party. Or maybe it'd better be described as a ball or gala."

"Are you serious?"

"Yep."

"The Cyfrin throws parties?" Toby asked.

"Only one," Mateo answered. "They do a huge blow out once a year for all the members. It's kind of a thank you to them for being on their side and supporting their message. Plus, it helps build rapport to mingle with everyone."

"When is it?" Kodi asked.

"In a couple weeks I think. Alexander is supposed to tell us about it tomorrow."

I let out a groan. This wasn't what I had been expecting.

"I'm sorry. I know it's not the information you were wanting," Mateo told me.

"It's not your fault. It's just frustrating."

"I know. But I'm not giving up. I'll live by Toshiro's side if I have to."

I smiled at him. "Thank you."

That night I stayed frazzled as I took a shower and got ready for bed. The longer I was here without success, the more anxiety filled me. Dawn's voice echoed in my head, and I fought back tears. I couldn't be the reason more people died.

Chapter Twenty-Five

The next morning, my body was stiff and sore. I eased out of bed slowly, grunting as the discomfort in my ribs spread through me. I walked into the bathroom and stood in front of the mirror. My eye was still slightly swollen but it looked better than yesterday. I gently lifted my shirt and grimaced. The bruise was big and splotchy, a multitude of colors spreading out along my side. I brushed my fingers over it and hissed in a breath with how tender it was.

"What the hell happened to you?"

I turned around and saw Claire standing in the doorway with Matthew behind her, both of their faces a mixture of anger and concern.

"Matthew!" I exclaimed, stepping towards him with a wide smile on my face. I stopped short when I remembered I couldn't hug him.

"What the hell happened to you?" he repeated.

"It's nice to see you too," I muttered.

"Are you okay?" Claire asked.

"Yeah, I'm fine. Alexander-"

"Alexander did this to you?" Matthew hissed before I could finish.

"Technically, but-"

"I'm going to kill him!"

"Matthew."

"I knew sending you here was a bad idea. But did anyone listen to me? No! And now look at what they've been doing to you. We have to get you out of there."

"Matthew," I repeated.

He turned towards Claire. "We have to get her out of there."

"Matthew!" I yelled, finally getting his attention. "Shut up and listen to me. I'm fine. Alexander and I had a bet. That's the only reason we had a fighting match. And I won."

"You won?" he asked doubtfully, crossing his arms, and positioning himself in a stance that reminded me of Alexander.

"Yes, I did."

He observed me for a second before concluding, "He let you win."

I pursed my lips. "Maybe."

"Why would he do that?" he asked.

"Because he didn't want to hurt me, and he knew I wouldn't back down."

Matthew narrowed his eyes at my explanation, so I sighed. "I'm fine, okay? Don't worry about me."

"Impossible," he replied.

"Then trust me. I'll tell you if I can't handle something."

"No, you won't."

I smiled softly. He knew me so well.

"I think I have information you'll be interested in," Claire spoke up, tired of being ignored.

"Wish I could say the same." I sighed. "All the Cyfrin are talking about is some party or gala or something."

Matthew snorted. "Of course they are. They wouldn't miss it. Not even with an impending battle upon them."

"What's it like?" I asked curiously.

"Gaudy. Very extravagant and over the top," he replied with disdain.

Claire put her hands on her hips. "Hello? What am I, invisible?"

"I'd say more translucent," Matthew told her with a thoughtful expression.

"Definitely translucent," I agreed, nodding my head.

"If this is how it's going to be I just won't bring Matthew with me again," she said, a sly smile playing at her lips.

"That's cruel," I responded with a pout.

"Then I guess you better start listening."

Matthew and I both closed our mouths and looked at her expectantly.

"That's right. *I'm* in control," she remarked with satisfaction. "But anyway, we finally traced all your trainees back to their families."

"That's great!" I exclaimed.

"It is . . . Mostly," Claire responded.

"What do you mean 'mostly'?"

"Not all of their parents are alive."

"Oh, no," I murmured, my heart dropping. "Who?"

"Donald Bryan, Latasha Crossley, and Theodore and Rachel McCoy."

"No, I meant whose parents are they?"

"Kodi's father, Andre's mother, and both of Toby's parents," she replied.

"No," I whispered. I didn't want any of them to have lost both their parents, but Toby was the worst option. He didn't have a family his whole life and now he didn't even have one to go to in Garridan.

"I'm sorry," Claire said.

"It's not your fault . . . I'm just sad for them. They're already struggling with everything. I'm not sure how to tell them that."

"Maybe you shouldn't," Matthew suggested.

"I can't keep it from them."

"You need them to be at their best at all times. This will just be a burden they can't do anything about, and it'll distract them."

"They deserve to know."

"It won't do them any good."

"You mean it won't do *me* any good," I accused, seeing through his words.

"Yes, that's what I mean," he agreed, unashamed. "They're your only allies there; your only means of help when you need to escape. I don't think your safety is worth risking."

"That's where we differ, Matthew. I don't care about my safety. I care about theirs," I told him softly.

He shook his head at me, his face grim. "Of course, you do."

"Is that such a bad thing?"

"It is when you're risking my best friend's life."

My heart clenched at his words. "I wish I could give you a hug. I miss you."

"I miss you too, Robin"

"And once again I'm over here like chopped liver," Claire muttered.

Matthew rolled his eyes at her. "Do you always have to be center of attention?"

She shrugged. "Where else is there to be?"

Just then, both their forms started to flicker.

"You have to go already?" I asked.

"Unfortunately so," Claire replied with a disappointed sigh. "Bringing Matthew has drained me faster than when I'm alone."

"I'm glad you brought him," I said, smiling at them sadly. "Thank you for telling me about their parents. And don't tell mine about all the bruises, okay?"

"Okay," she agreed, her voice sounding far away.

"Be careful, Robin," Matthew told me, and I nodded at nothing.

I took a deep breath, shaking off their visit, then went and got dressed. I pulled my knotty hair into a bun as a knock sounded at my door.

"Room service," I heard Alexander call out and I scrunched my brows.

When I opened the door, he was holding out some Tylenol and a bottle of water.

"Thanks," I said, accepting them gratefully.

"Nice cut," he told me, gesturing to my eye.

"Nice bruise," I rebutted, motioning to his temple.

The side of his mouth turned up in his signature half smile. "I had a good opponent. How's your side?"

I shrugged nonchalantly. "Fine."

"Really?" he asked, raising his eyebrows. He reached out and poked my ribs and I instinctively slapped his hand away as I grunted. "Thought so."

"What was that for?" I asked in annoyance.

"Just making sure Nedra's services were necessary since I called her all the way up here."

"Who's Nedra?"

"I am," an older woman with graying hair and a hunched back said as she entered my room. She smiled at me, her eyes squinted tight. "I'm a healer."

"You brought me Tylenol and a healer?" I asked Alexander. "Seems kind of counterproductive."

He chuckled. "The Tylenol is for your head. The healer is for your ribs."

"Come sit down, dear," Nedra instructed.

I sat on the couch where she pointed, lifting my shirt for her. Alexander's eyes tightened slightly at seeing my bruise before he looked away.

"I'll wait for your outside," he said.

Nedra ran her hands over my skin, her touch warm. She closed her eyes and the warmth of her hands spread into my side and through my entire torso. The feeling was appealing and relaxed me into a trance. I watched as the bruise slowly dissipated, the warmth leaving along with it.

"There you are. All fixed," Nedra declared.

"Thank you," I said, standing up and hesitantly stretching. I smiled when no pain came with the movement.

Nedra walked out of the room, and I followed to where Alexander stood waiting.

"Thank you," I told him as we began walking.

"Don't mention it," he replied, sounding like he seriously meant it.

"Why not heal the rest of our bruises and cuts though?" I asked curiously.

"Because they're good for your image. They show you're a badass who can hold her own in a fight with me. And trust me, that'll go a long way with everyone."

I nodded slightly but didn't reply. I would never get used to this lifestyle they had created. When we entered the dining room, we were both met with comments about our faces, but Alexander was right—they were all praises.

"What made you two decide to spar anyway?" Monique asked.

"We need outside opponents for the trainees. People who will give them a real fight. Robin wanted to choose so we wrestled for it," Alexander explained.

"A noble reason," Isaac approved.

"Speaking of which, it's time to tell our newcomers about our upcoming event," Toshiro spoke up.

Isaac gave him a look. "That wasn't related to the conversation at all."

Toshiro waved away his words, uncaring. "Alexander, if you would."

Alexander sighed. "We have our yearly gala in a couple weeks. It's a tremendously important event to us and you will all be required to attend and mingle with everyone."

The trainees exchanged glances, an appropriate amount of disgust and questioning on them despite already knowing the information.

"What's the dress code?" Emery asked.

"Formal. You will all be given appropriate attire."

"Yippee. Just what I always wanted," Emery popped off. "To play dress up in a castle."

"How lucky you'll have your chance to fulfill that soon enough then," Mallory shot back, just as sarcastic.

"This event means a great deal to everyone here," Toshiro informed us. "I expect you'll all be on your best behavior and do what's expected of you. Do I make myself clear?"

He was met with unintelligible mutters of agreeance, but he seemed satisfied by it and went back to his breakfast. I glanced over at Alexander and scrunched my nose in disgust at the thought of a gala. His lips lifted in a small grin, and I could tell he was just as displeased about it as I was. Apparently, it wasn't important to everyone after all.

Chapter Twenty-Six

"Your size reflects that you're slow but strong which means your greatest asset is your strength," Alexander was saying to Andre. "That makes Isaac a perfectly matched opponent for you."

Isaac grinned at them, his right hand twitching anxiously in excitement. "You ready, boy?"

"As ready as I'll ever be," Andre replied, stepping up across from him on the mat. They were the same height and build so it seemed like it would be an evenly matched fight.

Isaac crouched down in anticipation as Alexander counted them down. As soon as he said 'go', Isaac lunged at Andre, wrapping his arm around his neck, and pulling him to the ground. Andre landed with a heavy thud and coughed before quickly rolling over as Isaac attempted to stomp on him. He stood up, receiving a blow to his face then his stomach.

It was impressive seeing Isaac work as he used his single arm to block and hit masterfully. His handicap didn't seem to affect his ability to fight whatsoever, and Andre was paying the price. Isaac roundhouse kicked Andre in the chest then brought his knee up into Andre's face as he was doubled over. Blood poured out of Andre's nose, and he cursed, his eyes narrowing to slits before closing altogether.

As Isaac went in for another attack, Andre dodged his blow without opening his eyes. Isaac grunted in disapproval as he tried again with the same results. I eyed the pair in confusion, not sure what was happening as the scene continued in similar fashion. Finally, Isaac cocked his head at him, seeming to have a thought. He pulled his arm back before punching Andre straight in the jaw.

"Dammit," Andre grunted, his eyes opening.

"Nice try," Isaac told him with a grin. "But I can make your power moot, remember?"

Alexander held up his hand to stop Isaac from advancing again as he watched Andre. "How did you do that?" he asked.

"Do what?" I questioned, wanting to know what was happening.

"He was predicting Isaac's moves," Alexander explained.

I looked at Andre with wide eyes. "When did you learn to do that?"

"Right now, I guess," Andre replied. "I couldn't do it before, but I got so tired of being hit and kept thinking I wish I could see what he was going to do next. Then something just seemed to connect in my mind, and I was seeing it."

"That's an incredible advancement," Alexander told him. "It'll serve you well to be tapped into your power in this way."

Isaac crept up behind Andre, swinging his leg towards his feet. Andre reached down and caught his leg midway before pushing his unsteady body to the ground.

Andre grinned. "Oh, yeah. That's useful."

"Unfortunately for you, it's not useful on Isaac when he takes your power away," Alexander pointed out as Andre helped Isaac to his feet. "But don't be mistaken, this is a huge asset."

The morning training continued with similar pairings, none of the trainees winning their matches. They all came out with an assortment of bruises and cuts but a surprising new hunger to win next time.

"This is exactly what I wanted," Alexander said as they sat along the bench. "For you to *want* to win. But for that to happen, you must train harder and more seriously. This is your new normal. Get used to your body aching and tending to your wounds because the only way it's going to stop is for you to win against your opponent. You all have individual power training this afternoon. Until then, class dismissed."

He walked out of the room, and I walked over to the trainees. "You guys did really well. After some more practice you'll all be able to hold your own against any of them. But for now, let's go up to my room. We'll get you all cleaned up then get some lunch if you're up to it."

They shuffled out of the room with varying degrees of wincing. Kodi stopped before stepping out the door, turning towards me hesitantly.

"Will you do some extra training sessions with me?" she asked.

"If you'd like" I replied. "But you're doing fine, Kodi."

"I need to be more than fine. My power is useless in a battle. The only way I'll be helpful is if I'm physically capable. I can't sit by and let everyone else do the work. Or even worse, need everyone else's protection. I won't be a damsel in distress."

She looked so upset that I put my hand on her shoulder. "Okay. I understand. You can do more physical training when everyone else is doing their power training and then I'll work with you after. Alright?"

She nodded and swallowed loudly. "Alright."

"Come on, let's go catch up with the others," I said, wrapping my arm around her.

I helped tend to the deeper cuts on the trainees as they took turns wiping their faces and hands clean of blood. When everyone was more or less presentable, I rang for Roxy. She came quickly with her head bowed down as she entered the room.

"What can I do for you?" she asked.

"Is it possible to get food brought up here for us?" I questioned. "We don't really feel like eating in the dining room."

"Of course. Just tell me what you'd like, and I'll have it prepared."

We each told her our request and she exited the room with her eyes still on the ground. Our encounters had always been friendly, but she refused to acknowledge me with her gaze. She was probably too scared of Alexander or the other Cyfrin members punishing her again. It reminded me again that we were fighting for so many people, both with and without powers. I looked around the room, watching as Mateo, Toby, and Kodi compared their changing skin tones on my bed and Emery and Andre sat on the couch entranced in their own conversation. I bit my lip then cleared my throat to get their attention.

"I need to tell you guys something," I started, looking down at my shoes. "But it isn't all pleasant."

"What's wrong?" Andre asked.

"I had a friend in Garridan track down your families, your birth families, and she finally got back to me with information."

"Really?" Toby asked excitedly, and my heart crumbled as I nodded.

"She didn't have the time to give me specific details other than . . ." I trailed off, gazing up at the ceiling.

"Other than?" Emery pressed.

"Other than . . . not all of your parents are alive," I finished quietly. "Andre, your birth mother passed away. Kodi, your birth father."

Emery put her hand over Andre's as his face fell slightly. Kodi rubbed her lips together but didn't seem too bothered by it; she already had a father after all and never knew the man who helped create her.

"And Toby," I said, and his face instantly shrank. "I'm sorry but . . . both of your parents are gone."

"Oh, Toby," Kodi murmured as his eyes filled with tears.

His chin began to quiver, and a sob escaped his mouth as he covered his face with shaking hands. I ran over to him, wrapping him in a hug and pulling him to my chest as his body trembled. I blinked away my own tears as his heartache tore into me. Kodi and Mateo both looked on with sympathy in their eyes as they placed their hands on his back. Before I knew it, Andre and Emery joined in. Andre put one hand on my shoulder, his other intertwined with one of Emery's as she sat next to Mateo and leaned against him. We stayed like that, huddled around Toby as he continued to cry. His sobs rang out for the parents he would never know and the family he would never have.

Chapter Twenty-Seven

The next couple of weeks passed with lots of repeated activity as we all grew into new grooves. Kodi and I spent almost all of our free time in the training room, working out and sparring. As she honed in on her technique and strengthened her muscles, she was quickly becoming a force to be reckoned with. It was good practice for me as well, keeping me fit and perceptive. Toby also threw himself into training, his sadness and anger showing in his power usage. He was brutal as he destroyed the training room time after time. Alexander always made him fix it before he left, though, making it ready for another day of abuse. We all tried to talk to him about it, but he refused, shutting us out and letting it fester inside.

Andre and Emery seemed to be getting closer as they spent much of their time together and encouraged one another throughout the day. Andre's new abilities were everyone's favorite pass time, but he still couldn't see more than a couple minutes ahead of the present time. Mateo tried to stay near to Toby but frequently found himself kicked out of their room with Toby's request of wanting to be alone. He quickly learned he was a third wheel to Emery and Andre, so he often followed Kodi and I into our training sessions, yelling words of support to Kodi but refusing to fight her.

Since so much of my time was spoken for and Alexander was in party planning mode, we had almost no one-on-one interaction with one another, and I found myself missing his company. Even though he gave me emotional whiplash, I enjoyed being around him. I feared Matthew saw through my facade when he came visiting with Claire, but I couldn't shake the idea that Alexander could come home with us one day. He deserved a second chance, just like Matthew was getting.

As the gala approached, there was a lot more outside activity in the castle as the throne room was decorated and performers rehearsed. The trainees and I were lost in the shuffle and given little attention, which we were more than happy about as we plotted our own strategies against the Cyfrin. I knew once the gala was over, we'd go back to being under the microscope which meant we'd have little time to discuss our own endeavors. The morning before the big event, Claire came to visit.

"Guess what?" she said excitedly.

"What?"

"Your parents agreed. They said they'd be happy to!"

"I knew they would," I replied with a wide smile, but despite my words, relief washed through me at having it confirmed. "I can't wait to tell Toby! I hope he'll agree too."

"I'm sure he will."

"I think so too," I agreed. "Nice hair by the way."

She ran her fingers through her hair as I admired the hidden rainbow effect she had done. "Thanks! Do you know what you're going to do with yours for the gala tomorrow?"

"I honestly couldn't care less," I said with a roll of my eyes.

"Oh, come on! It's a chance to get dressed up and have fun. Who cares that it's with the Cyfrin."

"You remind me of Felicity," I told her. "You two would be perfect friends."

"Too bad her and my brother couldn't work out. I bet we'd be even better sisters-in-law."

"I know. How's she doing anyway?" Claire gave me a sideways glance and I placed my hands on my hips. "Don't act all innocent. I know you still check up on her."

"Okay, I do. But not because Matthew asks me to," she insisted. "I just want to make sure she's happy so I can tell him when he's feeling down about it."

"I believe you," I assured her. "So how is she?"

"She's really good. She's throwing herself into her drama class."

"No boyfriend?"

"No, she's taking time for herself."

I smiled at that. "Good."

Claire returned my smile but averted her eyes, causing suspicion to rise in me.

"What's wrong?"

"Nothing's *wrong*. It's just . . . I've been checking up on Ben as well," she said slowly, and my heart skipped a beat in my chest at the mention of his name.

"You really shouldn't spy on people," I chastised her. "But since you did . . . How is he?"

"He's good too."

The way she said it made me furrow my brows. "What aren't you telling me?"

She hesitated.

"What?" I demanded, folding my arms over my chest.

"I . . . I saw him kissing another girl."

The words were like a punch to the stomach, and I rubbed my lips together as my heart sank. "Oh," was all I managed to say.

"I'm sorry, Robin," Claire said, but I shook my head at her as I took a deep breath.

"No, it's a good thing," I murmured, my voice breaking slightly. "We both know we can't be together so it's good he's moving on. He deserves to be happy and . . . He can't be happy with me . . . So it makes sense for him to go out with someone else. Someone he *can* be with."

"You almost sound convincing," Claire commented, giving my shoulders a tight squeeze as I tried to accept my own words. "Do you want to be alone?"

When I nodded my head, she dissipated away without another word. I wrapped my arms around a pillow and hugged it tight, lying down as I stared at the ring on my finger. I gave myself permission to cry but no tears came. Instead, I stayed there silent and unmoving, feeling nothing but hollow. I wasn't sure how long I stayed like that, but a loud knock snapped me out of my state. I sat up as my door opened and Alexander peeked in.

"I know I'm entering without your permission, but I wanted to make sure you were okay," he said, his brows pulled together as he looked me over. "I got concerned when you didn't show up for breakfast."

"Sorry. I just had a lot on my mind and lost track of time," I told him, crossing my legs underneath me.

"Are you alright?" He walked closer to my bed, his eyes appraising me.

"I will be."

"Do you want to talk about it?"

"I'm not really sure how to."

I glanced at my ring again and Alexander must've noticed because realization dawned on his face. "Is this about the man you love?"

I looked up, searching his face for any sign of anger or irritation but saw none so I nodded. "He's moving on," I said quietly.

"What makes you say that?"

"Just a feeling," I lied.

"Are you upset because you don't want him to . . . Or because you do?"

"I guess a little bit of both," I admitted, turning the ring around on my finger. "I want him to be happy. I do. And I know the only way that'll happen is if he finds someone else and forgets about me . . . But that doesn't make it hurt any less."

A single tear slid down my cheek and I quickly wiped it away, annoyed that my body chose to cry now and not when I was alone. Alexander pressed his lips together tightly as he watched me swipe at another tear. He took a step closer and held his hands out.

"Come here," he instructed. I hesitantly put my hands in his and he helped pull me off the bed so I was standing in front of him. "I'm going to hug you now," he informed me, and my brows raised in surprise.

When I didn't object, he wrapped him arms around me firmly, resting his chin on my head as it leaned against his chest. I stood stiffly for a minute but as his heartbeat sounded in my ear and his hand rubbed against my back, I relaxed into his embrace. I let my tears flow freely as I hugged him back, but he didn't speak. He just held me as I fell apart with broken sobs. When I finally settled down, he leaned back to look at me. His eyes were unsettled, as if my tears hurt him as much as they hurt me. He gently brushed his thumbs against my cheeks, wiping away the wetness that lingered. I saw his Adam's apple contract as he swallowed.

"One day you'll be able to move on as well," he told me quietly. "He may always be in the back of your mind as the one that got away, but that doesn't mean you can't find happiness without him. You have options if you'll let yourself see them."

"Options as in you?" I asked sarcastically, my voice thick.

He gave me his signature half smile, but it didn't reach his eyes. "I'll always be an option. If you ever so choose."

His hand lingered on my cheek and as I stared into his big doe eyes, I saw nothing but sincerity. He leaned down and my breath caught in my throat as his lips gently brushed my forehead. The gesture left me dumbfounded and tingly as he pulled back, his smile sad.

"Go down to training when you're ready. Isaac and Monique are with them now. I have last minute party details to attend to, so I won't see you until tomorrow." He walked towards the door but before leaving, he glanced back at me. "Save me a dance?"

I nodded, unable to speak, and he closed the door behind him. Was it possible for me to ever love him like I did Ben? The answer resonated in me, relieving some of the hollow feeling that came with Ben's absence. It was entirely possible. In the time that I had been in the Cyfrin compound, he had already managed to steal a small portion of my heart and with time, I knew it could grow. But I also knew it heavily depended on the outcome of the war. If he came back to Garridan with me, there was a chance for a real future between us. But if he sat on a throne, ruling over the people of this planet, I couldn't sit idly by his side. I let out a sigh as I went to splash water on my face. Love was a complicated fiasco.

Chapter Twenty-Eight

I lingered at the door of the training room, watching as the five trainees went up against Monique and Isaac simultaneously. It was a mixture of physical battle and power usage which was a chaotic scene to witness. Kodi and Andre were keeping Isaac busy so the other three could use their powers against Monique. A leopard hissed at her as she turned her arms into spears to stab at it. Toby molded the metal of the workout equipment into a shield and moved it in front of Mateo as he pounced away from the sharp weapons.

At the same time, Emery brought down a line of electricity from the ceiling and it absorbed into Monique's spears. She let out a yell, her arms returning to normal as Isaac glanced over and silenced Emery's powers. The distraction was just enough for Kodi to land a blow to the back of his knee and Andre finished him off with a sweep of his leg, knocking him to the ground. I grinned as Isaac and Monique yielded, out of breath. They seemed impressed, and I walked in, clapping.

"That was awesome," I told them. "You guys are getting really good."

"You really are," Monique agreed. "You'll be huge assets to us when your training is complete."

"I know Monique wasn't using her power to her full capabilities because she didn't want to kill you three, but you two," Isaac stopped and pointed at Kodi and Andre. "You just gave me a run for my money. Fair and square, you win this round."

Kodi and Andre grinned at one another, pleased by the praise.

"You and Alexander have done an excellent job with them," Monique told me. "You make a good team."

"Thanks," I responded with a small smile.

"We'll leave you to it then," Isaac said. "I'm ready for a break. Let's go get some food."

"We just had breakfast," Monique pointed out.

"And?" Isaac replied as they walked out of the room.

"You know, I really want to know how he lost his arm," Kodi commented when they were gone. "But it seems rude to come out and ask."

"He had to cut it off-" Andre started.

"*He cut it off*?!" Kodi exclaimed, her eyes wide.

We all stared at her, bewildered by her assumption.

"*No*," Andre emphasized slowly. "Someone else did."

"Oh," Kodi murmured, hanging her head in embarrassment as color flushed to her cheeks.

"He had to cut it off because he got an infection from a wound he received in a battle. They didn't catch it in time so it spread, and they couldn't save his arm," Andre explained.

"That makes more sense," Kodi said, nodding her head vigorously.

"Ya think?" Mateo muttered and she punched him in the arm as we all laughed. She was kind, caring, and considerate and she was turning out to be an excellent fighter. But sometimes she was ditzy as hell.

"Why don't you guys take a quick break," I suggested. "I need to talk to Toby really quick."

Toby watched me sullenly as the others walked away. "I don't want to talk about it."

"I know you don't. This isn't about your parents," I told him. "Well, it's related but it's a different matter entirely."

His oily hair fell into his eyes, and he pushed it back, making it stand on end crazily.

"I know no one and nothing can replace your birth parents," I started, causing him to avert his eyes as they narrowed. "But how would you like some adoptive ones?"

His gaze shot to mine. "What?"

"I told my parents about you, and they want to make you a part of our family when we get back to Garridan."

"Your family?" he whispered, and I nodded earnestly.

"You can be my little brother."

He stared at me as his mouth dropped open. A smile slowly crept onto his face, and he let out an excited whoop as he threw his arms around me. He jumped up and down, turning me in circles with him and I couldn't help but laugh. I pulled back and saw his eyes glistening with unshed tears.

"Is that a yes?" I asked.

"Yes! Yes! Of course, it's a yes!" he exclaimed as the others came to see what all the commotion was about.

"What's going on?" Emery questioned.

"I have a family!" Toby announced gleefully.

"My parents want to adopt him when we get back to Garridan," I explained as he clung to me, and everyone else broke out with excited congratulations.

"It's so good to see you smile again," Mateo told him.

"It really is," Kodi agreed, giving him a hug. They were right. His smile was infectious, and we all stood there grinning at one another, sharing in his happiness. Sometimes life offered up happy endings after all. But only sometimes.

* * *

"I'm here to help you get ready," Roxy murmured, holding up a dress bag that I grabbed and hung on a rack.

"There's still two hours until the gala," I said after looking at the clock.

"I just do as I'm told."

"I have a better idea. How about you go get Emery and Kodi for me then you can sit in here and relax while we help each other get ready."

"Oh, I uh, I don't know," she stammered, clasping her hands together.

"It'll be okay," I assured her. "We can get you something from the kitchen and you can talk to us or watch TV or do whatever else you want to do."

"That sounds nice," she admitted, her voice quivering.

"Okay, then, it's settled."

She scurried out the door as I ordered her some room service. She came back with Emery and Kodi at her heels holding dress bags of their own and the food showed up not much later.

"Here," I told her as I set the platter in front of her. She eyed it and rubbed her lips together but didn't touch it, so I kneeled next to her. "It's okay. Really. You have nothing to fear from us."

She offered me a timid smile and slowly picked up the silverware. I turned on the TV and sat the controller next to her before going into the bathroom with the girls.

"She's so skittish," Emery commented.

"I guess that's what happens when you're treated so poorly for so long," I replied. "It makes me sad."

"Really? Because it makes me angry," Emery spat out.

"That too. But soon enough they'll be free from this life."

"We hope."

"Don't be so pessimistic. We need to believe it."

"I believe it," Kodi spoke up and I smiled appreciatively at her.

"Okay, so I was provided all makeup known to man and every possible hair tool we could ever need in our entire lives," I told them. "Who's first?"

"Not me," Emery said.

"Kodi it is then," I concluded, motioning for her to sit in the chair I had brought in front of the mirror.

We gabbed about nothing of importance as I curled her hair, then fashioned it with two clips holding up the sides. She was insistent on not wearing any makeup, but we were able to talk her into nude lip gloss and light mascara which made her eyes pop. Emery was more open to a wild look, despite not wanting to sit still for it to be done, so Kodi helped me tease her long hair into a high bump on top while the rest pulled into an elegant bun that rested against the nape of her neck. She informed us that her dress was best described as a moss green, so we decided on a dark green eyeshadow that blended into black at the corners of her eyes. We lined them with heavy eyeliner and mascara before covering her lips with a brown matte lipstick.

"You know, this might actually be fun if it wasn't being forced on us by the Cyfrin," Emery said as she stood in front of me to do my hair.

"I know what you mean," I agreed.

"I can start your makeup while Emery does your hair," Kodi offered.

"Don't take this the wrong way, but I don't think I want you doing my makeup," I told her gently.

"Why not?" she asked with her hands on her hips.

"I'm afraid you'll make me look like a clown."

"I would not!"

"How about you do her hair and I'll do her makeup," Emery intervened. "Can't do any harm with that."

"She could burn my hair off," I muttered. Kodi glared at me, but didn't argue.

"What color is your dress?" Emery asked.

"I actually don't know. I haven't even looked at it," I admitted.

I stood up and walked to the other room, surprised to see Roxy gone. She really was scared of getting in trouble. I unzipped the dress bag and my jaw dropped slightly. The dress was simple but beautiful and I loved it. It was a light blue, A-Line dress with a sweetheart neckline and an off the shoulder sleeve that was secured by skinny straps. There were white, lacy details along the entire dress and a small belt at the waist that framed the smallest amount of sheer material between it and the chest area.

"Say what you will, but they know how to pick out clothing," Kodi commented.

"How would you know? You wear the same thing every day," Emery said with a scoff, and Kodi scowled.

"Why are you picking on me today?" she asked.

"Because it's fun," Emery replied with a wink.

"Let me see your dresses," I requested, and they happily obliged.

Kodi's was a simple black, A-line, satin gown with a cowl neck bodice secured by cap sleeves. I also noticed a slit that went all the way to the thigh. Emery's had a white, long-sleeved top with a V-neckline and a green, trumpet styled bottom that was connected by a wide sash.

"I guess this thing really is going to be extravagant," I said.

The thought made me nervous, but I was also intrigued to see what the throne room looked like. I sat back down, ready to be pampered, and recalled the last time I had been so dressed up: junior prom. Hopefully tonight wouldn't end the same tragic way that night did.

When Emery and Kodi were done, I looked in the mirror and smiled. My eyes were shimmering with pale blue and white eyeshadow. Light eye liner made my already bright eyes pop even more and a natural pink layered my lips. The sides of my hair were pulled back in two loose French braids that were intertwined at the back of my head while the rest fell over my shoulders in tamed curls. A couple of loose strands of hair framed my face and a lace ribbon had been weaved through the braids expertly.

"Wow!" I exclaimed. "I'm impressed."

"I think you both owe somebody an apology," Kodi commented, looking pleased with herself.

I grinned. "I'm sorry I doubted your mad skills. And thank you."

We all got into our dresses and admired one another as we realized they were perfect fits. Kodi's tattoos helped ease the shocking contrast between her white skin and the black dress, but not much, while Emery's dress complemented her in every way. A short time later, there was a knock at the door.

"I'm here to escort Emery and Kodi to the gala," Roxy announced, her eyes resting on the floor by our feet.

"What about Robin?" Emery questioned.

"I'll come back for her."

"Why can't we just go together?" I asked.

"I don't make the rules," Roxy said. "I just follow them."

Emery, Kodi, and I exchanged glances before I shrugged. "Guess I'll see you guys in there."

They reluctantly agreed and followed Roxy down the hall. I fiddled with my dress, unsure what to do as I stood there and waited. When Roxy finally came back for me, my stomach churned, but I was surprised to see the foyer empty, and the throne room's doors closed.

"Where is everybody?" I asked.

"They've already gathered in the ballroom," Roxy replied.

"Then why wasn't I brought in earlier?"

Roxy didn't reply. Instead she ushered me towards the doors.

Chapter Twenty-Nine

I stepped up to the closed doors, confused as Roxy told me to stay put. I could hear music on the other side mixed with an array of voices conversing and laughing. I opened my mouth to ask Roxy why I couldn't go in, but she was already gone. A muffled voice rang out, silencing the noise in the throne room. I stepped closer, putting my ear against the door, to try to hear what they were saying.

"-so thankful for each and every one of you. We can never express how much your loyalty means, especially when we've been forced to endure so much pain and heartache to fight for our own well-being." Toshiro's voice was patronizingly sad, and I scoffed in disgust as murmurs of agreement rang out. "But soon, all our sacrifices will be worth it because our victory is near!"

Cheers filled the room, followed by bouts of excited chatter.

"Soon, we won't be ignored. We won't be forced to sit in hiding. We won't be held back by our greatest rivals in Garridan. We will take our rightful place as the world's leaders!"

The uproar in the room shook the ground and vibrated the doors as I leaned against them. Every time it started to die down, someone would start a new round of hollers. After another minute, the Toshiro's voice silenced the people. "Alright, alright, settle down. I love the enthusiasm but right now we have a more important matter to address: the new Keeper of Balance among us. We wanted to take this opportunity to introduce her to all of you."

Oh no.

"You've heard many rumors about her."

Oh no.

"-and you've all been patiently waiting to get a glance at her."

Please no!

"Here's your chance. Please give a warm welcome to our water element—Robin!"

The doors swung open, and I barely caught myself from falling over as I stared, wide-eyed, at the scene before me. My cheeks burned from the heat that rose to them while the curious crowd watched me as they clapped. They were split down the middle with a soft black carpet running in between them from the door to the place where the three Keepers of Balance sat. My legs threatened to give out as my eyes darted back and forth, unsure of what to do, before they landed on Alexander.

His black suit was accented by hues of green on his vest and tie, complimenting his skin tone. His gaze was set on me, his eyes unwavering from my own. He motioned at me to take a deep breath, trying to help calm me as I was ambushed by my unknowing reveal. I obeyed his instructions, taking one breath, then another. He beckoned me forward, and I swallowed around the dryness in my throat as my heart pounded in my chest. I took one shaky step after the other, my eyes never leaving Alexander's as he gave me the strength to force my legs to keep moving. When I got closer, his eyes darted to the empty chair next to him, so I stepped up onto the platform and took a seat, thankful for his silent guidance.

From here, I could see the room much better, and I took in the scene before me. Everyone was dressed in formal attire, matching the mood of the room as it sat decorated in gold and silver. All the bookcases and tables had been removed and were replaced by large, gaudy statues and artwork. Rings hung from the ceiling, occupied by exotic dancers who were weaving themselves in and out as their bodies literally stretched to go further. Emery, Kodi, Toby, Andre, and Mateo stood lined to the left of where I sat, as much of a spectacle as I was.

I glanced to my right and saw Mallory in a vibrant red dress that clashed with her hair and Toshiro in his usual suit but in yellow. I looked at the colors of green on Alexander then down at my own blue dress. We were representing our respective elements.

"We've entered into a new dawn!" Toshiro continued. "Tonight, we celebrate our upcoming vanquishment of Garridan!"

I fought the urge to cover my ears as screams rang out so loud my body quivered. They were all filled with such hate for a place that did nothing but keep the world safe. I tried to keep my face neutral, but anger swelled in the pit of my stomach at the scene I was being forced to watch. I looked over at the trainees and saw their expressions were much like my own. They were bothered by the people of the Cyfrin as much as I was.

"Please, dance, eat, enjoy!"

Mallory jumped down from where she sat as people ventured into the foyer where tables of food had been brought in during the Toshiro's speech. Many others partnered up and began twirling around as music filled the air.

"Care to dance?" I looked up and saw Alexander standing in front of me with one hand stretched out. He must've noticed my hesitation because he grabbed my hand with his own and pulled me up. "Come on, it'll take your mind off of what you're thinking."

"How do you know what I'm thinking?" I questioned as he walked me to the center of the room. He brought my hand up to his shoulder, then placed his on my waist as our other hands intertwined.

"You don't have a very good poker face." He guided me into a dance, and I looked down at my feet as my dress swayed. His finger landed under my chin, forcing me to look up into his eyes. "Look at me, not your feet. It'll only make your dancing worse."

I scoffed. "I am not a bad dancer!"

"I've been dancing with you for five seconds and already know you're a bad dancer."

I pursed my lips, and he grinned as I said, "Maybe you should find a different dance partner then."

"I'm sure it wouldn't be a problem, but I'd much rather have my feet stomped on by you than deal with any of these suck ups." I scrunched my brows, so he quickly explained, "Every year I'm subjected to dancing with anyone and everyone who requests it. It's a tedious job. They all want something and use this time to pitch for it."

"Oh."

"However, this year I have the perfect excuse to ignore them all."

"And that would be?"

"You."

"Glad I could be of service," I commented sarcastically. I glanced around the room and saw the five trainees spread out, all of them caught up in a conversation with someone.

Emery had a glare forming in her eyes and I said a silent prayer that she wouldn't cause a scene. Andre must've been watching her as well because he came up and interrupted the conversation, then pulled Emery onto the dance floor.

Everywhere I looked, I was met with stares. Some were curious, some judgmental, some even envious. Heat rose to my cheeks, hating the attention.

"What's wrong?" Alexander questioned, seeing the redness in my face.

"I'm just not accustomed to people watching me in this type of setting. I hate it."

He looked around the room, causing most people to divert their gazes quickly. Some braver ones continued to look on, uncaring of his stare. He stepped away from me, his hand still in mine, then began walking out of the room

"Where are we going?" I asked as people parted for us to get through.

"Away from all the people." He led me through the foyer and out the front door where more people lingered aimlessly. Alexander greeted them with a nod of his head as we passed.

The music became a dull thud in the background as we walked further away from the castle and into the garden. The night air was peaceful as crickets chirped and a breeze swept by. I shivered slightly, and Alexander immediately shook off his jacket and held it up to me.

"Here," he beckoned me to put it on, "this should help."

I gratefully pushed my arms through the sleeves and let the warmth of it envelope me as it warded off the winter cold. "Thank you."

"Of course. Can't have you freezing to death out here. We won't stay long. I just thought you needed time to recuperate if we expect you to last in there all night."

"It's a lot," I admitted.

"Your way of life is being altered. It's a shock."

"It is."

"It'll get easier."

I glanced over as him as he stared straight ahead. "Did it get easier for you?"

"I never objected to the ways of the Cyfrin. There was nothing for me to overcome morally."

Of course.

"Can I ask you a question?" I asked hesitantly as we walked through one of the paths lined by flowers.

"Of course."

"Why do you hate people without powers so much?"

"I don't hate them."

"You're lying," I said softly, and he looked to his feet. I watched him thoughtfully, trying to decipher his expression. "I know you're lying. Why do you hate them?"

"I don't," he repeated.

I could see through his lie easily. "Yes, you do. I just can't figure out why."

"I've told you before, they're beneath us."

"I know you think that, but I don't think that's the only reason you want to rule over them."

"They're a terrible people.".

"Why do you say that?"

"Because it's the truth."

"There are terrible people in any race or culture. That doesn't make them all bad."

"I've yet to be proven otherwise."

A connection started forming in my mind and I jumped on my hunch. "Is that because of your foster parents?" His eyes visibly hardened, and I knew I was right. "What you went through was awful and there's no excuse for it, but not everyone in the human race is like that. Most of them aren't, actually. You just got unlucky with your placement."

"Seven."

"Seven?"

"I had seven placements before I was rescued by the Cyfrin. All of them bad," he spat out.

I rubbed my lips together, sudden sorrowful for him. "I'm sorry. I can't imagine what you went through . . . But you can't punish everyone for the actions of a few." He scoffed and opened his mouth to argue but I cut him off. "I'm serious. You think there's no good people in the normal world? I can prove you wrong. My mom adopted me and loved me as her own regardless of not being blood. My best friend advocates for people who won't speak up for themselves even though she's the most popular person I know. My whole school even signed off on an anti-bullying rule because they wanted everyone to feel safe and accepted. There are good people everywhere you look. You just have to see past the bad ones that are easier to spot."

Alexander remained silent so I continued. "Do you really want to push *your* misfortunes onto people who don't deserve it?"

"Why are you always trying to analyze me?" he finally spoke up with a bite in his tone.

My lips lifted in a sad half smile as I answered, realizing the truth in the words as they came out. "Because I care about you."

Alexander stopped walking as his expression softened. "You do?"

"Yes. I do."

"Why?"

I thought about it for a moment before saying, "You can't spend as much time together as we do and not start to care."

We continued to walk, both wrapped up in our own thoughts as we made our way to the fountain I was always drawn to. Alexander turned to me, then hesitantly asked, "Do you think you could ever love me?"

Without thinking it through, I answered, "I think I could . . . But I don't want to."

Why did you say that?

"Why not?" he questioned. I pressed my lips together, internally kicking myself at opening this can of worms. I shouldn't have answered honestly. "Robin?"

It was too late to change it now, so I pressed forward with another honest answer. "Because you stand for something I don't want to ever see happen."

His lips tightened. "You'll never forgive me after it happens, will you?"

I shook my head lightly and whispered my response. "No."

His face fell slightly but then he met my eyes with a new fire inside them. "But until then I have a chance?"

"I'm not going to answer that."

"You don't have to," he said, taking a step towards me. "All you have to do is say 'no' . . ."

My heart hammered in my chest as he closed the distance between us. His gaze never wavered from mine as he brought his hands up to my cheeks and slowly leaned in. When I didn't object, his eyes began to close, then his lips gently met mine. My eyelids fluttered shut as his touch consumed me. His lips were cautious and sweet but I stood there, paralyzed. Warning sounds flooded my mind, but something made me ignore them as

Alexander pulled away. We searched each other's eyes for an answer to an unknown question, then I put my hand on the back of his neck and brought his lips to mine again.

Chapter Thirty

Alexander and I waltzed back into the throne room hand in hand as our kiss lingered in my mind. My feelings were muddled as guilt and regret fought with the satisfaction and enjoyment I was feeling.

What have I done?

"I have to go make the rounds now but," Alexander brushed his thumb over my chin, and I shivered at his touch, "I'll come back to you as quickly as possible."

"Okay. I'll just catch up with the trainees," I replied with a timid smile that he returned before turning away from me. I inhaled deeply then turned to find a familiar face waiting to intercept me.

"May I have this dance?" Toshiro asked.

"Uh . . . sure," I responded, placing my hand in his. We came together, swaying back and forth awkwardly.

"You seem to be enjoying yourself," he noted as he looked to Alexander.

"It's quite the party."

"It always is. However, I meant more so with our dear Alexander." I stayed quiet as he looked me over. "It appears continuing a pure blood line isn't going to be as hard as I initially thought."

I opened my mouth then snapped it shut as my blood boiled at his indiscreet comment. He raised his eyebrows, daring me to object, so I set my lips in a tight line and forced a smile onto my face.

"Maybe not," I managed to get out through clenched teeth. I told myself to calm down, knowing I couldn't afford to be on his bad side. As difficult as it was, I had to placate him whenever possible.

"Excellent to hear." He leaned in close, and his breath tickled my ear. "You're fitting in here quite nicely. Keep it up."

He released me suddenly and turned to greet the person closest to him with exuberance. I blinked rapidly, surprised by his sudden departure. Was I actually fooling him into thinking I was working on being a prominent part of the Cyfrin?

"Hey," Mateo said from behind me.

"Hey," I responded after turning around.

"These people are nuts."

I sighed heavily. "Yes, they are. Hopefully we don't have to deal with them much longer."

"I miss my family," he said, looking down at his hands.

I put my arm around his shoulders and laid my head against his. "I do too."

We stood and watched the people on the dance floor as they passed us by before Mateo pointed and said, "At least they're enjoying themselves."

I looked to where he indicated and saw Kodi dancing crazily with Toby, completely out of place from the formal dancing everyone else was doing, and Andre twirling Emery around before pulling her back in close. A smile crept onto my face as they stared at one another like there was nobody else in the room.

"They're falling in love, aren't they?" I asked.

"She's all he talks about in the room," Mateo noted with a grin. "At least one good thing could come from all this disaster."

"As long as we make it out of here alive." Mateo's face fell slightly, and I instantly regretted my words. "I'm sorry. I didn't mean to be such a downer."

"It's okay. I'm frustrated too that we haven't gotten any solid information that will help Garridan."

"We will though. We have to."

We offered each other reassuring looks as an outbreak of powers started to occur all around us. We, and most everyone else, took a step back towards the wall as some people flocked the middle of the room. One after another, they showed off their talents. The room came alive with different colors and noises as those with the same powers put on a show as a group. Animals growled as shapeshifters turned from one ferocious beast to the next. Body parts grew out of people where they weren't meant to be. The light was stolen from around us and projected in an array of shapes on the walls. People flew, lifted items ten times their size, and camouflaged in with their surroundings. It was a remarkable sight that left me amazed.

After a while, Mallory went up with a devilish grin on her face as the lights went out and candles illuminated the space around us. I noticed they were all strategically placed around the room, no doubt for her to be able to use them to show off. She seemed to take a breath then the flames from the candles slowly rose into the sky. She pulled them towards her, and they connected in the middle, creating a blanket of fire above us in lines that radiated heat. She spun them around in a circular motion, not caring who was in the way as people ducked to avoid being burned. Our eyes connected and she glared as she collected all the flames in a tight ball, letting it fester with energy. She let out a war cry then flung the fire at the doors, knocking them off their hinges as they caught fire.

"Not again," I heard Toshiro say with a heavy sigh as he ushered a woman towards it and the lights came back to life. The woman was tall and lanky with scars lining her body. She held one hand up to the doors and rotated her finger on her other hand counterclockwise. As she did, the fire died down before evaporating entirely, then the doors stood up and went back to their rightful place.

"What just happened?" I asked quietly.

"She can manipulate time," a man next to me replied.

"Then why didn't we all reverse back?" Mateo questioned.

"Because she's very skilled," the man responded with a nod of his head. "She can use time manipulation on a single object."

"Wow," Mateo and I breathed simultaneously. The gifts of our world would never cease to awe me.

As the room buzzed with conversation, Alexander stepped into the center of the circle and quietly raised his arms. The chatter died down almost immediately as two roots sprung from the cracks in the floor and rose to create two fully grown trees. He turned in a full circle and vines latched onto the walls from the floor to the ceiling with an eccentric display of flowers and fruits encasing us. I watched as he created massive boulders from seemingly empty air, then the ground began to rumble deep in the crust of the earth. I grabbed onto Mateo as I almost fell over before bringing my gaze back to Alexander. He stood with his eyes closed in deep concentration and I realized he was causing the trembling. I couldn't help but be mesmerized as I watched him. He was more powerful than I had thought.

When he opened his eyes again, he was staring directly at me, and a genuine smile lit up his face. He lightly twirled a single finger, and something tickled my ear. I reached up to find a flower tucked securely behind it and smiled sheepishly back at Alexander. With a single flick of his wrist, the room went back to normal, and applause filled the air.

"Too bad he's on their side," Mateo muttered as he joined in on the clapping.

"Yeah," I murmured, my voice faint, as Alexander bowed his head to accept the praise. "Too bad."

Toshiro strode up next to him, patting him on the back, then ushering him out of the circle. He came over to me and I opened my mouth to speak but Toshiro's voice rang out.

"How about a show from our new Keeper of Balance!" he suggested, and my eyes grew wide as people looked my way in interest.

I lightly began shaking my head, but Alexander quickly stopped me. "It's a power grab."

"What?"

"Didn't you notice how all the powers shown became more powerful and impressive, not the other way around?"

"I mean, I thought they were all pretty impressive," I replied, my hands beginning to sweat as Alexander rolled his eyes at me.

"You have to claim your place here. Great power earns great respect. This is your chance to show everyone why you're a Keeper of Balance and that you won't be questioned."

"Do I have to?"

"Toshiro won't have anything else. He needs our people to view you as a leader." I bit my lip as anxiety crept through me. "It'll be okay. Just pretend no one else is in the room."

"That's not really possible."

"Okay, then look at me. Only me," he instructed. "Go be one with your powers. No one else matters."

I nodded my head meekly before slowly walking to where Toshiro stood. He held both arms out in a grand gesture as if presenting me, then gave me an awkward hug that I didn't return.

"Be impressive." His breath smelled of wine and I retracted away from him as he smiled widely, always putting on a performance for his people.

I looked around the room. Mallory was watching with detest in her eyes. Kodi and Toby were giving me a thumbs up. Andre looked sympathetic, and Monique and Isaac were watching with curiosity. I found Alexander's eyes amongst all the people and my heart dropped into my stomach as he nodded at me encouragingly.

He's so supportive.

I let the cool tingle creep through me as I gathered the moisture in the air, working its way from my head to my toes.

He wants me to succeed here.

The force built up inside of me and I let it out through my fingertips, creating a small stream of water in front of me.

He really isn't a bad person.

Alexander mouthed the word 'more' and I knew the small show of my powers wouldn't suffice.

He always seems to be there when I need someone.

I took a deep breath and let it out slowly as I let my eyes slide shut.

But he isn't who I need now.

I thought back to a day when Matthew, Felicity, Ben, and I sat at the lake with a picnic lunch around us. The sun had shone high above us, but the air was still chilly, and we were cuddled up to keep warm. I remembered making shapes of water circle in front of us as Matthew petrified them, causing them to fall to the ground with loud thuds. Ben held me around my waist, whispering how amazing I was in my ear as Felicity yelled out different designs for me to create. It had been one of our best days together filled with nothing but laughter.

I need my family. Only they can get me through this.

I smiled as memories continued to fill my head and I let the happiness guide me. I separated the water in front of me, multiplying it into different sized balls that filled the room like bubbles. I raised them high into the ceiling then popped them one by one. As the water fell, I caught it and tightly wound it back up into a ball before it could drench the onlookers. I continued this, using all my concentration, before finally letting it all seep away in a misty cloud. I swept my arms up, ready to perform another trick.

"Robin, look out!" Andre yelled with his hand outstretched towards me.

Everyone glanced over at him, wondering, as I was, why he would risk punishment by interrupting my unwanted time in the spotlight. A quiet crackling noise caught my attention, and I looked above me as the crystals on the chandelier clanked together like they had when Alexander made the earth move. Before I knew what was happening, the chandelier dropped from its home on the ceiling and barreled towards where I stood beneath it. I manifested a shield of water above me, but the chandelier crashed into it before I had time to make it stronger. The water fell all around me a split second before I was hit by the outer edges of the light fixture.

* * *

I couldn't remember what happened as my eyes fluttered open. Alexander was red in the face as he screamed at people nearby, but I couldn't hear what he was saying around the ringing in my ears. I turned my head slightly and a dull pain radiated through my neck. A low moan of discomfort left my mouth and Alexander's head snapped my way. His eyes were full of relief as he gently touched my cheek and moved his mouth as if he were talking to me.

I reached behind me to push myself up, but the motion caused a severe pain to radiate in my torso and up my side. A small cry burst out of me, and I fell back to the floor as the burning sensation brought all my senses into overdrive. All at once, my brain focused, allowing me to hear the commotion around me as people spoke loudly over one another. I looked around, making sure not to move my head, and saw members of the Cyfrin looking on in shock. I noticed the trainees in the very front, all of them wearing expressions of fear. Toby was visibly sobbing as the others surrounded him, trying to hide his tears from everyone else. What had happened?

"You're going to be okay, Robin," Alexander was saying with a thick voice. "I promise, you're going to be just fine." He glanced around the room, his eyes blazing with anger. "*Where the hell is Akio?*"

My brows furrowed as my brain tried to process what was happening. Something ran down my stomach and I instinctively reached for it. My eyes widened as my fingers touched something warm and thick. I glanced down to see a piece of metal from the chandelier sticking through my torso. Blood covered the floor, and I realized it was mine.

"What happened?" I asked in a hoarse breath.

"The chandelier fell," Alexander replied. One side of his lips turned up in a small, humorless smile. "You must have the worst luck known to man. That chandelier has been there for hundreds, maybe thousands, of years with no problem. Then you step under it, and it decides to break."

"It didn't break," Andre spoke up, stepping towards us. His face was twisted with anger, a look that was foreign on him and extremely intimidating. "It was forced out of the ceiling on purpose."

"That is a very serious accusation," Toshiro hissed as he came up next to us with a man that was a mirror image of him. The man immediately knelt beside me and started assessing my wounds.

"It's the truth," Andre responded in an equally harsh tone.

"Who?" Alexander asked, seeming not to doubt Andre.

"Serafina."

Alexander's eyes narrowed into slits as Toshiro set his jaw.

"How do you know this?" Toshiro asked, not as hateful as when he last spoke.

"Premonition," is all Andre said, and Alexander and Toshiro shared a quick glance.

"Find her," Toshiro instructed a nearby guard.

"I need to extract this candelabra before I can heal her," the man I assumed to be Akio said. "Clear the room. This isn't anything anyone else needs to see."

Toshiro gave the order and guards immediately began ushering people out. I gave Toby a weak, reassuring smile as they filed away with everyone else. My mind was getting foggy, and I let out a barely audible moan as black spots started taking over my vision.

"I don't feel so good," I whispered as my head lulled to the side.

"Akio," Alexander said as he steadied my head with his hands.

"She's lost too much blood," Akio commented. "I need to get this out of her so I can start the healing process before it's too late."

"Then do it!" Alexander yelled.

"I need you to hold her down. This isn't going to be pleasant, and I can't have her thrashing around," Akio instructed.

Alexander watched me with apologetic eyes. "I'm sorry," he murmured as he tightly grabbed onto my shoulders and firmly held them against the floor. He leaned over me so I couldn't see anything past him as someone held my legs down.

"Are you ready?" Akio asked and my breaths started coming in short gasps as panic overtook me.

"Just do it!" Alexander commanded as I shook my head wildly.

I felt a strange pulling sensation inside my body followed quickly by an unbearable pain that ripped through every inch of me. A high-pitched screech filled the air around us as I writhed, desperately trying to get away from the cause of my suffering.

"One last pull," I heard Akio say as my head pounded against my skull.

I let out another scream as the pain became all-consuming but finally, just when it was at its worst, it began to vanish, leaving behind a dull throb. My tense body began to relax, and darkness surround me as my eyes closed.

"Hey, Robin, open your eyes," Alexander told me earnestly.

"I can't," I murmured. "I'm so sleepy."

"Akio," I heard Alexander cry out as a warm feeling filled my torso. I felt it begin to spread through me before everything faded away.

Chapter Thirty-One

"Bring him in," Alexander stated blatantly. I heard doors open and willed my eyes to do the same, but I couldn't bring them to obey. "Leave us alone."

A long stretch of silence followed after the doors closed again before Alexander sighed and a chair scraped the ground. "Do you know why I summoned you?"

"I think so," Andre replied.

"You saw the chandelier falling."

"Yes."

"But not with enough time to give anything but a 'heads up' as a warning."

Andre cleared his throat uncomfortably. "No."

"Tell me something. What good are you if you can't provide a rational time frame for an upcoming attack? What good are you if you can't keep people safe? Hmm?"

"I don't know," was Andre's quiet reply.

"Lucky for you I *do* know. You're *no* good. You're *useless*! Look at her. You claim her to be a friend to you, correct?"

"Yes."

"Then why would you allow this to happen to her? You could've prevented this, but your limitations were greater than your capabilities. If that's the only thing you can offer us, your purpose here is futile. What if it's that girl you're falling for that's a target next?"

"Is that a threat?" Andre asked angrily.

"No. It's simply an observation and perhaps a motivation," Alexander replied dryly. "If you can't make yourself more of an asset, you won't like the consequences. Understand?"

"I understand," Andre answered. I was surprised he was allowing Alexander to speak to him so callously, but I thought I heard the faintest sound of guilt in his voice. It was as if he agreed with what was being said. I hoped that wasn't the case.

"Get out."

Feet shuffled away, and Alexander sat back down in the chair. He let out a heavy breath right next to me, then took my hand in both of his.

"Wake up, Robin," he begged me quietly. "Please, wake up." The doors thudded open again and he let out a frustrated grunt. "Get out!"

"I beg your pardon, but you don't get to tell me what to do," Toshiro chastised.

"Sorry. I didn't know it was you," Alexander apologized halfheartedly.

"I brought my brother along to do a quick check up on our water element."

Brother?

"Why hasn't she woken up yet, Akio?" Alexander asked.

"Her body has been through a tremendous trauma. It needs time to recuperate, but she's fine," Akio assured him. "Just be patient."

"Not one of his stronger attributes," Toshiro commented with a laugh. Someone smacked their hand down aggressively. "What? Are we a little sensitive today?"

"What's your problem?" Alexander hissed. "Serafina tried to *kill* her and you're acting as unbothered as ever. Don't you ever take anything seriously?"

"Watch your tone, Alexander," Toshiro warned in a tight voice. "Serafina has been apprehended and will pay the consequences for her actions. It'll be a pity to lose her, but she's given us no choice after her atrocious behavior since our water element has joined us."

"She isn't just 'our water element'! She's a *person*. A *good* person. You can't keep seeing her as a pawn in our plans, Toshiro. She matters."

"The only reason she matters is for her power. That's all I care about."

"But I care about *her*!"

"Good. It'll help us keep a pure bloodline intact."

Alexander yelled out in frustration, knocking something to the ground as his temper got the best of him. "Get out," he demanded.

"Excuse me?" Toshiro questioned, clearly annoyed by the demand.

"*Get. Out.*"

I could only imagine the stare down that was happening between them but after a few tense moments, Toshiro gave in. "We'll discuss this later," he said. "Come, Akio."

"Akio can stay."

"You're going to make me think you like him better than me," Toshiro said in a disapproving tone.

"I do like him better than you," Alexander stated coldly to which Toshiro sighed theatrically.

"I'll let that slide because I know you're hyped up on useless emotions. Let me know when she wakes up."

After Toshiro was gone, Alexander spoke again. "I'm sorry, Akio. I didn't mean to put you in the middle of that "

"It's not the first time, nor will it be the last," Akio replied with a chuckle. "I got used to it a long time ago."

"Is she really okay?"

"Yes. She is. I promise."

"Akio . . ." Alexander trailed off.

"Yes?" Akio questioned curiously.

"What happened between you and Margo Flemming?" Alexander finally asked.

Akio's voice was sharp as he said, "You know Toshiro doesn't allow me to speak of her."

"I know but . . . "

"But you're in a similar situation," Akio finished for him quietly.

"No, of course not," Alexander replied harshly. He seemed to rethink his statement, though, because in a softer voice he added, "I don't know."

The air was tense; you could've heard a pin drop as the silence lingered.

"Margo," Akio cleared his throat. "Margo was the love of my life. We were high school sweethearts and had our whole life together planned out. We were perfect for one another . . . Until we weren't." Akio took a shaky breath, as if the topic were hard for him to talk about. "I wanted a simple life inside the walls of Garridan and she wanted to join the Cyfrin's efforts to seek 'our due recognition'. It tore us apart. She became someone I didn't recognize. As did everyone who banded together to form the Cyfrin, my brother included. But . . . I still loved her . . . I had to make sure she was safe so I decided to join them so I could keep an eye on her and Toshiro and all my other friends who revolted. I was hoping to be a light in their darkness. To keep them from falling too far into the evil they yearned for. Unfortunately, that didn't happen.

"Margo became one of the leaders of the Cyfrin and she did everything to earn that title. If you think the things Toshiro has done is bad, you couldn't handle the stories of what she and some of the past Keepers of Balance did. They were malicious and showed no mercy. They slaughtered many people, both from Garridan and the normal world. Despite that . . . I never stopped loving her." Akio paused for a long moment before continuing. "One day, she was wounded in battle. They brought her back to me to heal her but . . . I couldn't bring myself to. I couldn't bear the thought of her hurting more innocent people. So I held her hand and kissed her cheek . . . And I let her die."

"You let her die," Alexander repeated.

"Yes. I did."

"I think that's what Robin would do if I was hurt," Alexander said quietly, more to himself than to Akio. "She'd let me die. Because she doesn't agree with what I'm doing here."

"Sometimes a sacrifice is our greatest way of showing our love for someone."

"She doesn't love me," Alexander denied. "See that ring on her finger? It's from the man she *does* loves. A good man. She cares about me, and I think she could love me like she does him . . . But she'll never allow herself to because she hates what I stand for. In her eyes, I'm not a good man."

"That's a tough situation," Akio told him, sounding thoughtful. "The way I see it, there's three ways your story could end."

"And that would be what?" Alexander asked sarcastically.

"She changes for you-"

"*That* will never happen," Alexander cut him off with a humorless scoff.

"You change for her-"

"That won't happen either," Alexander said quietly with less conviction. "So what's my third option?"

"A tragedy."

* * *

I inhaled deeply and let out a low groan as I forced my eyes open. I was in my bedroom, tucked under the covers with a pair of pajamas on. A small snore caught my attention, and I saw Alexander sitting in a chair with his head lulled to the side. I carefully pushed myself up to a seated position, expecting pain, but none came. I shifted around on the bed, causing it to creak as I tested out my mobility. I didn't seem to have any limitations, so I pulled my top up to reveal my stomach but saw no evidence that I had ever been hurt.

"Pretty amazing, isn't it?" Alexander asked.

I looked over and saw him watching me with a smile. "It is," I agreed as I put my shirt back where it belonged.

"How are you feeling?"

"Pretty amazing, actually," I admitted. My whole body felt good as new.

"Good."

"Uhm . . ." I hesitated.

"What's wrong?" he asked in concern.

"Who got me dressed?" I asked warily.

He smiled softly at me. "Roxy."

"Oh, good," I said, relief running through me. He let out a chuckle that was quickly followed by a yawn. "Sorry I woke you."

"It's fine. I've been waiting nearly a week to see you awake."

"A week?" I asked in surprise. "I've been asleep for a *week*?"

"Just about. You've had quite a few visitors too," he informed me, and my stomach dropped as I thought of Claire. Had one of her visits been intercepted?

"I have?" I asked uneasily and he nodded.

"You've seemed to have made some friends since you've been here. The trainees obviously, Monique, Darnell, Isaac."

I breathed a sigh of relief. Our secret was still safe. "I'm not surprised about the trainees. They've become like family since we're together so much. The others I didn't expect."

"I think you've made an impression on them. None of them are happy about what Serafina did."

"I'm not exactly thrilled about it either," I commented sarcastically. "What's going to happen to her?"

"Toshiro sentenced her to death."

"He what?" I asked in horror.

"She committed a crime against a Keeper of Balance. There was no other option."

"There's always another option."

"Robin . . . Even in your world, the justice system sentences some criminals to the death penalty. We have rules and laws and if they're broken, appropriate actions are taken."

I rubbed my lips together. As much as I didn't want to admit it, there was no flaw to his logic that I could argue. "So . . . She's dead?"

"No. Toshiro postponed her execution until you could be present."

"What? No. I don't want to see that."

"I know," he replied, a hint of sympathy in his tone. "But you don't have a choice."

I averted my gaze unhappily. Something caught my attention through the bathroom door and my eyes widened as I realized it was the familiar hue of Claire's translucent body.

"Can you go get me some food?" I asked Alexander, trying to hide my panic.

"I can call Roxy to get you some," he replied, standing up.

"Uh, no, I need you to get it." His brows furrowed so I rushed to come up with a better explanation. "I mean . . . I could just use a couple minutes alone. This is a lot to process."

His forehead smoothed out as understanding dawned. "Of course. I'll have the cook whip up something fresh. It'll take longer."

"Thank you."

I played with my fingers, keeping my eyes on my hands as he walked to the doors. When it clicked shut, I jumped out of bed as Claire came running out of the bathroom. "What are you doing here?" I exclaimed.

"You're awake!" Claire cried out at the same time, throwing her arms around me. They went straight through my body, though, and I shivered at the feeling it left inside my bones. "Whoops. Are you okay?"

"I'm fine," I assured her.

"We've all been so worried! Your dad is a mess. Matthew is furious. I've been coming three times a day just waiting for you to wake up."

"You could've gotten seen!" I chastised her.

"Ye of little faith," she said with a roll of her eyes. "Don't worry, I've been careful. Although that first day I came pretty close to being caught. I didn't expect Alexander to sit by your bed the entire time."

"He was there the whole time?"

She nodded. "Every time I came, he was. He seemed really worried."

"Yeah, I think he was," I agreed, my heart fluttering a little faster at the thought.

"Everyone is going to be so happy you're okay, Robin. I can't believe what that telekinesis chick did!"

"You know?"

"Uh, yeah. I didn't just leave after seeing you were still healing. I was listening in to a bunch of Alexander's conversations with people in here and trying to snoop in other parts of the castle."

"Did you learn anything?"

"Plenty. But nothing that'll help Garridan, unfortunately."

"Of course not," I grumbled. "How's everyone doing?"

"Everyone is pretty frustrated with one another right now. It's been crazy tense between all the leaders and the weather has been so wacky because of it. Some of the Keepers of Balance were talking about coming here to attack but most of them are against that. There's a reason they stopped doing it. And a lot of them are still holding on to the hope that you'll come through with some big revelation."

I looked down dejectedly. I wasn't fulfilling my original purpose for being here very well, and it made me feel like I was failing everyone. But I reminded myself that I was still contributing with the trainees, and it was because of me that they had a chance for survival. Not only that, but Garridan didn't have to worry about them (specifically Emery and Toby) being threats which was a big advantage.

"Oh!" Claire broke through my thoughts. "Matthew is officially part of the guard now! He got sworn in last week."

"That's great! I know how much he wanted that." I looked down at my hands. "Selfishly, though, I wish he wouldn't be anywhere near the battlefield when the time comes."

"I understand. Trust me I do," Claire replied softly, and I gave myself a mental slap for being so inconsiderate. He was her brother, of course she wanted that too. "But he's really smart and tactical. He's been through worse, so I know he'll be fine. He's more concerned about you than he is for himself. So am I, honestly."

"I'll be fine. I'm pretty smart and tactical myself."

"I know but . . . A real battle is nothing like training. You're going to have to make some hard choices to survive."

"Hard choices like . . ." I trailed off, not wanting to say it and she nodded.

"It's either kill or be killed, Robin. You're going to have to come to terms with that before it's too late."

I looked away, knowing she was right but not wanting to accept it. Could I really compromise my morals just to live?

"Next time I come, I'll bring Matthew. But he's going to be really hard on you about that," Claire warned. "He literally won't shut up about your 'inability to see the greater picture'."

I rolled my eyes, just picturing him grumbling about it. "Of course he is."

"On a different note entirely," Claire said, a smirk coming to her face, "what's with you and lover boy?"

"What do you mean?" I asked, heat rising to my cheeks.

"I overheard a certain conversation and now I'm under the impression that you kissed the very person you told me you weren't falling for." I pursed my lips, my eyes not meeting hers, and she gasped theatrically. "It's true?"

"No, *he* kissed *me*," I clarified. I paused for a second as her eyes widened. "And then I kissed him back."

"Robin," she groaned.

"*What*?"

"You just made this very messy."

"You were the one egging it on!"

"I know but I didn't think you'd act on it!"

"*Claire*," I whined, frustrated by our exchange and, even more so, at the feelings I had but didn't want. My eyes widened as a thought crossed my mind. "Don't tell Matthew!"

"And be the receiver of his wrath?" Claire snorted. "I don't think so."

I sighed, already dreading when he would find out. Voices made their way to my ears and footsteps thudded in the distance.

“Guess that's my cue to go,” Claire announced, and I nodded sadly. “I really am glad you're okay, Robin.”

“Me too. Tell my parents I love them. And tell Matthew to chill out.”

Claire laughed quietly at my request, then waved before fading away and leaving me to wait for Alexander to knock at the door.

Chapter Thirty-Two

"I was a little out of it, but did I hear Toshiro call Akio his brother?" I asked Alexander as I ate the burger he brought me.

"That's correct," he confirmed.

"Why didn't I get introduced to him before?"

"Toshiro keeps him on a tight leash. He isn't allowed to socialize with people very often. Nedra is our main healer. Akio only gets brought in on severe cases because he's better equipped for it than Nedra is."

"But . . . Why?" I pressed, my brow furrowed.

"It's complicated."

"Is it because he doesn't agree with Toshiro and the Cyfrin's ways?"

"Why would you say that?" Alexander questioned with narrowed eyes.

I bit my lip, regretting bringing it up. "I uhm . . . I think I heard him talking to you at one point. I tried to open my eyes but it's like they were glued shut. Then I fell back asleep."

"What else did you hear?" he asked, his voice tight, and I knew he wanted to know if I had heard the latter part of that conversation.

"Just that he loved a woman who became a leader with the Cyfrin, and he joined to keep her safe."

"That's all?" he questioned accusingly.

I nodded slowly, trying to play it off. "Yeah. I think so. I don't remember anything else at least."

He scrutinized me for a moment, so I held onto my innocent expression. Finally, he looked away, and I breathed a silent sigh of relief.

"Toshiro scheduled Serafina's execution for tomorrow. I know it won't be easy for you to see but you can't show any emotion," he told me.

"Okay," I murmured, glancing down at my hands.

"I can escort you there in the morning if you'd like or Roxy can bring you. Whichever you prefer."

"If I'm freaking out on the way there, are you going to be supportive or an ass?"

He suppressed a grin. "We both know my personality, so would a supportive ass suffice?"

I pretended to ponder on it, then raised my arms in a shrug. "I suppose it'll do."

"Execution is at seven, so I'll be here at six-forty on the dot."

"Why so early?"

"So the rest of our day goes uninterrupted." I bit the inside of my cheek to keep myself from letting out a snarky comment. He already knew I thought they were callous. "Get dressed. There are some people who want to see you."

"Who?" I asked as I got off the couch and walked to where my clothes hung. I quickly grabbed the first things I saw.

"Your trainees."

I stopped and turned towards Alexander with a smile on my face. "Really?"

"Really." I ran into the bathroom and started changing as Alexander continued. "They've all been working extremely hard this past week. None of them wanted to disappoint you with no progress when you woke up."

"You sound kind of impressed," I commented, looking around the door to see his face. He scowled, and I grinned, knowing I was right. They had done something to make an impression.

"Hurry up before I change my mind," he growled and I rolled my eyes, unfazed.

We walked to the training room side by side, our hands nearly brushing at each step. My heart hammered in my chest, and I fought the urge to reach out and wrap my fingers in his. I remembered the kiss we shared, the memory seared into my brain like it happened yesterday. What would have happened if Serafina hadn't dropped that chandelier on me? Would Alexander have walked me to my room and left me with another kiss before Darnell came to put me to sleep?

I sighed inwardly, torn between what I should be feeling and what I was actually feeling. I loved Ben and I always would, but we were in two different worlds and always would be. Was it so wrong for me to find happiness with someone else? According to Claire, that's what he was doing too. Even though it broke my heart, that's what I wanted for him, so I knew it's what he would want for me as well. However, I didn't think he'd be particularly supportive of my choice.

I glanced up at Alexander, taking in his defined features. It was different being around him than it was with Ben. Ben was my rock, my safe place. Being around him was as easy as breathing. I was comfortable and happy, always knowing I was secure with him. Being around Alexander was the complete opposite. Our encounters were new and exciting, always leaving me on my toes and making my heart skip a beat as I wondered what would happen next. We pushed each other's buttons and never seemed to be in agreement, but still managed to find an appeal in one another. As frustrating as he could be, I looked forward to being around him.

"What are you thinking?" Alexander asked, catching my stare.

I looked away, my cheeks instantly heating up. "Nothing."

"I don't believe that for a second," he said, watching me as if he knew what was going through my mind. As we came up to the training room doors, he put his hand on my arm to stop me. "Robin, I-"

Before he could finish, a loud ripping sound echoed through the hall, and we both raised our hands to our ears. A second later, the doors swung open, and Monique and Isaac flew through the air, their backs hitting the opposite wall. They fell to the ground with a thud before standing up shakily.

"Are you okay?" I asked with wide eyes.

"Peachy," Isaac grumbled.

"Speak for yourself," Monique groaned, grabbing her head in her hands. "I think I'm gonna puke."

"Go see the healer," Alexander instructed. "We'll take it from here."

"Good to see you awake, Robin," Isaac said over his shoulder as they stumbled down the hall.

"What the hell happened to them?" I asked.

"I've been teaching Emery and Toby to combine their powers. The metal creates a conductor for electricity and it's the perfect combination for a deadly reaction. There's lots of built-up power between those two."

I opened my mouth, then shut it again, unsure how to respond. Alexander smirked, then walked into the training room. I quickly followed and saw Emery and Toby high fiving while

Mateo, Andre, and Kodi looked on with differing levels of amazement.

"I see you've mastered that technique," Alexander commented with his hands behind his back. All five of them quickly straightened up and looked towards him, but when they saw me, they lost that military-like composure.

"Robin!" Toby, Kodi, and Mateo yelled simultaneously as they ran towards me.

I laughed as they wrapped me in a group hug. "Hey, guys!" I greeted them as Andre and Emery walked up and gave me individual hugs. I looked over to Alexander but found he had left the room.

"I'm so glad you're okay!" Toby said, his lower lip pouting out some. My heart swelled as his eyes filled with tears and I instantly wrapped him in my arms again.

"We are too," Andre said, his voice full of regret.

"Hey," I told him as I remembered his conversation with Alexander. "It wasn't your fault. You know that, right? Don't let Alexander put that on you."

He shrugged and looked away. "It may not have been my fault, but he had a point. If I had worked harder to grow my powers, I could've prevented it."

"Maybe," Emery chimed in, putting her hand on his arm.

"Nonetheless, it was an eye opener," Andre continued. "And it pushed me to expand my powers."

"It did?"

He nodded. "I'm still extremely limited but Alexander has been working with me to figure out what I can continue to expand on and what's just a permanent limitation."

"That's awesome. I'm so proud of you guys!" I exclaimed.

"Just wait until you hear the best part," Mateo piped up.

"What's that?" I asked as they all shared glances with one another.

"We know their battle plan and what they want with Emery," Kodi answered quietly as she watched the doors. "Well, at least part of it."

"No way!" I gasped. "How?"

"Andre had a premotion about me," Emery said, "and Mateo has been eavesdropping on Toshiro and their guard members every day. Ever since the gala, the battle seems to be everyone's main focus. They've been having multiple planning meetings a day."

"They're preparing for it to be soon," I murmured, knowing I'd have to relay the information as quickly as possible. Hopefully Claire would come back tomorrow or the next day. "So tell me what you found out!"

Andre glanced around the room, making sure it was safe to speak. "They're going to use Emery to destroy Garridan's protective barrier. It's how they plan on getting in and attacking."

"Their protective barrier has been there for a really long time. My parents told me it's one of the most powerful things ever created and it can't be destroyed," I said.

Andre lifted one shoulder in a shrug. "It may be powerful, but I *saw* her destroy it. It almost killed her, but she did it."

"That's not good," I said. Without that, Garridan was a sitting duck, not just to the Cyfrin but to the people who lived near them. "So what's their plan after the barrier is down?"

"They have a member named Kiara," Mateo told me. "She has some sort of energy power and, from what I overheard, she can basically send a death wave over a certain distance, and it'll kill anyone or anything in its path." My eyes widened at this news. "They plan on targeting Garridan's force field users at full blast and, when they're out of the way, sending Kiara in to kill the first line of defense."

"That's . . . Awful," I managed to get out, swallowing around the dryness in my throat. "Wait, but if they have someone that powerful, why not just use her to kill everyone?"

"They said she can only use her powers once because after she does, she's in a sedative state for months. Mallory also said something about it taking five years off her life when she does it."

"It kills her when she uses it?" I asked in horror and Mateo nodded.

"That's what they said."

I shook my head, trying to wrap my mind around all the information being thrown at me. "The guard keeps half of their most powerful people at the front line. Without them, Garridan is doomed."

"I still say why don't we just kill her?" Emery asked, and I could sense she had brought it up to the others while I had been asleep. “Eliminate the problem before it actually becomes a problem.”

No,” I said. “We’re not killing anyone. We aren’t murderers.”

“Even if it’ll save everyone in Garridan?”

I hesitated before saying, “Yeah, even then.” But I wasn’t entirely convinced by my own answer.

“You couldn’t kill her even if you wanted to,” Mateo spoke up. “She’s heavily guarded and Toshiro won’t tell anyone where she is. Even Monique and Isaac don’t know.”

“So she’d still be a problem even if we could kill her,” Andre clarified.

“You have to warn them,” Kodi said to me. “You have to warn Garridan.”

“I know.” I stayed silent as thoughts collided in my head. With this Kiara person, the guard would lose whoever they put on the front lines. Even if it was some of the weaker members, it would still be a major blow with countless lives needlessly stolen. I knew the Keepers of Balance there would never allow that once they found out. But how could they avoid it? How could they one up the Cyfrin’s plans? That’s when it hit me.

“If they want any chance of winning . . .” I trailed off, the conclusion I had come to not sitting right with me. “They're going to have to come here.”

Chapter Thirty-Three

That night, dinner was served in the throne room. There were multiple tables placed in a large square with chairs lining the outside. I exchanged a look with Andre as I wondered what was going on. A servant led us to our seats, and I glanced uneasily at the chandelier that had been replaced in the ceiling above.

"Don't worry," Alexander said as he sat down next to me. "Serafina is safely locked away."

"Doesn't make it any less terrifying," I muttered, and he gave me a gentle smile.

We sat in silence as people filed in and were seated all around the tables. Soon enough, food was placed before us, and we began to eat. Silverware clinked around me, and I looked around the room, surprised by the silence. My brow furrowed as I watched people's mouths move and arm gestures thrown up.

"Why can't I hear them talking?" I asked Alexander.

"Because Toshiro doesn't want you to," he replied. "You, me, and the other trainees are in our own little sonic bubble right now."

"Why?" Emery asked.

"Because they're discussing things that you don't need to listen in on."

"About the war?" Andre questioned.

"Not that it's any of your concern, but yes," Alexander replied curtly.

"Why aren't you outside our sonic bubble discussing it with them?" I asked.

"Because someone needs to listen in to your conversation," Alexander said.

"Like we have anything to hide," Emery muttered with a roll of her eyes.

"I'm sure you have plenty," Alexander commented, and she brought her chin up defiantly as I shot her a look to keep her poker face in line.

"Why didn't we just get served dinner separately?" I asked. "Seems like that would've made more sense."

"To keep face," Alexander replied. "I told you before, we need our people to see you as a leader. It wouldn't very well make sense for a leader not to be a part of a war meeting."

"Doesn't very well make sense that a leader wouldn't participate in a war meeting either," I pointed out.

"Very true," Alexander agreed. "But they're under the impression that we're playing it safe with the trainees. No one expects us to fully trust them yet."

"Seems overly complicated if you ask me," Emery muttered.

"Good thing no one did then, isn't it?" Alexander retorted with narrowed eyes.

I saw Toby nudge Emery in the side, another hint to keep her mouth shut. Her inability to keep her snarky comments to herself could be the death of us all.

"If you expect us to be a part of your battle, shouldn't you tell us what you want us to do?" Emery continued.

"You'll know soon enough," Alexander responded, keeping his eyes on the people that sat far across from us.

"What if we don't want to cooperate? Hmm?" she pressed. "What then?"

"You'll all cooperate."

"How can you be so sure?"

"Because you all have someone you care about." Alexander glanced over at Andre. "And, yes, this time that was a threat."

We all exchanged unhappy looks as he turned his attention away from us. He was well aware that none of us would willingly help the Cyfrin, and that wasn't a good thing. I found slight comfort in knowing Toshiro didn't appear to be in the loop. If he knew, the trainees would have already had family members or friends killed as incentive. I only hoped that Alexander wouldn't tell him but, for some reason, I didn't think he would.

* * *

The next morning, I sat on the edge of my bed as nausea overwhelmed me. I stood up slowly as a knock sounded at my door but, before I could answer it, my stomach churned, and I bolted to the bathroom. I slid to my knees in front of the toilet and closed my eyes as a dry heave escaped my mouth. I placed my elbows on the toilet seat with my forehead resting against my hands as another wave threatened to overwhelm me. Someone's hands pulled my hair up from around my shoulders, holding it at the nape of my neck. I didn't have to look to see who it was.

"I thought we agreed you wouldn't enter my room without permission," I whispered weakly, the motion threatening to send me over the edge.

"This seemed like an obvious exception to the rule," Alexander replied in a low voice.

"You don't have to-"

"I know." We sat like that for a minute longer before I eased onto my butt, leaning against the wall for support, as Alexander gently dropped my hair. "Are you okay?" he asked.

I slowly blew out a breath. "I don't think I can do this."

"I'm afraid you don't have a choice."

"Of course I don't," I muttered in frustration, blinking rapidly as tears formed in my eyes.

"Hey, don't cry." He dropped to his knee in front of me.

"I'm about to be forced to watch someone be killed. Don't tell me not to cry."

"I didn't mean it as a command," he said with an eye roll. "She tried to kill you. Why do you care if she dies?"

"Even if I didn't care, I still wouldn't want to watch!"

"It's the way things are done here."

"Yeah, well, you're fully aware I don't agree with the way things are done here." I sniffled as I swiped at the tears on my cheeks, not bothering to hide my disdain.

"It'll get easier."

"Did it get easier for you? Or have you always been heartless?"

He stayed silent for a long minute before speaking again. "It gets easier."

"So you *used* to care but now you've just been completely desensitized to death?" I questioned sarcastically. He shrugged so I set my jaw and looked him straight in the eyes. "So you wouldn't care if I died?" A flicker of emotion passed in his eyes. "You wouldn't care if Matthew died?"

He broke eye contact with me, and I saw his Adam's apple contract as he swallowed. "I suppose everyone has at least one person they care about."

"What happens when the battle comes then?" I asked, and his head snapped up at the change of topic.

"What do you mean?"

"Would you be able to fight against me?"

"Why are you asking me that?"

"I'm not stupid and neither are you. I came here with the intent of fooling everyone into thinking I was on the Cyfrin's side but, clearly, I failed at that. We both know that I don't want to help the Cyfrin beat Garridan. So what happens when the battle comes?"

He pressed his lips into a tight line as he considered his response. "You didn't fail entirely. You've been putting on a good show in front of everyone . . . Except me. Trust me when I tell you, I'm the *only* one who's aware of the deep hatred you still possess for us. Toshiro has his doubts, but he has no idea how deeply your loyalty runs against him."

"Well, that's something at least," I mumbled more to myself than to him. "You didn't answer my question though."

He took a deep breath before speaking again. "Toshiro's left the decision about letting you join us in the battle or not up to me. I told him I wouldn't decide until I could be sure you wouldn't betray us. You've made me put on a front of my own because I've known since day one that that's exactly what you'd do if given the chance. But I can't let him know that. I can't put you in the path of his wrath . . . I won't." He laughed humorlessly. "We all have someone we care about." He banged his hand against the wall near my head, causing me to flinch as he ground his teeth together. "This would all be so much easier if you could just see the possibility of our ways."

"Your way will never be a possibility for me," I whispered as I watched the muscles in his neck tense up.

"Which is why, when the time comes, you'll be kept under lock and key. I can't have you fighting against us. More than that, I can't let Toshiro *see* you fighting against us."

"What about the trainees?" I asked, but he stood up and shook his head.

"You've already squeezed enough information out of me. You should know better than to expect more." He held his hand out and I took it, letting him help me off the floor as my stomach did another flip. "We need to go."

"I think I'm gonna be sick again," I muttered as he ushered me out of the room.

"Look above her head."

"What?"

"Look above Serafina's head. It'll appear as if you're watching but you really won't see much."

I nodded slowly, trying to come to terms with what I was about to witness. He led me outside to the back of the castle where a hoard of people stood a ways back on either side of a small wooden pedestal. The trainees were standing in between Monique and Isaac, front and center. Kodi and Toby looked close to tears while the other three appeared stone-faced, but I could see them struggling to hide their anger. Mallory and Toshiro were standing a couple feet back from the front of the pedestal and Alexander led us over to join them.

The air was still, silent. There wasn't a single sound— not from us, not from the birds, not from anything. That made Serafina's arrival all the more apparent as dead leaves crunched beneath her feet as she was escorted between two guards to the pedestal. Old bruises discolored her pale skin and her face sunk in as if she hadn't eaten in a while, causing her already sharp features to seem unnatural. As she stepped up on the wooden platform, her sharp eyes bore into mine with unwavering hatred. I tried to keep my face neutral, but a chill ran up my spine at her menacing glare. The guards placed two shackles around her ankles before walking away, leaving us all to stare at her.

"We are gathered here today to see justice served." Toshiro's voice rang out, strong and steady. "It's a sad day when one of our own betrays us. It hits deep, and they must pay the ultimate price for that." He paused, letting his words sink in before continuing. "Attacking a Keeper of Balance is a crime punishable only by death so death is what shall be given. Let this be a reminder to all that we do *not* tolerate disobedience. If you step out of line, you *will* be served with consequences."

He nodded to Mallory who slowly walked to where Serafina stood. She pulled a match out of her sleeve and lit it then slowly ran it across the edges of the pedestal. Small sparks caught here and there before Mallory stepped back and raised her arms, igniting the separate fires until they joined as one. My breathing quickened as I realized Serafina's death wasn't going to be a quick one. It was going to be excruciating. As the flames licked up the wood and crept closer to her, Serafina finally lost her composure. Panic filled her eyes, and she began to cry out as she tried to stomp the fire out.

I instinctively raised my hands to douse it, but Alexander grabbed my wrist and shook his head. My chin began to quiver as Serafina's cries of agony turned to high-pitched screams. Tears threatened to spill down my cheeks, and I knew I couldn't hold them back. In that same moment, I also realized that tears were just a different form of water, and I could probably control them. Smoke filled the sky as I concentrated on feeling the connection of my powers and gently began pulled the tears out of my eyes before letting them fall to the ground. I did this, over and over, as Serafina's screams began to fade, using it as a way to hide my emotion as well as a distraction from the smell of burnt flesh that threatened to make me hurl.

A short time later, Toshiro spoke again. “Go forth, my friends, and don't forget what happened here today.”

He turned his back on the fire as it continued to rage on, and Alexander ushered me to follow suit. As we walked away, I couldn't help but take one last glance over my shoulder at the place where Serafina's body continued to burn.

Chapter Thirty-Four

"That was a tragedy indeed," Toshiro said when we entered the castle, nodding sadly. "Well, back to our day. We all have important business to attend to."

He turned on his heel and briskly walked away from us as I stared at him in disbelief.

"He doesn't care about what just happened?" I questioned.

"He does, but he won't let anyone know it," Mallory replied with a shrug.

"Does that go for you too?" I asked her and she snorted.

"No. *I* really don't care," she responded curtly before following in Toshiro's direction.

"Are you okay?" Alexander asked me when she was out of ear shot.

I rubbed my lips together, trying to get the image of Serafina out of my head. "Did you know tears can be controlled?"

"What?" He looked at me as though I had lost my mind.

"Tears are just another form of water," I continued, pulling the moisture from his tear ducts.

He blinked rapidly and sniffled as his nose automatically began to run from the motion. "Stop that."

The side of my lips lifted in a half smile. "Probably the only time I'll ever see you cry," I said as he wiped the liquid from his cheeks.

He watched me as I observed him, his expression a mixture of confusion and concern. I sighed heavily, dropping my head as Serafina's screams echoed in my ears.

"That was the worst thing I've ever witnessed in my entire life," I told him, and he took my hand in his own, squeezing it gently.

"Look at the plus side," he replied. "At least *you* won't have to deal with the nightmares of her screams."

My brows furrowed as I tried to understand the meaning behind his words. Darnell putting me to sleep did mean I didn't have to worry about the nightmares but there was something in his tone that made me think there was more to it than that. I cocked my head to the side as a thought crept onto my mind. Was Serafina's death going to haunt *his* dreams? Had her punishment taken a toll on him? As I watched his expression, I realized it had. But why?

Because death does still faze you. Our previous conversation lingering in my mind. *But how much? Where's the line drawn? At what point do you not care?*

"Can I ask you something?" I questioned.

"Of course."

I hesitated, not sure how to approach the subject before deciding direct was best. "Did my sister's death affect you at all?"

He kept his gaze steady on me, his eyes suddenly on the defensive. "It bothered me."

"It *bothered* you?" I repeated, pulling my hand out of his and he nodded.

"Yes."

I clenched my jaw. "Like an annoying fly on a summers day, it bothered you," I continued, anger rising in me at his word choice. "My innocent little sister's murder *bothered* you, but sadistic Serafina's execution is going to leave you with nightmares?"

"I didn't know your sister," was all he said before his lips pressed together tightly.

Fire burned in my veins at his indifference and my hands balled into fists at my sides. I tried to calm myself down, but the anger won out as I once again saw the version of him that Matthew tried to warn me of.

"Well, let me tell you about her then," I snapped. "She was the sweetest little girl. She always made sure everyone around her was happy. She was bubbly and imaginative and playful. Oh, and we had nicknames for each other. She was my sunshine, and I was her little bird. She was my *baby sister* and had her whole life ahead of her still! My whole world revolved around her and there's a piece of me that will never be okay again because she was stolen from me!" I was yelling by then, my cheeks hot and wet as I sobbed loudly. "She was *six* . . . Only six . . . And you're just *bothered* by it?

"Oh, and how about my mom? Hmm? You want to hear about her too? She was the most selfless person I've ever met. She took me in as a baby and raised me as her own, no questions asked. She was hardworking and always made sure we had food on the table. She was *so* supportive of me and made sure I was taken care of even though she killed herself every day trying to provide for us because her no good husband didn't give us a second thought. She was my confidant. She may not have been my biological mother, but she was my mom in every sense of the word, and I miss her every single day! You didn't steal just one person away from me. You stole two. And your answer is it *bothers* you?"

Alexander looked away from me, and it sent me over the edge as my vision blurred with anger. Without thinking, I let my powers take over and raised my hands, forcing the moisture in the air down his throat. His head snapped back towards me as his throat gurgled, trying to expel the liquid that was cutting off his breath.

"What the hell is the matter with you? What kind of person murders people and just continues on like it's nothing? I can't believe I almost fell for your act! You're not a good person in any way shape or form! I mean . . . I thought . . . I thought maybe there was something good in you. I-I thought maybe you weren't as horrible as everyone made you seem. That maybe it was just a facade. I thought . . ." I swallowed loudly as he stared at me red-faced and equally as angry. "I guess it doesn't matter what I thought. Matthew was right. You're a monster and you'll never be anything more than that!"

Alexander cast his arm out, splitting the floor beneath my feet. I yelped as I fell through, banging my elbows on the cold stone as cool air brushed my legs. The motion broke my concentration and Alexander coughed violently as water spewed from his mouth and nose. His eyes blazed, and my heart skipped a beat as fear paralyzed me. The stone around my chest tightened and I gasped as it squeezed my breath away.

"You will *never* understand why I am the way that I am. You will *never* understand the things I've been through . . . The things I've seen . . . The things I've had to do to survive." His voice was low and full of hate, much worse than any yelling could've been. His narrowed eyes never left mine, and I could see him struggling to continue. "I may be a monster but don't ever assume I don't live every day burdened by the consequences of our choices."

He took a deep breath and looked up at the ceiling and I could see his throat contracting. He finally looked back down at me and reached for my hands, widening the gap just enough to pull me out of the hole in the ground before closing it up. He stood there with his arms crossed, his eyes unfocused on anything.

"I see the faces of the people I've killed every night. In my dreams, I hear the screams of the people we've tortured. I remember their tears, their fear, their pleas . . . They *all* haunt me and that's something I'll never be able to run away from."

I bit my bottom lip, his heartache matching my own. His words hit like a brick, smacking me in the face as he finally opened up to me and I saw all the pain he hid so well. Everything he could never tell anyone else he was choosing to trust me with. Or maybe he was just finally cracking. He glanced over at me, his eyebrows drawn together.

"I didn't want your family to die. I told Toshiro, as I always do, that there was another way, but he wouldn't listen. He never listens. He doesn't care who he kills. Your family's death did bother me in the beginning, and I don't mean that in any small sense, but now . . . It's unbearable. I'll always be responsible for the grief of the woman I'm falling for and for that, I am truly sorry. If I could go back, I'd take their place in an instant but . . . Unfortunately, I can't."

I swallowed once, then cleared my throat as it thickened with emotion. "Why do you do it?"

"Do what?" he asked quietly, almost defeatedly.

"You could do what Matthew did and leave. Why do you stay?"

He eyed his shoes for a long moment. "Because I believe in the Cyfrin's mission. I don't like the way Toshiro runs things but . . . He's brought us this far. He needs to be the one who sees us through to the end of our mission. I can't turn my back on him."

"Even if it means losing yourself in the process?" I asked softly. He didn't answer or look up from his shoes. "Alexander . . ." I paused, trying gather my thoughts, but nothing seemed right to say. I was once again overwhelmed by the possibilities of who he was and if I had a chance of helping him. He wasn't a monster. "I'm sorry."

I meant it. I was sorry for everything he'd been through. I was sorry he'd been turned into someone he couldn't face in the mirror. I was sorry he didn't think he could escape this way of life. They were two small words, but they held so much meaning and he seemed to understand as he offered me a small twitch of the mouth.

"I'm sorry too."

As I stared at his sad, withdrawn face, I noticed the faint signs of stress on it. His eyes were filled with a regret I could never comprehend, and I realized he was right. I would never understand the things he's been subjected to. I could never take away his pain or the hate he held for himself. But maybe I could help ease it. I slowly stepped up to him as he eyed my every move, then wrapped my arms around his back. He stiffened and I could feel his heart beating faster in his chest as my ear rested upon it. After a moment, his slid his arms around me, gripping me tightly as he leaned his head against mine. He just needed some guidance and love, and I was going to make sure he got it.

* * *

I opened the door to the training room to see the trainees all sitting against the wall. Andre and Emery were huddled up, their low voices intense as the other three leaned against one another quietly, their faces small and scared.

"Are you guys okay?" I asked as I went and sat across from them.

"Well, that's a stupid question," Emery commented, and I gave her a warning glare before turning my attention back to Toby, Kodi, and Mateo.

"I can still smell it," Toby whispered.

"We can *all* still smell it," Emery said.

I turned towards her in annoyance. "What's your problem?"

"My problem?" she repeated equally as annoyed. "What do you *think* my problem is? We *all* just saw that chick burned alive. We *all* smelled her flesh burning and we *all* heard her screams. None of us are okay but you don't hear me complaining about it."

"Sounds like you're complaining to me," I snapped, but it was quickly followed by a sigh. "I'm sorry. I didn't mean to snap at you, but I really need you to stop being so . . ."

"Rude, judgmental, unpleasant," Mateo offered up, and Emery shot him a scowl.

"Exactly," I agreed. "Listen . . . I understand you've been through more than they have and that you'd rather keep all your feelings bottled up but that doesn't mean you can't be sympathetic to what they're feeling. They're allowed to complain. They're allowed to cry. They're allowed to feel anything they want or need to survive being here." My voice continued to get louder. Emery's way of 'coping' reminded me much of Alexander's. "They don't have to hide it all like you or Alexander do so either be supportive or just shut the hell up."

They all stared at me with varying degrees of shock, and I bit the inside of my cheek as my gaze fell to the ground.

"Did you just compare me to Alexander?" Emery asked with disdain.

"Emery," I said sharply.

"Yeah, yeah, shut the hell up," she grumbled, leaning back into the wall.

"Is something wrong?" Andre questioned.

"There's a lot wrong," I replied rubbing my hands against my face.

"Is there something specifically wrong right now though?" he pressed. "You seem a little . . ."

"Snappy, tense, irritable," Mateo butted in again.

"Exactly," Andre responded, copying my earlier reply.

At that moment, I knew I couldn't tell them about my conversation with Alexander. They either wouldn't understand or wouldn't care, and I couldn't have them thinking I wasn't entirely committed to them and our escape. So I decided to tell a half truth.

"Before Serafina's execution, Alexander and I had a . . . Honest conversation," I said.

"What do you mean?" Kodi asked so I quickly relayed our exchange to them.

"I'm worried that we're all going to get separated whenever the battle comes," I continued. "I'm not even sure who's going to be where. Although if I had to guess, I would think they'd only take Emery and Toby. Which means the rest of us would be locked up here."

"We can't let that happen," Andre said, his voice tight.

"I don't think we'll be able to stop it," I responded. "It's not like we can make a run for it before the battle and there's no way we could hide among everyone if we could get out of our rooms."

No one was happy but I could tell they knew I was right.

"So what *do* we do?" Kodi asked.

"I'm not sure," I admitted.

"We get out," Mateo spoke up. "We get out of our rooms and out of the castle then we follow behind the Cyfrin until they get to Garridan."

"I'm afraid it won't be that easy," I said.

"It never is," Mateo replied. "But what's our other option? Sit here while Emery and Toby are in danger?"

"No, of course not," I answered.

"Then we start finding a way out now," Mateo continued. "We learn every nook and cranny of this castle and plan multiple escape routes. That way we'll be sure we can get out when the time comes. We should also find a way to make sure one of their planes stays here. Otherwise, we'll never make it to Garridan in time."

"Planes?" Kodi questioned.

"Yeah, they have a whole airbase camouflaged just west of here," Mateo explained. "How do you think they've gotten to Garridan before?"

"I don't know. Walk?" Kodi replied with her shoulders raised.

"Nine hundred miles?" Mateo pointed out with a roll of his eyes.

"Maybe," Kodi shot back.

"How do you know that?" I asked, cutting off the argument I knew was coming.

"I've been listening in on a lot of different conversations. The battle is almost all they talk about now."

"That's really helpful, Mateo," I praised him, and a sheepish grin spread across his face. "And you're right. About all of it. I know none of you have access to much of the castle so Mateo, you're going to have to take point on planning out escape routes. I'm not sure how we're going to get them to leave a plane behind though."

"I'll take care of that one," Andre spoke up. "I can tell Alexander I had a premonition of one of them having engine trouble when they take off for Garridan."

"That's perfect!" I exclaimed.

"What about Toby and me?" Emery asked. "What are we supposed to do?"

I pressed my lips together, knowing they would have the hardest job of all. "Stick together . . ."

"And survive," Toby finished for me, and I nodded unhappily. They'd probably be on the front lines of the battle, directly in harm's way. There was no way for us to help them. The only thing I could do was tell Garridan's guard to look out for them and hope for the best.

Chapter Thirty-Five

I sat in bed that night with a plethora of ill thoughts plaguing me. As well as the trainees were doing, fear consumed me knowing we'd be involved in a real battle soon enough. They had all quickly become like family to me the last few months, even Emery and her cynical attitude. She actually reminded me of Matthew in that way. Another person I couldn't bear to think of being in the battle. The possibility of any of them getting hurt set me on edge. I couldn't allow my family to die because of me again.

I thought of Adriana and Elijah. They would both be in the deepest depths of the fighting but, for some reason, I wasn't as worried about them. Maybe it was because I knew how powerful and experienced they were. They had a multitude of fights under their belts, and I knew they could take care of themselves. But what about everyone else in Garridan who wasn't a fighter? Would the guard be enough to protect them if the Cyfrin got there and destroyed the barrier?

My thoughts jumped to Alexander. How much death would he be responsible for? What would I do if he hurt someone I loved? My heart and my mind were torn. Our relationship was so complicated and each interaction we had only confused me more. It didn't help that he himself was so complicated. I had seen him wrestling with who he was, and I just wanted to help. Matthew was right. I was too nurturing. But was it my nurturing nature that made me want to save him, or was it that I actually cared for him?

"Penny for your thoughts?"

I looked up and saw Darnell peeking in around the door. I smiled softly, almost thankful for his intrusion. "Hi," I greeted him.

"All tucked in and ready for bed?" he asked.

"Actually . . . Can I ask you a question?"

"Sure."

"Why are you a part of the Cyfrin?"

He clasped his hands in front of him, a contemplative expression coming to his face as he considered it. "Well, I suppose it's because I believe in a better future for our people. A future where we can live as free as anyone else without being hunted down or persecuted." He looked over at me, his eyes full of hope. "Wouldn't that be a wonderful thing?"

"I'm sure it would," I replied, his sincere explanation foreign to me

He observed me for a moment before speaking again. "But you don't quite understand that yet, do you?"

"I'm afraid I don't, actually," I admitted.

"That's understandable. You've been living amongst the norms your whole life. You've never had to witness or learn what drove our ancestors into hiding." He sat down next to me. "Still, you're doing so well here despite that. You were very brave to come join us and we're very lucky to have you."

"Thank you," I told him, and he bowed his head forward slightly, their universal sign of respect that still threw me for a loop.

"Now, how about we send you off to dream world?" he suggested.

"I don't dream under your somnokinesis."

"I know," he responded with a chuckle. "It's just an expression. Goodnight, Robin."

"Goodnight, Darnell."

* * *

"Holy hell would you wake up already?" I heard above me. I cracked my eye open and saw Matthew standing above me, poking his finger through my head.

"Hello to you too," I grumbled, and he stood up straight.

"About time!" he exclaimed. "We've been waiting here forever."

"You know I don't exactly have control over my sleep patterns anymore, right?" I pointed out as I sat up in bed, rubbing my eyes as the familiar metal taste filled my mouth.

"You know I don't exactly care, right?" he shot back, and I made a face at him. He grinned, and I couldn't help but smile back, our familiar relationship always a comfort. "How are you doing?"

I glanced over at Claire who was sitting at the foot of my bed. She discreetly shook her head, so I knew she hadn't said anything about Alexander.

"I won't lie, I'm not great. Serafina's execution was yesterday, and it was . . . awful. They burned her alive," I told them, the emotion evident in my voice.

"That's horrible!" Claire exclaimed, her face twisted in horror.

"They must've really wanted to make an example out of her," Matthew said, shaking his head. "I only remember them doing that a couple of times and it was for extremely serious transgressions."

"You've seen people burned alive?" Claire asked him.

"I've seen every form of torture you could imagine," he replied, his tone flat.

"Oh, baby brother," Claire murmured, her eyes full of pain.

He turned his attention back to me, not wanting to address her sorrow for him. "I'm sorry you had to see that," he said.

"Me too. I'm sorry everyone had to see it."

"I'm sure some people enjoyed it," he muttered in disgust.

"I'm not so sure about that . . . Everyone seemed upset by it. Even Toshiro and Alexander."

Matthew scoffed. "Yeah, right."

"I'm serious, Matthew. I mean, I didn't see Toshiro act upset but Mallory said he was."

"Because you can take everything she says at face value."

"Well, no, but I still think he was. And Alexander . . . Well, let's just say I *did* see him upset. Really upset."

"I don't believe that."

"Why?"

"Because he's a monster, Robin!" he basically yelled. "How many times do I have to tell you that? He's. A. Monster."

"No! He really isn't!" I exclaimed, and he narrowed his eyes at my insistent tone.

"You're just blind about him."

"Have you ever considered that maybe *you're* the one who's blind about him?" I questioned. "You told me he protected you as a little boy. Did you ever stop and consider that maybe that's what he's been doing this whole time?"

"Are you trying to blame *me* for his actions?" he questioned angrily.

"No! Of course not." I sighed and rubbed my temples, knowing this was a conversation for another time. "Can we discuss this later? I have way more important things we need to talk about."

"You better believe we'll discuss this later," he assured me. "We'll also add in what you're hiding from me." He glanced over at Claire who had been watching in silence. "What you're *both* hiding from me."

Claire and I shared another quick look before she swiftly changed the subject as she avoided Matthew's gaze. "So what is it you want to tell us?" she asked me pointedly.

"The Cyfrin's battle plan."

"You know their battle plan?" Matthew asked urgently, all thoughts of Alexander slipping away, and I nodded.

"Garridan's guard needs to come here," I informed them.

They exchanged a look, their expressions matching with furrowed brows.

"The guard is safe behind the barrier. Why do you think they always had the upper hand against the Cyfrin? Them coming here wouldn't be very tactical," Matthew stated slowly.

"It would be if the barrier is gone," I replied.

"That's impossible," Claire spoke up. "The barrier is impenetrable."

"Unfortunately, that's not true. Andre had a premonition. They're going to use Emery to destroy it."

"But she won't be able to," Claire denied.

"Andre *saw* her do it. He said it nearly killed her, but she did it."

They shared another look, this time concerned. "That's not good," Claire said softly.

"No, it's not," Matthew agreed. "But even without the barrier, the guard is strong. We'd still be better off there than in the open here. Home field advantage and what not."

"I'm not so sure about that," I said. "Do you guys know anything about a member of the Cyfrin named Kiara?"

"No," Claire answered.

"Yes," Matthew responded at the same time.

Claire looked over at him. "Who is she?"

"She was a child of Garridan. She had a very rare energy power and could summon up a death wave. It killed on contact, getting rid of the enemy's first line of defense."

"Oh! I've learned about that," Claire exclaimed. "But I was told she was dead."

"Not dead, just uselessly old," Matthew replied.

"She couldn't be that old if she was a child of Garridan," Claire pointed out.

"She had an unfortunate side effect to her powers. Every person she killed took a year off her life."

"So if she killed twenty-five people-"

"She aged twenty-five years," Matthew finished as Claire and I stared wide-eyed at one another. "It's why the Cyfrin only got a couple uses out of her."

"Well, they're planning on getting one more out of her," I told him.

"There's no way. She's been in the care of Nedra for years. She's basically knocking on deaths door, has been for a while."

"I'm just telling you what was said," I replied, slightly annoyed that he brushed it off so easily.

Matthew got quiet, his brows furrowed together, and his mouth pulled downward as he thought. "Surely she wouldn't have enough energy to perform another death wave."

"Let's say, for argument's sake, she does," Claire said. "What would that mean?"

"It'd mean that the Cyfrin would have a huge advantage. We'd lose our front men and," he stopped for a minute to take in a loud breath, "possibly the entire war. Garridan is strong. Really strong. They have double the manpower. But the Cyfrin are cunning and they're not as weak as they once were. It's what I was trying to tell Dad and the other leaders when Robin and I first got to Garridan. This isn't going to be an easy fight like they expected it to be. They were underestimating the Cyfrin's numbers and powers by a long shot."

"I guess it's a good thing you came along when you did then," Claire murmured. "So what do you think the guard should do?"

Matthew lifted his shoulders slightly and shook his head. "I really don't know. The guard has played with the idea of coming here but always comes to the conclusion that it would be a huge disadvantage to us. However . . . If they're really planning on using Kiara . . . Staying there would put all of Garridan in danger. Doing a surprise attack *might* be our only chance at an upper hand but . . . I really don't know."

It was weird to see him so unsure. I could tell the possibility of Kiara knocked him off his rocker, and that scared me. "Sounds like you'll all have a lot to discuss today then," I commented. "But you have to tell the Keepers of Balance they need to decide soon. I doubt *they* want to be hit with a surprise attack."

"I think there's something else everyone is going to need to consider," Claire suddenly spoke up. "A survival plan."

"What do you mean?" I asked.

"Think about it. We've been planning this battle under the impression that we'd win. But with knowing what we do now, I think it's safe to say we need to think about what will happen if we lose . . . What will happen to Garridan and everyone in it."

Matthew and I shared a look, the thought never occurring to either of us. We had just found our place in Garridan, but Claire had lived there almost her whole life. She and William had been some of the lucky ones who were found almost immediately after Garridan started looking for their kids. They had spent their years away together, one of the few sets of siblings who weren't separated in the foster care system. Of course she'd worry about her home being destroyed.

"If the Cyfrin have the ability to destroy Garridan's protective barrier, whether they win here or there, they'll go and slaughter everyone. They couldn't take over the world if Garridan still existed. They need us completely annihilated."

"She's right," I said softly.

"I know," Matthew responded, his voice just as low. "That's definitely something to bring up to the council once we relay the rest of the information."

"What do you think is going to happen?" I asked, my stomach knotting up as dread filled me.

"I wish I could tell you." He sighed, scratching the back of his head. "The only thing I can say for sure is that we have a long day of meetings ahead of us."

"You'll come back as soon as things are decided, right?" I requested.

"Of course. I'll scour the whole castle to find you if I have to," Claire replied, and I smiled at her gratefully.

"I hate to say it, but I should probably get ready for breakfast," I told them, less than enthusiastic at their pending departure.

"Yeah, we really need to get this information back to the council anyway," Claire told me. "Thank you for getting it."

"Don't thank me. It was Andre and Mateo's doing."

She smiled. "Then thank them for us, will ya?"

"Of course," I said, returning her smile. I looked over at Matthew who was still deep in his own thoughts, the lines on his face prominent. "It's going to be okay."

The side of his lip barely twisted up. "If only any of us believed that," he replied. "We'll see you soon, okay?"

I nodded and watched as their bodies dissipated, leaving me alone. I threw myself back into my pillows as I was overwhelmed by all the unknowns to our situation. Garridan had to win. They just had to.

Chapter Thirty-Six

"Mateo, Kodi, would you knock it off and come here?" I requested with a roll of my eyes.

They were both glaring at the other, their hands intertwined as they pushed forward trying to knock each other down. Mateo glanced my way for a second, momentarily distracted, but that was all it took. Kodi placed her leg behind his and knocked him over, placing her knee into his chest as he grunted from the force of the fall.

"Ha, I win!" she proclaimed with a smirk.

Mateo huffed as she stood over him. "Just remember who would win if we were using powers."

She scowled, knowing she was inferior in that department, before offering her hand to him. He stood up then shoved her playfully before running over to where Toby, Emery, Andre, and I sat. Their interactions always left me smiling. They had taken to one another as siblings, and it showed in every argument, every fight, and every make up. I realized how special it was for both of them for completely opposite reasons. Mateo was making up for the adoptive siblings he had lost when he was kidnapped while Kodi was making up for the lone childhood she was given. Their relationship was special, and I couldn't be mad about that, no matter how annoying they were.

"Listen," I told them as Kodi and Mateo settled down next to us. "Garridan knows everything we do now, and they'll decide what to do soon. When they do, we'll plan accordingly. For now, I thought this might help."

I pulled out the map Alexander had given me and unfolded it on the ground so everyone could see.

"Is this the whole castle?" Toby asked.

"I think so. It's only marked with the places I needed to be so I don't know what else is where but at least we can all get a better idea of the layout of the castle. Once Mateo routes some escape paths, I figured we could draw them up on here so we'd have a visual. That way we'll all know exactly where we're going when the time comes."

"That's a great idea!" Toby exclaimed enthusiastically, always on board with any of my plans. "What's that mean though?" He pointed to Alexander's wispy handwriting.

"Oh, nothing. When I first got here, I sarcastically said that the castle needed road signs so people could get around," I explained. "That's why he made this for me."

Despite there being nothing more to the story, I blushed as they all exchanged glances with one another.

"You guys aren't . . . You know," Kodi said awkwardly.

"*Together*," Mateo added in, his clarification not needed. "Like dating together."

"No!" I denied loudly as my face continued to grow hot.

"Are you sure?" Toby asked as he began fiddling with his fingers.

"You guys *are* together a lot," Emery piped up. "And you seemed pretty friendly at their stupid dance. Actually, you were basically starry eyed for one another."

"And he was really distraught when you got hurt," Kodi pointed out.

"But he's kinda the enemy . . ." Toby said softly.

"No *'kinda'* about it," Emery scoffed. "Seems like you're giving in to psycho man's offspring plan."

"It's really none of our business," Andre interceded, his voice firm as he tried to give me an out.

I looked down at my hands, my thumbs tapping each other as rapidly as my heart was beating. I had figured this would be brought up eventually, but *I* still didn't know what it was so how could I explain it to anyone else? After a moment, I looked back up and my gaze jumped from each face that sat in front of me.

"It is your business actually," I finally said, not taking the opportunity Andre had tried to give me. "Our lives are literally going to be depending on one another eventually which means I need to be able to trust all of you and you all need to be able to trust me. So I think you have every right to question my relationship with Alexander."

"What is it then?" Emery pried.

"I can honestly tell you I don't know. I know that's a crappy answer but it's true." I twirled my ring around on my finger, always finding comfort in it, and a little guilt. "You all know what Toshiro has planned for us and that's why we're together all the time. It's not by choice. Neither one of us agrees with it and neither one of us likes it."

"Alexander doesn't agree with it?" Kodi asked, and I shook my head.

"No. But since we're together so much, I can't deny that we've gotten close in some ways. He's actually gotten me through a couple of rough spots here," I admitted quietly. "If I'm being perfectly honest . . . I do have feelings for him . . . I don't want to but they're there. . ." I trailed off as I looked to the ceiling, struggling with the vulnerability of the conversation. "But nothing will ever come of it."

"Why not?" Toby questioned.

"Because he *is* the enemy," I stated flatly. "I don't think he's as corrupt as some of the people here but that doesn't really matter, and I won't let my feelings for him blind me from the truth. No matter what happens between us . . . I'll do what needs to be done when the time comes, and that includes making sure none of you get hurt. I won't choose him over any of you. Ever. That's a promise."

Andre reached over and gave my shoulder a tight squeeze. "I believe you," he told me firmly. "And I trust you."

"I trust you too," Toby said, picking my hand up with both of his.

"Me too," Mateo echoed as Kodi nodded in agreement. We all looked over to Emery who sat with her arms crossed. She rolled her eyes at us and leaned back into her hands.

"Okay, yeah, I trust you too," she said in an annoyed tone.

I smiled, grateful they believed me. "Thank you, guys."

"That's what families are for," Toby replied, returning my smile. "Right?"

"Right," I assured him as I placed my arm around his shoulders, a weight lifted off me. "Now that that's out of the way, let's get to work."

"What's first, boss?" Mateo asked with a salute.

"More training," I replied with a shrug, to which they all groaned. "Hey, I don't like it any more than you do but that's really all we *can* do."

"What about learning the layout of the castle?" Kodi asked hopefully.

"We can definitely take turns doing that, but it'll be more beneficial once Mateo is able to give us some escape routes."

"Why don't I do that now then," Mateo offered.

"I think it'll be safer to wait until nighttime," Andre told him.

"Me too," I agreed. "We never know when Alexander or Monique or Isaac are going to show up to train with us and we don't want to risk getting caught."

"I guess that means it's time for me to kick all your butts," Emery inserted with a smirk as she stood up.

"Guess that depends on if we're using powers or not," Andre countered.

"Exactly," Kodi agreed with a sly smile shot at Mateo.

Just then the doors burst open, and I quickly folded up the map and shoved it in the pocket of my cardigan as Toshiro waltzed in followed quickly by Alexander, Mallory, Isaac, Monique, Darnell, and a couple others I didn't know the names of.

I stood up next to the trainees as Toshiro stopped in front of us with a smile playing at his lips. He looked out of place in a loose tank top and workout pants.

"Ready for some fun?" he asked.

"We were just about to start training," I replied.

"Excellent. That's just the fun I was referring to."

I looked around at all the faces in front of me, my brows furrowed in confusion. "Are you going to watch?"

Toshiro laughed. "No. I'm going to fight."

I opened my mouth, then shut it again, unsure what to say. I caught Alexander's eye, and he stepped forward. "Is that going to be a problem?" he asked me, his demeanor rigid.

"N-no, of course not," I stuttered. "Uhm . . . They're all yours."

Toshiro nodded his head at me, and I slowly made my way to the far wall in the room. The others joined me as the trainees lined up in front of Toshiro and Alexander.

"Why is Toshiro fighting?" I asked Monique quietly.

"He wanted to get a sense of their advancements," she responded.

"Does he do that often?"

She shook her head slowly. "Not really. He usually lets Alexander handle all that."

"So why now?"

"It's probably just the fact that we have an important battle upon us. He wants to make sure they're ready and not a liability."

I turned my focus back to the middle of the room where Toshiro stood with Toby.

"Your ferrokinesis is great, but your pudginess will be the death of you if you stand against someone who can cancel it," Toshiro said, looking down his nose at Toby.

My eyes narrowed into slits, but it was Emery who spouted off with, "Hey, he's come a long way, asshat."

"Yeah," Kodi added in as they all looked on in anger.

Toshiro gave them a side glance, the corner of his mouth turned up in a threatening smirk. "You were right," he said as his eyes traveled over the trainees. "They have gotten awfully close."

My gaze jumped to Alexander, but his eyes stayed on Toshiro, his face cold and distant. He was putting on his Cyfrin facade.

"Alexander, how would you rank them on hand-to-hand combat alone?" Toshiro asked.

"From worst to best: Toby, Mateo, Emery, Kodi, Andre," he immediately answered.

"I'll make you all a little deal," Toshiro said, pacing in front of them. "I'm going to start with Toby. No powers, strictly hand-to-hand combat, and when he can't take anymore, the next in line can take his place or I'll keep whaling on him. We'll move all the way up the chain, in the order Alexander just stated. If one of you wins, I'll spare you all from a punishment. If I win, one of you pays for all of you. Is that clear?"

Silence followed as Toshiro urged Toby to step up. Toby hesitated, his eyes meeting mine as he swallowed nervously, and I gave him an encouraging nod. I didn't want him to be in this position. I knew he wouldn't win against Toshiro. But I couldn't stop it. I just hoped one of the other trainees could beat him before anything worse happened.

Toby lifted his hands up by his face and spread his feet apart to better his balance. Toshiro didn't wait before striking out, immediately kicking Toby in the stomach. Toby bundled over and Toshiro took the opportunity to drive his knee into his nose which began bleeding. Toby grabbed Toshiro's leg and yanked up, knocking him off balance just enough to push him to the ground with a small shove. As soon as Toshiro hit the ground, he swung his legs under Toby, sweeping him to the ground. Toshiro pounced on top of him, placing his knee directly on Toby's windpipe before punching him in the face. Toby struggled to get up, pressing his hands against Toshiro's knee, but Toshiro didn't budge as he continued to pound on Toby's face with his fists.

"Sluggish," Toshiro stated, calm and collected. I watched in horror as Toby cried out, his face now covered in blood. "Uncoordinated. Weak."

"Enough!" Mateo yelled, running up and tackling Toshiro off Toby

Alexander pulled Toby up and pushed his slumped body into the wall as Mateo and Toshiro rolled on the ground. Mateo managed to gain some control and plopped himself atop Toshiro, punching him in the face repeatedly as he had just done to Toby. Toshiro easily shifted his weight, and knocked Mateo to the ground, pushing him onto his back and yanking his arms behind him. Mateo cursed as Toshiro pushed up then a howl of pain, closely resembling that of an animal, left his mouth as Toshiro snapped his elbow.

"Poor reflexes, no counterattack skills," Toshiro commented as Mateo cradled his arm. Toshiro stepped closer to him for another hit, but Emery cut him off.

"My turn, asshat," she told him as she waved for Mateo to leave.

Isaac chuckled and I gave him a sideways look. "What's so funny?"

"Nothing, really. It's just that no one else could get away with calling him names," he told me as they began to circle one another.

"Then why can she?"

He shrugged. "I think it's because she reminds him of Serafina."

"Were him and Serafina close?"

"Kind of," he responded as Emery lashed out at Toshiro repeatedly. "I really never understood their relationship dynamic, but she got away with a *lot*."

My brows furrowed, unsure what to think of that information as I turned my full attention back to the action in the center of the room. Emery got in some good hits, drawing blood from Toshiro, but he quickly began dodging them. He moved with grace as he sidestepped her forceful blows, then always wound up behind her, striking out with his own unforgiving hits. Their match lasted twice as long as the other two and Emery's motions began to slow down as fatigue settled in. Toshiro took the opportunity to go in full force, his moves now quicker and stronger than hers. In ten seconds flat, he had her on the ground.

"No thought process. No ability to pace yourself. Fueled by rage not tactic," he noted before lifting his leg up to drive a blow straight to her skull.

"Stop!" Kodi demanded.

Entertainment danced in Toshiro's eyes as he watched her help a pissed off Emery off the ground. "Ready?" he asked.

Kodi didn't answer. Instead, she charged him, no fear in her determined eyes. Toshiro blocked her first swing but when he went to land his own blow, she easily caught his wrist in her hand and twisted it around his back. He let out a small hiss as she shoved her foot into the back of his knee, causing him to fall forward. She took the opportunity to reach her arm around his neck, putting him in a tight choke hold.

Without hesitation, Toshiro grabbed her arm with both hands and lunged forward, the motion launching Kodi over his head and to the ground. She quickly got herself up but not before Toshiro kicked her straight in the jaw. She instinctively put her hand to the spot then spit out some blood as Toshiro swung his arm up in an uppercut. Kodi shrank back, barely missing it, then sent a roundhouse kick to his chest. He began coughing as he struggled to catch his breath from the blow.

I watched, barely blinking, as Kodi sent her elbow into his face. She was giving him a run for his money. Toshiro let out an irate grumble and I saw his eyes turn calculating as he assessed Kodi's every move. As she stepped forward, he somehow managed to find footing behind her and pulled her body backwards over his outstretched leg to where only her shoulders were touching it. In what I could imagine was an extremely hard balancing act, he put his other foot on top of her chest and pulled her hair, so her neck was stretched past a comfortable position.

"Just one tiny tug and your neck is snapped," he told her before looking up at Andre, signaling his time to take over. Toshiro shoved Kodi off him and looked her over as he straightened up, unbothered by the blood dripping down his face. "Agile, cunning, receptive. Not bad at all."

Kodi stood up without a word or reaction to his praise and Andre patted her shoulder as they passed one another. He stayed silent as he stared at Toshiro, and neither one of them made an attempt at the first move as they observed the other.

"Your size is intimidating," Toshiro finally said, slowly beginning to walk, "but it means nothing if you can't-"

Andre whipped his arm around, sucker punching Toshiro in the eye. Toshiro cursed as the force of it knocked him back and Andre used the opportunity to strike again, his knuckles connecting with Toshiro's face once, twice, three more times. Toshiro wasted no time, clearly over being hit, and maneuvered himself behind Andre, his only point of advantage. He slammed his hands over Andre's ears, causing him to yell as blood trickled out one of them. Andre swung his arm around, but Toshiro stayed directly behind him out of reach. Toshiro's lips were pressed in a firm line as he continued to play cat and mouse.

I realized that Andre was actually a match for him; that's why he was staying out of harm's way. Andre turned around once more, frustrated, then shoved his left leg back in an attempt to make contact with Toshiro. Toshiro grabbed onto it and twisted hard, the motion snapping Andre's ankle out of place. Andre's face showed the pain he was in but no sound left his mouth as he desperately swung his arm around again. Toshiro wasn't winning this one by sheer skill, though. He was playing dirty. He twisted Andre's foot again and, this time, Andre yelled out. He yanked his foot out of Toshiro's grasp with a new wave of pained screams but without being able to step on it, he was stuck, and everyone knew it.

"Shall we continue to the unavoidable result or just call it now?" Toshiro asked, his eyes gleaming at his foul play.

With sweat dripping down his face, Andre jumped forward trying to tackle Toshiro, but he easily avoided it, and Andre fell to the ground with a loud thud.

"You're a true opponent," Toshiro murmured, his hand stroking his chin. "Strong, even tempered, thoughtful. Well played."

Alexander walked forward and announced, "As expected, Toshiro wins."

Applause broke out around me. I looked over at the trainees and my heart ached as I saw them bloodied, bruised, and defeated.

"Well, I do believe that means one of you is paying the price for your futile efforts," Toshiro commented as his eyes drifted over them. When they landed on Toby, he stopped. "You."

"No!" I heard myself cry out.

Toshiro turned towards me with brows raised high. "Excuse me? Is there a reason you don't want him harmed? Hmm? Say . . . A sentimental attachment to him? To all five perhaps?"

It's a test.

I set my chin and stepped closer to him. "Yes! That's exactly why."

I could see Alexander shooting warning glares my way, but I ignored him as I watched Toshiro. I knew what I was doing this time. "I've spent almost all day every day with them for the last couple months. I've watched them all grow from nothing to earn their place here. Some by their power levels and the others by their combat skills. None of them are worthless. Which, by *your* standards, makes them *family* in this compound, and I would never want anyone in my family to get hurt." For good measure I added in, "Not them, not Alexander, not Monique or Isaac, no one."

Toshiro stayed silent as he listened. He slowly closed the space between us, gazing at me intently as he placed his hand on my cheek. His voice was low so only I could hear as he said, "I think you're finally getting it. Don't get me wrong— I'm not so daft as to think you're one of us, and maybe you never will be, but you've shown tremendous growth here. I can't give you my trust yet . . . But you're working towards it."

I held his gaze, finally feeling like maybe I had won him over with my charade. He dropped his hand and turned back around, heading for the door. His entourage immediately followed as he said, "There will be no punishment today. Alexander, have Nedra see to their wounds. Tomorrow, we battle with powers."

Chapter Thirty-Seven

As the trainees were being treated for their numerous wounds, I walked around the snow-covered garden. Even bundled up, the cold was overwhelming, and I could see my breath in front of me as I aimlessly followed the maze of shrubs to the fountain. The flowers looked out of place being so bright and healthy in the midst of the snow, but I welcomed their company. No one else was around—they were all too intimidated by the freezing temperatures—and I found peace in my still, quiet surroundings. I cleared off the edge of the fountain and sat down, looking at the layer of ice that sat atop the rest of the water.

I let the familiar tingle fill me as I sensed the water— the way it felt, the way it moved, the way it smelled. Then I raised up the smallest bit, forming a tiny hole in the ice for it to get through, and let it arch above me. I pried it wider until it was two arches then let them twist around each other like vines. A mixture of pink chrysanthemums and white daisies intertwined themselves in the holes where the water didn't touch, and I smiled at the beauty of it. I looked around, my eyes searching for Alexander, and I spotted him on the balcony that overlooked the garden. I lifted my hand in a small wave. He turned around, and somehow, I knew he was coming to join me.

I let the water fall back into the fountain and picked up the flowers before lining them along the ice in a pattern, knowing they'd wilt soon without Alexander's intervention.

"You're going to catch a cold out here," Alexander said as he walked through the gap in the brush with a blanket in his hands. It seemed to be his favorite line when he found me outside.

"It'll be worth it," I replied, and he smiled softly.

"So some say. Nevertheless, another layer can't hurt."

He shook out the blanket and wrapped it around my shoulders. The gesture warmed me more than any blanket could, and it reminded me of something Ben would do.

"Thank you," I told him quietly, blinking away unwanted tears.

"What's wrong?" he asked, sitting next to me.

I dropped my head and shook it. "Nothing. It's stupid."

He folded his hands in his lap as he leaned against his knees. "Your old boyfriend?"

"How do you always seem to know what I'm thinking?" I asked in frustration.

"I'm very perceptive." I looked over at him, and realized he was trying to joke. When I didn't respond he asked, "Do you want to tell me about him?"

"Is that something you really want to hear?" I questioned, borderline sarcastic.

"I do, actually."

His tone made me pause. "What? Why?"

"Because it'll make you happy . . . And I wouldn't mind learning what kind of man has such a tight grip on your heart." I bit the inside of my cheek, unsure if I should. "Really. Tell me about him."

I took a deep breath, the cold stinging my throat. "Okay . . . His name is Ben. Benjamin, actually, but I'm the only one who gets away with calling him that." I smiled at the ground as I remembered the fits he used to throw about me calling him by his full name when we were younger. "He's Native American and has this beautiful, long black hair that I love. His tribe and his family and his values mean everything to him. He's . . . Well, he's amazing. He's the most down to earth person I know. He's athletic and social and kind. He's so compassionate and understanding. He didn't even bat an eye when Matthew and I told him about our powers. He didn't call me crazy before I knew what was going on and said I thought I was controlling water . . . He was just there for me."

I paused as my voice grew thick, and I took another deep breath. "He's always been there for me. He was there when I was in the hospital with pneumonia, when I started my period and stained my pants, when I fell off the stage at eighth grade promotion, when my parents would fight . . . When my mom and sister died . . . He's been with me through everything. He's my best friend . . . So, really, I guess it's not a surprise we fell in love."

"No, I suppose it's not," Alexander responded quietly. "He sounds like an upstanding guy." A hint of jealousy played in his tone. "And the ring?"

I looked down at my hand before pulling it into hiding under the blanket. "It's a promise ring."

"A promise of?"

"Love."

Alexander scrunched his brows together. "I don't follow."

"You don't have promise rings here?" I asked, once again baffled by their lack of knowledge of some basic things. Alexander shook his head, so I contemplated how to explain what it was. "In the normal world, promise rings are usually used as a sign of commitment. Like a pre-engagement ring."

"So it's a promise of marriage."

"Technically."

"So he promised to marry you," he said with a small bite in his voice.

"No," I answered slowly, drawing out the word.

"I'm afraid I don't understand," he replied, sounding frustrated.

"Ben and I *can't* be together!" I said loudly, my own frustration now evident. "Our lives got screwed up and there's no way to fix it. I'm stuck here and he's stuck there, and we both know it." I sighed before speaking again with a softer voice. "This ring really is just a promise of love. When Ben gave it to me, he said: 'no matter where you are or what you're doing, you can look at it and know that I love you and I will always love you no matter where life takes us. Even if it's in opposite directions'. Which, unfortunately, is exactly where life took us."

Alexander and I sat in prolonged silence, both of us wrapped up in our own thoughts. Snow started to fall around us, and I sniffled as my frozen nose began to run.

"Let's get you inside," Alexander said, standing up and offering me his hand. We walked side by side through the courtyard and into the castle as the wind whipped wildly behind us. We handed off our coats to the servant manning the door, then headed for the stairs where Alexander finally broke the quiet.

"Upstanding guy, romantic, and the one that got away," he commented as we walked to the second floor. "I can't compete with that."

"It's not a competition."

"Oh, but it is," he murmured, his usually well-guarded eyes poorly hiding his pain. "And I think I lose in every scenario."

I wrapped my arms together in front of me before the words poured out of my mouth. “Not *every* one.”

His eyes raced to mine, but I quickly diverted them as heat ran through me at my admission.

“There's one in which I win?” he asked, quiet but intense as we came to my bedroom door.

I opened it and stepped inside before turning towards him. He was only a couple inches away from me but neither of us backed away. “It’s not a competition,” I repeated.

“But, in your mind, there’s a scenario in which you and I end up together?” He was watching me with anticipation, and I swallowed around the dryness in my throat as my heart beat wildly at my coming confession.

“Yes.”

“Which one?”

“Garridan wins the war. The Cyfrin are gone for good. You come back with me and show everyone you're not just a monster. Instead of waging war on the world, you settle down for a content life living in peace . . . With me.”

Alexander's Adam’s apple bobbed up and down as he swallowed, the scenario digging through his rough exterior. He opened his mouth then closed it again, speechless for once. After a moment he asked, “What about Ben?”

“What about him?”

“In that scenario, what about Ben?” he repeated.

“In that scenario and many others . . . I move on,” I replied quietly. “He finds someone he loves and is happy with . . . And so do I.”

“That someone being me,” he murmured, and I nodded.

The truth of it hit me harder than I thought it would and all my senses were on overdrive. We stood watching one another, neither of us speaking as we pondered the possibility I had just presented. My eyes traveled from his intoxicating stare to his plump lips that were slightly parted. When I looked back up, his eyes were traveling over me, matching my lustful thoughts, but he didn't make a move.

“Why aren't you trying to kiss me?” I wondered out loud, my voice barely audible as I inched towards him.

“I didn't know if you wanted me to,” he said as his fingertips brushed my hips.

"I do," I told him, but I didn't wait for him to make a move. I placed my hands on his cheeks and pulled his lips to mine.

Shivers crept up my spine and my head swirled at his touch. His arms wrapped around my lower back, dragging the rest of me to him, and our lips quickly intensified as we clung to one another. His hands brushed over my face lightly, and I could feel the muscle in his arms contracting as I held onto them. I heard the door shut as I began pulling him deeper into the room, and my fingers ran through his hair.

Suddenly, a loud bang echoed around us, and we pulled away from one another, looking around to locate the source of the noise. I pushed my lips together as the euphoric sensation evaporated with only dread left in its place. I knew what the sound was—or should I say *who*.

"Something must've fell," I said as I stepped further away from him.

"Yeah . . . I guess so," he agreed, the moment gone. I straightened my shirt out and cleared my throat as I stared at my shoes. "I'll uhm- I'll see you tomorrow," Alexander told me.

I glanced up and saw his face full of mixed feelings, just as I was. He reached up and gently pushed a stray hair out of my face then walked away, shutting the door behind him. I closed my eyes before turning around to face what was waiting.

"What the hell are you doing?!" Matthew yelled as he and Claire came through the bathroom door.

"Keep your voice down!" I hissed, nodding at the door Alexander had just walked through.

"Keep my voice down? *Keep my voice down*?!" he shouted incredulously, his eyes popping out of his head. "That's what you have to say for yourself? You're screwing my arch nemesis, the enemy to your whole community, the person who had a hand in killing Rebecca and Dawn, and all you have to say is keep your voice down?"

"I'm not screwing anybody," I denied quietly, avoiding his angry glare.

"Could've fooled me," he retorted. "If Claire hadn't knocked down that shampoo bottle we would've seen-"

"You knocked down the shampoo bottle?" I asked Claire. "How?"

"So much concentration that I feel like dying," she answered, her ashen face speaking to the truth of her words.

Matthew slammed his fist through the wall then kicked through the bed angrily, his projected body working against his attempted rage. He placed his hands behind his head then looked back at me. "Tell me it's just for the sex. You don't really have feelings for him, right? You're just banging everybody here trying to give your hormones an outlet like Felicity is with all her late-night dates."

"Matthew!" I exclaimed, both shocked and angry at his words.

"What?!" he roared, louder than before.

"Enough!" Claire cried out, raising both her arms up. Matthew disappeared, and I stared at the empty spot he had just been. "Sorry. I just couldn't let him keep yelling. He was going to get us caught."

"It's okay," I responded. I rubbed my hand across my face as I mentally beat myself up. "I really screwed up, didn't I?"

"Nah, we all have urges we need filled. Hell, I would've jumped on that one a *long* time ago," she joked with a grin that didn't quite reach her eyes. That stunt with the shampoo had really drained her.

"You should go back too," I told her. "You look awful."

"Thanks so much," she replied sarcastically. "But you're right. I can't stay much longer. I need to tell you what the council decided first though. They're coming here."

"They are?" I asked, not sure if I should be relieved or more worried.

"Yeah. It was a really difficult decision, but they all realized a surprise attack is going to be their only upper hand this time around. I'm supposed to bring Adriana to talk to you tomorrow, but I probably won't have the strength to. I'll try to bring her the day after though."

"Talk to me about what?"

"A strategy for your and the trainees' safety."

"Oh. Well, we've already started mapping out the castle for escape routes."

"Good. Buckle down on that. You won't have time to do anything else."

I paused, the one question I hadn't asked now unavoidable. "How long do we have?"

Her face turned grim as her tired eyes met mine. "One week."

Chapter Thirty-Eight

I exited my room after Claire left, too wound up to be alone. Emotions ran wild inside me as my thoughts were torn between Ben, Matthew, Alexander, and the suddenly all too real battle.

"Hey!" Mallory called out.

I turned around to see her stomping towards me, her face in its usual down turned expression. "What, Mallory?" I asked, not in the mood for her antics.

"What did you do to Alexander?"

That stopped me cold. "W-what do you mean?"

"He's pissed. He's in his room throwing a temper tantrum, and you were just with him, right?" She crossed her arms as she waited for my answer.

"Yeah. But I didn't do anything to make him mad."

Did I? Was he mad about what happened between us? Maybe that it got cut short?

"Doubtful. Go fix it."

"Excuse me?"

"Go. Fix. It. Before I have to listen to him all night long."

"There's nothing to fix!" I exclaimed. "Besides, I'm busy."

I turned back around and started walking away from her, but she quickly followed. "Where are you going?"

"To see the trainees."

"You're not allowed to."

"Says who?"

"Toshiro."

"Well, he's not here, is he?"

"He will be when I go get him."

I stopped and sighed. "Then go get him Mallory. We're testing out one of Andre's premonitions. I'm sure he'd love to see." Mallory eyed me and pursed her lips as she contemplated my words, but I didn't have the patience to wait for her to decide her next course of action, so I walked past her again. "Bye, Mallory."

I heard her muttering a slew of insults behind me, but I ignored them. When I reached the trainees' rooms, I nodded at the guards in greeting then knocked on the girls' door.

When Emery answered I asked, "Has everyone already seen Nedra?"

"Yeah, we're all in one piece again," she replied.

"Good. Let's go to the boys' room."

"Uhm, they're really not supposed to mingle," one of the guards spoke up hesitantly.

I looked at him with narrowed eyes, and he diverted his gaze to the ground. "They mingle all day every day in training and at meals. What's the difference?"

"They aren't supposed to be unattended," the guard replied.

"They aren't unattended. They're with me. Unless you think I'm nobody?"

The guard squirmed, clearly uncomfortable. "No, of course not."

"Then don't question me," I told him in my best authoritative tone.

"Of course. My apologies."

"Come on," I told Emery and Kodi, who had come up behind us.

"That was awesome," Emery whispered in my ear as I knocked on the boys' door. Instead of waiting for anyone to answer, I opened it and walked in, my patience thin. Andre sat up on his bed and Toby and Mateo looked up from their game on the ground.

"Come in," Mateo called out, and I made a face at him.

"I wouldn't mess with her right now," Kodi playfully warned him. "She seems a little . . . On edge."

"Why? Are you okay?" Toby asked as I sat on the edge of one of the beds.

"I'm fine," I assured him, but he came and sat next to me anyway. "But more importantly, how are all of you?"

"As good as new," Mateo answered, flexing his now fixed arm.

"That healing process is really something," Andre added, rolling his once hurt foot around.

Emery climbed onto the bed next to him and crossed her legs. "Yeah, I haven't felt this good in years."

"Same," Kodi agreed as she plopped onto the floor next to Mateo who scoffed at her.

"You barely had a scratch on you," he told her, and she nodded in agreement.

"Yeah . . . I *was* pretty much a badass, wasn't I?" she said to him with a sly grin, and he pushed her over as she laughed.

"What's wrong?" Toby asked, his eyes never leaving my face.

"A lot," I admitted in a whisper, and I closed my eyes to fight away the tears that threatened to come. When I opened them again, everyone was staring at me in concern. "Garridan is planning a surprise attack one week from today."

"One week?" Kodi repeated, all hints of humor gone in her small voice, and I nodded.

I watched as all their faces shifted, mostly to fear. We all knew this was coming, but it was different now. It was real. I knew they needed words of reassurance, and I struggled to get past my own anxiety-ridden thoughts to give them some.

"I know this is a really scary situation guys," I started, grabbing Toby's hand in my own. "And it's okay to be scared. *I'm* scared. But we've been training for this. We have a lot of skills between the six of us and there are lots of people who are going to be watching out for us to help. We're going to be okay. We're going to get through this." I pulled the map out of my pocket and held it up as I looked at Mateo. "I know it's a lot to ask but I need you to map everything out tonight if you can. Every single way out of here needs to be on there."

"I'll get it done," he said and held out his hands as I tossed the map to him. "I'll bring it back to you tomorrow."

"No. Keep it with you," I instructed. "Take turns memorizing it. We don't know what's going to happen, but I assume all obvious points of entry will be heavily guarded, and we can't risk getting stuck in here. If Garridan loses, we'll be on our own to run fast and far."

"Okay, so, I think we should play 'what if' for a minute here so we can have general plans for certain scenarios" Andre spoke up.

"Okay," I agreed.

"What if Garridan attacks and Toshiro decides to lock us all up in different places?" Andre asked.

"Well . . . first and foremost, we'll all have to find a way out of wherever we're locked up," I answered. "I doubt we'd know where the others were, so we'd all have to be able to escape on our own."

"We should have a meeting place then," Emery said. "That way we'll all be able to find each other in case that happens."

"That's a good idea," Mateo told her.

"I agree," I chimed in, my mind already spinning on where it could be. "There's this little room full of old artifacts on the east side of the castle. It's secluded and the few times I've walked around, no one has ever been over there."

"I'll find it and mark it on the map," Mateo promised.

"On that note, what if not everyone makes it?" Kodi asked. "How long do we wait before leaving?"

We all exchanged looks.

"I guess that's going to be up to whoever is there," I answered. "You're going to have to decide what's best for you and your chance of escaping."

"I don't like that idea," Toby murmured.

"None of us do," Andre told him. "But it's a possible reality we might have to face. I'd rather get four of us out than none of us."

"Me too," Emery agreed.

I could tell Kodi and Mateo didn't agree but they stayed quiet, probably knowing this wasn't the time to argue about it.

"What if Garridan *does* lose? Where do we run?" Toby asked.

"If that happens, you can go anywhere you want," I replied, pausing before speaking the rest, "except home. The Cyfrin will look for you there first, and you'll just put your families in danger."

"What's to say they won't go after them anyway?" Mateo asked, his voice panicked, and I rubbed my lips together.

"They might," I admitted quietly. "But if you go there, they will for sure."

"¡Pinche mierda!" he yelled, running his hands through his hair. His family meant so much to him. I knew how it felt for the people you loved to be in danger, but there was no way for me to ease that feeling for him.

"Hopefully it won't come to that," I said, and Kodi wrapped her arm around him. "But, also, if it does, you can't use your powers. Ever. Otherwise, Arthur will be led straight to you again."

"I don't like that 'what if' either," Toby muttered.

"None of us do, Toby!" Emery exclaimed. "None of us like any of them. Just suck it up."

"Emery," Andre said in a warning tone, shaking his head at her, and she sighed.

"I'm sorry, okay? But I'm not going to baby him," she said, looking to Toby. "This is real life. We're going to see some awful things and you can't shut down or cry. You can't make yourself a liability because it could cause one of us to get hurt or die."

"Emery," Andre said again.

"No, it's okay," Toby told him. "She's right. I needed to hear that." He looked over at her and smiled sadly. "Thank you."

She responded with her own sad smile and nodded once.

"So what's next then?" Toby asked. "What if . . .?"

"What if Emery or Toby or Mateo are on the battlefield?" Kodi asked.

I took a deep breath before answering. "I don't know."

"It won't be good," Andre said.

"Stay safe and get out," Emery said with a shrug. "Try to meet you guys at the meeting spot. Or die."

Silence stretched on as a curtain of doom enveloped us. My stomach churned as anxiety threatened to overwhelm me. "Anymore 'what ifs'?" I asked.

Everyone shook their heads, and I knew we were all trying to process the impending possibility of our demise.

"We're all going to be okay," I said quietly, trying to convince myself as much as I was them. "We're all going to be just fine."

Chapter Thirty-Nine

I was the last one seated around the table because I had been waiting for Alexander. He always stopped by my room so we could walk to breakfast together, but not today. Today, he was already there. The trainees were silent as always but everyone else was jubilant. Everyone except Alexander. I watched him from the corner of my eye as he stared at the wall, stone faced.

"Good morning," I greeted him to which he gave the smallest nod of the head. I furrowed my brows. We always conversed before Toshiro began his speeches. "Is something wrong?"

"No," he replied.

"Are you sure?"

"Yes."

"Ignore him," Isaac told me from across the table. "He's been like that all morning."

"Someone is back to his old mood swings," Monique added in with a sly grin.

Alexander yanked a knife from the table and hurled it in her direction. With catlike reflexes, she turned her arm into a metal shield and the knife bounced right off it with a loud clang.

"Aht, aht, aht," she tsked as most of the table filled with laughter. "Gotta be faster than that."

Our food was presented to us then, so I focused on it as Mallory and Arthur got into an argument. I stole glances at Alexander, but he never met my gaze nor added into the conversation. My throat grew dry as I thought of our interaction last night. Had it really been that bad for him?

"We have a busy week ahead of us," Toshiro suddenly announced, and everyone instantly quieted down. "Lots of battle prep."

My attention was immediately captured by those words. "We'll be working long and hard with every Cyfrin member to ensure we maximize all our talents in our favor. I need you all focused, and I expect each of you to help me make this prep time invaluable. Also," his eyes skirted over to the trainees, "our trainees. We'll be cluing you in on our plans and what we expect from you. Some of you will play a vital role in this operation. Alexander has kept me up to date on your progress since the beginning, but today I'll be seeing your power levels for myself, just as I saw your hand-to-hand combat yesterday . . . Well, that's all. You may all be excused."

The trainees, Alexander, and I stood to head for the training room as we did every morning after breakfast. When we were out of sight of the dining room, I grabbed Alexander's arm and pulled him into a corner.

"*What* are you doing?" he hissed as he pulled away from me.

"What are *you* doing?" I asked. "Why are you shutting me out? Why are you so angry?"

He glared at a spot above my head and remained silent. I rubbed my lips together, thinking of Mallory's words the night before.

"Was . . . was it me? I mean . . ." I looked down at my feet, embarrassed. "Was it because of last night? Are you mad about what happened between us? Was it . . . *Bad* for you?"

He finally looked at me, his eyes gentler than they had been a moment ago. "You think I'm upset about what happened between us?"

"I mean . . . Yeah, maybe. I don't know."

"Robin," he put his finger under my chin and pushed my head up so I was looking at him. "I am in no way upset about that. And it most definitely wasn't *bad* for me. Quite the opposite actually. It was one of the best moments I've had in a very long time."

"Yeah?" I asked, an annoying giddiness filling me at his words.

"Yeah," he reassured me with a miniscule smile.

"Then what *is* wrong?"

He pressed his lips together and dropped his hand away from me. "I can't tell you that. But I'll find a way to get over it. Just . . . give me some time to be angry."

He stalked past me, nearly bumping my shoulder, and I turned to watch him go as confusion took center place again. I grunted in frustration and muttered to myself as I followed him into the training room. He was standing in front of the trainees, his eyes skimming over them unhappily, and I realized I wouldn't have any time to talk to them.

"You know what happened yesterday, expect worse today," he told them. "Don't let your guard down or else you *will* die . . . Good luck."

As if on cue, Toshiro came through the doors with the same people following that did yesterday. He had changed out of his morning suit into workout clothes again, and he looked like a kid hyped up on sugar.

"Ready?" he asked happily, and Alexander nodded. "Rankings please."

"Kodi, Andre, Mateo, Toby, Emery," Alexander answered.

"You know the drill," Toshiro said. "Step on up."

I swallowed loudly, my nerves getting the best of me as I watched Kodi walk in front of him. She, too, looked nervous as did the other trainees. She could hold her own in a physical fight any day, but she had no chance against someone in a power battle, let alone someone whose powers were so strong. It didn't seem fair for Toshiro to even bring her up when he knew he was going to demolish her.

"Aren't you going to do anything?" he taunted as he walked around her and brought in small breezes. "Call in the attack dogs? Maybe a lion or two? Oh, wait." He laughed merrily before staring her down and strengthening the wind. "There's no animals around here."

He whipped one arm out, bringing with it a blast of air that knocked Kodi off her feet. He stood above her, and I could feel the air that radiated off her as it pressed her into the ground. She let out a small whimper of pain, desperately struggling to get free, when something crawled over my feet. I took a step back and gasped as an army of rats stampeded across the floor and found their way onto Toshiro's legs.

Toshiro looked down at the feeling, and a shrill scream escaped his mouth as the rats clung to him and made their way further up his body. He continued to shriek, whipping his arms around wildly as he tried to throw the rats off of himself, and I couldn't help but let out a laugh at the sight. Almost immediately, a large leaf covered my mouth. I ripped it off and looked at Alexander. He shook his head, a warning to shut up. Toshiro's face grew angry. He turned to Kodi, who was grinning on the floor, and reached up before slamming a huge gust of air into her. Her head wacked the ground but Toshiro didn't stop. He did it once again and Kodi was knocked unconscious as a small trickle of blood escaped her nose and ears. The rats quickly dispersed, but Toshiro went to hit Kodi again.

"Isaac!" Alexander called out, and Isaac quickly quenched Toshiro's powers.

Toshiro whirled on Alexander, his eyes crazy. "How dare you!"

"You told me not to let you kill them," Alexander replied calmly.

Toshiro moved his jaw side to side, and I could see him biting his inner lip, as if it was a way to regain his composure. After a moment he said, "You're right, I did. Thank you." He took one last look at Kodi before huffing out a breath. "Get her off my mat. Next, please."

Alexander pulled Kodi's limp body from the floor and surprisingly gently passed her off to Mateo and Toby. Toby held her head in his lap as Andre stepped up to Toshiro.

"Afraid of rats?" Andre asked, and Alexander lowered his head into his palm as Toshiro narrowed his eyes.

Without missing a beat, Toshiro swept his hands across where Andre stood, but he was no longer there. Each time Toshiro hit a spot, Andre was already two steps ahead as he predicted what was going to happen.

"You can run," Toshiro muttered, "but not far or fast enough."

He circled his hands around, creating a wind funnel around himself. Even on the back wall, I could feel its pull. Mallory grabbed onto my arm, nearly swept up in it, and it took everything in me not to push her off and give her to the mercy of Toshiro's powers. Everyone seemed to grab onto something to hold them in place as Toshiro sped it up, creating more of a pull. Andre quickly got picked up in it. His feet left the ground, and he was being tossed around close to the ceiling as Toshiro smirked. All at once, the wind stopped, and Andre fell to the floor with a loud thud. He groaned as he attempted to push himself up, but Toshiro took the opportunity to fling his powerful gusts into him and trapped him where he lay as he had just done to Kodi.

More in control this time, Toshiro stopped without hurting him further and said, "Next."

With some effort, Andre slowly rose to his feet and stumbled to the bench on the wall. Mateo took his place, his fingers twitching at his sides. In one fluid motion he sunk down onto all fours, his hands and feet disappearing with paws taking their place as he shifted into a snarling Doberman. He bared his teeth at Toshiro before his body grew twice as large, his dark fur replaced by a copper mane and his teeth sharpened and dripping with drool. He was a lion. I realized he was playing on Toshiro's earlier words to Kodi.

With an ear shattering roar, he jumped at Toshiro, knocking him to the ground and swiping his massive paw against his chest. Toshiro hissed as blood gushed from his open wounds. He held his hands up as Mateo swiped again but his paws never made contact. He tried again but every time he came near Toshiro, his paws seemed to ricochet.

"What's he doing?" I asked more to myself than anyone else.

"Concussive force," Monique replied as Mateo was thrown into the wall with such strength the stonework broke away.

Mateo got up, shaking out his mane before growing into a massive, wrinkly elephant that towered over us all. He charged Toshiro but Toshiro was ready with another powerful tactic. The air rippled around Mateo, and I could literally see it move as it began to shrink around him, encasing him in a box that he couldn't escape from. He rammed the sides, over and over, but he was stuck.

"Before I show you what more can come of this deadly skill, let's move on," Toshiro said, dropping the box from around Mateo.

Mateo shifted back into his normal form, his face unhappy as he stomped to the bench. I didn't care that he was angry; I was just happy he hadn't been seriously injured. It didn't matter that he could've been healed. Toshiro had already lost his temper once and nearly killed Kodi. I didn't want to see that again, so my heart pounded loudly as I watched Toby step up to Toshiro.

Toshiro immediately threw a powerful gust of wind his way, but Toby pulled up the metal from the workout equipment and stretched it out so it blocked the attempt. Toshiro continued to send waves of air his way, but Toby kept his makeshift shield in front of him as he walked, making sure he couldn't be touched as the rest of us got the aftermath of the bouncing wind. Toby drew more metal from around the room but instead of bringing it to him, he cast it at Toshiro, warping it to his body. Toshiro yelled profanities as Toby lined every inch of him with the alloy before completely covering his face as well. We could hear Toshiro's muffled voice as Toby looked around his wall.

"Did I just win?" he asked in disbelief, as I exchanged perplexed looks with the trainees.

"I wouldn't be so sure," Alexander told him as he watched Toshiro's statue.

His tone made all of us follow his gaze, and silence filled the room as we all waited for something to happen. I cleared my throat, then did it again when I got no relief. Everyone around me began doing the same thing. The air grew thinner, and my ears plugged up. Suddenly, all the metal around Toshiro ripped apart with a deafening screech that set me on edge. Pieces of the sharp, shattered substance hurtled towards everyone in the room, but Toby quickly stopped them all, throwing them to the ground before anyone could be hurt. Except himself. A strange gurgling noise escaped his mouth as his hand covered his throat. He took one step forward before falling to his side.

"Toby! I cried out, running over, and sliding onto my knees next to him. Emery and Mateo came up beside me with horrified expressions. Blood spilled over his neck onto the floor, and I quickly pressed my hands into the wound. "Somebody do something!"

"Let us take him," Isaac told me. "We'll get him to Nedra" He placed a piece of cloth over the wound, and I backed away as one of the women who had been watching lifted Toby with ease. They quickly left the room as I stared after them in shock.

"He's gonna be okay, right?" Mateo asked.

I swallowed around the lump in my throat. "He better be."

"And then there was one," Toshiro said from behind us. I turned towards him and saw deep red marks all over his body. The metal must've hurt him after all. "Robin, why don't you go clean that blood off yourself."

"I'm good, thanks," I replied with a voice like steel.

"It really is quite a disarming look on you," he pressed.

My eyes narrowed into slits as they met his humorous ones. Without looking away, I conjured up some water and shoved my hands into it, letting it wash away Toby's blood. He smirked at my show, and I dropped the water to the ground.

"Happy?"

"Someone is testy," he murmured playfully.

"Emery," I said quietly as I walked by her. "Electrify him, would you?"

"My pleasure," Emery replied with a wicked smirk.

When we were all back in our spectator positions, Emery held out her hands. The bright light of the electricity she created was blinding and I could feel my hairs standing on end. She brought her hands together, generating more energy that she wound into a tight ball. All the while, Toshiro stood still with a grin playing at his lips. Emery conducted the energy throughout the room, being careful not to electrify anyone as she made a scene of how vast her abilities were. Bolts of electricity bounced off the walls and into her body, causing her to almost glow. When she was satisfied with how much pent-up energy she had, she thrust her arms out in front of her, letting the electricity travel out of her fingertips straight towards Toshiro.

Toshiro barely blinked as he held up his hands, the electricity never touching him. His hair rose above his head and his palms blackened as if touched by soot, but he stayed upright and unharmed. After a moment of anticlimactic angst, Emery lowered her arms.

"How . . . How is that possible?" Emery stuttered, her voice small.

"Your powers are a match to almost everyone . . . except me," Toshiro answered, enjoying the dramatics of his words. "I learned to deal with electrokinesis a very long time ago, my dear."

"What did you do?" she asked, more shocked than I had ever seen her.

"I created an airtight wall of wind that worked as an insulator for your electricity. It can't get out, and it can't harm me more than this." He motioned to his hands. "That was quite a show though. Next time, it'll kill hundreds."

He turned to Alexander and pointed to Kodi and Andre. "Get those two fixed up. Then teach them all who they do and don't have a chance against. Tomorrow, we'll go over our battle plan with them."

Without another word, he left the room the same way he had yesterday. I met Emery's questioning gaze, and knew exactly what she was thinking: Was Toshiro unbeatable? Surely not . . . He just needed to go up against the right opponent.

Chapter Forty

After lunch, and once Toby had been healed, I sat in the background of the library as Alexander coached the trainees. Books were scattered about, and whiteboards were a mess of charts as Alexander outlined which power sources the trainees could defeat and which they couldn't. I hung onto every word, knowing it was important information, but it was tedious and confusing. Someone could be more advanced than someone else with the exact same power which meant the trainees could defeat one but not another.

"Which also means you may or may not be able to defeat someone with the same power as you. For example," Alexander was saying as he looked my direction, "Robin's father possesses an air element power just like Toshiro. However, Toshiro is more skilled than Elijah which means he'd win in a fight."

"That's not true," I heard myself say, immediately defensive.

"You may not like it, but it is the truth," he replied. "Toshiro may not be *much* more powerful overall, but he possesses one skill that puts him over the edge of every other air element."

"And what would that be?" I challenged.

"Wouldn't you like to know," he murmured with a mischievous gleam in his eye. "Now, same as Toshiro is the most powerful air element, Mallory is one of the weaker fire elements. As you already know, her need for a source greatly cripples her abilities."

"What about you and Robin? Where do you stand?" Emery asked.

"We're both extremely powerful in our respected elements. I'm one of the top earth elements, but not quite the highest. However, Robin," he looked over at me with observant eyes, "I don't believe we've seen the extent of her powers just yet. I wouldn't be surprised if she was the most gifted water element our kind has seen in a very long time."

He held my gaze for a moment longer before going back to his lessons as I was left sitting there dumbfounded. Did he mean that? Was there really more that I hadn't discovered about myself yet? I guess time would tell.

The trainees, Alexander, and I spent the rest of the day in there. Dinner was brought to us, and Alexander didn't allow us to leave for any reason. By the time he let us out, we were all cranky, tense, and ready for bed. My head pounded against my skull as I trailed behind everyone going upstairs. It was late. Way later than I had stayed up since I had Kodi and Emery sleep over in my room, and I could feel the effects of it starting to hit me. Alexander glanced over his shoulder.

"Are you okay?" he asked when he saw me falling behind.

"Just tired. It's past my bedtime," I joked with a waning smile.

"That it is. I'll be sure Darnell goes to your room immediately," he replied, his voice professional and distant.

"You're still angry," I noted dejectedly.

"I am."

"Are you ever going to tell me why?"

"You'll know soon enough."

We walked the rest of the way to my room in silence. When I stopped at my door, he didn't join me like he usually did. Instead, he walked right by.

"Alexander," I called out. He paused but didn't turn around. "How long is it going to be like this?"

He was quiet for so long I didn't think he was going to answer. Eventually, though, he looked back at me. "Don't worry. Tomorrow I'll be back to my normal moody, brooding self."

"You're not brooding," I denied, and he cocked one eyebrow. I tried to hide the smile that wanted to creep onto my face. "Okay, maybe you are . . . But I don't mind."

"Which is one of the many things I like about you," he said. He turned back around but not before I saw a hint of sadness in his eyes. "Goodnight, Robin."

"Goodnight." I went into my room and straight to bed, fighting with my eyes to stay open until Darnell came. I didn't want any more nightmares than I already had, but sleep couldn't come fast enough.

* * *

I had just gotten out of the shower and was wiping the steam from the mirror. When I was able to look into it, I gasped and spun around as my hand flew up to my chest.

"You scared me!" I yelled in a whisper.

"Sorry," Claire replied with a grin, obviously finding joy in my heart attack. "But look who I brought."

She motioned towards the bathroom door, and I saw Adriana standing there with a soft smile on her face. My throat contracted as I ran over to her, swinging my arms up to wrap her in a hug. I fell straight through and banged my head against the wall instead.

"You know, I'm real tired of this crap," I muttered as Claire and Adriana tried to suppress their laughter. "I miss physical contact."

"Clearly," Claire said, and I shot her a look to which she merely winked at.

"How are you doing, sweetie?" Adriana asked, her bright blue eyes, my eyes, full of love.

"Better now that you're here," I told her, realizing just how much I missed her and Elijah. Tears formed in my eyes and, this time, I couldn't contain them. My chin began to quiver as the tears ran down my cheeks, and I let out a sob.

"Oh, honey," Adriana murmured, reaching out to me before realizing what she was doing and stopping. "It's okay. It's all going to be okay."

I leaned against the wall and shrank down to the ground as I let out a frustrated grunt. "That's what I keep telling the trainees, but we don't know that. None of us know that. Some of us could get really hurt. Some of us could *die*. I just . . . I just don't know what to do anymore. What if I can't protect them? W-what if Garridan loses? It may not be okay and I'm actually getting really tired of that word. This whole situation isn't okay, what's coming isn't okay, and . . . *I'm* not okay." My voice was thick as I continued to cry. "The whole world is in danger, Matthew hates me, Ben and Felicity are gone, Alexander is bipolar, the trainees are a huge responsibility and I'm just *not* okay. I'm *scared* . . . I just need my mom."

Adriana looked as miserable as I felt as I rested my chin against my knees. "I know you miss your mom. I wish she was here for you-"

"I was talking about you," I whispered.

She pressed her lips together as her own tears started flowing. "We are going to get you out of there," she said with confidence. "You and all the trainees. Garridan *will* win and you'll be back home where you belong. I'm so sorry you've had the weight of the world put on your shoulders Robin and it's okay to not be okay. You've been so strong these past months. I just need you to be strong for a few more days. Can you do that for me?" I nodded and she smiled proudly. She opened her mouth to say more but a sharp knock sounded from the door.

"Robin," Alexander said.

I looked at the clock; he was way earlier than usual.

"We'll come back and discuss battle plans," Adriana assured me. "I love you, Robin."

Another loud knock. "Robin."

"Just a minute!" I called out.

"Why? Are you hiding something?" he asked with venom in his voice.

I picked myself off the floor and marched to the door, flinging it open angrily. Alexander's narrowed eyes widened, not expecting to see me in a towel with tears running down my face.

"Do my puffy red eyes and snot covered face give you a hint about what I could've possibly been hiding?" I asked sarcastically.

"Uhm . . . That you were crying?" he answered hesitantly, my attitude throwing him off.

"Congratulations. Give the man a gold star. You're not a complete bonehead after all!" I yelled before slamming the door in his shocked face.

I went over to my bed and stretched out, burying my face in a pillow as I let all the emotions that had been piling up escape. I cried for the trainees and the way their lives had been ripped away from them. I cried for the people in the guard who were about to put their lives on the line. I cried for the world who had no idea what was going on. And I cried for myself. I cried for the people I had lost, for the people I wanted to desperately protect, and for the way my happy, normal life had been shattered. Even more than that, though, I cried for the things I knew I'd have to do soon enough.

When I couldn't cry any more, I stayed huddled on my bed feeling small and broken. A gentle knock reached my ears, but I ignored it. A moment later, Alexander peeked around the door.

"May I come in?" he asked.

"Why not?" I replied, my hoarse voice not portraying the sarcasm I had intended.

He walked in and shut the door with his foot, his hands carrying a tray. "I told Toshiro we wouldn't be joining them for breakfast today. I figured you needed some time to yourself, so I brought you some food to eat here if you like." He placed the tray down on the table by the couch, then turned to me with his hands in his pockets. "I wanted to apologize if I upset you earlier. I didn't mean to cause you any more distress than you were already feeling."

"It's okay," I told him, using that lie of a word again.

"Do you need anything?"

I looked away. "All I need is a hug from my mom."

Alexander came over to the side of the bed and pressed his lips together. "I'm not your mom but . . . I can still give pretty good hugs."

The words were strange coming from him, and it actually made me smile just a little before nodding. "I could use a good hug."

He sat on the edge of the bed then swung his legs up and leaned back against the wall. I scooted over to him, painfully aware that I was still wearing only a towel, and let him wrap his arms around me as I placed my head against his chest. He held me tightly, and I could feel myself starting to cry again. He ran his hand up and down my back as all the 'what ifs' began to hit me again. The only difference this time was now I didn't feel so small and broken. The simple act of having someone hold me made me feel a little more hopeful; like things could work out. Even if the person holding me was a big cause of all the 'what ifs', I still felt comforted. It didn't make much sense, but I was only human.

I wasn't sure how long we stayed like that, but eventually I glanced up and saw Alexander's eyes were closed.

"Are you asleep?" I asked quietly.

Without opening them, he said, "No. Just resting my eyes."

"Shouldn't we get down to the trainees?"

"Darnell and Arthur are with them."

"Why aren't Monique and Isaac?"

"They're with Toshiro and Mallory. They've started their meetings with all the Cyfrin members today."

"Oh."

He peeked one eye open. "Are you feeling better now?"

"A little bit . . . Thanks for sitting with me."

"Of course. What was wrong?"

"Just overwhelmed."

"With?"

"Everything," I admitted. "This isn't a life I'm used to. The idea of a battle is just . . . A lot to handle."

"Everything you're doing *is* a lot to handle," he agreed, an underlying meaning there that I couldn't figure out. After another minute of quiet, I sat up.

"I should get dressed," I said as I patted down my hair. "I can only imagine how crazy my hair looks."

"It looks great," Alexander told me with a smile as he stood.

"Whatever."

"No, really. I like your crazy hair. It suits you."

"Are you calling me crazy?" I asked, raising my brows.

"Maybe just a little," he replied with a grin. "Want me to wait for you?"

"Sure. I'll just get ready in the bathroom," I said as I went around and grabbed the clothes I needed.

"You can eat your food before we go down. I'm sure you're hungry."

Right on cue, my stomach grumbled. "I could eat."

After another quick smile his way, I went into the bathroom and shut the door. He was definitely in a better mood than he was yesterday. I appreciated his support, but it only made me wearier of our ever growing back and forth relationship. I missed my normal, uncomplicated, easy times with Ben.

Chapter Forty-One

Aside from a few bruises and bloody noses, the trainees were in one piece when we entered the training room. I couldn't say the same for Darnell and Arthur.

"Are you guys okay?" I asked as they hobbled to the doors.

"We'll live," Arthur huffed, walking past us without another word.

Darnell stopped and patted Alexander's shoulder. "You've got a good group here. You two have trained them well." He winced and grabbed his side. "Maybe a little too well."

Alexander looked to the trainees who sat lined against the wall as Darnell walked out. "Who did that?" he asked.

"It was a group effort," Emery answered smugly.

Alexander watched them for a minute then nodded his head. "Well done."

Kodi and Emery exchanged grins, obviously proud of themselves, so I suspected they did of the most damage.

"Let's move on," Alexander said. "Today you'll be learning the roll we expect you to play in our coming battle."

"Why now?" Andre asked. "You've been keeping it secret up to this point."

"Because we're making our move soon," he replied, "and you all need to be ready and appropriately . . . *Motivated* to comply."

Despite knowing Garridan was going to attack first, his words still made my stomach drop.

"What do you mean by '*motivated*'?" Kodi asked with narrowed eyes.

"You all have people in your lives you care about. Just remember that," was Alexander cryptic response.

Daggers were thrown at him from every set of eyes in the room, including my own. Kodi put her hand on Mateo's arm as he took a step forward. He looked back at her, and she shook his head at him. After a minute he leaned back against the wall, his face full of anger.

"So what are our roles?" Andre asked, crossing his arms.

"Glad you asked," Alexander said. "First and foremost, Emery." We all looked to her, and she raised her chin as she stared him down. "You're going to be playing the biggest role in all of this, but you all already know that, right?"

His eyes traveled over the trainees as they held expressions of faked confusion or blank stares before he looked over to me and repeated himself. "Right?"

"I don't know what you're talking about," I told him, keeping my own expression neutral.

"Yes, you do. You all do. So why don't you just stop lying?" When I didn't say anything, he continued, "I know Andre had a premonition about it."

"How did you know that?" Toby asked incredulously, and I shot him a look as Alexander grimaced.

"I had a hunch," he explained dryly. "I didn't know for certain . . . until just now."

Toby bit his bottom lip, his eyes shooting back and forth as we all gave him varying looks of disappointment, disbelief, and anger. He looked down, ashamed, and I made a mental note to make sure he wasn't too hard on himself later.

"How did you even get a hunch like that?" I asked quietly, bothered by how much he always seemed to catch onto. It made me question how effective we had been with our sneaking around and my meetings with Claire. If he knew about that, though, he would've gone to Toshiro immediately and I would've been thrown in the torture chamber.

"Since we were trying to advance Andre's capabilities, Arthur has been monitoring his energy waves. Every time he has a premonition, we know. And since he's been telling us every premonition he's had for training purposes, I knew something was off when Arthur registered one that he didn't report. It didn't make sense for him to hide it, so, naturally, I assumed it was something he shouldn't have known."

"That seems like a far stretch to jump to," Kodi muttered, crossing her arms.

"Yet, that's exactly what it was," Alexander shot back. "So would you like to fess up to anything else before getting caught red-handed again?"

I shot the trainees a hard look to make sure none of them slipped up again. "That was it."

He turned to me with a blank stare. "Are you sure?"

"Yes, and I don't see what the big deal is anyway," I said as he raised his brows at me. "Not like we could do anything with any information."

He eyed me for a minute too long, making me squeamish. "No," he finally said. "I suppose not. Let's move on then."

I breathed a sigh of relief. My heart was pounding in my chest at how close he dipped into everything we had been planning and doing. If that was the only thing he knew, though, it was fine. That meant we were still safe.

"Toby and Mateo, you will both be expected to fight in the front lines. If you die while helping us, it's no loss to us. However, if you live while defying us, you'll *wish* you had been killed during the battle." Toby looked fear stricken and it took everything in me not to go comfort him. Mateo still looked pissed, and I just hoped he'd stay in line and not make things worse for himself. "Andre and Kodi, you'll both be kept here. You serve no purpose to us in battle, and you'll be expected to make up for it."

"What do you mean 'serve no purpose'?" Kodi asked rudely. "We're the best hand-to-hand combat people in this room."

"That may be true, but at the end of the day this is a power battle and nothing less," Alexander told her coldly as he began to pace in front of them. "Putting you two out there would be a waste of bodies and space."

"Then why have we been training so hard?" Kodi placed her hands on her hips, her eyes showing her anger as she scowled. "Why have we learned all this crap if you knew it was all for nothing? You knew it was pointless from the beginning!"

Alexander stopped in front of her and folded his arms over his chest. "Yes. It doesn't matter how physically strong you are, if your powers aren't worthwhile, you're *nothing* here. You're no better than a regular human. You. Are. *Nothing*."

Kodi reached up and slapped Alexander across the face, the sound echoing through the silent room as we stared at her in shock. Alexander moved his jaw around before turning his gaze back to her, his eyes blazing. Kodi reached up to her chest, her face now panicked as she clawed at her skin. She began gasping for air, then dry heaved as she fell to her knees.

"No!" Mateo cried out, but Alexander lifted his hand and encased him in thick vines, thrusting him into the wall before completely swallowing his body so he couldn't escape no matter how small he made himself.

Andre and Emery stepped forward and Toby reached out to Kodi, but Alexander was on a war path. He stretched the vines over Toby, pulling him into the same crippling fate as Mateo. Then he split the floor beneath Andre and Emery. Andre immediately side stepped it, but Emery fell through and clung to the side as she tried to keep herself from slipping further in. Andre launched himself at Alexander, but Alexander was ready. He clotheslined Andre then kicked him in the stomach before making him choke just like Kodi was.

As I watched the scene unfold, my anger manifested a seed inside me. The more Alexander hurt them, the bigger it grew. It attached itself to the root of my powers, latching on in a pronounced display of authority.

"Enough!" I screamed as this newfound feeling pushed up and out my fingertips.

Without having to concentrate to manifest it like I usually did, the water came all on its own, springing from the force of my hands in a vigorous line. The jet stream pierced Alexander, cutting straight through his skin and out of his back. He dropped his hands, staggering back as Kodi, Andre, Toby, and Mateo were freed from his powers. Mateo and Toby went to Emery, pulling her to safety, as I moved the water up and out of Alexander's shoulder. He yelled as it sliced cleanly through the bone, and blood poured from his now open wound. I lowered my hands as he pushed into his upper arm to create pressure on the wound. He stared at me, his eyes wide, as I looked at my hands in disbelief.

What was that and where did it come from?

"Are you guys okay?" I asked the trainees without looking up.

"All good," Kodi croaked.

"Good, good," I murmured distractedly. "Uhm . . . What the hell was that?"

"Pressurized water," Alexander answered, wincing as he walked closer to me.

"What?"

"Have you ever heard of abrasive jet technology?"

"No."

"It's basically technology that uses highly pressurized water to cut through materials like wood and metal," he explained as he stared at me.

"Okay . . ." I said slowly, not understanding. "And?"

"And that's what you just did!" he clarified urgently.

"So you're saying Robin can cut through metal or wood with her water?" Toby asked, summing it up for the rest of us.

"Or bone," Alexander confirmed with a grimace.

"That's . . . Crazy," I finally decided on as the trainees watched me with awed expressions.

"That it is," Alexander agreed, sounding just as impressed as they looked. "It's not a very common ability . . . I knew we weren't done seeing you grow yet."

A small smile played at his lips, and he looked at me like there was more he wanted to say, but he let out a groan instead as more blood spilled down his arm.

"You should really go get that healed," I told him.

"I think you're right," he mumbled. "Trainees, join me."

"What? Why?" Emery asked in a huff.

"Because I said so."

"You just tried to kill us," Mateo accused, crossing his arms.

"If I wanted you dead, you'd be dead," Alexander replied with malice. "I was simply teaching you a lesson like I'm about to do now. Nedra has seen many things in her time. When you've been with her before, you've been the ones being healed. This time, you can watch the process and ask questions. Now, let's go."

The trainees reluctantly followed with low mumbles of hatred. Andre hung back, his face gentle.

"Are you okay?" he asked me.

"I should be asking you that," I told him. "You're the one who had a flower wrapped around your heart."

"I think it was one of those vines actually," he joked, and I couldn't help but smile. "But seriously. Are you okay?"

"I'm . . . Shocked," I admitted. "I just maimed Alexander's arm. I could've cut him in half. That's insane and . . . Terrifying. But at the same time, I never felt so strong. It was like *I* was finally the one in control. If I had pierced him in his heart, he'd be dead."

"Two very opposite feelings," Andre noted.

"They definitely are. I mean, this could give me the chance to actually help Garridan; to help all of you."

"Having the power to kill someone . . . That's a heavy responsibility."

"It is," I took a deep breath, unhappy with the idea. "But is it so different than having a gun or knife and using it to kill someone?"

"No. I suppose it's not. But what does that have to do with this?" Andre asked.

I stayed quiet for a moment before answering. "Because I would never kill someone if I had a weapon in my hands so why would I use this to do the same? Don't get me wrong, I'll use it to help us all get out, but just as a deterrent. Like a bullet hole to the leg. But killing someone . . . It's never going to be an option. That's not who I am, and it never will be."

"You'd be surprised what you're willing to do when the life of someone you love hangs in the balance," he pointed out softly.

"That's true but . . . Every moment of every day, we get to choose who we are and who we want to be. If you cross that line, you'll never come back from it, and I won't compromise myself like that." Andre watched me with a look I couldn't distinguish. "What?" I questioned.

"A lot of the time I forget how young you are," he said. "You're wiser than most people your age, and you hold the weight of the world on your shoulders like it's nothing. I don't know how you do it."

If only you knew.

"This whole situation sucks but I'm thankful to have someone like you fighting on my side," he continued.

I pressed my lips together, his words warming my heart. This is why I stayed strong. This is why I was fighting. For them. I wrapped him in my arms, hugging him tight. "Thank you."

* * *

I was sitting in the library, aimlessly leafing through a history book as I waited for everyone to get back. The door creaked open and looked up to see Alexander. He had changed out of his bloodied clothes and seemed to be in one piece.

"What's the prognosis?" I asked as he walked over.

"Nothing short of a miracle," he joked. "Doc said I've already made a full recovery. I'll live to see another day."

"I'm glad."

"Are you?" he questioned as he sat across from me.

I furrowed my brows, his comment catching me off guard. "Of course. Why wouldn't I be?"

He shrugged. "Seems like me dying would be better for you overall."

"I won't lie, it would make some things easier," I said quietly. "But I don't want you to die, Alexander. Not today, not in the battle, not anytime soon."

He looked away, and I couldn't tell what he was thinking as he sat there silently. Finally, he leaned over and grabbed my hand. He brought it up to his lips, kissing it gently, and flutters swam through my stomach.

"I hope you know," he paused and swallowed, "I'm not looking forward to what's going to happen next."

"You mean you being a part of a war that could destroy everything good in this world?"

"Yeah. That."

I hesitated for a minute then said, "I'm sorry I hurt you. I didn't mean to."

"Yes, you did. You were trying to protect them."

"I mean, yeah . . . But I didn't mean to almost cut your arm off."

His lip lifted in a half smile. "No, I bet you didn't. That's a very strong gift you've acquired. Toshiro is extremely pleased by that development in your powers."

"I'm sure he is," I said with a roll of my eyes.

"It really is impressive. I don't know of another water element who can do that."

"You did say I was special," I said, trying to take the edge off the conversation.

"And I was right." He stared at me for a moment then stood. "Let's get back to training."

I pushed myself off the couch. "Only if you promise not to try to kill any of the trainees again," I told him as we began walking to the door.

"They deserved it."

"Okay," I muttered.

"She slapped me, Robin. *Slapped* me. She couldn't even give me the courtesy of a punch." His low voice was layered with anger, and I bit my lip to keep from smiling. "Oh, you think that's funny?"

"Yeah, actually, I do," I replied, letting the grin cover my face.

He made a face at me, the look so unnatural on him that I began laughing. He scowled and bumped my shoulder with his own, only making me laugh louder. As he watched me, a smile crept onto his face then he interlaced his fingers in mine. The gesture quickly sobered up my giggles and I glanced up at him.

He squeezed my hand and, after a moment, I squeezed back. The exchange was simple. To anyone else it would look meaningless, but, to me, it spoke loudly. He was dealing with a lot of mixed emotions under that hard facade. Maybe I still had a chance of getting him on our side after all.

Chapter Forty-Two

"Alexander told me a very interesting story yesterday," Toshiro informed us as we sat around the table. "It seems our Keeper of Balance here has developed a new skill. Robin, would you be a dear and demonstrate for us?"

"Oh, uh," I looked around at all the intrigued faces. "I don't want to break anything."

"Pish posh!" Toshiro laughed. "Our stuff gets damaged and replaced ten times a week. Break anything you like."

"Okay," I said slowly. I glanced around the room for something to target when my eyes landed on the armor in the corner behind Toshiro.

Perfect.

I stood and searched around for the feeling I had yesterday. When I locked onto it, it lit a fire inside me and I thrust my hands forward. The flow of it leaving my fingertips was all consuming and the water easily sliced through the metal on contact. With deep concentration, I moved the jet stream down, cutting past the helmet until the whole suit was in two pieces that clattered on the ground.

"Amazing," Toshiro murmured, his usual giddy attitude replaced by pure amazement. "Have any of you ever seen such power?"

"Uh, yeah," Mallory said in a 'duh' tone.

"Well, obviously, but I meant have you ever seen it shown in such a way?" he corrected himself. "I've never witnessed such power from a water element. There's very little they can actually accomplish but this . . . It's a whole new outlook on them."

I let his jab about my element pass, even though I wanted to call him out on it.

"Haven't there been water elements before who've been able to do this?" I asked as I sat back down.

"Oh, yes," he replied. "But none in my lifetime. I don't think there's been someone with that capability for . . . My I don't even know. Arthur?"

"About a hundred years," Arthur answered, the go to guru for all things power related.

"So why can I do it then?" I questioned, my curiosity piqued. "What determines someone's strength within their power?"

"Genetics, character, determination," Arthur shrugged. "No one really knows."

"No matter what the cause, we're just thankful to have the most powerful water element of our time on our side," Toshiro commented, a bite in his voice I didn't understand.

"It really is incredible," Monique spoke up, and I looked across the table to see Darnell and Isaac nodding in agreement.

"Our little Robin is amounting to great things," Isaac added, throwing a wink in my direction.

"Which just means we'll be keeping an extra close eye on her," Toshiro said.

My brows furrowed, his demeanor setting me on edge. I glanced over at Andre, the only trainee paying close attention, and he barely lifted one shoulder. He could sense something was off too.

"I wonder," Toshiro continued, "how much control of it do you actually have though? No one can argue the greatness of it, but do you really have the skill to use it? Are you really worthy of such a gift?"

"Even if I wasn't, you couldn't very well take it away from me," I replied with narrowed eyes.

He smiled maliciously. "Can't I?"

I looked at Alexander, but he didn't show any indication of what I should be doing. When I brought my gaze back to Toshiro, his eyes were dancing.

"Maybe you should prove you deserve it," he said.

"What do you mean?"

"Prove that you can use it for what it's best meant for. What will benefit us the most from it," he replied cryptically. As I watched his smug face, it finally dawned on me what he meant—use my powers to kill.

"No," I said.

"Do it, Robin," he urged, his low hiss of a voice reminding me of a snake. "When are you going to prove you're willing to do the hard things for us? Do it. *Do it*!"

I swept my hand forward. The water that erupted from me barely grazed his cheek, creating the tiniest cut that drew blood. He didn't even flinch as I stared him down.

"I said *no*." My voice was steel as rage brewed inside me.

Toshiro stared at me through narrowed eyes, his lips almost pouty as he scowled at me. "You'll get what's coming to you soon enough."

"What's that supposed to mean?" I questioned but he ignored me. Instead, he stood and left the room, quickly followed by Mallory and Arthur.

"Finish eating," Alexander instructed. "We have training to get to."

The rest of the meal passed in silence as I mulled over my exchange with Toshiro. The whole conversation had me on edge, all his words seeming to have deeper meaning that I couldn't decipher. When everyone had finished eating, we stood up to go to the training room. I quickly caught up to Andre.

"That was weird, right?" I asked quietly, not wanting Alexander to overhear.

"Something definitely didn't feel right," he agreed.

"Alexander was acting off the other day too," I told him. "He said he was just angry about something but . . . It felt like more."

"Do you think they're up to something?"

"They're always up to something. But I kind of have a bad feeling about it all right now."

"Why's that?"

"I'm not sure . . . Maybe I'm just overreacting because Garridan is attacking so soon."

"Could be," he agreed, "but usually our instincts aren't so far off."

"What could they be planning though?"

"I wish I knew."

"Yeah . . . Me too."

"Hopefully, whatever it is, they have it planned for after Garridan attacks, so it won't matter anyway."

"Hopefully," I said. We exchanged another look but didn't say anything else. All we could do was wait and see.

* * *

As I sat on the couch in my room flipping through TV channels, a heavy tingling crept up my arm. I looked over and saw a tiny mouse creeping near my face. I let out a yelp as I stood and shoved it off my shoulder, internally cringing as I ran my hands over the rest of my body to make sure there was nothing else on me.

"You'd think you'd all be used to that by now," Mateo laughed as he stood in front of me.

"Well, surprise! None of us like random creatures crawling on us still," I growled, making him grin. "How're Andre and Kodi?"

"As good as new," he answered, plopping down on my couch. "I don't understand why the Cyfrin have been so willing to break bones and push us to the brink of death this week. They always seemed to hold back past a certain point before."

"I'm not sure what changed," I said, looking at his scraped-up face. "But I don't like it."

"Me neither. But, bonus, when Nedra heals us, all the cuts and bruises disappear too so we don't even look like we went through a fight."

"Well, I like seeing the cuts and bruises on your face then."

"Why? Do you think it's . . . *Sexy*?" He wiggled his eyebrows as he showed off his black eye.

"*No*," I emphasized, shoving him away from me. "Because it means you weren't hurt badly enough that you needed to be healed."

"Makes sense in a twisted kind of way," he relented. "In that case, you'll be happy to hear Toby and Emery still have all their battle scars too."

"Yes, ecstatic," I agreed with a smirk.

"So any update?"

"Yes," I replied, both of us getting serious. "Remember that airplane hangar you told us about a while back?" He nodded. "Adriana said they're going to be positioning a lot of guard members there to make sure none of the Cyfrin can escape. She said that's where we need to go once we get out of the castle, so we'll be safe. She also said . . . Well, *demanded* that none of us go anywhere near the main fight. They can't keep us safe there."

"So our plan is get out of the castle and go to the airplane hangar?"

"Unless someone finds their way into the castle to break us out first, yes."

"But we don't even know where it is. Not specifically at least."

"I know. That's why I was going to ask another big favor of you. Think you can make your way out there and find it?"

"Of course. I'll stay out all night if I have to."

I smiled at his determination. "Okay, then that's what we'll do. Just make sure you get specific directions so we can all find it on our own if we get separated."

"Aye, aye captain," he said with his signature salute.

"Do you ever take anything seriously?" I asked with a roll of my eyes.

He thought about it for a moment before shaking his head. "No, not really."

His answer made me snort. "Go find that airspace."

"Hey . . ." he hesitated before continuing. "I'm worried about my family."

My heart clenched as his face became emotional. "I know you are, Mateo."

"If the Cyfrin win, and we were fighting against them . . . Do you really think they'd go after them?"

I took a deep breath, torn between making him feel better and being truthful. "I wish I could tell you something different but . . . Yes. I think they would."

"They killed your family, right?" he asked softly, and I nodded. "Why?"

"Because Matthew defied them."

"So it wasn't even because of anything *you* did?"

"Not technically," I replied, "but Matthew defied them *because* of me. That was reason enough in their book."

"I can't let my family die because of me," he whispered, his hands clenched into fists.

"They won't. I won't let them."

"You couldn't even protect your own family. Why would I believe you could save mine?" he snapped. Almost immediately after, his eyes grew sorrowful. "I'm so sorry. I didn't mean that."

His words were like a knife to my heart. I looked away and bit the inside of my cheek, trying to keep my composure as anger and guilt threatened to lash out. When I finally felt like I wouldn't snap back at him, I met his gaze.

"I'm so sorry, Robin," he repeated earnestly, his eyes pleading with me to understand.

"It's okay. Really," I assured him. "If I were in your shoes, I'd be the same way. You love your family and don't want to see them get hurt. I can't fault you for that."

He nodded vigorously but didn't say another word.

"Listen . . . I couldn't save my family because I didn't know they were in danger," I told him quietly. "I had barely learned about my powers and didn't understand how ridiculously crazy the Cyfrin were. You have no idea how much guilt I hang onto about their deaths and honestly . . . I'll probably never be able to forgive myself for it." I swallowed around the lump that rose in my throat. "But I won't let that happen to you. If the Cyfrin win, I *will* find a way to keep your family safe. I don't care what it takes. Okay?"

He was silent for a short moment. "Okay."

"Okay," I repeated. "Now get. You have a mission to fulfill."

"Aye, aye captain," he said softly. He got up from the couch and took a single step before turning back around and leaning down to wrap me in a hug. "Thank you."

"You're welcome," I replied, hugging him back tightly. When he released me, I watched him shrink down into his usual mouse choice and jimmy into the air vent, leaving me alone to think on the past and what could've been if I hadn't let my mom and sister die.

Chapter Forty-Three

"Where is everyone?" I asked, the quiet in the castle unusual.

"Toshiro has most everyone in the throne room laying out battle plans," Alexander responded as we walked through the kitchen. I grabbed a bushel of bananas, but Alexander stopped me. "You won't need that many."

"Why not?"

"You'll only be joining Kodi and Andre in the library," he responded as he pulled off three bananas and handed them to me.

"Where are the others?" I questioned, immediately concerned.

"Training. We need to focus on their powers to make sure they're where they need to be, and Kodi and Andre just get in the way of that."

"Because their powers are useless in battle," I said sarcastically.

"Yes," he replied sternly.

"So what are we supposed to do? Sit around and read all afternoon?"

"If you wish. Consider this a one-time break. We'll bring them back to train tomorrow."

"You mean to torture."

"I beg your pardon?"

"What?"

"Watch yourself," he cautioned, not in a threatening way.

I scoffed. "Why? It's true. What's the point in making them fight to the brink of death every single day when you're just going to throw them away after the battle?" I raised my arms incredulously. "I mean, that's what you're going to do, right? Make them servants like Roxy because their powers are beneath you?"

Alexander lifted his chin but cast his eyes downward. "Yes."

"That's crap!" I said with frustration. "You don't really believe that. I can tell. You've spent almost every day with them for months. You *know* they aren't worthless."

"I'll admit they do have excellent fighting attributes but-"

"I'm not talking about their fighting skills. I'm talking about who they are as *people*. You *like* them. You like *all* of them. You see how great they are—how caring and loyal and brave they are. They're *good* people. Their powers don't define who they are, their characters do, and you know it. You see it. So why are you pretending otherwise?"

I watched as he pressed his lips together, his eyes still not meeting mine. "That's not how things work here."

I shook my head slightly, baffled by him. "But you know it's wrong."

"It doesn't matter."

"Yes, it does!"

"No! It doesn't!" he yelled. "The Cyfrin are going to battle, and they *will* win. They'll move forward with their plans to take over the world and we will be sitting next to them. Because the only alternative is death."

"Is that really a worse option?" I exclaimed.

"Yes!"

I paused for a moment, processing his words. "So . . . What it all comes down to is that you're afraid to die," I accused. "You're going to stand by them just so you don't have to die." I swallowed around the bile rising in my throat. "But you'll watch as they slaughter so many others."

I pushed past him, purposely knocking my shoulder into his, and walked to the library on my own. From day one, I hadn't believed he was a bad person. A bad person wouldn't take a bookshelf to the back for someone they had just met. I only thought he was misguidedly set in the ways the Cyfrin had taught him. As time passed, though, I slowly started seeing cracks in his bravado. There were many times I could tell he didn't fully agree with the way the Cyfrin did things, but I never doubted his commitment to their overall mission . . . Until now.

I walked by the guards stationed at the doors. The trainees were never without them even though they'd all proved to be unproblematic.

"Hey!" Kodi greeted me from the ground where she was doing pushups.

"Hey," I replied, still lost in my own thoughts.

"Is something wrong?" Andre asked, looking up from a tattered, old book.

"I don't think so," I told him as I leaned against a wall and tossed a banana his way. "Just got a lot on my mind."

"Do you know why we're stuck in here?" Kodi questioned.

"They basically don't think you're worth their time when they could be focusing on the others' power training," I informed them with a roll of my eyes.

"They weren't joking when they said you're worthless without good powers," Andre said.

"So imagine how strongly they really feel about regular people," Kodi pointed out.

"Strongly enough they're willing to kill them all," I muttered.

"We won't let that happen though," Kodi said. "Well, Garridan won't."

"No, they won't," I agreed.

"What are we supposed to do all afternoon then?" Kodi asked, and I shrugged.

"Whatever we want apparently."

"Whatever we want inside these four walls," Andre corrected.

"Probably," I admitted.

"That's fine. I'm drained anyway," he said.

"Why?"

"I had premonitions all night. I barely slept. It's like everyone keeps changing their minds about things."

"What do you mean?"

"Well, for instance, I saw four different places they had Kodi and I locked up. I also saw Mateo and Toby locked up in one of them," he explained.

"Why would they be considering locking them up?" I wondered out loud. "They already said they'd be coming with them if they stormed Garridan."

"I don't know. Maybe it's a decision that's made after Garridan attacks."

"That's true."

"Plus, now that Garridan has decided to come here, I kept seeing different battles happening between people right outside of town."

"Right outside of town?" I repeated. "Why wouldn't everyone just be at the castle?"

Andre shrugged. “I mean, would you send all your resources to just one spot? Especially if there's more active threats somewhere else?”

“No, I guess I wouldn't,” I admitted. “Did you have any other premonitions? Any, like, really helpful ones?”

“I'm afraid not,” he said, his face withdrawn.

“Ugh, I wish you would just have one that says how it all ends,” I groaned.

“Trust me, me too. You have no idea how hard I've been trying to see something that big.” He sighed in frustration and rubbed his hand against his forehead. “But I still can't see past anything that only has a few people involved. It sucks! The most I saw in those battles last night were limited to three people. If there were more, they were blurry, and I just couldn't find a way to make them out.”

“It's okay, Andre,” I tried to reassure him, but he let out a low grunt and banged his book on the table in front of him.

“No, it isn't! I feel like such a disappointment. I have the one thing that could guarantee all of our safety, but I'm not powerful enough to do it. I can't even map out specifics on all of us so I can help us survive. If anyone dies . . . It's because I couldn't give enough warning.”

“That's a lot of pressure to put on yourself,” Kodi said as she walked up to join us.

“It really is,” I agreed. “No one expects that of you. I'm sorry if I made you feel that way. I shouldn't have even joked about it.”

“It's fine. I know you didn't mean anything by it,” Andre assured me. “I guess I'm just being sensitive. You'd expect premonitions to be . . . More.”

“Not really,” Kodi said with a shrug. “If you look at most every premonition user in any comic, TV show, whatever, they're all extremely limited. There are really none that are super powerful. If they are, it comes with severe side effects, so you're probably better off this way anyway.”

Andre and I both stared at her, and amusement filled me. When she finally realized we were silently judging her, she crossed her arms.

“What?” she asked defensively. “I like fantasy things. Kinda useful, don't you think?”

I grinned. “I mean, it could be if it wasn't all fake.”

"Is it though?" she shot back. "Can we really prove that at this point?"

I pursed my lips and glanced at Andre who shrugged. She had a solid argument.

"Point taken," I said.

"For real though, Andre," she continued, turning her attention back to him. "What you can do is amazing. Don't put yourself down just because you're not the most powerful one here."

"Realistically, I know that. But when all you hear is you don't mean anything without a lot of power, it's hard not to start thinking it yourself."

"You do have a lot of power though," I inserted. "Maybe not in the way the Cyfrin mean but look at your strength. You're one of the strongest people here, and to me, that's power."

"But what good does that do any of you?" he asked.

"Okay, let me break it down for you real quick," Kodi said. "You're the gentle giant of the group."

"Wha-" he started but Kodi quickly shushed him.

"You're the gentle giant. You're massive and can knock someone out with one punch, but you're sweet and kind and wouldn't resort to violence if you didn't have to. That's what you bring to us and even if you don't believe it, it does do us some good. So, stop feeling sorry for yourself and man up."

A smile crept onto my face as we listened to her description of him. It was spot on.

"Thanks, kid," he told her with a sincere smile. "I don't think I've ever heard you act so smart."

"Wow, thanks," she scoffed as she opened her banana.

"No, it's true," I agreed with a laugh. "If he's the gentle giant, you're the ditzy blonde."

"Excuse you, but I'm not even blonde," she denied as she pointed to her faded turquoise hair that had grown out enough to show her natural brown roots.

"Clearly, that doesn't matter," I replied with a smirk, and she scowled at me.

"Who's everyone else then?" Andre asked with a grin.

"Robin's the mom of the group," Kodi answered without a second thought. "Toby's the baby brother who everyone protects and spoils, Mateo's the class clown, and Emery's the drunk aunt who can't get her life together."

"That's mean," Andre told her, but he was visibly holding back a grin.

"Sounds pretty accurate to me," I said with a shrug.

We all exchanged glances then burst out laughing. It was an amazing feeling that I hadn't had in a long time, and I savored every second of it as my cheeks began to hurt from smiling so wide. We spent the rest of the afternoon with lighthearted chitchat filling the room. We could've trained or read more history books, but we didn't. For this one afternoon, we just sat around and relaxed while we could, enjoying one another's company.

Chapter Forty-Four

The day before Garridan was set to attack was finally here. Every part of me was on overdrive, my thoughts thoroughly consumed by what was coming. I stared in the mirror, looking at the person in the reflection who I barely recognized. This person was older, more mature, with light stress lines etched into her face. She was more serious with dark bags under her tired eyes, but she was also more than that. More than what could be seen on the outside.

She had grown. She was more vocal, more confident, and more capable. She wasn't the girl who was overshadowed by her boisterous best friend as they walked down the hallway. She wasn't the girl who couldn't express her emotions to the guy she loved. She wasn't the girl who doubted her self-worth. She was a woman now. She was a leader who had lives depending on her.

I finished brushing through my hair, pulling it up into its usual ponytail, then began brushing my teeth. It seemed so out of place doing such normal things when I knew what was coming.

"Knock, knock," Claire said.

I glanced over my shoulder then rinsed my mouth out with water before turning around. "He didn't come with you again."

She shook her head, and I looked down at my feet as she said, "He's just really busy preparing for tomorrow."

"We both know that's not why he isn't here," I said sadly. "Is he really still that upset with me?"

Claire hesitated before answering. "I'm not sure. He hasn't spoken to me much since it happened. After we left that day, he threw himself into training and preparations. I've barely seen him the past week."

"I'm sorry if I put you in a rough spot. I didn't think he'd hold such a grudge against you for keeping my feelings for Alexander a secret."

"He's just got big emotions," she said with a rueful smile. "He'll come around."

"I just wanted to make amends before tomorrow. I didn't want to stay on bad terms if . . ." I trailed off, unable to finish.

"I understand," Claire assured me, her own face more serious and withdrawn than usual. "All week long everyone's been getting things in order with their families and friends. It's been pretty somber."

"I bet. But it's better this way . . . It's better to have the chance to say goodbye to the people you love," I said firmly, thinking of my mom and Dawn and all the things I wished I could've said to them.

"I agree."

We stood in silence for a moment, both wrapped up in our own thoughts.

"How's the preparation going anyway?" I finally asked.

"All but done. The planes are geared up, the battle plans are all in place, and everyone seems prepared for their roles. My dad and William are confident they have a successful arrangement so . . . Everything should go as smoothly as it can with it being a war and whatnot."

"Good . . . Good," I murmured.

"It's okay to be scared," Claire said.

"That's good . . . because I am."

"Me too," she whispered before pressing her lips in a thin line. "Well, I better get back. I have my own affairs to get in order. Get that stubborn fool of a brother to talk to me."

I smiled at that. "Hey . . . Tell him I'm sorry, okay?"

"You don't have anything to be sorry for."

"I know, but . . . Tell him anyway."

"Okay. I will. And I'll see you back home in Garridan when this is all over." I nodded. "Please be safe, Robin," she requested, her wobbly voice serious.

"I'll try."

The corner of her mouth lifted slightly before she waved and disappeared. I stood there, blinking away tears as I thought of her family, the family I had grown to love, being on the front lines. This was going to be an excruciatingly long day, but I had no doubt tomorrow would be worse.

* * *

The hours dragged on as we stuck to our usual schedule: breakfast, training, lunch, training, time spent in the library studying for training, and lastly dinner. The trainees were jittery and distracted all day, their nerves getting the best of them. None of them succeeded in either training session which resulted in them all coming out with some form of broken bones or internal injuries. I tried my best to keep my own emotions in check, but I struggled as much as they were and happiness filled me when the day was finally over.

As soon as I got into my room, I changed into pajamas and snuggled under my comforter, ready to relax with the TV on until it was time for Darnell to come put me to sleep. I aimlessly flipped through the channels until I landed on something that caught my eye. Barely five minutes in, someone knocked at my door, and I grunted in annoyance.

"Room service," a high-pitched voice that I didn't recognize said.

I scrunched my brows together. I hadn't asked Roxy for anything from the kitchen. I walked to the door and cracked it open, peering out suspiciously. A smile crept onto my face when I saw Alexander standing there with a sundae in his hands.

"Room service, huh?" I mocked, opening the door wider and stepping aside so he could come in.

"With the day you and the trainees had, I thought you could use a treat before bed," he said.

"You brought sundaes to the trainees?" I asked in surprise.

"No," he stated. "I just know you absorb their pain and they seemed to be in a lot of it today."

"So I get a treat because I'm empathetic, but they don't even though they actually went through the pain?"

"Exactly."

I rolled my eyes, his flawed logic never failing to amuse me. "Well, thank you. I think."

"You're welcome." After handing me the sundae, he stood with his hands behind his back, and I could tell by the look on his face that he was contemplating saying something.

"What's wrong?" I questioned.

"So much," he replied with a sad half smile. "But in this exact moment, nothing."

"Okay," I responded slowly. We stood quietly for a moment, the silence that dragged on becoming awkward as I shifted from one foot to the other. Finally, I asked, "Did you need something else then?"

"Not really."

My brows furrowed again, his behavior confusing me. It was like he didn't want to leave. "Did you want to stay for a while?" I asked.

"Would you mind?" he questioned, a hopeful look flashing in his eyes.

"Of course not. Why didn't you just ask?"

"I don't know."

"You're acting stranger than normal," I told him as I closed my door. I walked back to my bed and climbed in as he stood awkwardly in the same spot. "You can come sit down."

He slowly sauntered over but just stared at the bed, so I patted the spot next to me encouragingly. And slightly condescendingly as well. After I short pause, he joined me, leaning against the wall.

"What's up with you?" I asked, and he shrugged.

"Just not in my right mind today, I suppose."

"Seems like none of us are."

He shot me a look I couldn't decipher, but it was gone before I could read more into it. "I just needed to get out of my own head for a while. Distract myself from things."

"So you chose to come here?"

He nodded. "I find . . . Comfort being around you."

I grinned at his hesitation. "Well, shucks. I like you too."

He rolled his eyes at my sarcastic remark, but it got a smile out of him which is what I'd been hoping for.

"There's that smile I love," I told him.

"You love my smile?" he asked, and I quickly looked away as a blush crept onto my face.

"It's a very attractive quality, yes."

"So you think I'm attractive," he commented, his voice teasing as he crossed his arms.

"I never said that."

"But you think it."

"No."

"Yes."

My face was redder than a tomato by then and Alexander grinned as I squirmed. He pushed my hair out of my face and ran his finger along the edge of my jaw before dropping his hand away.

"This is exactly the distraction I was needing," he told me softly.

"So glad I could oblige," I grumbled, leaning into the wall and taking a bite of my ice cream. I could feel him watching me and glanced over to see pure adoration in his eyes. Sheepishly, I questioned, "What?"

"Nothing," he replied, a small smile playing at his lips.

"Then turn around and watch the TV," I instructed, self-conscious.

"Whatever you say," he said with one last exploration of my face.

I peered over at him from the corner of my eye as he relaxed more. I could tell something was bothering him but didn't know what. All I knew was he needed a moment to be real, to be himself. Right now he couldn't put on the facade he usually did for everyone else just like I hadn't been able to the other day. He was there for me when I needed someone, so I would be here for him. Even if all that meant was sitting in a bed sharing ice cream so he could relax.

Plus, I didn't know what would happen tomorrow. This could be the last chance we got to spend together, and I'd be lying if I said I didn't want to have this time with him. No matter how everything turned out, we'd never have the dynamic we did now, so I was happy to have one last memory of our complicated relationship before it all ended.

Chapter Forty-Five

"Wake her up already!" a distant voice demanded.

"I'm working on it," someone replied calmly.

"Hurry up!"

"I'm going as fast as I can, Mallory."

The voices were getting louder, and I groaned as I turned over in my bed. I wasn't ready to wake up.

"Hey!" Mallory yelled in my ear.

I opened my eyes in annoyance and sat up before snapping, "*What*?"

"Let's go," she commanded, straightening up and stepping back.

"Go where?" I asked as I tried to rub the sleep from my eyes.

"Toshiro has summoned for you," Darnell explained, standing on the other side of the bed. The window behind him was pitch black, and I yawned.

"What time is it?"

"About five-thirty," Darnell answered.

"What could Toshiro possibly want at this hour?" I grumbled as I pushed my covers off and got out of bed. That's when I noticed they were both dressed in matching tactical suits and heavy-duty boots. The only difference was in color—Mallory's being red while Darnell's was grey. "What's going on?"

"Just come with us, please," Darnell requested.

"Can I at least get changed first?" I questioned, motioning towards my black satin pants and top.

"No," Mallory denied. "Let's go. Now."

She turned around and walked through the door, so I quickly pulled on the boots sitting by my bed and followed. Darnell trailed behind me, our brisk pace fully waking up my sleepy body and clearing my foggy head. As we made our way down the stairs, I remembered what today was and nerves filled me. We entered the throne room and my heart pounded in my chest at the sight before me.

The room was jammed full of people standing in straight lines with their eyes set to the front of the room. Grim and serious expressions were all they wore. It seemed as if every member of the Cyfrin were here, and they were all dressed in the same grey getup as Darnell. In their usual spot at the front of the thrones, Toshiro stood in a white tactical suit and Alexander in a green one. Mallory quickly joined them but as I stepped closer, Toshiro held his hand up for me to stop. Darnell walked to the side, joining Arthur, Monique, and Isaac who had the trainees—all dressed in their pajamas still too—lined up in front of them. Warning signals started screaming in my head like crazy.

"What the hell is going on?" I questioned, every part of me on overdrive.

"Don't you know?" Toshiro asked, his eyes gleaming. "It's battle day."

The world stopped spinning. My body ran cold. Deafening silence echoed in my ears as my heart skipped a beat and my lungs expelled all the air from inside them as if I'd been punched. "W-what?" I stammered.

Toshiro cackled, loud and obnoxious, before setting his sights back to me with a wicked grin. "We have visitors coming today. They failed to tell us what time they'd be here, so we had to make sure we were prepared for their arrival at any moment. Even at this early hour."

My breath came raggedly, and I blinked rapidly as I tried to come to terms with what he was saying: The Cyfrin knew about Garridan's surprise attack.

"How?" I choked out.

"Oh, I think Alexander is better suited to explain," Toshiro replied, enjoying the dramatics of the situation.

My eyes flickered to Alexander whose face was an emotionless pit. He slowly walked up next to me.

"The only person you have to thank for this is Matthew," he said in a monotone voice.

"Matthew?" I repeated, my brows furrowing.

"Remember that night we were . . . Together," he continued, his voice lowered so no one in the audience could overhear. "Well, I had stopped outside the door. I was trying to think of something to say because I thought maybe you were upset about what had happened between us. That's when that dimwit started screaming at you."

"No," I whispered.

"Yes," Alexander shot back.

I squeezed my eyes shut, and tunnel vision hit me as the last week replayed in my mind. Alexander's anger the day after we had made out. Toshiro lashing out at the trainees in training. The focus on only a couple of their powers. The ins and outs of all the Cyfrin members for planning. It all made sense now. They had known what was coming.

Toshiro let out a single, humorless laugh. "You should know, Robin, at first, I was angry at you. I could've torn your head off. But I came to realize this is the best possible thing that could've happened. Launching our own surprise attack against someone who thinks they're surprise attacking us. It's honestly just too perfect, so thank you. You may have just won this war for us."

My mouth opened, then closed just as quickly as emotions swelled inside me. I had just led everyone I cared about into a slaughter.

"Mateo," Toshiro suddenly called out, and I watched in silence as Mateo's face turned defiant as he was pushed next to me by Monique.

At the same moment, the rest of the trainees had their hands bound behind them in shackles and Isaac held up his hand, taking their powers away and leaving them helpless. Monique struck the back of Mateo's neck with her elbow, causing him to fall to the ground where she took the opportunity to kick him under the jaw. He fell onto his back with a groan, and I took only one step towards him before Alexander had my arms pinned behind my back, keeping me from going any further. I reached inward to conjure up a water attack but was met with an empty hole where my powers resided. I looked over to Isaac, but he diverted his gaze away from mine as he held my powers captive.

Monique held her foot over Mateo's throat and turned her hand into a knife. She slowly dragged it from his temple to his chin, creating a crescent moon shape as he thrashed around and tried to hold back cries of pain.

"Why are you doing this?" I yelled angrily as I watched the blood pour from his face. I fought against Alexander's firm grip, but he only tightened his hold on me.

"We don't take kindly to eavesdroppers around here," Toshiro replied bitterly. I looked up at him in surprise and he narrowed his eyes. "Oh, yes. We knew he was spying on us. What do you take us for? Fools?"

"But-"

"The only reason we didn't do anything," Toshiro cut me off, "is because we didn't believe you'd be able to do anything with the information he obtained. We had Darnell putting you to sleep so dream projection wasn't a possibility. But unfortunately, you had an alternative, didn't you?" He narrowed his eyes. "Fool me once, shame on you, fool me twice . . . Monique!"

Monique pulled back her arm, then thrust it forward, impaling the sharp blade into Mateo's chest.

"No!" Kodi and Toby cried out.

"Stop!" I screamed at the same time, trying desperately to get to him, but Alexander made sure I stayed put.

"Remove him from my sight," Toshiro instructed, the disdain evident in his voice. "We'll deal with him later."

Monique grabbed him by the collar of his shirt and dragged him down the middle of the room, his blood leaving a streaky mess behind him as he groaned from the pain. Even after he was out of sight, I stared after him, full of dread.

This is my fault.

"Now, one more order of business before we throw you all out so we can get ready," Toshiro said. "Alexander."

Alexander passed me off to the strong woman who I'd only seen a couple times before, and she grabbed my wrist in her hand, holding me in place as Alexander stepped up to Toshiro.

"You were in charge of Robin. It was your responsibility to keep an eye on her and either you failed to do that or failed to report her transgressions. Either way, you have fallen short of our expectations of you and for that, you must be punished as well."

"Of course, Toshiro," Alexander agreed, casting his eyes down in submission.

"I have a very important task for you," Toshiro continued.

"What about his punishment?" Mallory asked in annoyance.

"This task *is* his punishment," Toshiro said, and I noticed Alexander stiffen slightly.

"What's the task?" he asked through clenched teeth.

"I need you to kill Matthew."

Alexander's eyes shot up, wide and full of shock. "What?" he asked, his voice hoarse.

"Kill Matthew," Toshiro repeated.

"I . . . I can't."

"You *can* and you *will*," Toshiro told him with a razor-sharp slice to his voice. "Because if you don't, *I* will, and I can promise you it won't be a quick and painless death like you'll offer him."

Alexander ground his teeth together, and I could see his entire body trembling with anger as he stood rigid.

"Do I make myself clear?" Toshiro pressed, and Alexander nodded once as he tried to maintain his composure. "Very well. Now go."

The trainees were pushed forward, each of them led by a different person in opposite directions as they stumbled out the doors. Alexander grabbed onto my upper arm and pulled me with him as he walked. I sidestepped the areas of the floor that were stained with Mateo's blood, but Alexander charged through them without a second thought. As we stepped up to the doors, Toshiro called out to me one last time. Alexander paused, allowing me to look back.

"Thanks again for the assist," Toshiro told me with a wicked sneer.

My nostrils flared and my eyes narrowed as I exhaled angrily, but before I could do anything, Alexander yanked me into the foyer and the doors thudded shut behind us. Without wasting any time, Alexander hauled me to the hallway opposite the dining room, but I wasn't going to go down without a fight. I dug my heels into the ground, using all my strength to fight from going any further. Alexander didn't seem fazed, my strength nothing compared to his, so I went dead weight and fell to the ground.

"Would you *stop fighting*?" Alexander growled.

"No!" I yelled back, trying to pull my arm free.

"Fine. Have it your way," he muttered angrily. He wrapped his arms around my chest and pulled me up before slinging me over his shoulders like I was nothing but a rag doll.

"Put me down!" I pounded my fists into his back and wildly kicked my feet, desperately trying to free myself from his iron grip as he walked down the winding hallways.

He ignored my screams and pleas, his eyes staring straight ahead as he carried me along. I suddenly realized I recognized the corridor we were heading down and paused my outcries. I knew exactly where we were going.

"You're locking me in the torture chamber?" I asked in disbelief.

"It's deep in the castle's bones. Water will do you no good here, so we won't have to worry about you escaping. And I won't have to worry about you getting hurt."

"Don't act like you care about my safety! If push came to shove, you'd let me die to save yourself."

"You don't believe that," he murmured, and I could detect a hint of hurt in his voice.

"Don't I?" I responded, and we both grew quiet.

The walls pressed closer together, barely wide enough for two people to pass through simultaneously. The ceiling lowered as well, and my head nearly scraped the top of it as Alexander carried me. I hadn't remembered it being so tiny, and the thought of being trapped within this miniscule structure made my breath come in short rasps.

We reached the torture chamber and two armed guards stepped aside to let us pass through. Alexander set me on the ground, and as I looked around the room I was flooded with the memory of when Matthew was chained up here. Bloody, bruised, and broken, all because he had come to save me. Alexander pulled some chains off the floor and hooked them up to one of the heavy-duty padlocks that was inserted in the wall. He turned towards me, holding up the shackles.

"Please don't fight me, Robin," he said quietly. "You know you can't win."

I bit the inside of my cheek, weighing my options. In the end, I knew he was right and decided not to waste my energy. I walked to him and held my hands up.

"Please don't do this," I begged, tears forming in my eyes as he clicked the locks into place.

"I don't have a choice."

"That's bull crap!" I yelled angrily. "Alexander, please. *Please*."

"I have to go."

"You're really going to kill Matthew?" I questioned, desperately grasping at anything I could to change his mind. "Your *brother*?"

He swung around and stomped back towards me, his face twisted with fury. “Don't you understand? If I don't, Toshiro will, and it'll be agonizing. It'll be slow and painful and excruciating. What I'm doing is a mercy killing. I'm doing this *for* him!”

His face turned red as he yelled at me, and his eyes were glassy with unshed tears. Something I never thought I'd see from him.

“Alexander . . .”

He turned his head away from me. “Why'd you do it? Why did you have to betray us? Why couldn't you have just cooperated? None of this would be happening if you had just . . . If you hadn't . . .”

“You're blaming *me*?” I asked in astonishment.

“I have to go,” he said instead of answering, but he didn't move. He stared into my eyes, a million emotions flickering in his own. He swallowed before speaking again. “Sometime today, I'm going to come back for you and you're going to hate me for the things I had to do. I don't know if our relationship will ever overcome that. So, before I go, I just need you to know . . . I love you, Robin.”

My mouth fell open, but no sound came out. Had he really just said that to me?

“I just needed to say it at least once. Before you hate me,” he added in. “I'll see you soon.”

With that, he turned and walked away.

“Alexander . . . Alexander!” I pulled against the chains around my wrists, but it was useless. Alexander was gone and I was stuck in the middle of the castle with no way to help anyone. Garridan was walking straight into a trap, Mateo was bleeding out somewhere, Matthew was going to be ambushed, and it was all my fault.

Chapter Forty-Six

Mateo

The pain was almost gone, numbness taking its place. Mateo knew that was a bad sign and once again looked around at the steel box he was locked in. It was barely big enough for him to sit up and, as he shifted himself in the pool of blood that cumulated beneath him, he thought once again how lucky he was to not have claustrophobia. He coughed once, his breath coming in short gasps, and he knew his blood loss was significant. He was running out of time. He weakly banged his fist against the walls that encased him, but it was no use. He wasn't getting out of this alive.

He closed his eyes and began thinking of his home and his family. He remembered his siblings, all as different as could be with their looks and personalities. The twins, Susie and Sophia, were twenty-one. Their Hispanic descent made them look the most like him. They were polar opposites but never failed to be there for their younger siblings. Ronan was next at nineteen. His ginger hair and fair skin fit his unique personality and peculiar obsessions that the rest of them found unusual. Then there were the other set of blood siblings in the family: fifteen-year-old Kofi, thirteen-year-old Malik, and ten-year-old Zuri. They were from Morocco, and all had big hearts and unending energy. Kofi and Malik were avid sports players while Zuri was more of a book worm. That left the two youngest: Jun and Mai. Both from south Asia, Jun was nine with a love for animals and Mai was only six. She was the baby of the family and perfect in every way.

Their dynamic shouldn't work but thanks to the phenomenal people Mateo got to call Mom and Dad, it did. His eyes began to water as he thought about them. They were the most selfless people he'd ever met. Who else would open their home to nine children from across the world when they were at their most vulnerable? He banged his head against the wall behind him as his love turned to anger. He couldn't give up. He couldn't be the reason they were put in harm's way.

He kicked in front of him, the vibration shaking the whole box. He kicked again and again, desperate to escape, but nothing happened. He slumped to the side, his body a sweaty mess. He struggled to keep his eyes open, but they were growing heavier by the second. His body began to convulse as he fought to stay awake but finally, he gave in. He was done. His eyes closed and he could no longer feel any part of his body. He sensed this was the end and he began to drift away.

Akio struggled with the locks on the steel box. The castle shook as it weathered another round of attacks. Garridan's guard made it further than the Cyfrin anticipated, and the old building was dealing with the consequences. Akio focused on what was in front of him as people shouted from the hallways. Finally, he was able to pull the door open, and the overflow of blood spilled out of the box in a wave. His eyes widened when he saw Mateo hunched over his knees, his face deathly pale.

Akio gently pulled him from his prison and placed him on the bed with great care. He only hoped he wasn't too late. He raised his hands over Mateo's body and let them sense where the damage was. He closed his eyes and saw Mateo's weak pulse flashing in the dark as if on a monitor. He took a deep breath and let the yellow mist wash through his body and into Mateo's. With deep concentration, he allowed the mist to close Mateo's injuries, pulling the skin back together pore by pore. Then he directed it over the nerves and tendons, connecting them where they had split.

When everything was back in place, Akio dug deep and transferred a red mist into Mateo. It slowly latched onto the bone marrow in his body, strengthening them until they were producing millions of stem cells in a matter of seconds. The stem cells quickly began their job of making red cells, white cells, and platelets and Mateo's heartbeat picked up. Akio watched as Mateo's color began to return then pulled back his healing powers. He grabbed a jar of smelling salts from his pocket and ran it over Mateo's face. After a moment, Mateo scrunched his nose and his eyes fluttered open.

He groaned as he looked around the room. "What happened?" he moaned.

"You just about died, that's what happened," Akio informed him.

Mateo looked down at his blood-soaked clothes, and everything hit him all at once. He immediately became defensive as he turned his glare to Akio. "You're the Cyfrin's other healer. The one that helped Robin."

"I am."

"Why are you here? What do you want?"

Akio smiled sadly at the boy's mistrust. "I'm only here to help."

"I don't believe you," Mateo retorted.

"I'm not surprised but it's the truth. Why would I heal you if it wasn't?"

"To torture me to the brink of death again?" Akio had to chuckle at that, and Mateo scowled. "You think that's funny?"

"No. It's actually extremely accurate which isn't funny at all," Akio replied, thinking of all the times he had been asked to do that in the past.

Mateo examined him, taking in his tired stature and kind eyes. Something about him seemed sincere so Mateo decided to take a leap of faith. "Why do you want to help me?"

Akio glanced towards the door as feet thudded by. "We don't have much time so let me give you the short version. A long time ago, I let someone very near and dear to my heart die because of what she had become—what the Cyfrin had turned her into. After that, I reached out to Garridan and became a spy for them. Over the years, Toshiro has had his suspicions that there was a mole in our operation. Many people were tortured and killed because of it, but he never suspected his own brother. It was a perfect set-up aside from the fact that Toshiro never filled me in on some of the most important matters, so I haven't been much help. But that changes today. Today, I'm helping all you kids get out."

His words softened Mateo, and, in that moment, he knew he could trust him. It didn't take much for Mateo to like someone; he had excellent people skills and could read them like an open book. Akio was a friend.

"Okay," Mateo said with a nod. "Let's get to it then."

He swung his legs out of bed, but nausea took hold of his stomach, and he bent over as his head grew foggy.

"Easy there, son," Akio instructed.

"I thought you healed me," Mateo groaned.

"I did but sometimes the body needs time to recuperate. Remember when Robin got seriously injured? She was asleep for a week letting her body recover. Unfortunately, I had to wake you so you're going to feel pretty crappy."

"Duly noted," Mateo muttered, giving Akio a thumbs up.

Akio walked to one of the closets in the room and threw some clothes to Mateo. "Put these on. You won't make it two steps with those bloody clothes on."

"So what's the plan?" Mateo asked as he slowly pulled his clothes off, trying to avoid gagging.

"Garridan attacked about thirty minutes ago. The Cyfrin are split in half right now. Half of them are in or around the castle guarding it. The other half circled around Garridan's first line of defense when they attacked. From the sound of it, the guard advanced closer to the castle which is good for us because that means everyone will be distracted. So, hopefully, they won't look close enough to recognize you if they pass us by."

"You mean we're just gonna walk and keep our heads down?"

"Yes." Mateo eyed him skeptically, and Akio threw a hat at him. "Put this on. It'll help."

"Sure, it will," Mateo grumbled, but he did as he was told. With how miserable he was feeling, he was just grateful for any type of help.

"Think you can handle getting out?" Akio asked, worried about how pale Mateo still was.

"Yes," Mateo replied with determination. "But we can't get out yet. We have to go meet my friends."

"That's too risky."

"You said you were going to help us *all* get out, didn't you?" Mateo questioned.

"Yes, of course. But you're in no shape to-"

"I don't care if I'm stabbed and bleeding out again. I'm not leaving without every single one of my friends."

Akio examined Mateo's face and saw he was dead set in his goal. He sighed, knowing it wasn't going to be an easy trek, but nodded in agreement. "Okay. Let's go find your friends."

"They'll be in the old artifact room. We agreed on that being our meeting place last week."

"Alright," Akio said slowly, thinking of the safest route there. "If we go through the east tower, we shouldn't run into too many people."

"I know exactly which way you're talking about," Mateo said, picturing the map in his head.

"Let's hurry then."

Akio opened the bedroom door, peeking around the hallways before beckoning Mateo forward. Shouts sounded in the distance, followed by breaking glass and another shake of the ground. Mateo kept his head down, ignoring the pounding of it as he followed Akio through the back side of the second story. They got to the east stairs without bumping into anyone and they both sighed a breath of relief. As they rounded the corner, Mateo bumped into someone coming the opposite way. He fell, dry heaving at the impact as the person stared down at him.

"Hey, you're one of those trainees!" the man cried out.

"It's okay, Harley," Akio spoke up, putting himself between the two.

"What are you doing with him?"

"Transporting him to a different location."

"I don't think-"

Akio gripped the man's arm and yanked it behind his back, forcing him to turn around. With a remorseful heart, he snapped the man's neck to the side, tightening his lips at the sound of the bones breaking. The man fell to the floor as Mateo stared at his lifeless face in horror.

"Why did you do that?" Mateo choked out.

"He would've gone and told someone he saw us," Akio explained, his guilt overshadowed by logic. "It was the only way to ensure our safety."

Mateo didn't reply as Akio helped him off the ground. He knew Akio was right but was overcome with shame. This man just died because of him. He swallowed around the lump in his throat as the two continued down the corridors. The fighting outside grew louder as they approached the front of the castle again. They rounded one more corner and Mateo recognized the door at the end of the hall that was barely cracked open—it was the artifact room. They made it. As they walked towards it, voices reached their ears.

"We all agreed we'd leave if we had to," Andre was saying.

"No, you and Emery agreed to that," Kodi disagreed. "Toby and I never did."

"We'll be risking *all* our lives if we go looking for them," Emery said.

"I don't care," Toby replied stubbornly, and Mateo could picture him crossing his arms. "I'm not leaving without Robin."

"And I'm not leaving without Mateo," Kodi added in.

Akio and Mateo reached the door then and Mateo pushed it open with a playful grin on his face as he said, "Aw, I knew you cared."

Chapter Forty-Seven

Andre and Emery

"We all agreed we'd leave if we had to," Andre said, knowing they couldn't wait any longer for Mateo or Robin. He didn't want to leave them behind, the thought of it making him physically ill, but the fighting was getting closer to the castle. If they didn't leave now, they may not make it out at all.

"No, you and Emery agreed to that," Kodi shot back, placing her hands on her hips. "Toby and I never did."

"We'll be risking *all* our lives if we go looking for them," Emery spoke up from where she was peeking out of a window, watching Garridan's guard advance. She stretched her arms back, ignoring the throbbing in her shoulder from where it had been slammed into the wall.

"I don't care," Toby replied, crossing his cut-up arms with his chin set high. "I'm not leaving without Robin."

"And I'm not leaving without Mateo," Kodi added in.

Just then, the door creaked open, and everyone instantly jumped in defensive positions, not knowing what to expect.

"Aw, I knew you cared," Mateo said with a grin as he revealed himself.

"Mateo!" Kodi and Toby cried out, running up to him and wrapping him in a hug.

Andre noticed Mateo's whole body tense up as his smile turned into a grimace. Something was wrong. At the same time, Akio walked in, and Emery ran forward, ready for action.

"Who the hell are you?" she spat at him, her hands lifted and surging with electrical sparks.

"It's okay, Emery," Mateo spoke up. "He's a friend."

Emery eyed Akio suspiciously, always on the defensive, but slowly lowered her hands.

"We were so worried!" Kodi was telling Mateo.

"We thought . . . maybe . . . You were dead," Toby said, a tear sliding down his face.

"I would be if it wasn't for Akio here," Mateo informed them as he leaned on Kodi for support. "He's the healer that saved Robin, remember? He's been a spy for Garridan for years, and he's gonna help us get out."

Andre stood tall, using his size to try being intimidating as he stared at Akio. "Is that true?"

"Yes, it is," Akio replied, unfazed by Andre's tactic.

"If you're a healer, why does he look so unhealed?" Emery asked with narrowed eyes as she motioned to Mateo.

"He had traumatic injuries and severe blood loss. I was lucky I got to him in time. I patched his wounds and brought his blood levels up, but his body needs a significant amount of rest to fully recover," Akio explained for the second time that day. "He's going to need our help, and our protection, to make it out of here."

"So, basically, I'm a liability now," Mateo summarized.

"No, you aren't," Kodi assured him. "We're in this together."

A deafening explosion sounded, rocking the walls around them and taking out the glass in the window. Debris fell from the ceiling and the artifacts clattered to the floor.

"We need to go. *Now*," Akio instructed.

"What about Robin?" Toby cried out.

"She'll be fine," Emery told him firmly, believing with everything in her that it was true. "She's a big girl. She can take care of herself."

"Emery is right," Andre agreed. "She's so powerful, she'll have no trouble on her own."

"She won't be on her own anyway," Akio inserted, and they all turned to look at him. "Garridan already had a plan in place to retrieve her. She'll have all the help she needs."

"What if they can't find her though?" Toby asked, his eyes desperate for them to not leave her.

"They will. Matthew knows this castle like the back of his hand. He'll find her," Akio told him, gentle but resolute.

Toby opened his mouth to say more but Andre cut him off. "She wouldn't want us to stay for her. She would want us to get each other to safety."

"She wouldn't forgive herself if something happened to us because we were looking for her," Mateo added in, remembering their conversation about their families. "We have to go."

Toby's lower lip trembled slightly but finally he whispered, "Okay."

Akio didn't waste any time as he took a glance back out the door. "We can't go anywhere near the front, but the back will have Cyfrin members stationed too. Our best bet is to scale down the west tower."

"I'm sorry, scale?" Kodi asked.

"Yes. The way the window is positioned will give us cover from the fight. Once we're down though . . . It won't be pretty. We'll basically have to make a run for it."

"Let's just focus on getting there first," Andre said, noticing the uncertainty on everyone's faces. "We'll deal with the rest when we have to."

"Agreed," Emery said. "Let's get going."

Kodi and Toby positioned themselves on either side of Mateo, taking on most of his weight as Akio took the lead. They slowly made their way through the hallways, ducking back behind corners or into rooms when people would run by. It was a slow trek, but they were almost there.

"You there!" a voice yelled from behind Andre. "Stop!"

Andre glanced behind him and inhaled sharply when he saw a whole group of Cyfrin members heading towards them, all with angry expressions. "Run!" he instructed.

Everyone in front of him took off but Mateo couldn't keep up, dragging Kodi and Toby back with him. When Andre and Emery caught up, Andre scooped Mateo into his arms, knowing the extra weight wouldn't slow him down.

"Go, go, go," Andre yelled, pushing everyone in front of him as they made a beeline around another corner. At the end of the hall was the stairs to the tower and Akio stood waiting, beckoning them all to hurry. Toby reached the stairs first and began climbing as the people behind them continued to throw out threats. Kodi quickly followed but Emery ducked behind Andre, letting him go by her.

"What are you doing?" Andre questioned, worry instantly filling him.

"Get to the top," Emery replied as she sparked the electricity in her hands. "I'll be right behind you."

Andre hesitated but Emery didn't have the patience to deal with his distress, so she flicked a miniscule bolt of voltage at his feet. Andre let out a yelp as the shock ran up his toes and narrowed his eyes at her smirk.

"Go!" she yelled, and this time Andre obeyed, not wanting to get shocked again.

When her friends and Akio were safely out of range, she let the electricity course through her body. Each muscle spasmed at the interaction, a feeling of pleasurable pain filling her. It was almost comparable to how you felt after a good workout. She concentrated on the sound of feet slapping against the floor, getting closer and closer as she let her electricity grow bigger. As soon as their chasers rounded the corner, she shot a wave of energy at them.

The electricity that flowed out of her crackled as it jumped through the air. She felt the moment it shot through the people, jumping from one to another in an endless wave as it electrified them from the inside out. Her arm hairs stood on end as the static in the air became too much to handle. As their attackers fell to the ground one by one, she turned around and took the stairs two at a time. When she reached the top, the others were waiting with anxious faces.

"Told you I'd be right behind you," she remarked with a grin as everyone visibly let out sighs of relief.

"What did you do?" Toby asked as Akio closed the door to the room behind her and secured the lock. For good measure, Andre pushed a chest against it.

"Bought us some time," Emery replied, sparing him the details that she knew would make him cry again. She glanced around the tidy space they were in. It was small with just the bare necessities in it for someone to live. "Who's bedroom is this?"

"Mine," Akio responded as he rummaged through the back of the armoire. He came out with some heavy-duty rope and tossed it to Andre before opening the window. A cold breeze blew in, and everyone shivered. "Secure one end of that to the bed."

Andre immediately complied, trying to remember his knotting lessons from his Boy Scout days. When he was sure the rope wouldn't come undone, he stood and threw the other end of it out the window as the wind howled. "Okay, who's first?"

"I'll go," Kodi offered. She quickly hoisted herself onto the windowsill, her stomach churning at the height.

"Don't look down," Toby suggested, and she nodded in agreement.

"The wall might be slippery from the weather," Akio advised. "Place your feet carefully."

She grabbed onto the rope, making sure she had a tight grip on it, then lowered herself over the edge. The wall was curved here, creating the perfect cover from anyone who may be in front of the castle. The icy chill in the air went straight through her sweatpants, and she wished she had on something thicker. She planted her feet on the side of the castle and began her descent as the sound of battle echoed all around her. When she reached the bottom, she gave a thumbs up to the others before glancing around to make sure there were no threats nearby.

"Who's next?" Akio asked.

"I'll go," Mateo offered, despite his face being covered in sweat.

"There's no way you can make it down," Andre told him, his mind already working to figure out how they'd get him safely to the ground.

"What if . . ." Toby started, looking around the room. His eyes found all the metal pieces hidden around as they lit up for him like a beacon.

"What if what?" Emery asked quickly as the sound of voices coming from the stairway met her ears. They needed to hurry.

"I think there's enough metal in here that I can use to get us all down," Toby explained.

"Do it, Toby," Andre instructed as he stood next to Emery to help block the door.

Toby swiftly pulled all the metal to him. Each piece called out to him like a siren to a sailor. When he had every last inch of it, he bent it to his will, creating a landing just big enough for them all to stand on. He secured it over the windowsill with a large block of metal sitting on the inside to hold it in place.

"That should be enough to stretch almost all the way to the ground," Toby explained.

"So you've essentially made an elevator," Emery commented with a snort.

Toby rubbed the back of his head sheepishly. "Like an old timey one but yeah."

Someone began banging on the other side of the door. The old wood creaked in protest, and they all knew it wouldn't hold.

"You all need to go. Now," Emery ordered.

Akio and Toby helped Mateo over the windowsill, sitting him down on the metal before looking back in the room.

"Aren't you coming?" Toby questioned frantically.

Whoever was on the other side of the door punched a hole through it, splintering the wood.

"I'm going to stay and hold them back," Emery answered, her heart beating quickly in her chest. She never had a family before, so she only ever had to look after herself. When conflict arose, she would just run to save her own skin. But things were different now. She would stay so they could go. "It's the only way you'll have a chance of escaping."

"I'm staying too," Andre told them. Emery shot him a look of disapproval, but he ignored her. He wouldn't leave her alone. He looked to Akio, letting his next words echo in his eyes. "Please keep them safe."

"I will," Akio promised, their sacrifice pulling at his heart strings.

"Toby," Emery said, smiling at him gently as he began to cry. "Go. Be brave."

He nodded vigorously then began to stretch the metal out, slowly lowering them. Emery kept eye contact with him until she couldn't see him anymore then swallowed around the lump in her throat. *Damn kid*, she thought. The gap in the door widened, and wood shards began flying towards them as the person on the other side mercilessly chopped away at it.

"I'm proud of you," Andre told Emery, one side of his lips turning up in a smile.

"Whatever," she muttered, keeping her eyes on the threat ahead. "Stay focused."

"They'll get away," Andre said, somehow confident in his words. Between Emery's powers and his physical strength, they were ready for whatever came through that door. "We'll make sure of it."

Emery nodded, knowing he believed it. She believed it too. In an uncharacteristic move, she reached out and grabbed his hand. Andre raised his brows in surprise, then saw the fear in her eyes.

"Hey," he said, waiting until she looked at him to continue. "When *we* get away, I'm taking you on a proper date."

It was exactly what Emery needed to hear and she grinned, her fear minimizing. "You mean this isn't your idea of an ideal date?"

"No," Andre replied with his own small smirk.

Just then, the door cracked off its hinges and fell to the ground, ripping their attention back to the threat in front of them. Isaac stepped over the broken wood, his eyes searching the room unhappily as Monique stepped in behind him.

"Where are the others?" he demanded.

"What others?" Emery asked coyly, making sure to keep his line of sight away from the window.

"Don't play games," Monique instructed in annoyance. "We don't have time to deal with the lot of you right now."

"Yet here you are," Andre commented, his fingers twitching at his sides. "I thought you were the head of Toshiro's army. Why aren't you out there battling Garridan?"

"Toshiro seems to think my abilities are better suited to take care of you brats," Monique growled, clearly upset by that. "Let's make this easy so I can get my hands back where they really belong."

"Brats? And here I thought you liked us," Emery popped off with.

Monique narrowed her eyes. "Oh, I do, but that doesn't matter to me. I won't let you jeopardize our mission. I killed my own family for disagreeing with me. Don't think I won't do the same to you."

Andre and Emery exchanged a glance. They had never seen this side of Monique and it wasn't pleasant. Andre nodded slightly at Emery, ready to fight when she was.

"That's a shame," Emery said as she looked back to Monique and Isaac. "Because I'm pretty sure we beat you in training before."

She sent her electricity straight into Monique. Andre took the opportunity to dive into Isaac, knocking him over a chair and to the ground. The two rolled over one another, each getting in a round of punches before Isaac managed to get his arm around Andre's throat and his legs around his torso. Andre's eyes bulged from his head as Isaac tightened his grip. He threw his fist back wildly, getting lucky enough to hit Isaac square in the jaw. Isaac loosened his legs just a little but that was all Andre needed. He slammed his elbows into Isaac's inner thighs and with all the strength he could muster, forced them open so he could wiggle free.

He heard glass shatter and glanced over to see Monique slam Emery's face into the mirror on the wall. He took a step towards them, but Isaac kicked him in the back, sending him sprawling on the ground as Monique shaped one of her arms into a wooden shield and the other into an axe.

"I did my research this time," she said to Emery. "Wood is nonconductive."

Emery narrowed her eyes as she looked for an opening to shock Monique with again, but Monique was being tactical with every move. She peeked over at the boys as they crashed into a table, breaking it in two, and Monique took the opportunity to leap forward, slashing her axe hand directly towards Emery's head. Emery barely dodged it, hearing the whiz of it go by her ear as she dropped to the ground. Her heart beat wildly in her chest at the close call; she couldn't lose focus like that again.

Realizing she didn't have a clear opening for her electrokinesis, Emery relied on her own strength as Monique dove at her again. She rolled out of the way, letting Monique's axe hand barrel into the floor, then she stood up as Monique struggled to get her hand free. Seeing her stuck on the ground, Andre shoved Isaac back. He tripped over Monique and landed on top of her as she let out a spew of profanities.

"Get off of me you big oaf!" she yelled as he struggled to roll off her.

"Andre, the water!" Emery pointed to the glass pitcher next to the bed.

Despite being confused as to what she wanted with it, Andre tossed it over to her. She caught it with ease and dumped it over Monique and Isaac. In the same motion, she shot a stream of electricity towards them. The discharge spread over the length of the water, electrocuting the two. Emery highered her voltage, intensifying the stream of electricity that was flowing into their bodies. She watched as they started shaking uncontrollably, both their hair frying at the tips and their fingertips turning black.

"Emery, that's enough," Andre told her. He watched as her eyes danced with the reflection of the sparks and a shudder ran through him. She was scarier than anyone else here.

"I know," she replied, lowering her hands as her body jittered with the pent-up static inside her. "I wasn't going to kill them. I just wanted to incapacitate them."

"You succeeded," he said, wrinkling his nose at the smell that was now being omitted. "You're scary. You know that, right?"

She grinned, enjoying the fact that everyone saw her as a threat. "Yep. You still owe me that date though."

"I wouldn't dream of backing out," Andre replied with a chuckle before looking out the window. "I don't see the others. Hopefully that means they got away."

Emery wiped the blood from her face before saying, "Now we just have to meet them at the airspace."

"Only one problem with that." Andre held up the rope that has been burned in two by her electricity. "We have no way down."

"Well, I guess that means we have to go back through the castle," Emery said with a shrug. "You up for it?"

"Are you?" Andre shot back.

"Guess we're going to find out," she commented as more footsteps sounded on the stairs.

They looked at each other with grim expressions, both determined to make it back to their friends but neither of them sure if it would really happen.

Chapter Forty-Eight

Kodi and Toby

Kodi watched with narrowed eyes as a metal platform formed above her. She saw Akio, Toby, and Mateo get on before it began lowering to the ground. It stopped about a foot above her and Akio and Toby slid off before helping Mateo down.

"You couldn't have thought of that before I scaled the freaking wall in the snow?" she asked with a scowl on her face. Once again, she was handed the short end of the stick.

Toby smiled apologetically, hating that she was mad again. "No, sorry."

"Guys," Mateo said quietly.

Kodi let out a frustrated growl, holding out her hands to show the blisters and burn marks from the rope, and Toby looked down sheepishly.

"Sorry," he repeated.

"Guys," Mateo repeated a bit louder.

"I swear I'm going to kick your ass," Kodi continued, poking her finger into Toby's chest.

"Guys!" Mateo yelled, but it was too late. He mustered up all the energy he could and focused each cell of his body into turning into a cheetah. He felt each bone, each muscle, and each tendon shift, stretching and shrinking in whatever way necessary to become what he imagined. It was a pain he had grown accustomed to, barely noticing it anymore. In his mind, the shift felt like an eternity, but it only took a split second in reality. His body shuddered as it fought the shift, wanting to do nothing but give out, but he leapt over the others and charged the four men coming their way.

One of the men blinded him with what Mateo assumed was some sort of power, but his sense of smell was heightened so he didn't need his eyes. He knocked all four men down in one sweep, biting into one's shoulder as he slashed his paws at the others. One of them put their hands on his stomach, burning through his fur. He let out a loud hiss, chomping blindly at the hands. He made a connection and heard the man scream as the bone crunched between his jaws. He snarled as his paws started to go numb. Was this another power or his body threatening to go out on him? Just then, he heard the unmistakably sound of bending metal.

"Mateo, move!" Toby instructed as he tore half the metal from the platform and made it barrel towards where Mateo stood.

He shoved it into the ground under the four assailants. Mateo jumped out of the way as Toby shaped the metal into a ball, scooping the men—and a good chunk of earth—into an impenetrable dome. He could hear them banging against it but knew they couldn't escape without some sort of help. Kodi ran over to Mateo who had collapsed on the ground after shifting back to his human form. She bit her lower lip, her hands hovering over him helplessly as he lay face down in the muddy snow.

"Is he okay?" she asked Akio as he knelt next to them. She watched as he quickly ran his hands over Mateo's body.

"His body is exhausted. He won't be able to wake up for some time," Akio told them.

"How are we supposed to get to the airspace if he can't even walk?" Toby asked, his nerves setting in as he fiddled with his fingers.

"I'll carry him," Akio responded. "You two will have to cover us."

Kodi and Toby exchanged a glance, neither of them confident in that plan. Kodi knew she would be no help unless the fight was up close and personal, and Toby worried he wouldn't have the material needed to protect them. It's not like he could conjure up metal out of thin air like Robin did with water. He wasn't that powerful. He was limited. He started thinking about all the things that could go wrong, the fear becoming too much and nearly causing him to break down. Kodi sensed Toby's panic and put aside her own distress to comfort him.

"Hey," she said, waiting until he looked at her to speak again. "We're going to be fine. Don't let your fear control you. You're stronger than you know."

"What if I'm not?" he whispered, rubbing his sweaty palms on his tattered shirt. "What if I'm not good enough to keep us safe?"

"You are," Kodi told him, putting her hand on his shoulder. "I believe in you."

Toby's lower lip quivered as her words hit him like a freight train. All his life he had been told he wasn't good enough—by his peers, by the foster families that had given him up, by the perspective adoptive parents who had passed him by. But now, in this moment, someone was finally telling him he *was* good enough. Someone finally believed in him. He wrapped Kodi in a hug, and she held his trembling body tightly as she realized how much her words meant to him.

"Thank you," he told her before loosening his grip.

"You're welcome. Now, what do you say we get us all out of here safely?" she responded, and he nodded vigorously with his newfound confidence. Suddenly, Kodi realized they were two people short. "Where are Andre and Emery?"

"They stayed behind so we could get out," Toby told her, and she looked down at the ground. Of course they had.

Akio watched the exchange with adoration. This is how the world was meant to be—kind. It just renewed his conviction that the Cyfrin were the enemy. He looked around, taking in every detail of what was going on.

"I hate to say this," he told the kids, "but we're basically going to have to make a run for it."

Kodi glanced around. It was easy to tell the two groups apart since the Cyfrin members were all in grey uniforms and the guard from Garridan were in black. The front of the castle was lined with Cyfrin members, protecting it as they watched the courtyard being turned into a bloodbath. Further out, right on the edge of the town, a bigger battle was in session. Houses had been destroyed and the roads were filled with people fighting, some physically but a lot more with their powers.

Kodi breathed deeply, her eyes wide as she watched things she'd only ever seen in movies: people being thrown fifty feet in the air, people flying, forcefields, different colors leaving people's hands as their powers left them. It was insane.

More importantly, she saw that there was absolutely no cover of any kind for them once they left the castle. There were no other buildings, no trees, no bushes, nothing that they could hide behind. They would be sitting ducks until they hit the tree line that was at least a hundred yards away.

"There's really nothing else we can do?" Toby asked as he realized the same thing Kodi and Akio had.

"I'm afraid not," Akio replied. "The airspace is that way."

"We're going to be completely exposed though," Toby said, his video game experience telling him this was a bad idea. "We'll get seen immediately."

"And then killed," Kodi muttered, forgetting for a second that she was supposed to be comforting.

"It's either that or stay here," Akio told them, not liking their odds any more than they did.

"Then I guess we make a run for it." Kodi sighed. "How far is the airspace after that tree line?"

"Maybe half a mile?" Akio guessed.

"Great," Kodi grumbled. Not only did they have to make it to the tree line alive, but they had to go even further to reach safety.

Toby furrowed his brows, staring up at what was left of the metal platform. It wasn't much, but it could be useful. "What if I make the rest of that metal into a big shield? It would be thin and wouldn't wrap around us completely, but it would provide at least a little bit of protection if people started attacking us."

"That's a great idea!" Kodi exclaimed encouragingly. They were going to draw attention to themselves either way but at least this way they'd have a chance of not being killed right away.

Toby pulled the metal towards them, paying close attention to the way it glowed as it showed him its weak points. He pulled it into a square just big enough to cover all of them then rounded the top, so it covered their heads. He created two handles in it, one in the front and one in the back, so Kodi and him could hold it as they ran.

"You guys ready?" he asked, sliding his hand under the handle in the back.

Kodi copied him, grabbing the front as Akio gently picked Mateo off the ground and stood between them. "As ready as I'll ever be," she said.

"Keep a steady pace," Akio advised. "Fast but steady."

Kodi and Toby nodded, both their hands sweaty against the metal. Kodi looked over at him and nodded again. "One."

"Two," Toby said.

"Three!"

They picked up the metal and the three of them took off running. Toby's feet slid in the mush, but he managed to stay upright, knowing the others were depending on him. Kodi kept her eyes forward, her only thought being 'run'. She didn't know how far they had to go but she didn't care. She would just keep running. This was the last obstacle between her and her parents; the last thing she needed to overcome before she would be safe and could get back to her regular life with her sweet pups. Maybe she'd get another tattoo. Something to symbolize this life she barely had time to get to know before she'd leave it all behind.

They were a little over halfway across the open field and Toby pushed through his exhaustion as his breath came in small gasps. They were going to make it! Suddenly, Kodi and Toby were lifted off the ground with their metal shield. As it was lifted higher, they both let go and fell in a heap. Akio paused, further ahead of them since he hadn't been swept up.

"Keep going!" Kodi yelled at him. Akio hesitated for a moment but started running again when Kodi cried out, "Go! Please!"

Toby looked up and saw the strong woman hovering above them. She smiled wide, all her teeth showing, as she ripped the metal in two as if it were nothing but paper. Toby covered his ears at the noise as it set all his senses on overdrive. The woman tossed the metal to the side then cracked her knuckles as she stared at the two of them. They both quickly stood up and began backing away but were stopped by an invisible barrier. Toby banged his hands against it, but they just bounced off like he was on a trampoline.

"Welcome to the party, Fowley," the woman said as a short man came up beside her.

"Couldn't let you have all the fun, Anna," Fowley replied, and Anna grinned.

Kodi ran her hand along the barrier as she walked, but it seemed to lead in a circle.

"No use in trying to run," Fowley told her. "I've got you trapped."

"Clearly," Kodi responded with malice in her tone.

She stepped in front of Toby who wore his dread on his face. There had to be a way around Fowley's prison. Before she could do anything more, Anna stepped towards her and pulled her fist back. Kodi instantly ducked but Toby wasn't as quick, and Anna connected with his face. Toby's vision darkened as the pain swept through his jaw and up his ear as his eardrum ruptured. His eye instantly swelled, and he fell to the ground as blood flowed from somewhere on his face. A hard substance sat on his tongue, and he spit out a tooth that had been knocked out. One hit had done so much damage.

"And to think," Anna said with a purr in her voice. "That wasn't even half my strength."

Kodi wanted to make sure Toby was okay but knew she couldn't take her eyes off Anna. She was only a couple inches taller than Kodi, but it was clear her small stature didn't mean a thing. A hit at full strength would be deadly which meant Kodi couldn't let her get her hands on her.

Anna inched closer as Fowley sat on the ground away from them, clearly not a fighter. Kodi slowly circled her, keeping her attention away from Toby who was still trying to get up from the ground. Anna lunged forward, but Kodi quickly evaded her. Anna didn't lose her stamina though. She repeatedly dove after Kodi, but Kodi ducked around all her attacks. After a minute of playing cat and mouse, Anna glared and set her jaw. She turned around and launched her foot into Toby's stomach.

"No!" Kodi cried out, reaching her hand up helplessly as Toby hunched over.

He coughed out blood as he fell to his hands and knees, everything inside him seeming to explode with pain. He couldn't see, couldn't feel the cold that seeped into his clothes, couldn't even breathe. In one final effort to help Kodi make it, he called out to the metal that sat as broken and stagnant as he was. His vision blurred as he shaped part of it into a sharply edged spear. He breathed in as he began to lose consciousness then propelled the spear directly into Fowley's chest.

Anna shoved Kodi back into the barrier, rattling her brain. She did it over and over but then, Kodi didn't stop. She flew back past where the barrier had been. When she rolled onto the ground, she looked up and saw Fowley slouched over his knees. The barrier was gone. She glanced over at Toby, who's eyes were barely open and saw him mouth 'go' as his finger weakly pointed towards the trees. He had given her a way out.

Kodi looked to the trees then back to Toby who had passed out. She was so close to being free but as she watched Anna stomp over to him, she knew she couldn't leave him there. She took a calming breath then stood up and rushed Anna, jumping on her back and wrapping her in a headlock. She yanked back, causing Anna to fall away from Toby as she clung onto her. Anna let out an angry grunt then reached back with both her hands. She managed to grab the back of Kodi's shirt and heaved her over her head, propelling her directly into the ground. All the air rushed out of Kodi's lungs, and she wheezed as she tried to draw in a breath. Anna was done playing though. She slammed her foot into Kodi's shoulder, shattering the bones.

Kodi let out a high-pitched scream as pure agony filled her. She sobbed once, cradling her limp arm as she sat up. Anna raised her up by the wrist on her other arm then drew back her fist before hitting her in the chest. It wasn't hard enough to break her chest plate, but Kodi couldn't breathe again. It was as if Anna wanted to make her suffer as much as possible before killing her. She methodically hit Kodi as soon as she'd catch her breath, making sure she felt the torment in her lungs.

"It was nice knowing ya," Anna spat at Kodi, pulling her fist back one more time.

"Stop!" Kodi heard a familiar voice scream before she was suddenly wrapped in a curtain of water and safely pulled away from her attacker.

Chapter Forty-Nine

Robin

I sat on the floor with my back pressed against the damp wall. My wrists were rubbed raw, swollen and bleeding in spots from my attempts to free them from their cuffs. I leaned my head back against the cold stone as I listened to the sounds of war that made their way to my ears. Every so often I could feel the ground rumble and debris would fall on my head. Each time it happened, a new wave of panic filled me as I imagined the roof caving in and burying me alive.

The fighting hadn't been going on for long, but I was already on edge as my mind raced with thoughts and was overrun by fears. My parents and Matthew's family were somewhere out there, and I worried for their safety. I didn't know if they were all on the front lines, but I could only assume they were heavily involved in the fight already. Then I thought of the trainees. Was Mateo even alive? I had faith they'd all get out of wherever they were locked up, but their trek to the airspace made me uneasy. I needed to be there to protect them but instead I was stuck here, wallowing in my own anxieties.

I pulled at my cuffs again, pressing my lips together in a tight line as my wrists begged me to stop. I dropped my hands into my lap and let out a sob. After all the physical training and power growth, one lousy pair of handcuffs was going to do me in. How pathetic was that? I closed my eyes, letting the images of everyone I cared about flash in my mind. I had so much to fight for but here I was on the verge of giving up.

A commotion outside the door drew my attention. I sat up straighter, my mind immediately focusing as I waited to see what was going to happen. After a moment of quiet, the door creaked open. I jumped to my feet and eyed it suspiciously. A dark figure finally walked through, and a smile crept onto my face.

"Matthew!" I exclaimed happily, the relief of seeing him overwhelming me as more tears formed in my eyes.

He rushed over and quickly unlocked my cuffs before wrapping me in a tight hug as they clattered to the ground. I hugged him back just as hard and buried my head in his shoulder as his hand drifted to the back of my head. He wasn't normally one for physical affection, so I knew he had missed me as much as I had him.

"You came for me," I murmured, and he pushed me away so he could see my face.

His brows were furrowed at my comment. "You didn't think I would?"

I looked down. "I thought you were still mad at me."

"Of course, I am. But I would never be so mad that I'd leave you locked in a castle dungeon." His eyes were intense, silently chastising me for having such a thought.

I smiled softly and pulled him in for another hug. "I love you, Matthew."

"I know," he replied mockingly, so I shoved him away from me with a scowl. He grinned and slung one arm over my shoulders. "I love you too."

"I'm all for sappy reunions but we really have to go," William announced as he came around the door. "Hi, Robin."

"Hi, William," I replied with a wide smile on my face as I went over and gave him a quick hug.

"I'm glad to see you in one piece," he said, the closest he'd ever get to expressing his emotions. "The fight is getting dangerous. All our plans have been thrown out the window, and I'm not sure what's going to happen so we need to get you out while we can."

I nodded as Matthew put his hand on my lower back to usher me forward. Now that I wasn't locked up, I had a sense of determination again. I was ready for whatever was coming, and I knew I was going to get to the trainees.

"What the hell happened anyway?" Matthew asked as William led us out of the room. The guards were passed out on the ground, and I sidestepped around them. "Our first line of defense was completely ambushed. It's like they knew we were coming."

I hesitated, unsure how to explain without placing the blame on him.

"Robin?" William pressed, glancing back at me.

"It uhm . . . Well . . ." I paused, not wanting to say the words.

"What is it?" Matthew questioned.

I bit my lip but knew no matter what I said, his reaction would be the same. "Alexander heard you yelling at me that night."

I watched as realization dawned on him and he looked down, his eyes distraught.

"And?" William urged.

"And because he heard him yelling, he listened outside the door and heard Claire tell me when Garridan was going to attack."

William stopped in his tracks. "They knew we were coming?"

"They knew you were coming," I confirmed.

"Why didn't you warn us?" William asked with an accusing tone. "You saw Claire last night and you didn't say anything?!"

"I didn't know!" I cried out, almost angry at him for what he was insinuating. "I didn't find out until this morning when I was yanked out of bed and marched downstairs in my pajamas before being locked up here!"

William sighed. "I'm sorry. I didn't mean that . . . I just wish you could've done something before so many of us died."

"Don't put that on her," Matthew said quietly. "This is entirely my fault. I caused this . . . All because I couldn't keep my temper in check."

I could see him struggling with himself, the guilt evident on his face. I placed my hand on his shoulder and gave it a light squeeze, knowing how much he was beating himself up.

"We need to keep moving," William told us, his eyes sympathetic towards his little brother.

As we began walking again, William's words kept bugging me. I knew it wasn't the time to ask but I had to know. "What did you mean by 'so many of us died'?"

"Our first line of defense was wiped out by that old lady," William explained.

"Kiara," Matthew clarified, and my heart sank.

"How many?" I asked.

"Fifty, give or take," William answered. "Including three Keepers of Balance."

"Who?" I questioned intently as fear swelled inside me.

"Your parents are fine," William replied, immediately knowing what I was really asking, and relief filled me. "They were set to go in the second and third wave." He glanced at his watch.

"Which, with the way things were going, may have already been sent out."

An intense rumbling echoed in the walls around us as the ground began to shake. We all covered our heads and grabbed onto the wall to help keep us steady as we pushed on.

"What is that?" I asked as my legs wobbled beneath me.

"Probably one of the earth elements," William grunted.

"It's Alexander," Matthew said.

"How do you-"

"It's Alexander," he repeated with so much conviction that I didn't question him again.

"Speaking of which," I said, clearing my throat before continuing, "Alexander is going to try to kill you."

"Not if I get to him first," Matthew muttered with narrowed eyes.

"I'm serious," I told him, and he rolled his eyes.

"Alexander would never kill me."

I cocked one eyebrow at him. "Really? I thought you said he was a monster."

"He is."

"A monster would kill you."

"What can I say? I'm special," he half joked. I turned around and socked him in the arm. "Ow!"

"I'm serious!" I repeated angrily.

"So am I," he replied, ignoring my anger. "Alexander won't kill me. He can't. As much as I hate it, I'm his family."

I stayed quiet for a minute as I processed his words. It was so different from the other conversations we'd had about Alexander. Matthew held so much hate for him, but he couldn't honestly believe he was all bad if he thought Alexander wouldn't harm him. Could he?

"Why do you think Alexander is going to go after Matthew?" William asked, his concern evident in his voice.

"It's a punishment," I answered. "Toshiro blames him for me and Garridan's attack, so he told him to kill Matthew."

"Toshiro has told him that before," Matthew said. "He always gets around it."

"Not this time. He said if Alexander doesn't kill you, he would, and he'd make sure it was a slow and painful death. Alexander doesn't want that for you. He thinks he's giving you a mercy killing because it'll be quick."

Matthew pressed his lips into a tight line, and I could see that he finally understood the seriousness of what I was saying.

"Well, we'll just keep them both away from him then," William decided. Matthew and I exchanged a look, both of us knowing that wouldn't be possible, but we didn't say anything aloud as we reached a main corridor. "Okay, Matthew, direct us out of here."

"No," I denied. "We have to get to the old artifact room. That's where the trainees and I agreed to meet."

"We don't have time-" William started but I cut him off.

"We're going to *make* the time," I instructed firmly. "I'm not leaving them behind."

"Robin," William started, his patronizing tone making me narrow my eyes.

"If you want to leave then leave. I'm not going anywhere until I know they're all safe."

I stared him down, unwavering in my decision. He glanced at Matthew who only shrugged then sighed and rubbed his forehead. "Fine. Let's get your friends."

Matthew took the lead with William and I close behind. As we ran down the halls, I could hear the ongoing fight right outside the walls. I wanted to peek out of a window but knew there was no time. We paused as Matthew looked around a corner. He motioned us forward when he decided it was safe but a sudden searing pain in my shoulder blade caused me to cry out.

William immediately turned around and lifted his hands, encasing us in a force field. I peeked over my shoulder and saw multiple people running towards us. William bent his knees slightly and pushed out one arm. Part of his force field broke off and torpedoed towards the men. They sailed back on impact, striking the far wall behind them and falling to the ground in a huge limp pile.

"Are you okay?" Matthew asked as he checked out my wound.

"I'll live," I replied through clenched teeth as his touch sent a new wave of pain through me.

"What hit her?" William questioned.

"Looks like some form of a laser. But on the plus side, it cauterized the wound, so you won't bleed out."

"Tiny victories," I muttered, avoiding looking at the hole in my shoulder.

"Are you alright to keep going?" William asked, and I nodded.

"We're just around the corner from it," Matthew informed us as we started forward again.

We arrived with no other problems, but my heart dropped when I saw the room empty, all the artifacts on the ground smashed and shattered.

"No one's here," William stated.

I slowly turned in a circle, taking in every inch of the room. "Not anymore but they were."

"How can you tell?"

"I just can," I replied.

"Well, where are they now?" Matthew asked as he watched the door.

"Hopefully safe at the airspace."

"Which is where we need to be," William inserted in a no-nonsense voice. "Let's go."

We headed out again, this time with William staying behind me. We ran into little problems, and easily took care of the ones that we came across. We were on the opposite end of the castle when two beat up figures appeared, the smaller one limping as the larger one held them up. I squinted my eyes as they came closer and both Matthew and William stopped as they got in defensive positions.

"Wait!" I cried out to them as a smile crept onto my face. "It's Andre and Emery."

I ran past Matthew despite his objections and threw my arms around them.

"Robin!" Andre exclaimed as he wrapped his bleeding arm around me.

"Are you guys okay?" I asked as I took in their injuries.

"We'll be better when we get the hell out of here," Emery replied. "I swear there's more people around every corner."

"Where are the others?"

"They got out of the castle," Andre answered. "Last I could see they were running towards the airspace. Who are they?" He nodded to Matthew and William who had slowly come up behind me.

"This is Matthew and his brother William," I told them. "They're going to help us get the rest of the way out."

A large blast resonated through the castle just as a blinding light hit me. I held up my hands to protect my eyes as stones crashed around us. The floor gave way underneath me and I was suddenly free falling. William enveloped us all in his bubble of safety, keeping us unharmed by the castle walls as they caved in around us, but we all let out various degrees of groans as we smacked into the floor.

My lungs begged for air as I tried to catch my breath then I slowly sat up, my limbs screaming at me to stop. "Is everyone okay?"

"Dandy," Emery said, followed by a cough.

"All good," William replied, and Matthew and Andre nodded in agreement.

"What happened?" I asked, trying to see past the billows of dirt.

"Looks like the whole side of the castle got hit," Matthew answered as he stood up and looked around. "But hey, at least we're outside now."

He was right. The entire outside wall had caved in not far from where we were. The bleak sky looked dangerously close to producing more snow and a shiver ran up my spine as the cold air hit me. I walked over the rubble until my feet landed on the damp ground. A bloodcurdling scream reached my ears, and I searched around to find the source.

"No," I whispered.

Kodi was being held up by Anna, who had an angry expression on her face. Anna drew her fist back before slamming it into Kodi's chest. Without giving it a second thought, I was running towards them. I pushed my legs harder and faster than I ever had before as Anna continued pounding on Kodi. As I got closer, I saw two bodies on the ground. A mixture of rage and grief filled me when I realized one of them was Toby. Anna brought her fist back once again and I saw red.

"Stop!" I screamed before sending a jet wave into Anna's arm.

She dropped Kodi as I pulled a wall of water between them. I quickly wrapped Kodi in the stream just enough to be able to pull her out of harm's way before blasting my powers full speed at

Anna. She fell over from the force of it and I collected more water, building it until it was a steady torrent. With lots of concentration, I propelled it forward and it became a torrent as it cascaded away from us with Anna trapped in its midst. When I was sure she wouldn't be able to come back, I dropped my arms and ran to where Kodi lay on the ground. She was shivering intensely, and I realized how cold she must be now that she was wet.

"I'm so sorry I got you wet!" I exclaimed as I sat her up.

"It's o-okay," she said around her chattering teeth. "Just glad you came when you d-did."

"Are you okay?" I asked as Emery and Andre reached us.

"Yeah. How's T-Toby?"

"I don't know," I replied as I looked to him, afraid to know the answer.

Andre quickly made his way to him and put two fingers on the side of his neck. "He's alive."

I breathed out a sigh of relief. "What about Mateo?"

"He's s-safe. Akio got him to the airspace."

"Akio?"

"Long story."

"For another time," I said as I looked at the devastation happening around us. "We have to get you guys to the airspace too. Where's Matthew and William?"

"Alexander got them," Emery told me, and my heart sank.

I have to help them too.

"Do you think you can make it alone?" I asked.

"Why? What about you?" Kodi asked.

"I'm not don't here yet."

"Neither are we!" Emery declared. "We can help."

"No, you can't. You're all hurt. You'll only get in the way," I told them. "Please. Go to the airspace." They exchanged glances, none of them happy by that prospect. "Please. Get Toby there and get him help."

"Okay," Andre finally agreed.

"Okay," Emery echoed, and Kodi nodded.

"You're going to meet us there though, right?" Kodi asked.

"Yes. As soon as I can."

"Stay safe, Robin," Andre told me as he gently picked Toby up in his arms.

"I will."

As they began to jog away, I kept my eyes peeled for any signs of danger. When they hit the tree line, Kodi glanced back, and I nodded encouragingly before turning away. I ran headfirst into the battle, dodging high energy attacks and striking anyone who got in my way with an outflow of water. I surveyed the land around me, hell-bent on finding Alexander and Matthew, when my eyes landed on Elijah instead. He was locked in a struggle with Toshiro, and it looked like he was about to lose.

I watched with wide eyes as Toshiro launched him back, then Elijah was pushing his arms and legs out as if fighting off an invisible force. My brows furrowed as I watched Elijah's limbs being pressed closer into his body even though I still couldn't see anything around him. My eyes drifted to Toshiro who had a maniacal smile upon his face, and I realized it was him who was still attacking Elijah. Elijah's face was full of determination, but his body was folding up as if a box were closing in around him.

Without giving it a second thought, I bolted forward. I wouldn't lose another family member to this man. Instead of using my powers, I launched myself at Toshiro's back. He fell to the ground with a grunt, and I connected my fist to his face. I let all my anger towards him pour into my punches as I remembered everything he had done to uproot my life. I struck him for my mom and Dawn. I clobbered him for Matthew. I hit him for the trainees. For Alexander. Ben. Felicity. Elijah. Adriana. Me.

Toshiro lay still on the ground, his face covered in blood. I could feel him breathing but he wasn't fighting back. Had he passed out? I slowly slid myself off his chest and turned around to see if Elijah was safe. As soon as my back was turned, Toshiro swept his foot forward, knocking my legs out from under me. I fell onto my back, and he pinned me down, his hands wrapped tightly around my neck.

"I'm just about tired of you," he hissed as he applied more pressure to my throat. I clawed at his arms as my windpipe was crushed. "You're more hassle than you're worth!"

I pushed his face away from mine, desperately trying to latch onto something that would hurt him

"You know," he said with a sneer, "I think we can find a different way to produce a pure blood line. Let's call this a second punishment for our dear Alexander, shall we? Say goodbye, Robin."

Not today you bastard.

I conjured up all the energy I could muster and shot it out at his chest. The force of the water flung him off of me and I rolled over, coughing incessantly as my lungs dragged in air through my throbbing throat. I pushed my hands in front of me and lugged myself off the ground as my eyes tried to refocus. When I managed to stand upright, Toshiro was limping towards me with pure hatred in his eyes. I narrowed my own at him and let my lips travel down into a scowl. It was time to end this once and for all.

Chapter Fifty

Matthew and Alexander

"Robin, wait!" Matthew yelled as she took off past the demolished wall. Unsurprising to him, she didn't listen.

He made his way over the rubble with William, Emery, and Andre close behind. The cold didn't bother him as he ran after her. All he knew was he had to help her. She was stronger and more powerful than he was, and he knew she could take care of herself, but he still had to be there in case she needed him. He had promised Ben he'd keep her safe and so far, he'd been failing. Before they could make it any further, a new tree line popped up directly in front of them, blocking their way. Matthew turned around, already knowing what he'd see.

"Hello, Matthew," Alexander said as he stepped forward with his hands laced behind his back.

"Alexander," Matthew replied as Andre and Emery began backing away.

Alexander saw them from the corner of his eye but chose to ignore them as he focused on what he was about to do.

"Stay away from him," William growled, stepping in front of his little brother and forming a force field around the two of them.

Alexander observed him, noticing the similarities in their features. "This must be your brother."

"Yeah. He is. My *real* brother," Matthew answered, throwing the jab in there just to hurt him.

Alexander kept his face neutral despite the sadness that filled him. He was genuinely happy that Matthew had found his family. He was relieved when Robin told him how well Matthew had adjusted in Garridan. All he ever wanted was for Matthew to be safe and secure, but it was always hard to see the hate he had for him. Alexander couldn't blame him though. The way he had chosen to protect him only harmed him worse in the long run. But Alexander was only a child himself when they were brought here. He didn't know any better back then and now it was too late to change the things he wished he could.

"I've been waiting for you," Alexander said.

"So I've heard," Matthew replied.

"I knew she'd warn you," Alexander told him. Matthew furrowed his brows at the way he said it. It was as if he *wanted* Robin to warn him. "I just wish you had heeded it."

"I'm not afraid of you, Alexander."

"I know, but that's because you've never had a reason to fear me before."

Matthew couldn't deny the truth in that. Alexander had tortured him in numerous ways over the years, but he had never truly harmed him. He'd even saved his life a time or two from leaders of the Cyfrin. Despite the animosity Matthew felt for him, he knew Alexander had always been there for him even if it wasn't in the conventional way. Even now, in his own twisted way, he thought he was doing right by Matthew.

"You're not going to kill me," Matthew told him, setting his jaw defiantly.

"I don't have a choice," Alexander said through gritted teeth.

"A mercy killing," Matthew mocked.

"Would you rather Toshiro be in charge of your death?"

"I'd rather not die at all."

"Unfortunately, that's not an option."

"It is in my book."

"Matthew."

"Alexander."

They stared each other down, both their hands balled into fists at their sides.

"I think we should go," William said softly to Matthew.

Alexander laughed. "Go? You think you can just *go*? Fine, you want to leave? Be my guest."

He shot a thick vine into the ground, working it underneath William's force field before crumbling the earth under William's feet. He wrapped the vine all the way up William's leg then yanked him through the broken ground and pulled him through the earth until he was in front of Alexander.

"Alexander, stop!" Matthew yelled as William's forcefield evaporated but Alexander ignored him.

"Goodbye, real brother," he told William before flinging him far into the air.

Matthew knew William's forcefield would keep him safe from the fall but that didn't ease his anger any. "You're psychotic!"

"Why can't you understand the predicament I'm in?" Alexander questioned in frustration.

"Because it's your own fault you're in it!" Matthew yelled.

"Damn it, Matthew!" Alexander roared, his anger finally getting the best of him, and he yanked Matthew into the castle wall by the rubble, fastening him to it with strong tree roots. At the same time, he created a thick barrier of vines around them, almost completely blocking them from the dangers that lurked a few feet away. "You don't get it. You've *never* gotten it. I've taken your hate, your anger, and everything else all these years because you needed someone to blame. I understood. I was okay with bearing that load so you could feel better about yourself but not anymore. I need you to realize something very important and now is the last chance you'll get to."

"What's that?" Matthew asked as he tried to yank his arms free.

"I was barely older than you when we were brought here," Alexander replied. His answer made Matthew pause. "I was only a child myself. I didn't *bring* us here. I didn't *choose* this for us. We were taken. This life was forced on me as much as it was on you."

"You could've run. You could've taken us both away from here," Matthew stated, but there was no conviction behind his words as feelings stirred deep inside him.

"I was six years old with a four-year-old brother in the middle of nowhere. Where would I have run? How would I have taken care of us?" Alexander diverted his gaze. "Besides, they treated us so much better than our foster parents. Or don't you remember how much we loved being here?"

Matthew stayed silent, unsure what to say. He talked a big game about how much he despised Alexander and how much of a monster he was. However, when it came down to it, Alexander was just another pawn grown by the Cyfrin. He hated the things Alexander had done but it was a hypocritical stance since he himself had done things just as awful. What he said about Matthew made sense, but Matthew had never seen it that way before. To the outside eye, it was painfully obvious, and Matthew realized it's exactly what he had been doing.

"You're right," Matthew finally said.

"What?" Alexander questioned, not expecting those words.

"You're right," Matthew repeated as he met Alexander's gaze. "It wasn't your fault. None of it was." He took a deep breath, working up the courage to continue. He wasn't one to speak his feelings. He despised it, actually, but Alexander deserved an explanation and maybe, just maybe, it would change Alexander's mind about killing him. "I grew to hate who I had become, and I needed someone to blame for all the things I did for the Cyfrin. I didn't have the guts to take responsibility for myself . . . But there you were. It was easy to place it all on you because you seemed so in sync with everything they wanted, everything they stood for. So . . . I started directing all the rage and resentment I felt for the Cyfrin onto you because it was the easy way out. And you just took it like it was nothing."

The battle noise faded into the background as Alexander listened to Matthew speak. He hadn't expected Matthew to own up to the truth so easily and he wasn't sure if it made him feel any better or not. Before he could think on it anymore, Matthew continued.

"But the truth is . . . I never hated you, Alexander." He caught Alexander's gaze. "I could never hate you . . . As much as I'd like to deny it, you're still my family."

Alexander swallowed loudly as he tried to ward off the emotions Matthew was stirring in him. "Why do you have to go and say crap like that now?"

"Just hoping you won't kill me," Matthew replied, playing it off at a joke despite it being the truth.

Alexander looked down. "You know I can't disobey Toshiro."

"So you'll have killing me on your conscience all because of his say so?" Alexander stayed quiet so Matthew kept going. "What happens when he commands you to kill Robin? Will you do that too?"

"Toshiro needs her," Alexander said, narrowing his eyes at the change of subject. "He won't have me kill her."

"Not right now. But what if he decides he doesn't need her in a year or two? How can you guarantee her safety if you'll do whatever he tells you to?"

Matthew could tell he struck a nerve and decided this was his one opportunity to get free. As Alexander contemplated what he had said, Matthew let the mushy feelings of his powers fill his body. It was like slightly hardened clay traveling through his veins. He let it roll out his hands in a sluggish stream, molding it to the outside of the tree roots. It ate through the inside until it connected on the opposite end then Matthew used all his strength, straining as hard as he could, until the petrified roots cracked and crumbled around him.

Alexander saw him start running, petrifying the barrier around them as he went. Matthew continued headfirst into it, breaking through and not stopping.

Alexander sighed and shook his head before walking after him. "Oh, Matthew."

As Matthew ran, he looked towards the tree lining for Robin but didn't see her. Maybe she had gotten away already! He looked straight ahead, concentrating on getting away himself, when a familiar voice met his ears. He stopped and glanced around quickly. His eyes widened when he saw Toshiro and Robin locked in a power struggle. He took one step their way, but his other leg was yanked from underneath him as Alexander dragged him back.

Matthew let out a frustrated growl. He didn't have time for this. He had to help Robin. He petrified the vine around his leg and broke free, but Alexander just wrapped another one in its place. Alexander towered over him, but Matthew wasn't done fighting. He reached his free leg up and forcefully kicked Alexander's knee. Alexander fell to the ground, wincing in pain, and Matthew sucker punched him in the face. Then Matthew barreled into him, knocking him backwards as he slammed his head into Alexander's jaw. Alexander used Matthew's momentum to throw him over his head and Matthew landed with a loud thud on his back as Alexander stood up.

Matthew let his powers roll out of him, petrifying Alexander's feet so he couldn't move but Alexander immediately wrapped both Matthew's arms inside an unbloomed corpse flower while dropping the rest of his body into the ground. Matthew looked over to Robin again and saw her being beaten down. Her face was covered in blood and Toshiro had her locked inside one of his air condensing boxes. Panic filled him as the space around Robin started closing in around her. Without intervention, she'd face a painful death.

"Alexander!" Matthew yelled, the desperation evident in his voice. "Look!"

Alexander glanced over to where Matthew nodded and instantly froze. What was Toshiro doing? He watched as Robin hopelessly clawed at the invisible box shrinking around her. It was Toshiro's unbeatable skill.

"You have to help her!" Matthew shouted, knowing Alexander was the only person who could stop Toshiro.

Alexander opened his mouth, but no words came out as he stared at Robin. Even bleeding and bruised, she was beautiful to him but the fear on her face made him want to go primal. His protective side screamed for him to do something, but frustration overtook him. She could've easily ended the fight with Toshiro before it even began. She could've used her jet stream to pierce his heart, and this wouldn't be happening. But she hadn't. Of course she hadn't. She still had a heart untouched by the darkness. She would never kill anyone, even if it meant saving herself.

"Alexander!" Matthew called out again, his voice pleading and near hysteria. He couldn't watch her die. He had promised Ben she'd be safe with him. She was his best friend, and he couldn't fathom the thought of losing her. "Alexander!"

"He won't kill her," Alexander murmured as he watched. "He won't."

"Open your eyes! He *is* killing her!" Matthew stared at Alexander as he continued to watch what was happening and he knew he had to say the one thing he didn't want to think about. "You can't let him kill her . . . You love her."

Alexander whipped his head around. "How do you know that?"

"Because I know *you*. So don't let her die. Please. *Please*!"

All of Alexander's senses were on hyperdrive. He had a choice to make, and he didn't know what to do. He couldn't let Robin die but betraying Toshiro would mean the end for him. He thought back to Matthew's earlier words: *You could've run. You could've taken us away from here*. He was right. Alexander couldn't have done anything when they were so young but there had been plenty of opportunities to escape as they grew older. Alexander had just chosen not to.

Matthew broke away from the Cyfrin and Alexander could've done the same, but he didn't. He chose to rule. He chose to be on the side he thought had more power, the side he thought would win the war. He had killed. He had treated good people like they were worth nothing. He had conspired to end the world. When it came down to it, he did all that just so he could live. He chose his own well-being over everything else, and he realized now just how sickening that was.

He looked back to Robin. Toshiro had tightened the box around her to the point that she couldn't move anymore. Alexander watched as her knees started compressing against her chest and pain showed on her expression. A split second later, her eyes rolled into the back of her head. Anger filled him and, in that moment, he made his choice.

Today, all his misgivings would be thrown out the window. Today, he'd do right by someone no matter the consequence. Today, he'd choose someone else's life over his own.

"Unpetrify my feet, Matthew! *Now*!" he roared as he freed Matthew's arms.

Matthew quickly complied, then pulled himself out of the ground as Alexander took off running. Matthew watched as Alexander raised his arms, shaking the ground all around as he thrust his hands forward. A large boulder rumbled out of the earth and slid onto its side, landing directly on Toshiro's leg and pinning him to the ground as he cried out in pain. The box around Robin immediately disappeared and Matthew lurched forward, running over to her and falling to his knees.

He cradled her limp body in his arms as he petrified two Cyfrin members coming their way but many more were following behind, seeing their leader in distress. Matthew's eyes jumped around, trying to figure out how to fight while also keeping Robin safe when static met his ears. He scanned the perimeter as a force field circled around him and smiled with relief when he saw William running up the courtyard.

The ground opened between Matthew and the Cyfrin members, then a thick tree trunk swept over him and knocked into the people standing in its way. He glanced over to where Alexander had been with Toshiro and saw Alexander walking towards him while fighting off the Cyfrin members who were around them. They made eye contact and Alexander nodded once as he continued to take down those left standing. Toshiro's rule had finally come to an end.

Chapter Fifty-One

I opened my eyes and blinked rapidly as they adjusted to the light. Matthew was holding onto me but staring at something in the distance. I noticed the glow of a force field around us, and the earth rumbled continuously underneath me. I shifted in Matthew's arms, and his gaze was immediately drawn to my face.

"You're awake!" he exclaimed.

"How long was I out for?" I asked, struggling to sit up.

Matthew gently pushed me off his arms until I was upright, and I fought the urge to throw up as all my internal organs protested the movement. "Only a couple minutes. How do you feel?"

"Like my insides want to burst."

"That'll happen when you're squished to death," Matthew commented, and I inhaled sharply as I remembered being pushed together inside an invisible threat.

"Where's Toshiro?"

"He's dead."

My mouth fell open, the words not completely registering. "What?"

"Alexander killed him."

"Alexander . . . Killed him?" I repeated.

"Turns out he couldn't watch you die. He stopped Toshiro and finished him off," Matthew said. "Now he's trying to stop the rest of the fighting."

"Why?" I asked softly, my brows furrowed as I thought back to our last conversation. He wanted the Cyfrin to win; he wanted to live.

"By some small miracle," Matthew paused and shook his head, "you turned the monster into just a beast."

His voice wasn't cynical like I expected it to be, and his eyes were gentle as he watched me. He was being sincere, and it threw me off. Something told me there was an underlying meaning to his words, but I didn't have time to question it as another loud rumble tore through the earth. I searched around for Alexander but got distracted as my eyes took in the scene before me. The town was in ruins, the ground was ripped open in unnatural ways, and bodies littered the ground. My stomach dropped at the sight. The casualty number was going to be high.

"We have to end this now," I told Matthew, and he nodded in agreement just as William ran up to us.

"Are you two okay?" he asked as he lowered the forcefield.

"We're fine thanks to you," Matthew told him as he helped me stand.

"We need to get you both out of here," William instructed.

"We can't leave," I said. "We have to stop the fighting."

"You're not going to be able to do that," William replied with a shake of his head.

"Toshiro is dead," Matthew informed him, stopping him cold in his tracks. "And Alexander is fighting against the Cyfrin members. Once they realize that, the majority of them will cower."

"Which means we just need to find a way to let everyone know that," I added in, already trying to figure out how we could do it.

"Okay," William agreed. "But how?"

"Let's find Alexander," Matthew instructed. "I have the feeling he and Robin might be our only hope at getting everyone's attention."

"He was heading down the courtyard into town where the fighting is the worst," William said.

"Then let's go!" I replied.

"Run and don't stop," William told us. "I'll keep the forcefield around us as we go so we can get through the courtyard. Don't stop for anything." He looked over at me. "That means you, Robin. Even if you see someone you know, we can't stop."

"Better yet," Matthew spoke up, "just keep your eyes forward."

I nodded in agreement, knowing they were right in calling me out. I couldn't help that I wanted to keep everyone safe, but it was my downfall at times. I needed to stay focused on what was important: stopping the battle entirely so *everyone* was safe.

William quickly sparked a forcefield and we took off, weaving in and out of countless duels as we made our way through the courtyard. It took everything in me not to look to see who was fighting. It took even more strength not to stop to help every single member of Garridan who was in trouble. Matthew suddenly stopped in front of me, and I bumped into him, knocking us down as William tripped over our legs.

"A little warning would've been nice," William growled, but Matthew ignored him as we stood.

"There's Alexander," he announced.

I looked to where he pointed and saw Alexander knocking a building onto some of the Cyfrin members. He said something I couldn't hear to the Garridan guards, and they took off running as he turned around.

"Alexander!" I yelled.

He froze as my voice reached him and he looked over his shoulder to find me. When our eyes met, the relief showed on his face, and he quickly jogged to where we stood. "You're okay," he said when he reached us.

"Thanks to you, I hear," I replied, one side of my lips turning up in a grateful smile, and he returned it with a half-smile of his own.

"I owed you."

"Can the pleasantries wait until later?" Matthew grumbled, and Alexander glanced his way.

"You're right. This needs to end. Got any ideas?"

"I do actually," Matthew retorted before looking up at William. "I need you to lower the forcefield."

William glowered at Alexander. "I don't trust him."

"You don't have to," Matthew told him. "Just trust me."

William tore his gaze away from Alexander and observed Matthew. After a moment, he nodded and slowly dissolved his shield of protection from around us before telling Alexander, "I'm watching you."

Alexander rolled his eyes, clearly not intimidated by the threat. "What's your big idea, Matthew?"

"Mud."

"I beg your pardon?"

"Mud," Matthew repeated as we all stared at him with confusion. "If you lift up enough dirt, Robin can create mud with her water. Then you can raise it high enough to where everyone is stuck in it."

"That won't work," Alexander denied. "We'd have to have the perfect combination of the water with the dirt otherwise it wouldn't be thick enough to immobilize anyone."

"But if we raised it high enough around everyone, Matthew could just petrify it all," I inserted. "Then they'd all be stuck no matter what."

"Some people could still manage to get out of it with their abilities," Alexander said.

"Then we need to be quick about telling them what we need to tell them," I responded.

"How are you going to get everyone to hear what you need to say though?" William asked.

"I think I can help with that," someone said, and I looked over to see Malachi limping towards us with a teenage boy at his side. I recognized him almost immediately. He was a senior at our school.

"Good to see you, Robin," Malachi greeted me with a hug. "This is Javier. He can manipulate sound." He looked over to Alexander, his face professional but full of contempt. "Say what you need to say to stop the Cyfrin and Javier will make sure they hear it."

Alexander nodded in understanding before turning to me and Matthew. "Are you ready?"

"Ready," I replied.

"Let's finish this," Matthew answered.

"Stand back," Alexander instructed Malachi and Javier as he closed his eyes in concentration.

The earth began to rumble under our feet, and I watched with wide eyes as he conjured up the loose dirt as far as the eye could see. It was thick and chunky as it circled around everyone fighting, and they all stopped as they watched the strange sight. Alexander's lips were pressed together tightly, and a bead of sweat dropped down his temple as his eyebrows began to twitch. This was taking a lot out of him.

"Robin," he said without opening his eyes, and I took my cue to call upon the water around me.

I felt it in the air as it swirled around us and in the ground as it pulsed under the crust. I pulled it all together, allowing it to travel to the dirt mounds Alexander had created. The wide terrain was difficult to cover but I pushed past my limitations, making sure every inch was touched by the liquid. When it connected, I integrated the molecules into the sod and let it soak down until it was a dense mixture between solid and liquid. I felt Alexander's energy as he began to shape it around people, but it was slow going, and I realized it was too watered down for him to control fully. I had to help.

I connected with the water again and worked to push it where Alexander was wanting it to go. Our energies surged together, intertwining as they worked as one. I could feel his power like it was my own and our combined strengths made easy work as we molded the mud up high enough to incapacitate anyone within our radius.

"Matthew, now," Alexander instructed through gritted teeth.

Matthew stepped up and slowly raised his arms. He turned in a circle, each of his fingers operating in their own tune and I felt the moment the mounds were petrified as the water was stolen from me. People yelled out all around, some angry, some confused. Alexander and I both dropped our arms as Matthew finished, then he nodded over to us. Alexander looked back at Javier and motioned him forwards.

"Say what you need to say," Javier told him.

Alexander took a deep breath and let it out slowly before starting. "Cyfrin members," he said, his voice strong and unwavering. "Toshiro is dead. *I* killed him and I'll do the same to any of you if you choose to keep fighting . . . Let this mark our time in history as coming to an end. Our purpose is obsolete. It always has been, and it always will be. You have no leaders. So stop fighting . . . The Cyfrin is no more."

* * *

"There's my mom! She's okay!" I exclaimed, running towards her as we came closer to the organized chaos going on just past the town limits.

A group of Keepers of Balance were directing the last of the Cyfrin members around. They were being separated into smaller groups with twice as many guards watching over them, each lot containing at least one guard member who could silence powers so no one could try anything funny. Many of them ceased fire at Alexander's say so, their own self-preservation worth more than the lost cause they were fighting for once they realized Alexander had turned against them. There were plenty of others who had kept fighting, their anger igniting new rounds of battle, but with so many people against them and not enough backup, they quickly were captured or killed, ending the fighting entirely.

"Mom!" I called out when I got closer.

She didn't look up and I realized it's because she never had to answer to that name before. I chose to call her and my dad by their first names to preserve my other family but now I saw how silly that was. She was my mom just as much as my other mom was and that didn't smear her memory in any way. I was just lucky enough to have had two amazing mothers at different points in my life.

She looked up just before I reached her and gasped as I threw my arms around her. She enveloped me in an embrace, squeezing me tightly. "Oh, honey. I'm *so* happy to see you!" She pushed me back and looked me over, taking in every visible injury on me. "Are you okay?"

"I'm fine, Mom," I replied, and her eyes widened at my words. I saw her chin quiver slightly and rushed to continue before she had a chance to say anything. "Are *you* okay?"

"Yes," she said, then cleared her throat as her voice cracked from the emotion she was feeling. "I never even set foot on the battleground. I was stationed in the last line of defense."

"What about Dad?"

"What about Dad?" I heard him say from behind me. I turned to see him with a wide smile that filled his entire bruised-covered face. He wrapped his arms around us, and Mom buried her face in his chest.

"I was so worried!" she told him.

"I got lucky," he responded before giving me a knowing look. He didn't want her to know just how close he had come to being killed.

"I can't believe it's over," she said quietly as we look around us.

Healers were working quickly to save everyone they could, but there was already a significant line of bodies that hadn't made it. I knew their job wasn't going to be over anytime soon as guard members continually added more injured soldiers to their area.

"What happens now?" I asked.

"We'll start transporting people back to Garridan," Dad replied. "The Cyfrin members will be locked up and they'll each stand trial. Some might be rehabilitated and spared but I'm afraid many more won't. It'll be a long road. No one will forget what's happened here anytime soon."

"Speaking of which," Mom said as she watched Alexander walk up with the Alastair family.

She immediately shifted from concerned mom and wife to Keeper of Balance, standing taller and getting that air of authority about her. Alexander stopped in front of us with William and Malachi staying close to him as Matthew came and stood next to me. There was a brief moment of silence as my parents observed him, but he held his ground, his eyes unwavering from theirs.

"Are you really responsible for Toshiro's death?" Dad asked.

"I am," Alexander answered.

Mom and Dad exchanged a look with Malachi, then with Matthew who nodded in confirmation.

"That and the fact that you helped stop the fighting will give you a chance of not being executed," Mom told him. "But the transgressions against you are high and no one will look forgivingly to you. With no one on your side, it's very likely you'll be charged with the death penalty."

"*I'm* on his side," I spoke up, my head pounding with tension at the idea of him being killed.

"I'm afraid that won't mean much to anyone on the council," Dad told me gently.

"Then both of you need to be on his side," I told them, and their eyebrows creased simultaneously. "He was just a child when he was brought here. It's not his fault he ended up the way he did. What if the Cyfrin had found me when I was younger and I turned out just like him? Would you blame me? Would you not fight for me to have a chance?" I could tell I rattled them with that comparison but they weren't on board yet so I hit them with the thing I knew they couldn't write off. "He saved my life."

Mom glanced at Alexander before turning back to me. "What?"

"Toshiro almost killed me. I was fighting him, and I was losing. Alexander jumped in to save me and that's when he killed him. I'd be dead if it wasn't for him."

Mom and Dad shared another long look. "We'll discuss this more later. In private," Dad told me.

"Take him to the loading center," Mom instructed Malachi who nodded and pushed Alexander forward.

As he was passing us, Dad grabbed him by the arm and said, "Thank you."

"It wasn't for your benefit," Alexander stated.

"I'm well aware, but thank you anyway," Dad responded as he let go of his arm.

Alexander's eyes met mine and I offered him a timid smile. He didn't return it, but I could see how badly he wanted to speak to me. Malachi pushed him forward again and he glanced back at me once more before walking away. I knew I'd have to advocate for him.

"Let's get you all seen by a healer, then we'll head out," Mom said.

"No," I denied with a shake of my head. "Let them focus on everyone who needs it. Our injuries aren't life threatening. We'll be fine."

"I agree," Matthew said.

"Me too," Dad added as he appraised me with proud eyes.

Mom smiled at us all affectionately as she placed her hand in Dad's. "Then let's go home."

Chapter Fifty-Two

Garridan was still. It looked so serene and peaceful compared to the battleground we just came from. It seemed unaffected from the horrors that had occurred, but I knew that wasn't true. In the courthouse, Cyfrin members were being sorted into the underground prison system. In the hospital, wounded guard members were being healed. In the morgue and churches, family members were being told their loved ones had fought valiantly to the very end. No one had come out untouched by the battle.

"It's weird being back," I told Matthew as I looked around. "Everything's changed yet nothing's different."

"Hey," he said, pulling my attention to him as he put his hand on my shoulder. "You did good, Robin. You know that right?"

I didn't answer, mixed emotions going through me. I thought I'd feel a bigger sense of relief at the Cyfrin's downfall, but it didn't feel real yet. It didn't feel complete. Maybe after all the members had been dealt with that feeling would change but for now, I needed closure on my own problems.

"Where are the trainees?" I asked.

"They're in the hospital," Mom answered.

"I need to see them."

"Of course. We'll take you there now."

When we arrived, it was surprisingly calm for a hospital considering the circumstances. Then again, this wasn't your normal hospital. Akio was sitting in a chair in the waiting room, and I remembered Kodi saying he had gotten Mateo to safety. I didn't know how or why but he must've had answers about him.

"How's Mateo?" I asked as we walked up to him.

He looked up, then immediately stood when he saw my parents. "Elijah. Adriana."

"Hello, Akio," Dad said as Mom placed her hand on his arm. "It's been a long time. Welcome back."

Matthew and I exchanged a glance and he asked, "What's going on?"

"Akio has been our guy on the inside for a while now," Dad explained.

"You were a *spy*?" Matthew questioned, turning on him with disbelief in his voice.

Akio nodded and I raised my eyebrows in surprise as Mom spoke up. "We had a handful of them actually."

"How do you think Garridan was always one step ahead of the Cyfrin in the past?" Dad asked. "Unfortunately, Toshiro started to suspect so he began limiting who knew what. We never could manage to wiggle someone into his tight circle."

"Which is when we stopped getting concrete information," Mom added. "It was a huge disappointment."

"I'm sure," I said, my tone borderline sarcastic. It's not that I didn't care. I wanted to hear all this, just not right now. I had higher priorities at the moment. "How's Mateo?"

"He's asleep," Akio told me. "It was touch and go there for a while, but we finally got him stable enough to not be concerned. Priya will finish the process tomorrow after his body has had some time to rest."

"So he's going to be okay?" I confirmed. Akio nodded and relief surged through me. "What about the others?"

"As far as I know, they're all fine. The chubby one—what's his name?"

"Toby?"

"Yes, Toby. His injuries weren't nearly as bad as Mateo's, but he took a good hit. He'll probably be asleep for a while as well but the other three are awake and being kept overnight for observation"

"Am I allowed to see them?"

"Of course," Mom answered. "I'll find out what rooms they're in."

As she walked away, I observed Akio. His face was sad and withdrawn. "I'm sorry about your brother."

"I'm sorry about my brother too," he responded, more depth to his words than most would realize.

I hesitated before saying, "Thank you. For helping them get out."

"I really didn't do much."

"You kept them alive." I gave him a grateful smile, then heard my mom call me. "Are you coming?" I asked Matthew and Dad as they hung back.

"I'm going to stay here with Akio," Matthew replied. "I have some questions. Besides, I'm sure you want to see your friends alone."

"I'll see you later then?"

"You can count on it."

"Dad?" I pressed.

"Go see your friends. I'll be here waiting when you come back," he told me, giving me a quick peck on the head before ushering me away.

I followed my mom to the second story. When the elevator door opened, she said, "They're all in room 215. They wanted to stay together."

"Don't you want to meet them?" I asked as I stepped out.

"Of course I do but that can wait. Go spend some time with them. Malachi and I are going to notify their families that they're here."

"That's going to be rough, isn't it?"

"It's never easy," she replied sadly.

The door closed as she said goodbye and I made my way down the hall, checking the door numbers as I went. When I got to room 215, I lightly knocked on the door before opening it. It was a standard shared room, but three rollaway beds had been jammed into the small space around the two hospital beds.

"You're okay!" Kodi exclaimed when she saw me. She hopped off her bed and ran to give me a hug that I happily returned. "We were so worried."

"And here I thought you guys had confidence in me," I joked with a shake of my head.

"Of course we do," Andre assured me as he wrapped me in his arms, "but that doesn't make us worry any less."

"I don't know what they're blabbing about," Emery spoke up from where she sat on her bed. "I wasn't worried for a second."

"Uh huh," Andre said at the same time Kodi sarcastically muttered, "Okay."

"Good to see you too, Emery," I told her with a grin that she returned.

"Why haven't you seen a healer?" Kodi asked as she looked over my battered body.

"There were people who needed them more than me. I'll go when things die down." I walked in between where Mateo and Toby lay and watched as they slept. "They look so peaceful."

"Just wait until they start snoring," Andre commented, and I smiled.

As I stared down at them, my emotions started to get the best of me, and I swallowed around the lump forming in my throat. "I'm so thankful you're all okay. I don't know what I would've done if one of you hadn't made it."

"Then it's a good thing we don't have to find out," Andre said, grabbing my shoulder and giving it a tight squeeze.

I nodded, not trusting my voice as Kodi grabbed my hand in her own and said, "We got lucky."

"Luck didn't haven't anything to do with it," Emery told her with a roll of her eyes.

"I meant with Robin," Kodi clarified, flipping Emery the bird before continuing. "If it wasn't for you, none of us would've made it out of there. Half of us probably wouldn't have even made it through training. I really believe you're the only reason we're here right now, so thank you."

My eyes watered as she spoke, and a tear spilled onto my cheek.

"I agree," Andre said, his voice quiet. "Thank you."

"Yeah . . . Thanks, Robin," Emery chimed in softly, her usual scowl turned up in a grateful smile.

I nodded my head vigorously as I began to cry. They weren't the reason I had gone to the Cyfrin compound, but they were the reason I made it through. They gave me something to fight for every day and a reason to be strong. They all helped me just as much as I helped them. I took a deep breath and let it out in a shaky laugh as I wiped at my eyes.

"Thanks for making me cry," I told them.

"If Toby was awake, he'd cry with you," Emery said, and I laughed at the truth in it.

"And Mateo would crack a joke to make you smile," Kodi added.

"They'll be awake soon enough," Andre said.

"Then you'll all get to meet your families," I told them, and they all paused with uncertainty on their faces, so I quickly added in, "Only if you want to, of course."

They exchanged glances and I regretted saying anything. "I'm sorry. That's a conversation for a different day. Just forget I said anything." I brought up a different subject, but I could tell none of them were fully invested in it, so I asked, "Do you guys want me to stay here with you tonight?"

"Nah, go be with your family," Emery replied. "We'll be okay."

"Are you sure?"

"Of course she's sure," Andre answered for her.

"What happens . . ." Kodi hesitated before continuing. "What happens when we're released tomorrow?"

"You'll come home with me," I told her, knowing my parents wouldn't have it any other way. "So will Toby and Mateo whenever they're released."

"What about our families?" she asked.

"You guys can figure out if you want to meet them or not and go from there."

"No . . . I meant our other families. In the real world," Kodi clarified quietly. "We get to go home, right?"

"I . . ." My shoulders lifted in a small shrug as I shook my head. "I really don't know what's going to happen, Kodi. But we'll figure it out. If going home is what you want, I'll help you get back. Okay?"

She nodded and looked away, and I could tell she was trying not to cry. I visited with them until a healer came in to tell me visiting hours were over. He also chastised me for not being seen then worked his magic on me, healing the chaffed skin around my wrists and the rest of the small wounds I'd received in battle. I told Andre, Emery, and Kodi I'd see them in the morning then headed down to the first floor. To my surprise, Dad was still sitting in the waiting room and Mom had come back and joined him at some point.

"You're still here," I said as I walked up to them.

"I told you I would be," Dad replied as he stood up and stretched. "Can't have you thinking I'd break my word to you."

"I would never think that," I told him with a smile as he wrapped me in hug.

"How are your friends doing?" Mom asked as we began walking out of the building.

"Physically, they're fine. Emotionally . . . They have a lot to process. I don't know if they're going to want to meet their families."

"That's normal," Mom said, "and their families will respect that if it's what they decide."

"Garridan has a lot of experience with all that, huh?"

"Unfortunately so."

"It never gets any easier either," Dad added in with a sigh.

"What if some of them want to go back home?" I asked.

They exchanged a glance before Mom said, "Let's talk about that later."

I opened my mouth to protest but stopped, knowing there was no point in arguing. I just wondered why she didn't want to talk about it now. Her car was waiting in the parking lot, so we didn't have to walk home in the unwelcoming cold. The drive was quick and, as I stared at our house, a smile formed on my face as the familiarity of it welcomed me. I hadn't lived there very long, but it had become my home. It was the safe haven that I never had in Milton with my fake dad being around. When I thought about home, this was what I pictured, not the house I grew up in.

I walked inside and a weight seemed to be lifted off my shoulders. It was as if walking through the doorframe gave me the ability to relax. The stress and worry I'd been burdened with the last few months melted away as I sank into the couch. I leaned my head back and closed my eyes as my parents sat on either side of me.

"It's weird," I said.

"What is, honey?" Mom asked.

"Closing my eyes without being afraid."

Even though I couldn't see it, I knew they exchanged a look. Their concern for me was painfully obvious.

"Is there anything you'd like to talk about?" Mom offered.

"Not really."

"Robin . . ." Dad hesitated. "We don't know what you've gone through since being in the Cyfrin compound. I mean, we know a little from what Claire told us but I'm sure that was the bare minimum . . . So if there's anything you need to . . . Work through or talk to someone about we'll help you in any way we can."

Behind my closed eyes, images flashed through my mind like a slideshow: the first time I saw the trainees, all of them dirty and reclusive; when Arthur began beating a servant for spilling his lunch; the sharp edges of the candelabra from the chandelier crashing towards me; Toshiro cutting down a member of the Cyfrin just because he could; Serafina's putrid body being disposed of. There were many things I'd never be able to unsee.

I finally opened my eyes, blinking away the tears that threatened to form. "I appreciate it. I really do. But . . . I don't want you to know what happened there." I looked down at my hands, feeling an odd sense of shame. "I don't want anyone to know what happened there. It's my burden to bear."

"Honey," Mom said with sadness in her voice, "that's not true. You're only eighteen. There's no reason you should hold onto this for the rest of your life. There's no reason you should've had to go through it at all!" She was upset now, her rarely seen anger showing. "We should've stopped you. We shouldn't have let you go. You're just a child and we-we shouldn't have let you go. We're your *parents*. We should've protected you. We should've-"

"It was my decision," I told her, meeting her gaze. "You couldn't have stopped me. None of this was your fault."

"We just don't want you to go through this alone any more than you already have," Dad said quietly.

"But I'm not alone. I never was. I had Andre and Emery and Kodi and Mateo and Toby . . . They were there with me the whole time. They saw the same things I did, and they went through everything I did. If I need someone to talk to, they'll be there for me. So, please, don't worry about me."

Mom took a deep breath as Dad sighed then said, "We'll always worry about you, kiddo."

"Thanks," I replied with a grateful smile. "I'm just happy to be home."

"We're happy that you're home too," Mom responded. "It's been a long day. Do you want to get some sleep?"

"Actually, you know what I really want?" I asked and they both waited expectantly. "Some of Dad's famous sticky buns."

Dad let out a loud bellow of a laugh. "How about I make us all dinner, then the sticky buns."

"Fine," I grumbled, crossing my arms playfully as he hoisted himself off the couch. Mom wrapped her arm around me, and I leaned into her. I inhaled her perfume, letting it comfort me as she turned on a movie. “I can't wait for you to meet Toby. He's such a good kid.”

“Your father and I are excited to meet him too,” she told me with a gentle smile. “We always wanted another child but, well, you know.”

“You're going to love him,” I continued. “He's such a sweetheart, and I already think of him as a brother. You don't know how much this means to him.”

“It goes both ways, Robin. I promise,” she assured me. “We already set up a room for him, but we were waiting for him to be here to pick out how to decorate it.”

I grinned happily, the idea of that making me giddy as I pictured Toby's reaction. “Oh, I told the others that they could stay here after they were discharged. Just until they figure out what they're doing. I hope that's okay.”

“Of course it is.” She looked at me with affection. “You're such a compassionate person, honey. I'm so proud of the woman you’ve grown up to be.”

I snuggled in closer to her and we sat there watching the TV as Dad clanged pots around in the kitchen. It was good to be home.

Chapter Fifty-Three

The icy night enwrapped me like an unpleasant blanket I couldn't get out from under. My fingers and toes had gone numb a while ago, and my lungs burned from inhaling the frigid air for so long. Still, I sat there in the snow under my favorite tree that was long dead. I stared at the frozen lake ignoring the water that called to me. My mind was too distracted by the voices that haunted me and plagued my dreams.

"Robin?"

I ignored him.

"Robin," he repeated as he lowered himself next to me. When he looked me over, he cursed and pulled his jacket off then threw it over my shoulders. "We need to get you inside."

"No," I answered, my throat recoiling from the motion.

"Robin."

"Matthew."

"Your lips are blue, and your hands are icicles. You're going to get hypothermia if you stay out here."

"I don't care."

Matthew looked at me in concern, his brows furrowed together. "What's wrong?"

"They won't stop. They won't leave me alone," I whispered.

"Who won't?"

"The voices."

Matthew paused, not expecting that answer. Realization dawned not long after and he looked at me with sympathy. "Somnokinesis withdrawal."

"I can hear their voices so clearly," I told him, the pain of it just as bad as the first time I experienced it. "All of them. It's like they're standing right next to me telling me it's my fault. It's all my fault. I'm the reason they're unhappy. I'm the reason they're dead."

"Come on, Robin," Matthew coaxed. "Let's get you home."

"I lost my ring."

"What?" he questioned incredulously.

"The ring Ben gave me. My promise ring."

"Oh," he said, the uncertainty in his voice ringing loud.

"It was on my nightstand in my room in the castle. I took it off when I went to sleep then I got locked away. I never got to put it back on."

"It's okay, Robin."

"Ben's angry at me," I whimpered, hearing his voice all too clearly in my head. "I lost his family heirloom. I lost his love."

"That ring didn't make him love you. It's okay, Robin," he repeated. "Please let me take you home."

I allowed him to pull me up, but my frozen limbs protested, and I nearly fell over. Without a second thought, Matthew swept me into his arms and began walking. I didn't have the energy to protest so I rested my head against his shoulder instead.

"How did you know I was out here?" I asked, my voice cracking slightly.

"Your mom went to check on you and freaked out when she found your bed empty. She called our house to see if you were with me which obviously you weren't. Since you weren't at the hospital either, I had a pretty good idea where you'd be."

"I didn't mean to scare her," I murmured. "I just couldn't lay in bed . . . I had to get out. I thought the fresh air might clear my head but . . . it didn't."

"The long-term use of somnokinesis has some pretty awful side effects," he told me with a frown.

"I know. Alexander told me. I experienced it once before because I wanted to have Emery and Kodi sleep over. He warned me against it, but I didn't listen. I didn't understand."

"Of course you didn't. You didn't know what would happen."

"Alexander found me outside too." My lips turned up in a humorless smile, the deja vu of it ironic. "He brought me a coat and I started crying. Then I begged him to have Darnell put me to sleep and he did."

"I'm afraid you won't get off that easy this time," he said. "You're going to have to get through it without being put back to sleep."

"Why?" I asked in a whimper. The thought of the voices staying was too overwhelming to bear.

"Think of it as a detox to a drug addiction. You just have to get past the worst of it, then you'll be fine."

"How long?"

"What?"

"How long will it take to get past the worst of it?"

Matthew grimaced. "With how long they did it to you, probably a couple weeks."

Panic surged through me, and I grasped onto his shirt. "I can't do this for a couple weeks, Matthew! I can't. I can't!"

My hysteria caused him to almost drop me, so he knelt and sat me on the ground as I continued to spew incoherent words.

"Hey. Hey!" He grabbed my face in his hands and my tear-filled eyes met his troubled ones.

He had never seen me like this, no one had, and I could see how worried he was. Or maybe he was just concerned for my sanity. I *was* acting like I had gone off the deep end. But my mind wasn't my own right now; it belonged to others who were blaming me for everything that had gone wrong in life.

"Take a deep breath," he commanded, and I did as I was told. "Again."

I took one deep breath after the other, exhaling them slowly. He made me focus on his face while doing it then instructed me to count to twenty. As I did, my mind started to clear up slightly. The voices lowered their tone, and I could think again.

"Better?"

I nodded. "It's tolerable . . . Thank you."

"You're welcome," he replied, finally releasing my face, and picking me up again. "I know how hard this is, but I'm going to help you through it. Okay?"

"Okay."

"The effects are far from pleasant, but there are ways to make it manageable. And I'll stay with you every night until it's better if it means not finding you frozen to death by the lake."

"I'm sorry," I said, knowing I had messed up. I hadn't been trying to die, I just wanted relief.

"It's not your fault." He paused then added, "It's Alexander's."

"What?" I asked in disbelief at his jump in thought. "How?"

"That night you told me about. He could've shown you how to contain the effects but did he? *No.* He probably didn't want to see you suffering so he just gave you the easy way out."

"And that's a bad thing?" I questioned, sarcasm playing at my voice.

Matthew cocked one eyebrow at me. "Yeah, you're feeling better."

"Don't avoid the question." I looked him over for a minute before continuing. "We never got a chance to talk about him."

"What about him?"

"You know what."

He sighed. "I really don't think now is the best time."

"There will never be a good time," I pointed out. "So what's better than when you're carrying me home and can't stomp off angrily?"

"You did this on purpose," he accused with narrowed eyes.

"Yes, I purposely had Darnell use somnokinesis on me for months so I'd lose my mind and force you to come rescue me from freezing to death *just* so I could talk to you about me and Alexander. Clearly."

Matthew rolled his eyes. "Clearly."

"Come on, Matthew. I just want to clear the air about it."

"Fine . . . I'm trying not to be mad at you for it, but I am," he admitted. "Why him? Out of everyone in the world why *him*? And what about Ben? I thought you loved him."

"I do love Ben!" I exclaimed. "I'll *always* love Ben. If I had it my way, I'd be with him right now. But, if you haven't noticed, we're from two different worlds that aren't allowed to mingle with one another. Not to mention, he's got a new girlfriend. He's trying to move on and that's a *good* thing. He deserves to be happy. I *want* him to be happy. Even if it's not with me." I inhaled shakily, the thought of him with anyone but me stinging. "So is it wrong for me to try to move on too?"

"Of course not," he replied. "But do you have to try to move on with Alexander?"

"It's not like I did it intentionally."

He hesitated before quietly asking, "Do you love him?"

He purposely didn't look at me as I tried to gather my thoughts around the faint sound of my sister crying out to me to help her. I thought back on everything Alexander and I had been through together. The good and the bad were equal in parts. I'd been angry at him as much as I'd been happy with him. But when I *was* happy with him, I was *really* happy. He understood me in ways Ben didn't, not that it was Ben's fault, and I found comfort in his presence. I had some mixed feelings about him but was it love? The fact that I had to ask that gave me my answer.

"No," I finally said. "I don't."

It could've been a trick of the light, but I thought I saw the side of Matthew's lip twitch as if my answer made him happy.

"I do care about him though. A lot. If he was to get pardoned and stayed in Garridan . . . I think I would end up falling in love with him." Matthew grimaced at my words, so I added in, "He's not a bad person, Matthew. Look at what he did for us yesterday."

"I know."

"Would you hate me forever if I ended up with him?"

He sighed heavily. "Of course not. I want you to be happy, Robin. I just . . . I struggle when it comes to Alexander. You know that. It's not going to be easy for me to think of him as 'not a bad person'. Maybe that's not fair but it is what it is."

"Do you think you'll ever be his friend again?" I asked, cautious but curious. "His brother?"

"I honestly don't know." He was quiet for less than a minute before an amused look crossed his face. "So if you two end up married, don't expect me to go to the wedding."

"Wow," I replied, drawing the word out. "That's how it's going to be, huh?"

"It may very well be, yes," he responded with a grin, and I returned it as the seriousness of the conversation melted away. "I'm glad you're back. I missed you."

"I missed you too," I told him, laying my head back on his shoulder.

He tightened his grip on me and I let the swaying motion of his walk lull me. My eyes closed and he must've noticed because he quietly instructed, "Focus on your breathing. Count to twenty again. And again. And again."

His voice was soothing, as I'm sure he intended it to be, and the voices in my head stayed in the background as I counted. The next few weeks were going to be brutal as I fought to win against them. If that weren't enough, I'd have to sit through all the trials for the Cyfrin members and relive so many unwanted memories. Plus, I'd need to get the trainees adapted and settled, or help them get home if that's what they wanted. I'd also have to help advocate for Alexander so he wouldn't be killed. Then, somehow, I would need to try to find my place here once again.

Despite all that, I found peace in knowing that I had people who would help me through all of it. I had a village surrounding me, supporting me, and making sure I was alright. Because of them, I knew I was going to be okay. Besides, I had been through worse. What could possibly compare to the rollercoaster of a year I just had?

Chapter Fifty-Four

“I still can’t believe some of them got away,” Matthew grumbled as he paced behind my chair.

“It just had to be Mallory.” I sighed and rubbed my temples as Mom patted my arm.

“We’ll find them,” Dad assured me as he put the last of the food on the table.

It had been a long and busy week as the Cyfrin members were charged and assigned cells. After everyone had been processed, someone finally realized that a few important people were missing. At some point during the battle, Mallory must’ve run off because she managed to escape being captured. Darnell and Arthur were also missing, and I could only assume they were all together. The council was visiting with Alexander to try and figure out if anyone else was unaccounted for but all I could think about was Mallory running free.

“She’s going to cause problems,” I said. “I don’t know how but she will. She’s crazy.”

“I second that notion,” Matthew agreed.

“I understand you’re worried,” Mom told us, “but try not to obsess over it. The council will be very diligent trying to find her and the others. Besides, they can’t do much to us outside the barrier.”

“Except expose all our secrets of course,” Dad inserted dryly. Mom narrowed her eyes and he smiled sheepishly. “We won’t think like that though.”

The doorbell rang and I jumped up from my seat excitedly as I let the thought of Mallory melt away.

“They’re here!” I announced as I strutted towards the front door. The others followed as I opened it to let in Andre, Emery, and Kodi.

“Mom, Dad, Matthew. This is Andre, Emery, and Kodi,” I pointed to them as I said their names. “Guys, these are my parents and Matthew.”

“It's so nice to meet you all,” Mom told them, shaking each of their hands as they walked inside.

"You too, ma'am," Andre responded. "We appreciate you letting us stay here while we figure things out."

"It's our pleasure," Dad told him sincerely.

"It's a beautiful home," Kodi spoke up.

"Thank you!" Mom said. "We have a room set up for the girls and, Andre, you'll be in Toby's room. Whenever he and Mateo get discharged it'll be a little tight in there, but it should do."

"That's okay. We're used to tight quarters with being raised in foster care and then a dungeon and what not," Emery spouted off with.

"Right," Mom replied, and an awkward silence followed. "Well, anyway, are you hungry? Elijah made lunch and I'm sure we could all use the time to get to know one another a little bit. Make the transition here somewhat easier for everyone."

"You mean you don't like awkward silences?" Emery asked sarcastically, and Kodi shoved an elbow into her side.

"Ignore her," I told my parents with a roll of my eyes. "She's not pleasant to be around nine times out of ten."

"Robin," Dad chastised with a shake of his head. "That's not a very nice way to talk about your friend."

"Don't worry about it," Emery told him with an amused smirk. "It's the truth."

My parents glanced at one another before Dad asked, "Should we go to the dining room then?"

"Yes, please," Andre accepted, shooting Emery a look before they followed my parents out of the room.

"They're an interesting bunch," Matthew commented as we brought up the rear.

"You have no idea," I replied. "Just wait until Mateo and Toby join in. It's a full-on circus."

"You've had your hands full the last few months, haven't you?"

"You have *no* idea," I repeated, and we shared a knowing look.

We got settled at the table, passing the bowls of food around, and Emery, Andre, and Kodi dug in. My dad watched them happily, always pleased when people enjoyed his food.

"Didn't you guys eat at the hospital?" Matthew asked with raised brows at how they were shoveling it in.

His comment must've made them realize how quickly they were eating because they all immediately stopped and wiped at their faces.

"Yes," Kodi answered, "but hospital food for a whole week gets old."

"I told you guys to come here every day," I pointed out.

"We know. We just wanted to stay with Mateo and Toby in case anything happened," Andre said.

"Actually, we knew they were fine. Andre just thought it would be nice if we let you have some alone time with your family before we crashed the party," Emery informed me.

I smiled over at him, but he purposely stared at his plate. Of course that's the real reason they camped out at the hospital all week.

"That was a very kind gesture," Mom told him, patting his hand with a grateful look on her face. "But please don't think of yourselves as a burden. You're more than welcome to stay here as long as you need."

"Speaking of which, have any of you decided if you want to meet your families or not?" Dad asked.

Silence filled the room as we waited for an answer. Just when I thought none of them were going to say anything at all, Emery spoke up. "I want to meet my parents . . . and I want to stay in Garridan."

A relieved smile crossed Dad's face, and something told me he knew her parents well. "We'll arrange it as soon as you want," he told her. "They'll be so excited."

"I think I'd like to meet my father as well," Andre said. "I'm not sure if I can make Garridan my home, but whether I stay or go I want to know my birth parents, even if it's just through pictures for my mother since she's deceased."

"Your dad, Levoy, already has a whole album ready to show you," Mom responded, her eyes sad. "If you decide not to stay, I'm sure he'll let you keep some pictures."

Andre nodded once, his eyes still cast downward, and I looked to Kodi who was pushing her food around on her plate. She put the fork down and sat up straighter as she met my eyes.

"I don't want to stay here, and I don't want to meet anyone. I just want to go home," she conveyed quietly. "And I'm pretty sure Mateo feels the same way. He misses his siblings like crazy."

I rubbed my lips together, saddened for everyone involved. Her parents would never know her, and she would never know them. I didn't want her or Mateo to go but I knew how difficult it was to leave people behind. They had to do what was right for them.

"Okay," I responded. "We'll get you both home then. Right, Mom?"

Mom hesitated before answering. "We can get you home, of course . . . At a cost."

"We know that they'll have to give up their powers," I said, and Kodi nodded.

"I'm afraid it's not just the powers," Mom replied. "It's all the memories associated with the powers as well."

Everyone stopped what they were doing and stared at her.

"What are you talking about?" I asked, noticing that Matthew was also looking confused.

"It's an unfortunate side effect to Joey's powers," she answered. "When he eliminates the powers, it eliminates all the memories someone has regarding that power too."

"You mean I'd forget Robin and Mateo and everyone else?" Kodi questioned, her brows furrowed deeply.

"Yes," Dad told her. "It's a great asset when using it to punish people, like the Cyfrin members who will get banished, but not so much for situations like this."

"I don't understand. You guys took all the kids' powers from them when they were sent away," I pointed out. "No one ever said anything about them losing their memories."

"Because they didn't," Mom replied.

"Joey . . ." Matthew finally spoke up. "I thought the power eliminator's name was Joseph and the Cyfrin's Keepers of Balance had him killed after you sent the kids into hiding."

"That's right," Dad said. "Joey is Joseph's son. He was sent away with the rest of the kids and found not long after we started searching. His dad was extremely talented, and his powers didn't have the side effects Joey's does. But, yes, the Cyfrin did kill him which is why our only option now is Joey since their power is so rare."

"I don't want to forget everything I've been through," Kodi said. "I don't want to forget all my new friends or this place. Can't I just keep my powers and still go home?"

"The Keepers of Balance will never allow that," Mom told her. "It's too big of a risk to our people."

"Isn't there anything else we can do then?" Andre asked, probably thinking he didn't want to forget either if he chose to leave.

I glimpsed over to Matthew, a thought swirling around my head. I remembered the conversation he had started when I was the one desperately trying to figure out a way to keep Ben. Adriana's words played in my head: *Alternatively, if they come from our world and wish to leave, he will take away someone's powers.*

"What . . . What about that tree?" I asked slowly.

"What tree?" Emery questioned, judgement in her voice at the seemingly ridiculousness of my question.

"The Keeper of Balance tree," Matthew said, nodding as he instantly picked up what I was talking about. "He could take away their powers without damaging their memories."

"Matthew, I told you before we don't know anything about that legend," Mom chastised him. "We have no way of finding him or even knowing if it's true."

"You said there are records of people being granted powers," I reminded her. "That's proof enough for me that there's *something* out there. Something that can grant powers and something that can probably take them away like the legend says."

"Even if there's the smallest chance that's true, we have to try it," Kodi spoke up, her voice desperate. "We have to. *Please*."

Mom opened her mouth then shut it again as she looked to Dad. They had one of those silent conversations with their eyes as we all looked on waiting for an answer.

Finally Dad said, "We'll talk to the council. See what information we can get."

"Thank you! Thank you, thank you, thank you," Kodi exclaimed, relief crossing her face.

"I'm not making any promises," he added in. "There's a very slim chance that the legend is true. Who turns a man into a tree?" He let out a nervous laugh and I eyed him suspiciously.

Why is he acting so strange?

"Okay, is this a person or a tree?" Emery asked in frustration.

As Matthew started explaining, a sharp knock rang out from the front door. Before anyone could get up to answer, the doorbell rang.

"Someone's impatient," I commented as I rose from my seat. I walked to the foyer and twisted the doorknob as another knock sounded. "Oh, hi, Claire."

"Robin," she acknowledged, her eyes skittering past me.

"We were just eating lunch. Do you want some?" I offered as Matthew came up behind me.

"No."

"What's wrong, Claire?" Matthew asked tensely, and I stopped to look at her.

She was nervously messing with her fingers and biting her inner lip. Her eyes were full of sorrow as she stared at me.

"What's wrong?" I echoed.

"It's Ben. There's been an accident."

Made in the USA
Columbia, SC
29 October 2022